"The Lean, High House of the Gnoles"

*(from "How Nuth Would Have Practised His Art
upon the Gnoles")*

GODS, MEN AND GHOSTS

The Best Supernatural Fiction of

LORD DUNSANY

Selected, with an introduction by
E. F. BLEILER

With 20 illustrations by
SIDNEY H. SIME

DOVER PUBLICATIONS, INC.
NEW YORK

Gods, Men and Ghosts: The Best Supernatural Fiction of Lord Dunsany, first published by Dover Publications, Inc., in 1972, is a new selection of stories by Lord Dunsany (reprinted without abridgment) taken from the sources indicated on page 259. The selection was made by E. F. Bleiler, who also wrote the Introduction.

International Standard Book Number: 0-486-22808-8
Library of Congress Catalog Card Number: 75-164735

Manufactured in the United States of America
Dover Publications, Inc.
180 Varick Street
New York, N.Y. 10014

Introduction
to the Dover Edition

AROUND 1904 a new universe was created, the first original, detailed cosmogony in English literature since the time of William Blake. Great primal gods appeared from nothingness and formed a cosmos; lesser godlings emanated or congealed; forces of nature assumed personality and warred with one another, as neomyth succeeded neomyth in brilliant profusion. The occasion was *The Gods of Pegana* by the Irish poet, storyteller and dramatist, Lord Dunsany. This book marked the first emergence of a small but strong, steady, self-walled stream of idea and prismatic beauty.

This new universe also showed a stability and capacity for growth that must have surprised even its author. After the Gods there appeared further myths, tales of great heroes and rogues in days that never were, and ultimately stories of the smaller people. "Dunsanean" is the term usually applied to this dream-cosmos, a term that has specific meaning to the reader of fantastic fiction. This word marks an honor that few men share in modern supernatural literature: "Lovecraftian" and "Wellsian" come to mind as parallel words, with "Vernesque" and "Merrittesque" and a few others as poor thirds. The common factor is that each of these men created work so fully formed, so iconized that it is in a sense ideal.

The circumstances under which Dunsany began to write are not known beyond the fact that he felt he had something to say and did not care about everyday matters in literature. "I never write of the things I have seen—which hundreds of others can do as well,—but only of the things I have imagined," he wrote in 1921. While this is not entirely correct, since he did occasionally write about everyday matters, it is probably 90% true. In his autobiography *Patches of Sunlight,* years later, he added: "I did not feel as though I was inventing, but rather as though I wrote the history of lands I had known, in forgotten wanderings."

Edward John Moreton Drax Plunkett, 18th Baron Dunsany, was born in 1878, succeeding to his title in 1899. His family, seated at Castle Dunsany, Meath, not far from Dublin, was one of the oldest in the British peerage, well-known in the Middle Ages as a robber barony. Following the family tradition Dunsany was intended for an Army career, attending Eton and Sandhurst, the British equivalent of West Point. He served in the Boer War and was wounded in World War I.

Dunsany travelled a great deal, and spent much of his time hunting big game in Africa. As he once commented, although he had some reputation as a literary man, he had really devoted most of his life to soldiering and hunting. Indeed, *While the Sirens Slept,* one of his autobiographical books, is in large proportion a record of kills. He was a good cricket player, and as might have been guessed from his stories, a chess enthusiast. He created many published chess problems, won the chess championship of Ireland, and even managed to hold the World Champion, Capablanca, to a draw in a simultaneous exhibition in London.

In his old age, Dunsany occasionally lectured at universities. He was guest Byron Professor of English at the University of Athens during World War II, and barely escaped at the height of the German invasion. He died in 1957, not long after a visit to the United States.

In person, Dunsany was a very tall, gaunt man, who put on flesh in later life. Genial and hearty in his earlier days, he seems to have become crotchety and irascible in his later years. All in all, he gave the impression of a traditional British hunting squire like Jorrocks more than he did a semimystical playwright and storyteller. Mrs. Littlefield's personality sketch of Dunsany, based on his stay in California during the coronation of Queen Elizabeth II (which he refused to attend because he felt slighted), is likely to surprise anyone who believes that "he who writes fine poetry himself finely poetic should be."

During his lifetime, Lord Dunsany had two worldwide reputations. He was known as a playwright, loosely attached for a time to the new Irish drama of Synge, Lady Gregory and Yeats.

At one time Dunsany considered financing their enterprises; at another his plays shared the stage with theirs in England and the United States. It was a forced association, however, for Dunsany really had little enthusiasm for Irish cultural nationalism, whether Synge's romantic realism or Yeats's poetic antiquarianism. Dunsany's world lay sometimes in his own dreams, sometimes in the present, where he savagely attacked elements of our world he did not like. Among his better-known plays are *A Night at an Inn,* possibly the finest, in which Toff discovers that his worldly wisdom is powerless against the supernatural; *The Glittering Gate,* in which two burglars try to break into Heaven; and *Cheezo,* in which a young man whose clerical career is faltering because he cannot believe in eternal damnation, sees his error after a glimpse at big business.

Dunsany the dramatist, however, was not wholly a happy entity, for his talents did not really lie on the stage. The best that can be said of his plays today is that they are occasionally original, ingenious, shimmeringly decorated with language, but stiff, dull and pointless. They bear some anticipations of the theatre of the absurd, but the resemblance is surface rather than essence. Dunsany stated emphatically, many times, that he was not an allegorist or symbolist, that he was not writing for interpretation, and that he had no higher truths to offer or disclaim, beyond what emerged unconsciously.

Dunsany's second reputation, the more lasting one, was as a writer of fantasy. Here he wrote two types of stories, the earlier dreamland works and the later everyday adventures and prevarications.

The Gods of Pegana (1905) and *Time and the Gods* (1906) established the worlds of private wonder in terms of myth and legend. Within their ambience there took place many stories of heroes, demigods, petty gods, ephemeral beings and creatures of twilight: *The Sword of Welleran* (1908), *A Dreamer's Tales* (1910), *The Book of Wonder* (1912), *Tales of Wonder* (1916). These collections also contain occasional stories that have some foothold in our own world.

In the 1920's Dunsany tried his hand at three longer works, two of which are still in the tradition of gods and heroes. These were *The King of Elfland's Daughter* (1924), the only work in which he succeeded in enlarging one of his facet-universes into a full globe; *The Charwoman's Shadow* (1926), a traditional fairytale reworked, and *The Blessing of Pan* (1927), in which the Great God Pan emerges to awaken ecstasy in a dreary, modern English village.

During the late 1920's Dunsany started to explore a different fictional territory, a series of stories based on his own travel experiences, narrated by a drunken old liar at a London club to cadge drinks. Dunsany started this series at the request of friends, but with great reluctance, since he disliked using untransformed experience. Eventually he worked out a compromise that satisfied his aesthetics: "the background is all true; the cactus forests of Kenya are there . . . the lie is the tale itself, worked up with this material as a goldsmith will make a winged goddess from honest gold." These Jorkens stories, which are occasionally excellent, are related in several books: *Travel Tales of Mr. Joseph Jorkens* (1931), *Jorkens Remembers Africa* (1934), *Jorkens Has a Large Whiskey* (1940), *The Fourth Book of Jorkens* (1948) and *Jorkens Borrows Another Whiskey* (1954). In the same vein is *Little Tales of Smethers* (1953). Untypical and unmemorable is his last important work, *The Last Revolution* (1953), which is concerned with self-reproducing, intelligent machines.

This is only a partial list of Dunsany's works, for he was a prolific writer and worked in (or out of) many literary forms. He also wrote a good deal of poetry, with a goose-quill pen that splattered badly; most of this harks back to the 1890's in manner. There were also books of reminiscences, autobiographical fragments, stories of contemporary Irish life, war propaganda, aesthetic essays and a fair amount of material that does not fit into exact categories. Of all, the short story seems to have been his favorite form, especially where it approached the peripheral ranges of the prose poem or the narrative-of-point. Most of his work is short, since he apparently did not have the patience to work at length, and believed in putting his ideas into final form immediately. He was a lapidary rather than an architect.

Much of this work is now half-lost in the periodicals of his life-span, or is to be found in out-of-print books that no one reads anymore. Most of it, unfortunately, is ephemeral, and has little survival value except as tour de force. Like Chesterton, Dunsany had the fatal faculty of being able to turn almost anything into a saleable story. Indeed, he once claimed that he could write a story about the mud of the Thames, which he did. Probably no one else in modern literature has had this gift as strongly, and probably no one else has suffered so much from it a generation or so later.

Yet despite material that is too slight to survive, or repeats themes which had previously been exhausted, Lord Dunsany wrote some first-class work that is unique in English and will be read well into the future. If his range is narrow, his power is great within that range. If he had few ideas to offer, he had the power of awakening secondary ideas in others. If he is indifferent or hostile to the literary flow around him, he offers an individual beauty of language that is an inimitable mixture of cerebral and half-dream. There have been many imitators of Dunsany's work, but no successors. "The Three Sailors' Gambit" is still the best chess story that has ever been written, while the sly humor and outrageous plotting in "Nuth" and "Thangobrind" make their exploits inexhaustible. Dreams and dreaminess have seldom travelled beyond Bethmoora and the Yann, while epic grandeur is miniaturized in many of the sketches of *Time and the Gods*. The permanent Lord Dunsany may not be large in bulk, but it is uniquely personal, brilliant, and high.

Associated in this book with Lord Dunsany, as he was in many books, is Sidney H. Sime, 1867–1942), pronounced "seem." Sime came to be more than simply an illustrator of Dunsany's stories; he became an active collaborator, and in their later association even contributed the first creative impulse.

Born into an impoverished Yorkshire family, Sime worked for a time as a child coal miner, but eventually escaped from his environment. After a succession of small jobs he studied art at the Liverpool School of Art, did occasional journalistic work, and gradually became known in the London publishing world. In later life he inherited money, edited *The Idler* for a time, and retired outside London. Martin Gardner, in his excellent essay "Sidney Sime of Worplesdon," gives many details about his fantastic later life. Today, however, Sime is remembered for his illustrations to Dunsany stories, together with similar work for Arthur Machen.

Just how Sime and Dunsany came to work together is not clear, since Dunsany has given two different accounts of the incident.

For several books, they collaborated in the usual manner, with Sime preparing illustrations to a story that had already been written. In *The Book of Wonder,* however, this situation became reversed. Dunsany visited Sime, examined a series of pictures that were in various stages of completion, and wrote stories that he thought would fit them. Dunsany's interpretation may not always have been Sime's intention, however. In his autobiography, *Patches of Sunlight,* Dunsany says, "I had particularly asked Mr. Sime not to tell me what the pictures were about, and he only tried to explain one to me, but I could not quite follow. When I showed him a story, and asked him if it accurately described what was going on in the picture, he said, 'It sounds extremely probable.' "

Four of the stories in the present collection (taken from *The Book of Wonder*) were composed in this fashion: "The Distressing Tale of Thangobrind," "The Hoard of the Gibbelins," "How Nuth Would Have Practised His Art" and "The Coronation of Mr. Thomas Shap."

After Sime's death Lord Dunsany prepared an obituary tribute to him in the *Fortnight.* "There was in his pictures a sombre grandeur showing all the majesty of night or the mystery of dark forests, like a joke by a god whom nobody worships . . . and yet his sombre shadows . . . are always lit by the rays of his merry humor. Now that vast imagination has left us, having enriched our age with dreams that we have not entirely deserved. . . ."

This could stand equally well for Dunsany at his best.

E. F. BLEILER

New York, 1971

Contents

JORKENS

GODS

List of Illustrations

The Fortress
(from "The Fortress Unvanquishable, Save For Sacnoth")

MEN

The Edge of the World
(from "The Probable Adventure of
the Three Literary Men")

The Three Sailors' Gambit

SITTING some years ago in the ancient tavern at Over, one afternoon in spring, I was waiting as was my custom for something strange to happen.

In this I was not always disappointed, for the very curious leaded panes of that tavern, facing the sea, let a light into the low-ceilinged room so mysterious, particularly at evening, that it somehow seemed to affect the events within. Be that as it may, I have seen strange things in that tavern and heard stranger things told.

And as I sat there three sailors entered the tavern just back, as they said, from sea and come with sun-burned skins from a very long voyage to the South; and one of them had a board and chessmen under his arm, and they were complaining that they could find no one who knew how to play chess. This was the year that the Tournament was in England. And a little dark man at a table in a corner of the room, drinking sugar and water, asked them why they wished to play chess; and they said that they would play any man for a pound. They opened their box of chessmen then, a cheap and nasty set, and the man refused to play with such uncouth pieces, and the sailors suggested that perhaps he could find better ones; and in the end he went round to his lodgings near by and brought his own, and then they sat down to play for a pound a side. It was a consultation game on the part of the sailors, they said all three must play.

Well, the little dark man turned out to be Stavlokratz.

Of course he was fabulously poor, and the sovereign meant more to him than it did to the sailors, but he didn't seem keen to play, it was the sailors that insisted; he had made the badness of the sailors' chessmen an excuse for not playing at all, but the sailors had overruled that, and then he told them straight out who he was, and the sailors had never heard of Stavlokratz.

Well, no more was said after that. Stavlokratz said no more, either because he did not wish to boast or because he was huffed that they did not know who he was. And I saw no reason to enlighten the sailors about him; if he took their pound they had brought it on themselves, and my boundless admiration for his genius made me feel that he deserved whatever might come his way. He had not asked to play, they had named the stakes, he had warned them, and gave them first move; there was nothing unfair about Stavlokratz.

I had never seen Stavlokratz before, but I had played over nearly every one of his games in the World Championship for the last three or four years; he was always, of course, the model chosen by students. Only young chess-players can appreciate my delight at seeing him play first hand.

Well, the sailors used to lower their heads almost as low as the table and mutter together before every move, but they muttered so low that you could not hear what they planned.

They lost three pawns almost straight off, then a knight, and shortly after a bishop; they were playing in fact the famous Three Sailors' Gambit.

Stavlokratz was playing with the easy confidence that they say was usual with him, when suddenly at about the thirteenth move I saw him look surprised; he leaned forward and looked at the board and then at the sailors, but he learned nothing from their vacant faces; he looked back at the board again.

He moved more deliberately after that; the sailors lost two more pawns, Stavlokratz had lost nothing as yet. He looked at me, I thought, almost irritably, as though something would happen that he wished I was not there to see. I believed at first he had qualms about taking the sailors' pound, until it dawned on me that he might lose the game; I saw that possibility in his face, not on the board, for the game had become almost incomprehensible to me. I cannot describe my astonishment. And a few moves later Stavlokratz resigned.

The sailors showed no more elation than if they had won some game with greasy cards, playing amongst themselves.

Stavlokratz asked them where they got their opening. "We kind of thought of it," said one. "It just come into our heads like," said another. He asked them questions about the ports they had touched at. He evidently thought, as I did myself, that they had learned their extraordinary gambit, perhaps in some old dependency of Spain, from some young master of chess whose fame had not reached Europe. He was very eager to find who this man could be, for neither of us imagined that those sailors had invented it, nor would anyone who had seen them. But he got no information from the sailors.

Stavlokratz could very ill afford the loss of a pound. He offered to play them again for the same stakes. The sailors began to set up the white pieces. Stavlokratz pointed out that it was his turn for first move. The sailors agreed but continued to set up the white pieces and sat with the white before them waiting for him to move. It was a trivial incident, but it revealed to Stavlokratz and myself that none of these sailors was aware that white always moves first.

Stavlokratz played on them his own opening, reasoning of course that as they had never heard of Stavlokratz they would not know of his opening; and with probably a very good hope of getting back his pound he played the fifth variation with its tricky seventh move, at least so he intended, but it turned to a variation unknown to the students of Stavlokratz.

Throughout this game I watched the sailors closely, and I became sure, as only an attentive watcher can be, that the one on their left, Jim Bunion, did not even know the moves.

When I had made up my mind about this I watched only the other two, Adam Bailey and Bill Sloggs, trying to make out which was the master mind; and for a long while I could not. And then I heard Adam Bailey mutter six words, the only words I heard throughout the game, of all their consultations, "No, him with the horse's head." And I decided that Adam Bailey did not know what a knight was, though of course he might have been explaining things to Bill Sloggs, but it did not sound like that; so that left Bill Sloggs. I watched Bill Sloggs after that with a certain wonder; he was no more intellectual than the others to look at, though rather more forceful perhaps. Poor old Stavlokratz was beaten again.

Well, in the end I paid for Stavlokratz, and tried to get a

game with Bill Sloggs alone; but this he would not agree to, it must be all three or none. And then I went back with Stavlokratz to his lodgings. He very kindly gave me a game: of course it did not last long, but I am more proud of having been beaten by Stavlokratz than of any game that I have ever won. And then we talked for an hour about the sailors, and neither of us could make head or tail of them. I told him what I had noticed about Jim Bunion and Adam Bailey, and he agreed with me that Bill Sloggs was the man, though as to how he had come by that gambit or that variation of Stavlokratz's own opening he had no theory.

I had the sailors' address, which was that tavern as much as anywhere, and they were to be there all that evening. As evening drew in I went back to the tavern, and found there still the three sailors. And I offered Bill Sloggs two pounds for a game with him alone and he refused, but in the end he played me for a drink. And then I found that he had not heard of the *en passant* rule, and believed that the fact of checking the king prevented him from castling, and did not know that a player can have two or more queens on the board at the same time if he queens his pawns, or that a pawn could ever become a knight; and he made as many of the stock mistakes as he had time for in a short game, which I won. I thought that I should have got at the secret then, but his mates who had sat scowling all the while in the corner came up and interfered. It was a breach of their compact apparently for one to play chess by himself; at any rate they seemed angry. So I left the tavern then and came back again next day, and the next day and the day after, and often saw the three sailors, but none were in a communicative mood. I had got Stavlokratz to keep away, and they could get no one to play chess with at a pound a side, and I would not play with them unless they told me the secret.

And then one evening I found Jim Bunion drunk, yet not so drunk as he wished, for the two pounds were spent; and I gave him very nearly a tumbler of whiskey, or what passed for whiskey in that tavern in Over, and he told me the secret at once. I had given the others some whiskey to keep them quiet, and later on in the evening they must have gone out, but Jim Bunion stayed with me by a little table, leaning across it and talking low, right into my face, his breath smelling all the while of what passed for whiskey.

The wind was blowing outside as it does on bad nights in November, coming up with moans from the south, towards which the tavern faced with all its leaded panes, so that none but I was able to hear his voice as Jim Bunion gave up his secret.

They had sailed for years, he told me, with Bill Snyth; and on their last voyage home Bill Snyth had died. And he was buried at sea. Just the other side of the line they buried him, and his pals divided his kit, and these three got his crystal that only they knew he had, which Bill got one night in Cuba. They played chess with the crystal.

And he was going on to tell me about that night in Cuba when Bill had bought the crystal from the stranger, how some folks might think that they had seen thunderstorms, but let them go and listen to that one that thundered in Cuba when Bill was buying his crystal and they'd find that they didn't know what thunder was. But then I interrupted him, unfortunately perhaps, for it broke the thread of his tale and set him rambling awhile, and cursing other people and talking of other lands, China, Port Said and Spain: but I brought him back to Cuba again in the end. I asked him how they could play chess with a crystal; and he said that you looked at the board and looked at the crystal and there was the game in the crystal the same as it was on the board, with all the odd little pieces looking just the same though smaller, horses' heads and whatnots; and as soon as the other man moved the move came out in the crystal, and then your move appeared after it, and all you had to do was to make it on the board. If you didn't make the move that you saw in the crystal things got very bad in it, everything horribly mixed and moving about rapidly, and scowling and making the same move over and over again, and the crystal getting cloudier and cloudier; it was best to take one's eyes away from it then, or one dreamt about it afterwards, and the foul little pieces came and cursed you in your sleep and moved about all night with their crooked moves.

I thought then that, drunk though he was, he was not telling the truth, and I promised to show him to people who played chess all their lives so that he and his mates could get a pound

whenever they liked, and I promised not to reveal his secret even
to Stavlokratz, if only he would tell me all the truth; and this
promise I have kept till long after the three sailors have lost
their secret. I told him straight out that I did not believe in the
crystal. Well, Jim Bunion leaned forward then, even further
across the table, and swore he had seen the man from whom Bill
had bought the crystal and that he was one to whom anything
was possible. To begin with, his hair was villainously dark, and
his features were unmistakable even down there in the South,
and he could play chess with his eyes shut, and even then he
could beat anyone in Cuba. But there was more than this, there
was the bargain he made with Bill that told one who he was. He
sold that crystal for Bill Snyth's soul.

Jim Bunion, leaning over the table with his breath in my
face, nodded his head several times and was silent.

I began to question him then. Did they play chess as far away
as Cuba? He said they all did. Was it conceivable that any man
would make such a bargain as Snyth made? Wasn't the trick well
known? Wasn't it in hundreds of books? And if he couldn't
read books, mustn't he have heard from sailors that that is the
Devil's commonest dodge to get souls from silly people?

Jim Bunion had leant back in his own chair quietly smiling
at my questions, but when I mentioned silly people he leaned
forward again, and thrust his face close to mine and asked me several times if I called Bill Snyth silly. It seemed that these three
sailors thought a great deal of Bill Snyth, and it made Jim
Bunion angry to hear anything said against him. I hastened to
say that the bargain seemed silly, though not, of course, the man
who made it; for the sailor was almost threatening, and no
wonder, for the whiskey in that dim tavern would madden a nun.

When I said that the bargain seemed silly he smiled again,
and then he thundered his fist down on the table and said that
no one had ever got the better of Bill Snyth, and that that was
the worst bargain for himself that the Devil ever made, and that
from all he had read or heard of the Devil he had never been so
badly had before as the night when he met Bill Snyth at the inn
in the thunderstorm in Cuba, for Bill Snyth already had the
damnedest soul at sea; Bill was a good fellow, but his soul was
damned right enough, so he got the crystal for nothing.

Yes, he was there and saw it all himself, Bill Snyth in the

Spanish inn and the candles flaring, and the Devil walking in out of the rain, and then the bargain between those two old hands, and the Devil going out into the lightning, and the thunder-storm raging on, and Bill Snyth sitting chuckling to himself between the bursts of the thunder.

But I had more questions to ask and interrupted this reminis-cence. Why did they all three always play together? And a look of something like fear came over Jim Bunion's face; and at first he would not speak. And then he said to me that it was like this; they had not paid for that crystal, but got it as their share of Bill Snyth's kit. If they had paid for it or given something in exchange to Bill Snyth that would have been all right, but they couldn't do that now because Bill was dead, and they were not sure if the old bargain might not hold good. And Hell must be a large and lonely place, and to go there alone must be bad; and so the three agreed that they would all stick together, and use the crystal all three or not at all, unless one died, and then the two would use it and the one that was gone would wait for them. And the last of the three to go would bring the crystal with him, or maybe the crystal would bring him. They didn't think, he said, they were the kind of men for Heaven, and he hoped they knew their place better than that, but they didn't fancy the notion of Hell alone, if Hell it had to be. It was all right for Bill Snyth, he was afraid of nothing. He had known perhaps five men that were not afraid of death, but Bill Snyth was not afraid of Hell. He died with a smile on his face like a child in its sleep; it was drink killed poor Bill Snyth.

This was why I had beaten Bill Sloggs; Sloggs had the crystal on him while we played, but would not use it; these sailors seemed to fear loneliness as some people fear being hurt; he was the only one of the three who could play chess at all, he had learnt it in order to be able to answer questions and keep up their pretence, but he had learnt it badly, as I found. I never saw the crystal, they never showed it to anyone; but Jim Bunion told me that night that it was about the size that the thick end of a hen's egg would be if it were round. And then he fell asleep.

There were many more questions that I would have asked him but I could not wake him up. I even pulled the table away so that he fell to the floor, but he slept on, and all the tavern was dark but for one candle burning; and it was then that I noticed for the first time that the other two sailors had gone; no one remained at all but Jim Bunion and I and the sinister barman of that curious inn, and he too was asleep.

When I saw that it was impossible to wake the sailor I went out into the night. Next day Jim Bunion would talk of it no more; and when I went back to Stavlokratz I found him already putting on paper his theory about the sailors, which became accepted by chess-players, that one of them had been taught their curious gambit and the other two between them had learnt all the defensive openings as well as general play. Though who taught them no one could say, in spite of enquiries made afterwards all along the Southern Pacific.

I never learnt any more details from any of the three sailors, they were always too drunk to speak or else not drunk enough to be communicative. I seem just to have taken Jim Bunion at the flood. But I kept my promise; it was I that introduced them to the Tournament, and a pretty mess they made of established reputations. And so they kept on for months, never losing a game and always playing for their pound a side. I used to follow them wherever they went merely to watch their play. They were more marvellous than Stavlokratz even in his youth.

But then they took to liberties such as giving their queen when playing first-class players. And in the end one day when all three were drunk they played the best player in England with only a row of pawns. They won the game all right. But the ball broke to pieces. I never smelt such a stench in all my life.

The three sailors took it stoically enough, they signed on to different ships and went back again to the sea, and the world of chess lost sight, for ever I trust, of the most remarkable players it ever knew, who would have altogether spoiled the game.

The Three Infernal Jokes

THIS is the story that the desolate man told to me on the lonely Highland road one autumn evening with winter coming on and the stags roaring.

The saddening twilight, the mountain already black, the dreadful melancholy of the stags' voices, his friendless mournful face, all seemed to be of some most sorrowful play staged in that valley by an outcast god, a lonely play of which the hills were part and he the only actor.

For long we watched each other drawing out of the solitudes of those forsaken spaces. Then when we met he spoke.

"I will tell you a thing that will make you die of laughter. I will keep it to myself no longer. But first I must tell you how I came by it."

I do not give the story in his words with all his woeful interjections and the misery of his frantic self-reproaches, for I would not convey unnecessarily to my readers that atmosphere of sadness that was about all he said and that seemed to go with him wherever he moved.

It seems that he had been a member of a club, a West End club he called it, a respectable but quite inferior affair, probably in the City: agents belonged to it, fire insurance mostly, but life insurance and motor-agents too; it was, in fact, a touts' club.

It seems that a few of them one evening, forgetting for a moment their encyclopaedias and non-stop tyres, were talking loudly over a card-table when the game had ended about their personal virtues and a very little man with waxed moustaches who disliked the taste of wine was boasting heartily of his temperance. It was then that he who told this mournful story, drawn on by the boasts of others, leaned forward a little over the green baize into the light of the two guttering candles and revealed, no doubt a little shyly, his own extraordinary virtue. One woman was to him as ugly as another.

And the silenced boasters rose and went home to bed leaving him all alone, as he supposed, with his unequalled virtue. And yet he was not alone, for when the rest had gone there arose a member out of a deep arm-chair at the dark end of the room and walked across to him, a man whose occupation he did not know and only now suspects.

"You have," said the stranger, "a surpassing virtue."

"I have no possible use for it," my poor friend replied.

"Then doubtless you would sell it cheap," said the stranger.

Something in the man's manner or appearance made the desolate teller of this mournful tale feels his own inferiority, which probably made him feel acutely shy, so that his mind abased itself as an Oriental does his body in the presence of a superior, or perhaps he was sleepy, or merely a little drunk. Whatever it was he only mumbled "Oh yes," instead of contradicting so mad a remark. And the stranger led the way to the room where the telephone was.

"I think you will find my firm will give a good price for it," he said; and without more ado he began with a pair of pincers to cut the wire of the telephone and the receiver. The old waiter who looked after the club they had left shuffling round the other room putting things away for the night.

"Whatever are you doing of?" said my friend.

"This way," said the stranger. Along a passage they went and away to the back of the club, and there the stranger leaned out of a window and fastened the severed wires to the lightning conductor. My friend has no doubt of that, a broad ribbon of copper, half an inch wide, perhaps wider, running down from the roof to the earth.

"Hell," said the stranger with his mouth to the telephone; then silence for a while with his ear to the receiver, leaning out of the window. And then my friend heard his poor virtue being several times repeated, and then words like Yes and No.

"They offer you three jokes," said the stranger, "which shall make all who hear them simply die of laughter."

I think my friend was reluctant then to have anything more
to do with it, he wanted to go home; he said he didn't want jokes.
"They think very highly of your virtue," said the stranger.
And at that, odd as it seems, my friend wavered, for logically if
they thought highly of the goods they should have paid a higher
price.

"O all right," he said.

The extraordinary document that the agent drew from his
pocket ran something like this:

"I . . . in consideration of three new jokes received from Mr.
Montagu-Montague, hereinafter to be called the agent, and war-
ranted to be as by him stated and described, do assign to him,
yield, abrogate and give up, all recognitions, emoluments, per-
quisites or rewards due to me Here or Elsewhere on "account of
the following virtue, to wit and that is to say . . . that all women
are to me equally ugly." The last eight words being filled in in
ink by Mr. Montagu-Montague.

My poor friend duly signed it. "These are the jokes," said the
agent. They were boldly written on three slips of paper. "They
don't seem very funny," said the other when he had read them.
"You are immune," said Mr. Montagu-Montague, "but anyone else
who hears them will simply die of laughter: that we guarantee."

An American firm had bought at the price of waste paper a
hundred thousand copies of *The Dictionary of Electricity*,
written when electricity was new—and it had turned out that
even at the time its author had not rightly grasped his subject,—
the firm had paid £10,000 to a respectable English paper (no
other in fact than the Briton) for the use of its name, and to
obtain orders for *The Briton Dictionary of Electricity* was the
occupation of my unfortunate friend. He seems to have had a way
with him. Apparently he knew by a glance at a man, or a look
round at his garden, whether to recommend the book as "an absolutely up-to-date achievement, the finest thing of its kind in the
world of modern science" or as "at once quaint and imperfect,
a thing to buy and to keep as a tribute to those dear old times
that are gone." So he went on with this quaint though usual business, putting aside the memory of that night as an occasion on
which he had "somewhat exceeded" as they say in circles where a
spade is called neither a spade nor an agricultural implement,
but is never mentioned at all, being altogether too vulgar.

And then one night he put on his suit of dress clothes and found the three jokes in the pocket. That was perhaps a shock. He seems to have thought it over carefully then, and the end of it was he gave a dinner at the club to twenty of the members. The dinner would do no harm he thought—might even help the business, and if the joke came off he would be a witty fellow, and two jokes still up his sleeve.

Whom he invited or how the dinner went I do not know, for he began to speak rapidly and came straight to the point, as a stick that nears a cataract suddenly goes faster and faster. The dinner was duly served, the port went round, the twenty men were smoking, two waiters loitered, when he after carefully reading the best of the jokes told it down the table. They laughed. One man accidentally inhaled his cigar smoke and spluttered, the two waiters overheard and tittered behind their hands, one man, a bit of a raconteur himself, quite clearly wished not to laugh, but his veins swelled dangerously in trying to keep it back, and in the end he laughed too. The joke had succeeded; my friend smiled at the thought; he wished to say little deprecating things to the man on his right; but the laughter did not stop and the waiters would not be silent. He waited, and waited, wondering; the laughter went roaring on, distinctly louder now, and the waiters as loud as any. It had gone on for three or four minutes when this frightful thought leaped up all at once in his mind: *it was forced laughter!* How ever could anything have induced him to tell so foolish a joke? He saw its absurdity as in revelation; and the more he thought of it as these people laughed at him, even the waiters too, the more he felt that he could never lift up his head with his brother touts again. And still the laughter went roaring and choking on. He was very angry. There was not much use in having a friend, he thought, if one silly joke could not be overlooked; he had fed them too. And then he felt that he had no friends at all, and his anger faded away, and a great unhappiness came down on him, and he got quietly up and slunk from the room and slipped away from the club. Poor man, he scarcely had the heart next morning even to glance at the papers, but you did not need to glance at them, big type was bandied about that day as though it were common type, the words of the headlines stared at you; and the headlines said: Twenty-two Dead Men at a Club.

Yes, he saw it then: the laughter had not stopped, some had probably burst blood-vessels, some must have choked, some succumbed to nausea, heart-failure must have mercifully taken some, and they were his friends after all, and none had escaped, not even the waiters. It was that infernal joke.

He thought out swiftly, and remembers clear as a nightmare the drive to Victoria Station, the boat-train to Dover and going disguised to the boat: and on the boat pleasantly smiling, almost obsequious, two constables that wished to speak for a moment with Mr. Watkyn-Jones. That was his name.

In a third-class carriage with handcuffs on his wrists, with forced conversation when any, he returned between his captors to Victoria to be tried for murder at the High Court of Bow.

At the trial he was defended by a young barrister of considerable ability who had gone into the Cabinet in order to enhance his forensic reputation. And he was ably defended. It is no exaggeration to say that the speech for the defence showed it to be usual, even natural and right, to give a dinner to twenty men and to slip away without ever saying a word, leaving all, with the waiters, dead. That was the impression left in the minds of the jury. And Mr. Watkyn-Jones felt himself practically free, with all the advantages of his awful experience, and his two jokes intact. But lawyers are still experimenting with the new act which allows a prisoner to give evidence. They do not like to make no use of it for fear they may be thought not to know of the act, and a lawyer who is not in touch with the very latest laws is soon regarded as not being up to date, and he may drop as much as £50,000 a year in fees. And therefore though it always hangs their clients they hardly like to neglect it.

Mr. Watkyn-Jones was put in the witness-box. There he told the simple truth, and a very poor affair it seemed after the impassioned and beautiful things that were uttered by the counsel for the defence. Men and women had wept when they heard that. They did not weep when they heard Watkyn-Jones. Some tittered. It no longer seemed a right and natural thing to leave one's guests all dead and to fly the country. Where was Justice, they asked, if anyone could do that? And when his story was told the judge rather happily asked if he could make him die of laughter too. And what was the joke? For in so grave a place as a Court of Justice no fatal effects need be feared. And hesitatingly the prisoner pulled from his pocket the three slips of paper: and perceived for the first time that the one on which the first and best joke had been written had become quite blank. Yet he could remember it, and only too clearly. And he told it from memory to the Court.

"An Irishman once on being asked by his master to buy a morning paper said in his usual witty way, 'Arrah and begorrah and I will be after wishing you the top of the morning.'"

No joke sounds quite so good the second time it is told, it seems to lose something of its essence, but Watkyn-Jones was not prepared for the awful stillness with which this one was received; nobody smiled; and it had killed twenty-two men. The joke was bad, devilish bad; counsel for the defence was frowning, and an usher was looking in a little bag for something the judge wanted. And at this moment, as though from far away, without his wishing it, there entered the prisoner's head, and shone there and would not go, this old bad proverb: "As well be hung for a sheep as for a lamb." The jury seemed to be just about to retire. "I have another joke," said Watkyn-Jones, and then and there he read from the second slip of paper. He watched the paper curiously to see if it would go blank, occupying his mind with so slight a thing as men in dire distress very often do, and the words were almost immediately expunged, swept swiftly as if by a hand, and he saw the paper before him as blank as the first. And they were laughing this time, judge, jury, counsel for the prosecution, audience and all, and the grim men that watched him upon either side. There was no mistake about this joke.

He did not stay to see the end, and walked out with his eyes fixed on the ground, unable to bear a glance to the right or left. And since then he has wandered, avoiding ports and roaming lonely places. Two years have known him on the Highland roads, often hungry, always friendless, always changing his district, wandering lonely on with his deadly joke.

Sometimes for a moment he will enter inns, driven by cold and hunger, and hear men in the evening telling jokes, and even challenging him; but he sits desolate and silent, lest his only weapon should escape from him and his last joke spread mourning in a hundred cots. His beard has grown and turned grey and is mixed with moss and weeds, so that no one, I think, not even the police, would recognise him now for that dapper tout that sold the *Briton Dictionary of Electricity* in such a different land.

He paused, his story told, and then his lip quivered as though he would say more, and I believe he intended then and there to yield up his deadly joke on that Highland road and to go forth then with his three blank slips of paper, perhaps to a felon's cell, with one more murder added to his crimes, but harmless at last to man. I therefore hurried on, and only heard him mumbling sadly behind me, standing bowed and broken, all alone in the twilight, perhaps telling over and over even then the last infernal joke.

The Exiles' Club

It was an evening party; and something someone had said to me had started me talking about a subject that to me is full of fascination, the subject of old religions, forsaken gods. The truth (for all religions have some of it), the wisdom, the beauty, of the religions of countries to which I travel have not the same appeal for me; for one only notices in them their tyranny and intolerance and the abject servitude that they claim from thought; but when a dynasty has been dethroned in heaven and goes forgotten and outcast even among men, one's eyes no longer dazzled by its power find something very wistful in the faces of fallen gods suppliant to be remembered, something almost tearfully beautiful, like a long warm summer twilight fading gently away after some day memorable in the story of earthly wars. Between what Zeus, for instance, has been once and the half-remembered tale he is to-day there lies a space so great that there is no change of fortune known to man whereby we may measure the height down which he has fallen. And it is the same with many another god at whom once the ages trembled and the twentieth century treats as an old wives' tale. The fortitude that such a fall demands is surely more than human.

Some such things as these I was saying, and being upon a subject that much attracts me I possibly spoke too loudly. Certainly I was not aware that standing close behind me was no less a person than the ex-King of Eritivaria, the thirty islands of the East, or I would have moderated my voice and moved away a little to give him more room. I was not aware of his presence until his satellite, one who had fallen with him into exile but still revolved about him, told me that his master desired to know me: and so to my surprise I was presented, though neither of them even knew my name. And that was how I came to be invited by the ex-King to dine at his club.

At the time I could only account for his wishing to know me by supposing that he found in his own exiled condition some likeness to the fallen fortunes of the gods of whom I talked unwitting of his presence; but now I know that it was not of himself he was thinking when he asked me to dine at that club.

The club would have been the most imposing building in any street in London, but in that obscure mean quarter of London in which they had built it it appeared unduly enormous. Lifting right up above those grotesque houses, and built in that Greek style that we call Georgian, there was something Olympian about it. To my host an unfashionable street could have meant nothing, through all his youth wherever he had gone had become fashionable the moment he went there: words like the East End could have had no meaning to him.

Whoever built that house had enormous wealth and cared nothing for fashion, perhaps despised it. As I stood gazing at the magnificent upper windows draped with great curtains, indistinct in the evening, on which huge shadows flickered, my host attracted my attention from the doorway, and so I went in and met for the second time the ex-King of Eritivaria.

In front of us a stairway of rare marble led upwards. He took me through a side-door and downstairs and we came to a banqueting-hall of great magnificence. A long table ran up the middle of it, laid for quite twenty people, and I noticed the peculiarity that instead of chairs there were thrones, for everyone except me, who was the only guest and for whom there was an ordinary chair. My host explained to me when we all sat down that everyone who belonged to that club was by rights a king.

In fact none was permitted, he told me, to belong to the club until his claim to a kingdom, made out in writing, had been examined and allowed by those whose duty it was. The whim of a populace or the candidate's own misrule were never considered by the investigators, nothing counted with them but heredity and lawful descent from kings, all else was ignored. At that table there were those who had once reigned themselves, others lawfully claimed descent from kings that the world had forgotten, the kingdoms claimed by some had even changed their names. Hatzgurh, the mountain Kingdom, is almost regarded as mythical.

I have seldom seen greater splendour than that long hall provided below the level of the street. No doubt by day it was a little sombre, as all basements are, but at night with its great crystal chandeliers, and the glitter of heirlooms that had gone into exile, it surpassed the splendour of palaces that have only one king. They had come to London suddenly, most of those kings, or their fathers before them or forefathers; some had come away from their kingdoms by night, in a light sleigh, flogging the horses, or had galloped clear with morning over the border; some had trudged roads for days from their capital in disguise, yet many had had time just as they left to snatch up some small thing without price in markets, for the sake of old times as they said, but quite as much, I thought, with an eye to the future. And there these treasures glittered on that long table in the banqueting-hall of the basement of that strange club. Merely to see them was much, but to hear their story that their owners told was to go back in fancy to epic times on the romantic border of fable and fact, where the heroes of history fought with the gods of myth. The famous silver horses of Gilgianza were there, climbing their sheer mountain, which they did by miraculous means before the time of the Goths. It was not a large piece of silver, but its workmanship out-rivalled the skill of the bees.

A yellow Emperor had brought out of the East a piece of that incomparable porcelain that had made his dynasty famous though all their deeds are forgotten, it had the exact shade of the right purple.

And there was a little golden statuette of a dragon stealing a diamond from a lady, the dragon had the diamond in his claws, large and of the first water. There had been a kingdom whose whole constitution and history were founded on the legend, from which alone its kings had claimed their right to the sceptre, that a dragon stole a diamond from a lady. When its last king left that country, because his favourite general used a peculiar formation under the fire of artillery, he brought with him the little ancient image that no longer proved him a king outside that singular club.

There was the pair of amethyst cups of the turbaned King of Foo, the one that he drank from himself, and the one that he gave to his enemies: eye could not tell which was which.

All these things the ex-King of Eritivaria showed me, telling me a marvellous tale of each; of his own he had brought nothing, except the mascot that used once to sit on the top of the water tube of his favourite motor.

I have not outlined a tenth of the splendour of that table, I had meant to come again and examine each piece of plate and make notes of its history; had I known that this was the last time I should wish to enter that club I should have looked at its treasures more attentively, but now as the wine went round and the exiles began to talk I took my eyes from the table and listened to strange tales of their former state.

He that has seen better times has usually a poor tale to tell, some mean and trivial thing has been his undoing, but they that dined in that basement had mostly fallen like oaks on nights of abnormal tempest, had fallen mightily and shaken a nation. Those who had not been kings themselves, but claimed through an exiled ancestor, had stories to tell of even grander disaster, history seeming to have mellowed their dynasty's fate as moss grows over an oak a great while fallen. There were no jealousies there as so often there are among kings, rivalry must have ceased with the loss of their navies and armies, and they showed no bitterness against those that had turned them out, one speaking of the error of his Prime Minister by which he had lost his throne as "poor old Friedrich's heaven-sent gift of tactlessness."

They gossiped pleasantly of many things, the tittle-tattle we all had to know when we were learning history, and many a wonderful story I might have heard, many a sidelight on mysterious wars, had I not made use of one unfortunate word. That word was "upstairs."

The ex-King of Eritivaria having pointed out to me those unparalleled heirlooms to which I have alluded, and many more besides, hospitably asked me if there was anything else that I would care to see; he meant the pieces of plate that they had in the cupboards, the curiously graven swords of other princes, historic jewels, legendary seals; but I who had had a glimpse of their marvellous staircase, whose balustrade I believed to be solid gold, and wondering why in such a stately house they chose to dine in the basement, mentioned the word "upstairs." A hush as at sacrilege came down on the whole assembly, the hush that might greet levity in a cathedral.

"Upstairs!" he gasped. "We cannot go upstairs."

I perceived that what I had said was an ill-chosen thing. I tried to excuse myself but knew not how.

"Of course," I muttered, "members may not take guests upstairs."

"Members!" he said to me. "We are not the members!"

There was such reproof in his voice that I said no more, I looked at him questioningly, perhaps my lips moved, I may have said, "What are you?" A great surprise had come on me at their attitude.

"We are the waiters," he said.

That I could not have known, here at least was honest ignorance that I had no need to be ashamed of, the very opulence of their table denied it.

"Then who are the members?" I asked.

Such a hush fell at that question, such a hush of genuine awe, that all of a sudden a wild thought entered my head, a thought strange and fantastic and terrible. I gripped my host by the wrist and hushed my voice.

"Are they too exiles?" I asked.

Twice as he looked in my face he gravely nodded his head.

I left that club very swiftly indeed, never to see it again, scarcely pausing to say farewell to those menial kings, and as I left the door a great window opened far up at the top of the house and a flash of lightning streamed from it and killed a dog.

Thirteen at Table

In front of a spacious fire-place of the old kind, when the logs were well alight, and men with pipes and glasses were gathered before it in great easeful chairs, and the wild weather outside and the comfort that was within, and the season of the year—for it was Christmas—and the hour of the night, all called for the weird or uncanny, then out spoke the ex-master of fox-hounds and told this tale.

"I once had an odd experience too. It was when I had the Bromley and Sydenham, the year I gave them up—as a matter of fact it was the last day of the season. It was no use going on because there were no foxes left in the country, and London was sweeping down on us. You could see it from the kennels all along the skyline like a terrible army in grey, and masses of villas every year came skirmishing down our valleys. Our coverts were mostly on the hills, and as the town came down upon the valleys the foxes used to leave them and go right away out of the country, and they never returned. I think they went by night and moved great distances. Well, it was early April and we had drawn blank all day, and at the last draw of all, the very last of the season, we found a fox. He left the covert with his back to London and its railways and villas and wire, and slipped away towards the chalk country and open Kent. I felt as I once felt as a child on one summer's day when I found a door in a garden where I played left luckily ajar, and I pushed it open and the wide lands were before me and waving fields of corn.

"We settled down into a steady gallop and the fields began to drift by under us, and a great wind arose full of fresh breath. We left the clay lands where the bracken grows and came to a valley at the edge of the chalk. As we went down into it we saw the fox go up the other side like a shadow that crosses the evening, and glide into a wood that stood on the top. We saw a flash of primroses in the wood and we were out the other side, hounds hunting perfectly and the fox still going absolutely straight. It began to dawn on me then that we were in for a great hunt; I took a deep breath when I thought of it; the taste of the air of that perfect spring afternoon as it came to one galloping, and the thought of a great run, were together like some old rare wine. Our faces now were to another valley, large fields led down to it with easy hedges, at the bottom of it a bright blue stream went singing and a rambling village smoked, the sunlight on the opposite slopes danced like a fairy; and all along the top old woods were frowning, but they dreamed of spring. The field had fallen off and were far behind and my only human companion was James, my old first whip, who had a hound's instinct, and a personal animosity against a fox that even embittered his speech.

"Across the valley the fox went as straight as a railway line, and again we went without a check straight through the woods at the top. I remember hearing men sing or shout as they walked home from work, and sometimes children whistled; the sounds came up from the village to the woods at the top of the valley. After that we saw no more villages, but valley after valley arose and fell before us as though we were voyaging some strange and stormy sea; and all the way before us the fox went dead up-wind like the fabulous flying Dutchman. There was no one in sight now but my first whip and me; we had both of us got on to our second horses as we drew the last covert. Two or three times we checked in those great lonely valleys beyond the village, but I began to have inspirations; I felt a strange certainty within me that this fox was going on straight up-wind till he died or until night came and we could hunt no longer, so I reversed ordinary methods and only cast straight ahead, and always we picked up the scent again at once. I believe that this fox was the last one left in the villa-haunted lands and that he was prepared to leave them for remote uplands far from men, that if we had come the following day he would not have been there, and that we just happened to hit off his journey.

"Evening began to descend upon the valleys, still the hounds drifted on, like the lazy but unresting shadows of clouds upon a summer's day; we heard a shepherd calling to his dog, we saw two maidens move toward a hidden farm, one of them singing softly; no other sounds but ours disturbed the leisure and the loneliness of haunts that seemed not yet to have known the inventions of steam and gunpowder.

"And now the day and our horses were wearing out, but that resolute fox held on. I began to work out the run and to wonder where we were. The last landmark I had ever seen before must have been over five miles back, and from there to the start was at least ten miles more. If only we could kill! Then the sun set. I wondered what chance we had of killing our fox. I looked at James' face as he rode beside me. He did not seem to have lost any confidence, yet his horse was as tired as mine. It was a good clear twilight and the scent was as strong as ever, and the fences were easy enough, but those valleys were terribly trying, and they still rolled on and on. It looked as if the light would outlast all possible endurance both of the fox and the horses, if the scent held good and he did not go to ground, otherwise night would end it. For long we had seen no houses and no roads, only chalk slopes with the twilight on them, and here and there some sheep, and scattered copses darkening in the evening. At some moment I seemed to realize all at once that the light was spent and that darkness was hovering. I looked at James, he was solemnly shaking his head. Suddenly in a little wooded valley we saw climb over the oaks the red-brown gables of a queer old house; at that instant I saw the fox scarcely leading by fifty yards. We blundered through a wood into full sight of the house, but no avenue led up to it or even a path, nor were there any signs of wheelmarks anywhere. Already lights shone here and there in windows. We were in a park, and a fine park, but unkempt beyond credibility; brambles grew everywhere. It was too dark to see the fox any more, but we knew he was dead-beat, the hounds were just before us—and a four-foot railing of oak. I shouldn't have tried it on a fresh horse at the beginning of a run, and here was a horse near his last gasp, but what a run! an event standing out in a life-time, and the hounds, close up on their fox, slipping into the darkness as I hesitated. I decided to try it. My horse rose about eight inches and took it fair with his breast, and the oak log flew into handfuls of wet decay,—it was rotten with years. And then we were on a lawn, and at the far end of it the hounds were tumbling over their fox. Fox, horses, and light were all done together at the end of a twenty-mile point. We made some noise then, but nobody came out of the queer old house.

"I felt pretty stiff as I walked round to the hall door with the mask and the brush, while James went with the hounds and the two horses to look for the stables. I rang a bell marvellously encrusted with rust, and after a long while the door opened a little way, revealing a hall with much old armour in it and the shabbiest butler that I have ever known.

"I asked him who lived there. Sir Richard Arlen. I explained that my horse could go no further that night, and that I wished to ask Sir Richard Arlen for a bed.

" 'O, no one ever comes here, sir,' said the butler.

"I pointed out that I had come.

" 'I don't think it would be possible, sir,' he said.

"This annoyed me, and I asked to see Sir Richard, and insisted until he came. Then I apologized and explained the situation. He looked only fifty, but a 'Varsity oar on the wall with the date of the early seventies made him older than that; his face had something of the shy look of the hermit; he regretted that he had not room to put me up. I was sure that this was untrue, also I had to be put up there, there was nowhere else within miles, so I almost insisted. Then, to my astonishment, he turned to the butler and they talked it over in an undertone. At last they seemed to think that they could manage it, though clearly with reluctance. It was by now seven o'clock, and Sir Richard told me he dined at half-past seven. There was no question of clothes for me other than those I stood in, as my host was shorter and broader. He showed me presently to the drawing-room, and then he reappeared before half-past seven in evening dress and a white waistcoat. The drawing-room was large and contained old furniture, but it was rather worn than venerable; an aubusson carpet flapped about the floor, the wind seemed momently to enter the room, and old draughts haunted corners; stealthy feet of rats that were never at rest indicated the extent of the ruin that time had wrought in the wainscot, somewhere far off a shutter flapped to and fro, the guttering candles were insufficient to light so large a room. The gloom that these things suggested was quite in keeping with Sir Richard's first remark to me after he entered the room.

" 'I must tell you, sir, that I have led a wicked life. O, a very wicked life.'

"Such confidences from a man much older than oneself after one has known him for half an hour are so rare that any possible answer merely does not suggest itself. I said rather slowly, 'O, really,' and chiefly to forestall another such remark, I said, 'What a charming house you have.'

" 'Yes,' he said, 'I have not left it for nearly forty years. Since I left the 'Varsity. One is young there, you know, and one has opportunities; but I make no excuses, no excuses.' And the door slipping its rusty latch, came drifting on the draught into the room, and the long carpet flapped and the hangings upon the walls, then the draught fell rustling away and the door slammed to again.

" 'Ah, Marianne,' he said. 'We have a guest to-night. Mr. Linton. This is Marianne Gib.' And everything became clear to me. 'Mad,' I said to myself, for no one had entered the room.

"The rats ran up the length of the room behind the wainscot ceaselessly, and the wind unlatched the door again and the folds of the carpet fluttered up to our feet and stopped there, for our weight held it down.

" 'Let me introduce Mr. Linton,' said my host. 'Lady Mary Errinjer.'

"The door slammed back again. I bowed politely. Even had I been invited I should have humoured him, but it was the very least that an uninvited guest could do.

"This kind of thing happened eleven times, the rustling, and the fluttering of the carpet, and the footsteps of the rats, and the restless door, and then the sad voice of my host introducing me to phantoms. Then for some while we waited while I struggled with the situation; conversation flowed slowly. And again the draught came trailing up the room, while the flaring candles filled it with hurrying shadows. 'Ah, late again, Cicely,' said my host in his soft mournful way. 'Always late, Cicely.' Then I went down to dinner with that man and his mind and the twelve phantoms that haunted it. I found a long table with fine old silver on it, and places laid for fourteen. The butler was now in evening dress, there were fewer draughts in the dining-room, the scene was less gloomy there. 'Will you sit next to Rosalind at the other end?' Sir Richard said to me. 'She always takes the head of the table. I wronged her most of all.'

"I said, 'I shall be delighted.'

"I looked at the butler closely; but never did I see by any expression of his face, or by anything that he did, any suggestion that he waited upon less than fourteen people in the complete possession of all their faculties. Perhaps a dish appeared to be refused more often than taken, but every glass was equally filled with champagne. At first I found little to say, but when Sir Richard, speaking from the far end of the table, said, 'You are tired, Mr. Linton?' I was reminded that I owed something to a host upon whom I had forced myself. It was excellent champagne, and with the help of a second glass I made the effort to begin a conversation with a Miss Helen Errold, for whom the place upon one side of me was laid. It came more easy to me very soon; I frequently paused in my monologue, like Mark Antony, for a reply, and sometimes I turned and spoke to Miss Rosalind Smith. Sir Richard at the other end talked sorrowfully on; he spoke as a condemned man might speak to his judge, and yet somewhat as a judge might speak to one that he once condemned wrongly. My own mind began to turn to mournful things. I drank another glass of champagne, but I was still thirsty. I felt as if all the moisture in my body had been blown away over the downs of Kent by the wind up which we had galloped. Still I was not talking enough: my host was looking at me. I made another effort; after all I had something to talk about: a twenty-mile point is not often seen in a lifetime, especially south of the Thames. I began to describe the run to Rosalind Smith. I could see then that my host was pleased, the sad look in his face gave a kind of a flicker, like mist upon the mountains on a miserable day when a faint puff comes from the sea and the mist would lift if it could. And the butler refilled my glass very attentively. I asked her first if she hunted, and paused and began my story. I told her where we found the fox and how fast and straight he had gone, and how I had got through the village by keeping to the road, while the little gardens and wire, and then the river had stopped the rest of the field. I told her the kind of country that we crossed and how splendid it looked in the spring, and how mysterious the valleys were as soon as the twilight came, and what a glorious horse I had and how wonderfully he went.

"I was so fearfully thirsty after the great hunt that I had to stop for a moment now and then, but I went on with my description of that famous run, for I had warmed to the subject, and after all there was nobody to tell of it but me except my old whipper-in, and 'the old fellow's probably drunk by now' I thought. I described to her minutely the exact spot in the run at which it had come to me clearly that this was going to be the greatest hunt in the whole history of Kent. Sometimes I forgot incidents that had happened, as one well may in a run of twenty miles, and then I had to fill in the gaps by inventing. I was pleased to be able to make the party go off well by means of my conversation, and besides that the lady to whom I was speaking was extremely pretty: I do not mean in a flesh-and-blood kind of way, but there were little shadowy lines about the chair beside me that hinted at an unusually graceful figure when Miss Rosalind Smith was alive; and I began to perceive that what I first mistook for the smoke of guttering candles and a tablecloth waving in the draught was in reality an extremely animated company who listened, and not without interest, to my story of by far the greatest hunt that the world had ever known: indeed, I told them that I would confidently go further and predict that never in the history of the world would there be such a run again. Only my throat was terribly dry.

"And then, as it seemed, they wanted to hear more about my horse. I had forgotten that I had come there on a horse, but when they reminded me it all came back; they looked so charming leaning over the table, intent upon what I said, that I told them everything they wanted to know. Everything was going so pleasantly if only Sir Richard would cheer up. I heard his mournful voice every now and then—these were very pleasant people if only he would take them the right way. I could understand that he regretted his past, but the early seventies seemed centuries away, and I felt now that he misunderstood these ladies, they were not revengeful as he seemed to suppose. I wanted to show him how cheerful they really were, and so I made a joke and they all laughed at it, and then I chaffed them a bit, especially Rosalind, and nobody resented it in the very least. And still Sir Richard sat there with that unhappy look, like one that has ended weeping because it is vain and has not the consolation even of tears.

"We had been a long time there, and many of the candles had burnt out, but there was light enough. I was glad to have an audience for my exploit, and being happy myself I was determined Sir Richard should be. I made more jokes and they still laughed good-naturedly; some of the jokes were a little broad perhaps, but no harm was meant. And then,—I do not wish to excuse myself, but I had had a harder day than I ever had had before, and without knowing it I must have been completely exhausted; in this state the champagne had found me, and what would have been harmless at any other time must somehow have got the better of me when quite tired out. Anyhow, I went too far, I made some joke,—I cannot in the least remember what— that suddenly seemed to offend them. I felt all at once a commotion in the air; I looked up and saw that they had all risen from the table and were sweeping towards the door. I had not time to open it, but it blew open on a wind; I could scarcely see what Sir Richard was doing because only two candles were left, I think the rest blew out when the ladies suddenly rose. I sprang up to apologize, to assure them—and then fatigue overcame me as it had overcome my horse at the last fence, I clutched at the table, but the cloth came away, and then I fell. The fall, and the darkness on the floor, and the pent-up fatigue of the day overcame me all three together.

"The sun shone over glittering fields and in at a bedroom window, and thousands of birds were chaunting to the spring, and there I was in an old four-poster bed in a quaint old panelled bedroom, fully dressed, and wearing long muddy boots; someone had taken my spurs and that was all. For a moment I failed to realize, and then it all came back— my enormity and the pressing need of an abject apology to Sir Richard. I pulled an embroidered bell-rope until the butler came; he came in perfectly cheerful and indescribably shabby. I asked him if Sir Richard was up, and he said he had just gone down, and told me to my amazement that it was twelve o'clock. I asked to be shown in to Sir Richard at once.

"He was in his smoking-room. 'Good morning,' he said cheerfully the moment I went in. I went directly to the matter in hand. 'I fear that I insulted some ladies in your house . . .' I began.

" 'You did indeed,' he said. 'You did indeed.' And then he burst into tears, and took me by the hand. 'How can I ever thank you?' he said to me then. 'We have been thirteen at table for thirty years, and I never dared to insult them because I had wronged them all, and now you have done it, and I know they will never dine here again.' And for a long time he still held my hand, and then he gave it a grip and a kind of a shake which I took to mean 'good-bye,' and I drew my hand away then and left the house. And I found James in the disused stables with the hounds and asked him how he had fared, and James, who is a man of very few words, said he could not rightly remember, and I got my spurs from the butler and climbed on to my horse; and slowly we rode away from that queer old house, and slowly we wended home, for the hounds were foot-sore but happy and the horses were tired still. And when we recalled that the hunting season was ended, we turned our faces to spring and thought of the new things that try to replace the old. And that very year I heard, and have often heard since, of dances and happier dinners at Sir Richard Arlen's house."

The Wonderful Window

THE OLD MAN in the Oriental-looking robe was being moved on by the police, and it was this that attracted to him and the parcel under his arm the attention of Mr. Sladden, whose livelihood was earned in the emporium of Messrs. Mergin and Chater, that is to say in their establishment.

Mr. Sladden had the reputation of being the silliest young man in Business; a touch of romance—a mere suggestion of it—would send his eyes gazing away as though the walls of the emporium were of gossamer and London itself a myth, instead of attending to customers.

Merely the fact that the dirty piece of paper that wrapped the old man's parcel was covered with Arabic writing was enough to give Mr. Sladden the idea of romance, and he followed until the little crowd fell off and the stranger stopped by the kerb and unwrapped his parcel and prepared to sell the thing that was inside it. It was a little window in old wood with small panes set in lead; it was not much more than a foot in breadth and was under two feet long. Mr. Sladden had never before seen a window sold in the street, so he asked the price of it.

"Its price is all you possess," said the old man.

"Where did you get it?" said Mr. Sladden, for it was a strange window.

"I gave all that I possessed for it in the streets of Baghdad."

"Did you possess much?" said Mr. Sladden.

"I had all that I wanted," he said, "except this window."

"It must be a good window," said the young man.

"It is a magical window," said the old one.

"I have only ten shillings on me, but I have fifteen-and-six at home."

The old man thought for a while.

"Then twenty-five-and-sixpence is the price of the window," he said.

It was only when the bargain was completed and the ten shillings paid and the strange old man was coming for his fifteen-and-six and to fit the magical window into his only room that it occurred to Mr. Sladden's mind that he did not want a window. And then they were at the door of the house in which he rented a room, and it seemed too late to explain.

The stranger demanded privacy while he fitted up the window, so Mr. Sladden remained outside the door at the top of a little flight of creaky stairs. He heard no sound of hammering.

And presently the strange old man came out with his faded yellow robe and his great beard, and his eyes on far-off places. "It is finished," he said, and he and the young man parted. And whether he remained a spot of colour and an anachronism in London, or whether he ever came again to Baghdad, and what dark hands kept on the circulation of his twenty-five-and-six, Mr. Sladden never knew.

Mr. Sladden entered the bare-boarded room in which he slept and spent all his indoor hours between closing-time and the hour at which Messrs. Mergin and Chater commenced. To the Penates of so dingy a room his neat frock-coat must have been a continual wonder. Mr. Sladden took it off and folded it carefully; and there was the old man's window rather high up in the wall. There had been no window in that wall hitherto, nor any ornament at all but a small cupboard, so when Mr. Sladden had put his frock-coat safely away he glanced through his new window. It was where his cupboard had been in which he kept his tea-things: they were all standing on the table now. When Mr. Sladden glanced through his new window it was late in a summer's evening; the butterflies some while ago would have closed their wings, though the bat would scarcely yet be drifting abroad —but this was in London: the shops were shut and street-lamps not yet lighted.

Mr. Sladden rubbed his eyes, then rubbed the window, and still he saw a sky of blazing blue, and far, far down beneath him, so that no sound came up from it or smoke of chimneys, a mediaeval city set with towers. Brown roofs and cobbled streets, and then white walls and buttresses, and beyond them bright green fields and tiny streams. On the towers archers lolled, and along the walls were pikemen, and now and then a wagon went down some old-world street and lumbered through the gateway and out to the country, and now and then a wagon drew up to the city from the mist that was rolling with evening over the fields. Sometimes folk put their heads out of lattice windows, sometimes some idle troubadour seemed to sing, and nobody hurried or troubled about anything. Airy and dizzy though the distance was, for Mr. Sladden seemed higher above the city than any cathedral gargoyle, yet one clear detail he obtained as a clue: the banners floating from every tower over the idle archers had little golden dragons all over a pure white field.

He heard the motor-buses roar by his other window, he heard the newsboys howling.

Mr. Sladden grew dreamier than ever after that on the premises, in the establishment, of Messrs. Mergin and Chater. But in one matter he was wise and wakeful: he made continuous and careful inquiries about golden dragons on a white flag, and talked to no one of his wonderful window. He came to know the flags of every king in Europe, he even dabbled in history, he made inquiries at shops that understood heraldry, but nowhere could he learn any trace of little dragons *or* on a field *argent*. And when it seemed that for him alone those golden dragons had fluttered he came to love them as an exile in some desert might love the lilies of his home or as a sick man might love swallows when he cannot easily live to another spring.

As soon as Messrs. Mergin and Chater closed, Mr. Sladden used to go back to his dingy room and gaze through the wonderful window until it grew dark in the city and the guard would go with a lantern round the ramparts and the night came up like velvet, full of strange stars. Another clue he tried to obtain one night by jotting down the shapes of the constellations, but this led him no further, for they were unlike any that shone upon either hemisphere.

Each day as soon as he woke he went first to the wonderful window, and there was the city, diminutive in the distance, all shining in the morning, and the golden dragons dancing in the sun, and the archers stretching themselves or swinging their arms on the tops of the windy towers. The window would not open, so that he never heard the songs that the troubadours sang down there beneath gilded balconies; he did not even hear the belfries' chimes, though he saw the jackdaws routed every hour from their homes. And the first thing that he always did was to cast his eye round all the little towers that rose up from the ramparts to see that the little golden dragons were flying there on their flags. And when he saw them flaunting themselves on white folds from every tower against the marvellous deep blue of the sky he dressed contentedly, and, taking one last look, went off to his work with a glory in his mind. It would have been difficult for the customers of Messrs. Mergin and Chater to guess the precise ambition of Mr. Sladden as he walked before them in his neat frock-coat: it was that he might be a man-at-arms or an archer in order to fight for the little golden dragons that flew on a white flag for an unknown king in an inaccessible city. At first Mr. Sladden used to walk round and round the mean street that he lived in, but he gained no clue from that; and soon he noticed that quite different winds blew below his wonderful window from those that blew on the other side of the house.

In August the evenings began to grow shorter: this was the very remark that the other employés made to him at the emporium, so that he almost feared that they suspected his secret, and he had much less time for the wonderful window, for lights were few down there and they blinked out early.

One morning late in August, just before he went to Business, Mr. Sladden saw a company of pikemen running down the cobbled road towards the gateway of the mediaeval city—Golden Dragon City he used to call it alone in his own mind, but he never spoke of it to anyone. The next thing that he noticed was that the archers on the towers were talking a good deal together and were handing round bundles of arrows in addition to the quivers which they wore. Heads were thrust out of windows more than usual, a woman ran out and called some children indoors, a knight rode down the street, and then more pikemen appeared along the walls, and all the jackdaws were in the air. In the street no troubadour sang. Mr. Sladden took one look along the towers to see that the flags were flying, and all the golden dragons were streaming in the wind. Then he had to go to Business. He took a 'bus back that evening and ran upstairs. Nothing seemed to be happening in Golden Dragon City except a crowd in the cobbled street that led down to the gateway; the archers seemed to be reclining as usual lazily in their towers, then a white flag went down with all its golden dragons; he did not see at first that all the archers were dead. The crowd was pouring towards him, towards the precipitous wall from which he looked, men with a white flag covered with golden dragons were moving backwards slowly, men with another flag were pressing them, a flag on which there was one huge red bear. Another banner went down upon a tower. Then he saw it all: the golden dragons were being beaten—his little golden dragons. The men of the bear were coming under the window; whatever he threw from that height would fall with terrific force: fire-irons, coal, his clock, whatever he had—he would fight for his little golden dragons yet. A flame broke out from one of the towers and licked the feet of a reclining archer; he did not stir. And now the alien standard was out of sight directly underneath. Mr. Sladden broke the panes of the wonderful window and wrenched away with a poker the lead that held them. Just as the glass broke he saw a banner covered with golden dragons fluttering still, and then as he drew back to hurl the poker there came to him the scent of mysterious spices, and there was nothing there, not even the daylight, for behind the fragments of the wonderful window was nothing but that small cupboard in which he kept his tea-things.

And though Mr. Sladden is older now and knows more of the world, and even has a Business of his own, he has never been able to buy such another window, and has not ever since, either from books or men, heard any rumour at all of Golden Dragon City.

The Bureau d'Echange de Maux

I OFTEN think of the Bureau d'Echange de Maux and the won-
drously evil old man that sate therein. It stood in a little street
that there is in Paris, its doorway made of three brown beams of
wood, the top one overlapping the others like the Greek letter pi,
all the rest painted green, a house far lower and narrower than
its neighbours and infinitely stranger, a thing to take one's fancy.
And over the doorway on the old brown beam in faded yellow
letters this legend ran, "Bureau Universel d'Echange de Maux."

I entered at once and accosted the listless man that lolled on a
stool by his counter. I demanded the wherefore of his wonderful
house, what evil wares he exchanged, with many other things
that I wished to know, for curiosity led me: and indeed had it not
I had gone at once from the shop, for there was so evil a look in
that fattened man, in the hang of his fallen cheeks and his sinful
eye, that you would have said he had had dealings with Hell and
won the advantage by sheer wickedness.

Such a man was mine host, but above all the evil of him lay in
his eyes, which lay so still, so apathetic, that you would have sworn
that he was drugged or dead; like lizards motionless on a wall
they lay, then suddenly they darted, and all his cunning flamed
up and revealed itself in what one moment before seemed no
more than a sleepy and ordinary wicked old man. And this was
the object and trade of that peculiar shop, the Bureau Universel
d'Echange de Maux: you paid twenty francs, which the old man
proceeded to take from me, for admission to the bureau, and
then had the right to exchange any evil or misfortune with anyone

on the premises for some evil or misfortune that he "could afford," as the old man put it.

There were four or five men in the dingy ends of that low-ceilinged room who gesticulated and muttered softly in twos as men who make a bargain, and now and then more came in, and the eyes of the flabby owner of the house leaped up at them as they entered, seemed to know their errands at once and each one's peculiar need, and fell back again into somnolence, receiving his twenty francs in an almost lifeless hand and biting the coin as though in pure absence of mind.

"Some of my clients," he told me. So amazing to me was the trade of this extraordinary shop that I engaged the old man in conversation, repulsive though he was, and from his garrulity I gathered these facts. He spoke in perfect English though his utterance was somewhat thick and heavy, no language seemed to come amiss to him. He had been in business a great many years, how many he would not say, and was far older than he looked. All kinds of people did business in his shop. What they exchanged with each other he did not care, except that it had to be evils; he was not empowered to carry on any other kind of business.

There was no evil, he told me, that was not negotiable there; no evil the old man knew had ever been taken away in despair from his shop. A man might have to wait and come back again next day and next day and the day after, paying twenty francs each time, but the old man had the addresses of his clients and shrewdly knew their needs, and soon the right two met and eagerly changed their commodities. "Commodities" was the old man's terrible word, said with a gruesome smack of his heavy lips, for he took a pride in his business and evils to him were goods.

I learned from him in ten minutes very much of human nature, more than I had ever learned from any other man; I learned from him that a man's own evil is to him the worst thing that there is or could be, and that an evil so unbalances all men's minds that they always seek for extremes in that small grim shop. A woman that had no children had exchanged with an impoverished half-maddened creature with twelve. On one occasion a man had exchanged wisdom for folly.

"Why on earth did he do that?" I said.

"None of my business," the old man answered in his heavy indolent way. He merely took his twenty francs from each and

ratified the agreement in the little room at the back opening out of
the shop where his clients do business. Apparently the man that
had parted with wisdom had left the shop upon the tips of his
toes with a happy though foolish expression all over his face, but
the other went thoughtfully away wearing a troubled and very
puzzled look. Almost always it seemed they did business in opposite evils.

But the thing that puzzled me most in all my talks with that
unwieldy man, the thing that puzzles me still, is that none that
had once done business in that shop ever returned again; a man
might come day after day for many weeks, but once do business
and he never returned; so much the old man told me, but, when
I asked him why, he only muttered that he did not know.

It was to discover the wherefore of this strange thing, and for
no other reason at all, that I determined myself to do business
sooner or later in the little room at the back of that mysterious
shop. I determined to exchange some very trivial evil for some
evil equally slight, to seek for myself an advantage so very small
as scarcely to give Fate as it were a grip; for I deeply distrusted
these bargains, knowing well that man has never yet benefited by
the marvellous and that the more miraculous his advantage ap-
pears to be the more securely and tightly do the gods or the
witches catch him. In a few days more I was going back to
England and I was beginning to fear that I should be sea-sick:
this fear of sea-sickness, not the actual malady but only the mere
fear of it, I decided to exchange for a suitably little evil. I did
not know with whom I should be dealing, who in reality was the
head of the firm (one never does when shopping), but I decided
that no one could make very much on so small a bargain as that.

I told the old man my project, and he scoffed at the small-
ness of my commodity, trying to urge me on to some darker bargain, but could not move me from my purpose. And then he
told me tales with a somewhat boastful air of the big business,
the great bargains, that had passed through his hands. A man
had once run in there to try to exchange death; he had swallowed
poison by accident and had only twelve hours to live. That sinister old man had been able to oblige him. A client was willing
to exchange the commodity.

"But what did he give in exchange for death?" I said.

"Life," said that grim old man with a furtive chuckle.

"It must have been a horrible life," I said.

"That was not my affair," the proprietor said, lazily rattling together as he spoke a little pocketful of twenty-franc pieces.

Strange business I watched in that shop for the next few days, the exchange of odd commodities, and heard strange mutterings in corners amongst couples who presently rose and went to the back room, the old man following to ratify.

Twice a day for a week I paid my twenty francs, watching life with its great needs and its little needs morning and afternoon spread out before me in all its wonderful variety.

And one day I met a comfortable man with only a little need, he seemed to have the very evil I wanted. He always feared the lift was going to break. I knew too much of hydraulics to fear things as silly as that, but it was not my business to cure his ridiculous fear. Very few words were needed to convince him that mine was the evil for him, he never crossed the sea, and I, on the other hand, could always walk upstairs, and I also felt at the time, as many must feel in that shop, that so absurd a fear could never trouble me. And yet at times it is almost the curse of my life. When we both had signed the parchment in the spidery back room and the old man had signed and ratified (for which we had to pay him fifty francs each) I went back to my hotel, and there I saw the deadly thing in the basement. They asked me if I would go upstairs in the lift; from force of habit I risked it, and I held my breath all the way up and clenched my hands. Nothing will induce me to try such a journey again. I would sooner go up to my room in a balloon. And why? Because if a balloon goes wrong you have a chance, it may spread out into a parachute after it has burst, it may catch in a tree, a hundred and one things may happen, but if the lift falls down its shaft you are done. As for sea-sickness I shall never be sick again, I cannot tell you why except that I know that it is so.

And the shop in which I made this remarkable bargain, the shop to which none return when their business is done: I set out for it next day. Blindfold I could have found my way to the unfashionable quarter out of which a mean street runs, where you take the alley at the end, whence runs the cul-de-sac where the queer shop stood. A shop with pillars, fluted and painted red, stands on its near side, its other neighbour is a low-class jeweller's with little silver brooches in the window. In such incongruous company stood the shop with beams, with its walls painted green.

In half an hour I stood in the cul-de-sac to which I had gone twice a day for the last week. I found the shop with the ugly painted pillars and the jeweller that sold brooches, but the green house with the three beams was gone.

Pulled down, you will say, although in a single night. That can never be the answer to the mystery, for the house of the fluted pillars painted on plaster, and the low-class jeweller's shop with its silver brooches (all of which I could identify one by one) were standing side by side.

The Ghosts

THE argument that I had with my brother in his great lonely house will scarcely interest my readers. Not those, at least, who I hope may be attracted by the experiment that I undertook, and by the strange things that befell me in that hazardous region into which so lightly and so ignorantly I allowed my fancy to enter. It was at Oneleigh that I had visited him.

Now Oneleigh stands in a wide isolation, in the midst of a dark gathering of old whispering cedars. They nod their heads together when the North Wind comes, and nod again and agree, and furtively grow still again, and say no more awhile. The North Wind is to them like a nice problem among wise old men; they nod their heads over it, and mutter about it all together. They know much, those cedars, they have been there so long. Their grandsires knew Lebanon, and the grandsires of these were the servants of the King of Tyre and came to Solomon's court. And amidst these black-haired children of grey-headed Time stood the old house of Oneleigh. I know not how many centuries had lashed against it their evanescent foam of years; but it was still unshattered, and all about it were the things of long ago, as cling strange growths to some sea-defying rock. Here, like the shells of long-dead limpets, was armour that men encased themselves in long ago; here, too, were tapestries of many colours, beautiful as seaweed; no modern flotsam ever drifted hither, no early Victorian furniture, no electric light. The great trade routes that littered the years with empty meat tins and cheap novels were far from here. Well, well, the centuries will shatter it and drive its fragments on to distant shores. Mean-

Oneleigh

"A Herd of Black Creatures"

while, while it yet stood, I went on a visit there to my brother, and we argued about ghosts. My brother's intelligence on this subject seemed to me to be in need of correction. He mistook things imagined for things having an actual existence; he argued that second-hand evidence of persons having seen ghosts proved ghosts to exist. I said that even if they had seen ghosts, this was no proof at all; nobody believes that there are red rats, though there is plenty of first-hand evidence of men having seen them in delirium. Finally, I said I would see ghosts myself, and continue to argue against their actual existence. So I collected a handful of cigars and drank several cups of very strong tea, and went without my dinner, and retired into a room where there was dark oak and all the chairs were covered with tapestry; and my brother went to bed bored with our argument, and trying hard to dissuade me from making myself uncomfortable. All the way up the old stairs as I stood at the bottom of them, and as his candle went winding up and up, I heard him still trying to persuade me to have supper and go to bed.

It was a windy winter, and outside the cedars were muttering I know not what about; but I think that they were Tories of a school long dead, and were troubled about something new. Within, a great damp log upon the fireplace began to squeak and sing, and struck up a whining tune, and a tall flame stood up over it and beat time, and all the shadows crowded round and began to dance. In distant corners old masses of darkness sat still like chaperones and never moved. Over there, in the darkest part of the room, stood a door that was always locked. It led into the hall, but no one ever used it; near that door something had happened once of which the family are not proud. We do not speak of it. There in the firelight stood the venerable forms of the old chairs; the hands that had made their tapestries lay far beneath the soil, the needles with which they wrought were many separate flakes of rust. No one wove now in that old room —no one but the assiduous ancient spiders who, watching by the deathbed of the things of yore, worked shrouds to hold their dust. In shrouds about the cornices already lay the heart of the oak wainscot that the worm had eaten out.

Surely at such an hour, in such a room, a fancy already excited by hunger and strong tea might see the ghosts of former occupants. I expected nothing less. The fire flickered and the shadows danced, memories of strange historic things rose vividly in my mind; but midnight chimed solemnly from a seven-foot clock, and nothing happened. My imagination would not be hurried, and the chill that is with the small hours had come upon me, and I had nearly abandoned myself to sleep, when in the hall adjoining there arose the rustling of silk dresses that I had waited for and expected. Then there entered two by two the high-born ladies and their gallants of Jacobean times. They were little more than shadows—very dignified shadows, and almost indistinct; but you have all read ghost stories before, you have all seen in museums the dresses of those times—there is little need to describe them; they entered, several of them, and sat down on the old chairs, perhaps a little carelessly considering the value of the tapestries. Then the rustling of their dresses ceased.

Well—I had seen ghosts, and was neither frightened nor convinced that ghosts existed. I was about to get up out of my chair and go to bed, when there came a sound of pattering in the hall, a sound of bare feet coming over the polished floor, and every now and then a foot would slip and I heard claws scratching along the wood as some four-footed thing lost and regained its balance. I was not frightened, but uneasy. The pattering came straight towards the room that I was in, then I heard the sniffing of expectant nostrils; perhaps "uneasy" was not the most suitable word to describe my feelings then. Suddenly a herd of black creatures larger than bloodhounds came galloping in; they had large pendulous ears, their noses were to the ground sniffing, they went up to the lords and ladies of long ago and fawned about them disgustingly. Their eyes were horribly bright, and ran down to great depths. When I looked into them I knew suddenly what these creatures were, and I was afraid. They were the sins, the filthy, immortal sins of those courtly men and women.

How demure she was, the lady that sat near me on an old-world chair—how demure she was, and how fair, to have beside her with its jowl upon her lap a sin with such cavernous red eyes, a clear case of murder. And you, yonder lady with the golden hair, surely not you—and yet that fearful beast with the yellow eyes slinks from you to yonder courtier there, and whenever one drives it away it slinks back to the other. Over there a lady tries to smile as she strokes the loathsome furry head of another's sin, but one of her own is jealous and intrudes itself under her hand. Here sits an old nobleman with his grandson on his knee, and one of the great black sins of the grandfather is licking the child's face and has made the child its own. Sometimes a ghost would move and seek another chair, but always his pack of sins would move behind him. Poor ghosts, poor ghosts! how many flights they must have attempted for two hundred years from their hated sins, how many excuses they must have given for their presence, and the sins were with them still—and still unexplained. Suddenly one of them seemed to scent my living blood, and bayed horribly, and all the others left their ghosts at once and dashed up to the sin that had given tongue. The brute had picked up my scent near the door by which I had entered, and they moved slowly nearer to me sniffing along the floor, and uttering every now and then their fearful cry. I saw that the whole thing had gone too far. But now they had seen me, now they were all about me, they sprang up trying to reach my throat; and whenever their claws touched me, horrible thoughts came into my mind and unutterable desires dominated my heart. I planned bestial things as these creatures leaped around me, and planned them with a masterly cunning. A great red-eyed murder was among the foremost of those furry things from whom I feebly strove to defend my throat. Suddenly it seemed to me good that I should kill my brother. It seemed important to me that I should not risk being punished. I knew where a revolver was kept; after I had shot him, I would dress the body up and put flour on the face like a man that had been acting as a ghost. It would be very simple. I would say that he had frightened me—and the servants had heard us talking about ghosts. There were one or two trivialities that would have to be arranged, but nothing escaped my mind. Yes, it seemed to me very good that I should kill my brother as I looked into the red depths of this creature's eyes. But one last effort as they dragged me down—"If two straight lines cut one another," I said, "the opposite angles are equal. Let AB, CD, cut one another at E, then the angles CEA, CEB equal two right angles (prop. xiii.). Also CEA, AED equal two right angles."

I moved toward the door to get the revolver; a hideous exultation arose among the beasts. "But the angle CEA is common, therefore AED equals CEB. In the same way CEA equals DEB. Q.E.D." It was proved. Logic and reason re-established themselves in my mind, there were no dark hounds of sin, the tapestried chairs were empty. It seemed to me an inconceivable thought that a man should murder his brother.

The Probable Adventure of the Three Literary Men

WHEN the nomads came to El Lola they had no more songs, and the question of stealing the golden box arose in all its magnitude. On the one hand, many had sought the golden box, the receptacle (as the Aethiopians know) of poems of fabulous value; and their doom is still the common talk of Arabia. On the other hand, it was lonely to sit round the camp-fire by night with no new songs.

It was the tribe of Heth that discussed these things one evening upon the plains below the peak of Mluna. Their native land was the track across the world of immemorial wanderers; and there was trouble among the elders of the nomads because there were no new songs; while, untouched by human trouble, untouched as yet by the night that was hiding the plains away, the peak of Mluna, calm in the after-glow, looked on the Dubious Land. And it was there on the plain upon the known side of Mluna, just as the evening star came mouse-like into view and the flames of the camp-fire lifted their lonely plumes uncheered by any song, that that rash scheme was hastily planned by the nomads which the world has named The Quest of the Golden Box.

No measure of wiser precaution could the elders of the nomads have taken than to choose for their thief that very Slith, that identical thief that (even as I write) in how many school-rooms governesses teach stole a march on the King of Westalia. Yet the weight of the box was such that others had to accompany him, and Sippy and Slorg were no more agile thieves than may be found to-day among vendors of the antique.

So over the shoulder of Mluna these three climbed next day and slept as well as they might among its snows rather than risk a night in the woods of the Dubious Land. And the morning came up radiant and the birds were full of song, but the forest underneath and the waste beyond it and the bare and ominous crags all wore the appearance of an unuttered threat.

Though Slith had an experience of twenty years of theft, yet he said little; only if one of the others made a stone roll with his foot, or, later on in the forest, if one of them stepped on a twig, he whispered sharply to them always the same words: "That is not business." He knew that he could not make them better thieves during a two days' journey, and whatever doubts he had he interfered no further.

From the shoulder of Mluna they dropped into the clouds, and from the clouds to the forest, to whose native beasts, as well the three thieves knew, all flesh was meat, whether it were the flesh of fish or man. There the thieves drew idolatrously from their pockets each one a separate god and prayed for protection in the unfortunate wood, and hoped therefrom for a threefold chance of escape, since if anything should eat one of them it were certain to eat them all, and they confided that the corollary might be true and all should escape if one did. Whether one of these gods was propitious and awake, or whether all of the three, or whether it was chance that brought them through the forest unmouthed by detestable beasts, none knoweth; but certainly neither the emissaries of the god that most they feared, nor the wrath of the topical god of that ominous place, brought their doom to the three adventurers there or then. And so it was that they came to Rumbly Heath, in the heart of the Dubious Land, whose stormy hillocks were the ground-swell and the after-wash of the earthquake lulled for a while. Something so huge that it seemed unfair to man that it should move so softly stalked splendidly by them, and only so barely did they escape its notice that one word rang and echoed through their three imaginations—"If—if—if." And when this danger was at last gone by they moved cautiously on again and presently saw the little harmless mipt, half fairy and half gnome, giving shrill contented squeaks on the edge of the World. And they edged away unseen, for they said that the inquisitiveness of the mipt had become fabulous, and that, harmless as he was, he had a bad way with secrets; yet they probably loathed the way that he nuzzles dead white bones, and would not admit their loathing, for it does not become adventurers to care who eats their bones. Be this as it may, they edged away from the mipt, and came almost at once to the wizened tree, the goal-post of their adventure, and knew that beside them was the crack in the World and the bridge from Bad to Worse, and that underneath them stood the rocky house of Owner of the Box.

This was their simple plan: to slip into the corridor in the upper cliff; to run softly down it (of course with naked feet) under the warning to travellers that is graven upon stone, which interpreters take to be "It Is Better Not"; not to touch the berries that are there for a purpose, on the right side going down; and so to come to the guardian on his pedestal who had slept for a thousand years and should be sleeping still; and go in through the open window. One man was to wait outside by the crack in the World until the others came out with the golden box, and, should they cry for help, he was to threaten at once to unfasten the iron clamp that kept the crack together. When the box was secured they were to travel all night and all the following day, until the cloud-banks that wrapped the slopes of Mluna were well between them and Owner of the Box.

The door in the cliff was open. They passed without a murmur down the cold steps, Slith leading them all the way. A glance of longing, no more, each gave to the beautiful berries. The guardian upon his pedestal was still asleep. Slorg climbed by a ladder, that Slith knew where to find, to the iron clamp across the crack in the World, and waited beside it with a chisel in his hand, listening closely for anything untoward, while his friends slipped into the house; and no sound came. And presently Slith and Sippy found the golden box: everything seemed happening as they had planned, it only remained to see if it was the right one and to escape with it from that dreadful place. Under the shelter of the pedestal, so near to the guardian that they could feel his warmth, which paradoxically had the effect of chilling the blood of the boldest of them, they smashed the emerald hasp and opened the golden box; and there they read by the light of ingenious sparks which Slith knew how to contrive, and even this poor light they hid with their bodies. What was their joy, even at that perilous moment, as they lurked between the guardian and the abyss, to find that the box contained fifteen peerless odes in the alcaic form, five sonnets that were by far the most beautiful in the world, nine ballads in the manner of Provence that had no equal in the treasuries of man, a poem addressed to a moth in twenty-eight perfect stanzas, a piece of blank verse of over a hundred lines on a level not yet known to have been attained by man, as well as fifteen lyrics on which no merchant would dare to set a price. They would have read them again, for they gave happy tears to a man and memories of dear things done in infancy, and brought sweet voices from far sepulchres; but Slith pointed imperiously to the way by which they had come, and extinguished the light; and Slorg and Sippy sighed, then took the box.

The guardian still slept the sleep that survived a thousand years.

As they came away they saw that indulgent chair close by the edge of the World in which Owner of the Box had lately sat reading selfishly and alone the most beautiful songs and verses that poet ever dreamed.

They came in silence to the foot of the stairs; and then it befell that as they drew near safety, in the night's most secret hour, some hand in an upper chamber lit a shocking light, lit it and made no sound.

For a moment it might have been an ordinary light, fatal as even that could very well be at such a moment as this; but when it began to follow them like an eye and to grow redder and redder as it watched them, then even optimism despaired.

And Sippy very unwisely attempted flight, and Slorg even as unwisely tried to hide; but Slith, knowing well why that light was lit in that secret upper chamber and *who* it was that lit it, leaped over the edge of the World and is falling from us still through the unreverberate blackness of the abyss.

The Coronation of
Mr. Thomas Shap

IT was the occupation of Mr. Thomas Shap to persuade customers that the goods were genuine and of an excellent quality, and that as regards the price their unspoken will was consulted. And in order to carry on this occupation he went by train very early every morning some few miles nearer to the City from the suburb in which he slept. This was the use to which he put his life.

From the moment when he first perceived (not as one reads a thing in a book, but as truths are revealed to one's instinct) the very beastliness of his occupation, and of the house that he slept in, its shape, make and pretensions, and of even the clothes that he wore; from that moment he withdrew his dreams from it, his fancies, his ambitions, everything in fact except that ponderable Mr. Shap that dressed in a frock-coat, bought tickets and handled money and could in turn be handled by the statistician. The priest's share in Mr. Shap, the share of the poet, never caught the early train to the City at all.

He used to take little flights with his fancy at first, dwelt all day in his dreamy way on fields and rivers lying in the sunlight where it strikes the world more brilliantly further South. And then he began to imagine butterflies there; after that, silken people and the temples they built to their gods.

They noticed that he was silent, and even absent at times, but they found no fault with his behaviour with customers, to whom he remained as plausible as of old. So he dreamed for a year, and his fancy gained strength as he dreamed. He still read halfpenny papers in the train, still discussed the passing day's ephemeral topic, still voted at elections, though he no longer did these things with the whole Shap—his soul was no longer in them.

He had had a pleasant year, his imagination was all new to him still, and it had often discovered beautiful things away where it went, south-east at the edge of the twilight. And he had a matter-of-fact and logical mind, so that he often said, "Why should I pay my twopence at the electric theatre when I can see all sorts of things quite easily without?" Whatever he did was logical before anything else, and those that knew him always spoke of Shap as "a sound, sane, level-headed man."

On far the most important day of his life he went as usual to town by the early train to sell plausible articles to customers, while the spiritual Shap roamed off to fanciful lands. As he walked from the station, dreamy but wide awake, it suddenly struck him that the real Shap was not the one walking to Business in black and ugly clothes, but he who roamed along a jungle's edge near the ramparts of an old and Eastern city that rose up sheer from the sand, and against which the desert lapped with one eternal wave. He used to fancy the name of that city was Larkar. "After all, the fancy is as real as the body," he said with perfect logic. It was a dangerous theory.

For that other life that he led he realized, as in Business, the importance and value of method. He did not let his fancy roam too far until it perfectly knew its first surroundings. Particularly he avoided the jungle—he was not afraid to meet a tiger there (after all it was not real), but stranger things might crouch there. Slowly he built up Larkar: rampart by rampart, towers for archers, gateway of brass, and all. And then one day he argued, and quite rightly, that all the silk-clad people in its streets, their camels, their wares that came from Inkustahn, the city itself, were all the things of his will—and then he made himself King. He smiled after that when people did not raise their hats to him in the street, as he walked from the station to Business; but he was sufficiently practical to recognize that it was better not to talk of this to those that only knew him as Mr. Shap.

Now that he was King in the city of Larkar and in all the desert that lay to the East and North he sent his fancy to wander further afield. He took the regiments of his camel-guard and went jingling out of Larkar, with little silver bells under the

camels' chins, and came to other cities far-off on the yellow sand,
with clear white walls and towers, uplifting themselves in the
sun. Through their gates he passed with his three silken
regiments, the light-blue regiment of the camel-guard being upon
his right and the green regiment riding at his left, the lilac
regiment going on before. When he had gone through the streets
of any city and observed the ways of its people, and had seen the
way that the sunlight struck its towers, he would proclaim
himself King there, and then ride on in fancy. So he passed from
city to city and from land to land. Clear-sighted though Mr.
Shap was, I think he overlooked the lust of aggrandizement to
which kings have so often been victims: and so it was that when
the first few cities had opened their gleaming gates and he saw
peoples prostrate before his camel, and spearmen cheering along
countless balconies, and priests come out to do him reverence,
he that had never had even the lowliest authority in the familiar
world became unwisely insatiate. He let his fancy ride at
inordinate speed, he forsook method, scarce was he king of a
land but he yearned to extend his borders; so he journeyed
deeper and deeper into the wholly unknown. The concentration
that he gave to this inordinate progress through countries of
which history is ignorant and cities so fantastic in their bulwarks
that, though their inhabitants were human, yet the foe that they
feared seemed something less or more; the amazement with which
he beheld gates and towers unknown even to art, and furtive
people thronging intricate ways to acclaim him as their sovereign;
all these things began to affect his capacity for Business. He
knew as well as any that his fancy could not rule these beautiful
lands unless that other Shap, however unimportant, were well
sheltered and fed: and shelter and food meant money, and money,
Business. His was more like the mistake of some gambler with
cunning schemes who overlooks human greed. One day his
fancy, riding in the morning, came to a city gorgeous as the
sunrise, in whose opalescent wall were gates of gold, so huge
that a river poured between the bars, floating in, when the gates
were opened, large galleons under sail. Thence there came
dancing out a company with instruments, and made a melody
all round the wall; that morning Mr. Shap, the bodily Shap in
London, forgot the train to town.

Until a year ago he had never imagined at all; it is not to be

The Coronation of Mr. Thomas Shap

"Little Cottages . . . Whose Looks We Did Not Like"
(*from "Poor Old Bill"*)

wondered at that all these things now newly seen by his fancy should play tricks at first with the memory of even so sane a man. He gave up reading the papers altogether, he lost all interest in politics, he cared less and less for things that were going on around him. This unfortunate missing of the morning train even occurred again, and the firm spoke to him severely about it. But he had his consolation. Were not Aráthrion and Argun Zeerith and all the level coasts of Oora his? And even as the firm found fault with him his fancy watched the yaks on weary journeys, slow specks against the snow-fields, bringing tribute; and saw the green eyes of the mountain men who had looked at him strangely in the city of Nith when he had entered it by the desert door. Yet his logic did not forsake him; he knew well that his strange subjects did not exist, but he was prouder of having created them with his brain, than merely of ruling them only; thus in his pride he felt himself something more great than a king, he did not dare to think what! He went into the temple of the city of Zorra and stood some time there alone: all the priests kneeled to him when he came away.

He cared less and less for the things we care about, for the affairs of Shap, a business-man in London. He began to despise the man with a royal contempt.

One day when he sat in Sowla, the city of the Thuls, throned on one amethyst, he decided, and it was proclaimed on the moment by silver trumpets all along the land, that he would be crowned as king over all the lands of Wonder.

By that old temple where the Thuls were worshipped, year in, year out, for over a thousand years, they pitched pavilions in the open air. The trees that blew there threw out radiant scents unknown in any countries that know the map; the stars blazed fiercely for that famous occasion. A fountain hurled up, clattering, ceaselessly into the air armfuls on armfuls of diamonds, a deep hush waited for the golden trumpets, the holy coronation night was come. At the top of those old, worn steps, going down we know not whither, stood the king in the emerald-and-amethyst cloak, the ancient garb of the Thuls; beside him lay that Sphinx that for the last few weeks had advised him in his affairs.

Slowly, with music when the trumpets sounded, came up towards him from we know not where, one-hundred-and-twenty archbishops, twenty angels and two archangels, with that terrific crown, the diadem of the Thuls. They knew as they came up to him that promotion awaited them all because of this night's work. Silent, majestic, the king awaited them.

The doctors downstairs were sitting over their supper, the warders softly slipped from room to room, and when in that cosy dormitory of Hanwell they saw the king still standing erect and royal, his face resolute, they came up to him and addressed him: "Go to bed," they said—"pretty bed." So he lay down and soon was fast asleep: the great day was over.

Poor Old Bill

ON an antique haunt of sailors, a tavern of the sea, the light of day was fading. For several evenings I had frequented this place, in the hope of hearing something from the sailors, as they sat over strange wines, about a rumour that had reached my ears of a certain fleet of galleons of old Spain still said to be afloat in the South Seas in some uncharted region.

In this I was again to be disappointed. Talk was low and seldom, and I was about to leave, when a sailor, wearing earrings of pure gold, lifted up his head from his wine, and looking straight before him at the wall, told his tale loudly:

(When later on a storm of rain arose and thundered on the tavern's leaded panes, he raised his voice without effort and spoke on still. The darker it got the clearer his wild eyes shone.)

"A ship with sails of the olden time was nearing fantastic isles. We had never seen such isles.

"We all hated the captain, and he hated us. He hated us all alike, there was no favouritism about him. And he never would talk a word with any of us, except sometimes in the evening when it was getting dark he would stop and look up and talk a bit to the men he had hanged at the yard-arm.

"We were a mutinous crew. But Captain was the only man that had pistols. He slept with one under his pillow and kept one close beside him. There was a nasty look about the isles. They were small and flat as though they had come up only recently from the sea, and they had no sand or rocks like honest isles, but green grass down to the water. And there were little cottages there whose looks we did not like. Their thatches came almost down to the ground, and were strangely turned up at the corners, and under the low eaves were queer, dark windows whose little leaded panes were too thick to see through. And no one, man or beast, was walking about, so that you could not know what kind of people lived there. But Captain knew. And he went ashore and into one of the cottages, and someone lit lights inside, and the little windows wore an evil look.

"It was quite dark when he came aboard again, and he bade a cheery good-night to the men that swung from the yard-arm, and he eyed us in a way that frightened poor old Bill.

"Next night we found that he had learned to curse, for he came on a lot of us asleep in our bunks, and among them poor old Bill, and he pointed at us with a finger, and made a curse that our souls should stay all night at the top of the masts. And suddenly there was the soul of poor old Bill sitting like a monkey at the top of the mast, and looking at the stars, and freezing through and through.

"We got up a little mutiny after that, but Captain comes up and points with his finger again, and this time poor old Bill and all the rest are swimming behind the ship through the cold, green water, though their bodies remain on deck.

"It was the cabin-boy who found out that Captain couldn't curse when he was drunk, though he could shoot as well at one time as another.

"After that it was only a matter of waiting, and of losing two men when the time came. Some of us were murderous fellows, and wanted to kill Captain, but poor old Bill was for finding a bit of an island, out of the track of ships, and leaving him there with his share of our year's provisions. And everybody listened to poor old Bill, and we decided to maroon Captain as soon as we caught him when he couldn't curse.

"It was three whole days before Captain got drunk again, and poor old Bill and all had a dreadful time, for Captain invented new curses every day, and wherever he pointed his finger our souls had to go; and the fishes got to know us, and so did the stars, and none of them pitied us when we froze on the masts or were hurried through forests of seaweed and lost our way—both stars and fishes went about their businesses with cold, unastonished eyes. Once when the sun had set and it was twilight, and the moon was showing clearer and clearer in the sky, and we stopped our work for a moment because Captain seemed to be looking away from us at the colours in the sky, he suddenly turned and sent our souls to the Moon. And it was colder there than ice at night; and there were horrible mountains making shadows; and it was all as silent as miles of tombs; and Earth was shining up in the sky as big as the blade of a scythe, and we all got homesick for it, but could not speak nor cry. It was quite dark when we got back, and we were very respectful to Captain all the next day, but he cursed several of us again very soon. What we all feared most was that he would curse our souls to Hell, and none of us mentioned Hell above a whisper for fear that it should remind him. But on the third evening the cabin-boy came and told us that Captain was drunk. And we all went to his cabin, and we found him lying there across his bunk, and he shot as he had never shot before; but he had no more than the two pistols, and he would only have killed two men if he hadn't caught Joe over the head with the end of one of his pistols. And then we tied him up. And poor old Bill put the rum between Captain's teeth, and kept him drunk for two days, so that he could not curse, till we found a convenient rock. And before sunset of the second day we found a nice bare island for Captain, out of the track of ships, about a hundred yards long and about eighty wide; and we rowed him along to it in a little boat, and gave him provisions for a year, the same as we had ourselves, because poor old Bill wanted to be fair. And we left him sitting comfortable with his back to a rock singing a sailor's song.

"When we could no longer hear Captain singing we all grew very cheerful and made a banquet out of our year's provisions, as we all hoped to be home again in under three weeks. We had three great banquets every day for a week—every man had more than he could eat, and what was left over we threw on the floor like gentlemen. And then one day, as we saw San Huëlgédos, and wanted to sail in to spend our money, the wind changed round from behind us and beat us out to sea. There was no tacking against it, and no getting into the harbour, though other ships sailed by us and anchored there. Sometimes a dead calm would fall on us, while fishing boats all around us flew before half a gale, and sometimes the wind would beat us out to sea when nothing else was moving. All day we tried, and at night we laid to and tried again next day. And all the sailors of the other ships were spending their money in San Huëlgédos and we could not come nigh it. Then we spoke horrible things against the wind and against San Huëlgédos, and sailed away.

"It was just the same at Norenna.

"We kept close together now and talked in low voices. Suddenly poor old Bill grew frightened. As we went all along the Siractic coast-line, we tried again and again, and the wind was waiting for us in every harbour and sent us out to sea. Even the little islands would not have us. And then we knew that there was no landing yet for poor old Bill, and every one upbraided his kind heart that had made them maroon Captain on a rock, so as not to have his blood upon their heads. There was nothing to do but to drift about the seas. There were no banquets now, because we feared that Captain might live his year and keep us out to sea.

"At first we used to hail all passing ships, and used to try to board them in the boats; but there was no rowing against Captain's curse, and we had to give that up. So we played cards for a year in Captain's cabin, night and day, storm and fine, and every one promised to pay poor old Bill when we got ashore.

"It was horrible to us to think what a frugal man Captain really was, he that used to get drunk every other day whenever he was at sea, and here he was still alive, and sober, too, for his curse still kept us out of every port, and our provisions were gone.

"Well, it came to drawing lots, and Jim was the unlucky one. Jim only kept us about three days, and then we drew lots again, and this time it was George. George didn't keep us any longer, and we drew again, and this time it was Charlie, and still Captain was alive.

"As we got fewer one of us kept us longer. Longer and longer a mate used to last us, and we all wondered how ever Captain did it. It was five weeks over the year when we drew Mike, and he kept us for a week, and Captain was still alive. We wondered he didn't get tired of the same old curse; but we supposed things looked different when one is alone on an island.

"When there was only Jakes and poor old Bill and the cabin-boy and Dick, we didn't draw any longer. We said that the cabin-boy had had all the luck, and he mustn't expect any more.

Then poor old Bill was alone with Jakes and Dick, and Captain was still alive. When there was no more boy, and the Captain still alive, Dick, who was a huge, strong man like poor old Bill, said that it was Jakes' turn, and he was very lucky to have lived as long as he had. But poor old Bill talked it all over with Jakes, and they thought it better that Dick should take his turn.

"Then there was Jakes and poor old Bill; and Captain would not die.

"And these two used to watch one another night and day, when Dick was gone and no one else was left to them. And at last poor old Bill fell down in a faint and lay there for an hour. Then Jakes came up to him slowly with his knife, and makes a stab at poor old Bill as he lies there on the deck. And poor old Bill caught hold of him by the wrist, and put his knife into him twice to make quite sure, although it spoiled the best part of the meat. Then poor old Bill was all alone at sea.

"And the very next week, before the food gave out, Captain must have died on his bit of an island; for poor old Bill heard Captain's soul going cursing over the sea, and the day after that the ship was cast on a rocky coast.

"And Captain's been dead now for over a hundred years, and poor old Bill is safe ashore again. But it looks as if Captain hadn't done with him yet, for poor old Bill doesn't ever get any older, and somehow or other he doesn't seem to die. Poor old Bill!"

When this was over the man's fascination suddenly snapped, and we all jumped up and left him.

It was not only his revolting story, but it was the fearful look in the eyes of the man who told it, and the terrible ease with which his voice surpassed the roar of the rain, that decided me never again to enter that haunt of sailors—the tavern of the sea.

The Ominous Cough

(from "The Distressing Tale of Thangobrind the Jeweller, and of the Doom That Befell Him")

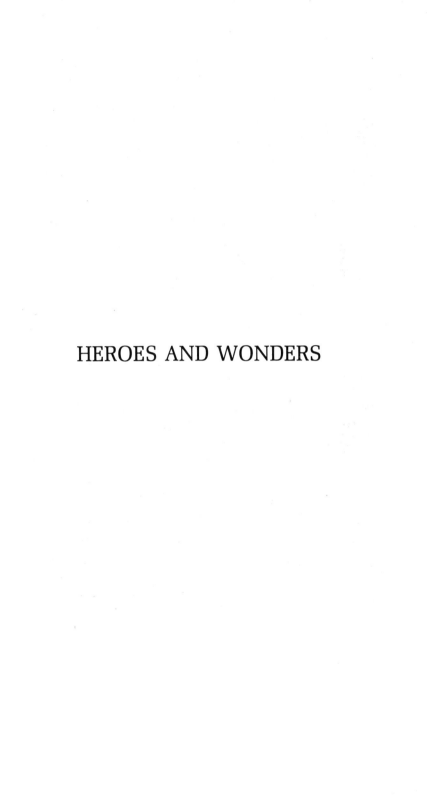

HEROES AND WONDERS

"There the Gibbelins Lived and Discreditably Fed"

The Hoard of the Gibbelins

THE Gibbelins eat, as is well known, nothing less good than man. Their evil tower is joined to Terra Cognita, to the lands we know, by a bridge. Their hoard is beyond reason; avarice has no use for it; they have a separate cellar for emeralds and a separate cellar for sapphires; they have filled a hole with gold and dig it up when they need it. And the only use that is known for their ridiculous wealth is to attract to their·larder a continual supply of food. In times of famine they have even been known to scatter rubies abroad, a little trail of them to some city of Man, and sure enough their larders would soon be full again.

Their tower stands on the other side of that river known to Homer—ὁ ῥόος ἀχεανοίο, as he called it—which surrounds the world. And where the river is narrow and fordable the tower was built by the Gibbelins' gluttonous sires, for they liked to see burglars rowing easily to their steps. Some nourishment that common soil has not the huge trees drained there with their colossal roots from both banks of the river.

There the Gibbelins lived and discreditably fed.

Alderic, Knight of the Order of the City and the Assault, hereditary Guardian of the King's Peace of Mind, a man not unremembered among the makers of myth, pondered so long upon the Gibbelins' hoard that by now he deemed it his. Alas that I should say of so perilous a venture, undertaken at dead of night by a valorous man, that its motive was sheer avarice! Yet upon avarice only the Gibbelins relied to keep their larders full, and once in every hundred years sent spies into the cities of men to see how avarice did, and always the spies returned again to the tower saying that all was well.

It may be thought that, as the years went on and men came by fearful ends on that tower's wall, fewer and fewer would come to the Gibbelins' table: but the Gibbelins found otherwise.

Not in the folly and frivolity of his youth did Alderic come to the tower, but he studied carefully for several years the manner in which burglars met their doom when they went in search of the treasure that he considered his. *In every case they had entered by the door.*

He consulted those who gave advice on this quest; he noted every detail and cheerfully paid their fees, and determined to do nothing that they advised, for what were their clients now? No more than examples of the savoury art, mere half-forgotten memories of a meal; and many, perhaps, no longer even that.

These were the requisites for the quest that these men used to advise: a horse, a boat, mail armour, and at least three men-at-arms. Some said, "Blow the horn at the tower door"; others said, "Do not touch it."

Alderic thus decided: he would take no horse down to the river's edge, he would not row along it in a boat, and he would go alone and by way of the Forest Unpassable.

How pass, you may say, by the unpassable? This was his plan: there was a dragon he knew of who if peasants' prayers are heeded deserved to die, not alone because of the number of maidens he cruelly slew, but because he was bad for the crops; he ravaged the very land and was the bane of a dukedom.

Now Alderic determined to go up against him. So he took horse and spear and pricked till he met the dragon, and the dragon came out against him breathing bitter smoke. And to him Alderic shouted, "Hath foul dragon ever slain true knight?" And well the dragon knew that this had never been, and he hung his head and was silent, for he was glutted with blood. "Then," said the knight, "if thou would'st ever taste maiden's blood again thou shalt be my trusty steed, and if not, by this spear there shall befall thee all that the troubadours tell of the dooms of thy breed."

And the dragon did not open his ravening mouth, nor rush upon the knight, breathing out fire; for well he knew the fate of those that did these things, but he consented to the terms imposed, and swore to the knight to become his trusty steed.

It was on a saddle upon this dragon's back that Alderic afterwards sailed above the unpassable forest, even above the tops of
those measureless trees, children of wonder. But first he pondered that subtle plan of his which was more profound than
merely to avoid all that had been done before; and he commanded a blacksmith, and the blacksmith made him a pickaxe.

Now there was great rejoicing at the rumour of Alderic's
quest, for all folk knew that he was a cautious man, and they
deemed that he would succeed and enrich the world, and they
rubbed their hands in the cities at the thought of largesse; and
there was joy among all men in Alderic's country, except per-
chance among the lenders of money, who feared they would soon
be paid. And there was rejoicing also because men hoped that
when the Gibbelins were robbed of their hoard, they would
shatter their high-built bridge and break the golden chains that
bound them to the world, and drift back, they and their tower,
to the moon, from which they had come and to which they
rightly belonged. There was little love for the Gibbelins, though
all men envied their hoard.

So they all cheered, that day when he mounted his dragon,
as though he was already a conqueror, and what pleased them
more than the good that they hoped he would do to the world
was that he scattered gold as he rode away; for he would not
need it, he said, if he found the Gibbelins' hoard, and he would
not need it more if he smoked on the Gibbelins' table.

When they heard that he had rejected the advice of those that
gave it, some said that the knight was mad, and others said he
was greater than those that gave the advice, but none appreciated
the worth of his plan.

He reasoned thus: for centuries men had been well advised
and had gone by the cleverest way, while the Gibbelins came to
expect them to come by boat and to look for them at the door
whenever their larder was empty, even as a man looketh for
a snipe in the marsh; but how, said Alderic, if a snipe should
sit in the top of a tree, and would men find him there? Assuredly
never! So Alderic decided to swim the river and not to go by the
door, but to pick his way into the tower through the stone.
Moreover, it was in his mind to work below the level of the
ocean, the river (as Homer knew) that girdles the world, so
that as soon as he made a hole in the wall the water should
pour in, confounding the Gibbelins, and flooding the cellars

rumoured to be twenty feet in depth, and therein he would dive
for emeralds as a diver dives for pearls.

And on the day that I tell of he galloped away from his home
scattering largesse of gold, as I have said, and passed through
many kingdoms, the dragon snapping at maidens as he went,
but being unable to eat them because of the bit in his mouth,
and earning no gentler reward than a spur-thrust where he was
softest. And so they came to the swart arboreal precipice of the
unpassable forest. The dragon rose at it with a rattle of wings.
Many a farmer near the edge of the world saw him up there
where yet the twilight lingered, a faint, black, wavering line;
and mistaking him for a row of geese going inland from the
ocean, went into their houses cheerily rubbing their hands and
saying that winter was coming, and that we should soon have
snow. Soon even there the twilight faded away, and when they
descended at the edge of the world it was night and the moon
was shining. Ocean, the ancient river, narrow and shallow there,
flowed by and made no murmur. Whether the Gibbelins ban-
queted or whether they watched by the door, they also made
no murmur. And Alderic dismounted and took his armour off,
and saying one prayer to his lady, swam with his pickaxe. He did
not part from his sword, for fear that he met with a Gibbelin.
Landed the other side, he began to work at once, and all went
well with him. Nothing put out its head from any window, and
all were lighted so that nothing within could see him in the
dark. The blows of his pickaxe were dulled in the deep walls.
All night he worked, no sound came to molest him, and at dawn
the last rock swerved and tumbled inwards, and the river poured
in after. Then Alderic took a stone, and went to the bottom
step, and hurled the stone at the door; he heard the echoes roll
into the tower, then he ran back and dived through the hole in
the wall.

He was in the emerald-cellar. There was no light in the lofty
vault above him, but, diving through twenty feet of water, he
felt the floor all rough with emeralds, and open coffers full of
them. By a faint ray of the moon he saw that the water was
green with them, and, easily filling a satchel, he rose again to
the surface; and there were the Gibbelins waist-deep in the
water, with torches in their hands! And, without saying a word,
or even smiling, they neatly hanged him on the outer wall—
and the tale is one of those that have not a happy ending.

How Nuth Would have Practised His Art upon the Gnoles

Despite the advertisements of rival firms, it is probable that every tradesman knows that nobody in business at the present time has a position equal to that of Mr. Nuth. To those outside the magic circle of business, his name is scarcely known; he does not need to advertise, he is consummate. He is superior even to modern competition, and, whatever claims they boast, his rivals know it. His terms are moderate, so much cash down when the goods are delivered, so much in blackmail afterwards. He consults your convenience. His skill may be counted upon; I have seen a shadow on a windy night move more noisily than Nuth, for Nuth is a burglar by trade. Men have been known to stay in country houses and to send a dealer afterwards to bargain for a piece of tapestry that they saw there—some article of furniture, some picture. This is bad taste: but those whose culture is more elegant invariably send Nuth a night or two after their visit. He has a way with tapestry, you would scarcely notice that the edges had been cut. And often when I see some huge, new house full of old furniture and portraits from other ages, I say to myself, "These mouldering chairs, these full-length ancestors and carved mahogany are the produce of the incomparable Nuth."

It may be urged against my use of the word incomparable that in the burglary business the name of Slith stands paramount and alone; and of this I am not ignorant; but Slith is a classic, and lived long ago, and knew nothing at all of modern competition; besides which the surprising nature of his doom has possibly cast a glamour upon Slith that exaggerates in our eyes his undoubted merits.

It must not be thought that I am any friend of Nuth's, on the contrary such politics as I have are on the side of Property; and he needs no words from me, for his position is almost unique in trade, being among the very few that do not need to advertise.

At the time that my story begins Nuth lived in a roomy house in Belgrave Square: in his inimitable way he had made friends with the caretaker. The place suited Nuth, and, whenever anyone came to inspect it before purchase, the caretaker used to praise the house in the words that Nuth had suggested. "If it wasn't for the drains," she would say, "it's the finest house in London," and when they pounced on this remark and asked questions about the drains, she would answer them that the drains also were good, but not so good as the house. They did not see Nuth when they went over the rooms, but Nuth was there.

Here in a neat black dress on one spring morning came an old woman whose bonnet was lined with red, asking for Mr. Nuth; and with her came her large and awkward son. Mrs. Eggins, the caretaker, glanced up the street, and then she let them in, and left them to wait in the drawing-room amongst furniture all mysterious with sheets. For a long while they waited, and then there was a smell of pipe-tobacco, and there was Nuth standing quite close to them.

"Lord," said the old woman whose bonnet was lined with red, "you did make me start." And then she saw by his eyes that that was not the way to speak to Mr. Nuth.

And at last Nuth spoke, and very nervously the old woman explained that her son was a likely lad, and had been in business already but wanted to better himself, and she wanted Mr. Nuth to teach him a livelihood.

First of all Nuth wanted to see a business reference, and when he was shown one from a jeweller with whom he happened to be hand-in-glove the upshot of it was that he agreed to take young Tonker (for this was the surname of the likely lad) and to make him his apprentice. And the old woman whose bonnet was lined with red went back to her little cottage in the country, and every evening said to her old man, "Tonker, we must fasten the shutters of a night-time, for Tommy's a burglar now."

The details of the likely lad's apprenticeship I do not propose to give; for those that are in the business know those details already, and those that are in other businesses care only for their own, while men of leisure who have no trade at all would fail to appreciate the gradual degrees by which Tommy Tonker came first to cross bare boards, covered with little obstacles in the dark, without making any sound, and then to go silently up creaky stairs, and then to open doors, and lastly to climb.

Let it suffice that the business prospered greatly, while glowing reports of Tommy Tonker's progress were sent from time to time to the old woman whose bonnet was lined with red in the laborious handwriting of Nuth. Nuth had given up lessons in writing very early, for he seemed to have some prejudice against forgery, and therefore considered writing a waste of time. And then there came the transaction with Lord Castlenorman at his Surrey residence. Nuth selected a Saturday night, and by eleven o'clock the whole house was quiet. Five minutes before midnight Tommy Tonker, instructed by Mr. Nuth, who waited outside, came away with one pocketful of rings and shirt-studs. It was quite a light pocketful, but the jewellers in Paris could not match it without sending specially to Africa, so that Lord Castlenorman had to borrow bone shirt-studs.

Not even rumour whispered the name of Nuth. Were I to say that this turned his head, there are those to whom the assertion would give pain, for his associates hold that his astute judgment was unaffected by circumstance. I will say, therefore, that it spurred his genius to plan what no burglar had ever planned before. It was nothing less than to burgle the house of the gnoles. And this that abstemious man unfolded to Tonker over a cup of tea. Had Tonker not been nearly insane with pride over their recent transaction, and had he not been blinded by a veneration for Nuth, he would have—but I cry over spilt milk. He expostulated respectfully: he said he would rather not go; he said it was not fair, he allowed himself to argue; and in the end, one windy October morning with a menace in the air found him and Nuth drawing near to the dreadful wood.

Nuth, by weighing little emeralds against pieces of common rock, had ascertained the probable weight of those house-ornaments that the gnoles are believed to possess in the narrow, lofty house wherein they have dwelt from of old. They decided to steal two emeralds and to carry them between them on a cloak; but if they should be too heavy one must be dropped at once. Nuth warned young Tonker against greed, and explained that the emeralds were worth less than cheese until they were safe away from the dreadful wood.

Everything had been planned, and they walked now in silence.

No track led up to the sinister gloom of the trees, either of men or cattle; not even a poacher had been there snaring elves for over a hundred years. You did not trespass twice in the dells of the gnoles. And, apart from the things that were done there, the trees themselves were a warning, and did not wear the wholesome look of those that we plant ourselves.

The nearest village was some miles away with the backs of all its houses turned to the wood, and without one window at all facing in that direction. They did not speak of it there, and elsewhere it is unheard of.

Into this wood stepped Nuth and Tommy Tonker. They had no firearms. Tonker had asked for a pistol, but Nuth replied that the sound of a shot "would bring everything down on us," and no more was said about it.

Into the wood they went all day, deeper and deeper. They saw the skeleton of some early Georgian poacher nailed to a door in an oak tree; sometimes they saw a fairy scuttle away from them; once Tonker stepped heavily on a hard, dry stick, after which they both lay still for twenty minutes. And the sunset flared full of omens through the tree trunks, and night fell, and they came by fitful starlight, as Nuth had foreseen, to that lean, high house where the gnoles so secretly dwelt.

All was so silent by that unvalued house that the faded courage of Tonker flickered up, but to Nuth's experienced sense it seemed too silent; and all the while there was that look in the sky that was worse than a spoken doom, so that Nuth, as is often the case when men are in doubt, had leisure to fear the worst. Nevertheless he did not abandon the business, but sent the likely lad with the instruments of his trade by means of the ladder to the old green casement. And the moment that Tonker touched the withered boards, the silence that, though ominous, was earthly, became unearthly like the touch of a ghoul. And Tonker heard his breath offending against that silence, and his heart was like mad drums in a night attack, and a string of one of his sandals went tap on a rung of a ladder, and the leaves of the forest were mute, and the breeze of the night was still; and Tonker prayed that a mouse or a mole might make any noise at all, but not a creature stirred, even Nuth was still. And then and there, while yet he was undiscovered, the likely lad made up his mind, as he should have done long before, to leave those colossal emeralds where they were and have nothing further to do with the lean, high house of the gnoles, but to quit this sinister wood in the nick of time and retire from business at once and buy a place in the country. Then he descended softly and beckoned to Nuth. But the gnoles had watched him through knavish holes that they bore in trunks of the trees, and the unearthly silence gave way, as it were with a grace, to the rapid screams of Tonker as they picked him up from behind—screams that came faster and faster until they were incoherent. And where they took him it is not good to ask, and what they did with him I shall not say.

Nuth looked on for a while from the corner of the house with a mild surprise on his face as he rubbed his chin, for the trick of the holes in the trees was new to him; then he stole nimbly away through the dreadful wood.

"And did they catch Nuth?" you ask me, gentle reader.

"Oh, no, my child" (for such a question is childish) . "Nobody ever catches Nuth."

Chu-bu and Sheemish

IT was the custom on Tuesdays in the temple of Chu-bu for the priests to enter at evening and chant, "There is none but Chu-bu."

And all the people rejoiced and cried out, "There is none but Chu-bu." And honey was offered to Chu-bu, and maize and fat. Thus was he magnified.

Chu-bu was an idol of some antiquity, as may be seen from the colour of the wood. He had been carved out of mahogany, and after he was carved he had been polished. Then they had set him up on the diorite pedestal with the brazier in front of it for burning spices and the flat gold plates for fat. Thus they worshipped Chu-bu.

He must have been there for over a hundred years when one day the priests came in with another idol into the temple of Chu-bu, and set it up on a pedestal near Chu-bu's and sang, "There is also Sheemish."

And all the people rejoiced and cried out, "There is also Sheemish."

Sheemish was palpably a modern idol, and although the wood was stained with a dark-red dye, you could see that he had only just been carved. And honey was offered to Sheemish as well as Chu-bu, and also maize and fat.

The fury of Chu-bu knew no time-limit; he was furious all that night, and next day he was furious still. The situation called for immediate miracles. To devastate the city with a pestilence and kill all his priests was scarcely within his power, therefore he wisely concentrated such divine powers as he had in commanding a little earthquake. "Thus," thought Chu-bu, "will

I reassert myself as the only god, and men shall spit upon Sheemish."

Chu-bu willed it and willed it and still no earthquake came, when suddenly he was aware that the hated Sheemish was daring to attempt a miracle too. He ceased to busy himself about the earthquake and listened, or shall I say felt, for what Sheemish was thinking; for gods are aware of what passes in the mind by a sense that is other than any of our five. Sheemish was trying to make an earthquake too.

The new god's motive was probably to assert himself. I doubt if Chu-bu understood or cared for his motive, it was sufficient for an idol already aflame with jealousy that his detestable rival was on the verge of a miracle. All the power of Chu-bu veered round at once and set dead against an earthquake, even a little one. It was thus in the temple of Chu-bu for some time, and then no earthquake came.

To be a god and to fail to achieve a miracle is a despairing sensation; it is as though among men one should determine upon a hearty sneeze and as though no sneeze should come; it is as though one should try to swim in heavy boots or remember a name that is utterly forgotten: all these pains were Sheemish's.

And upon Tuesday the priests came in, and the people, and they did worship Chu-bu and offered fat to him, saying, "O Chu-bu who made everything," and then the priests sang, "There is also Sheemish," and again the people rejoiced and cried out, "There is also Sheemish"; and Chu-bu was put to shame and spake not for three days.

Now there were holy birds in the temple of Chu-bu, and when the third day was come and the night thereof, it was as it were revealed to the mind of Chu-bu, that there was dirt upon the head of Sheemish.

And Chu-bu spake unto Sheemish as speak the gods, moving no lips nor yet disturbing the silence, saying, "There is dirt upon thy head, O Sheemish." All night long he muttered again and again, "There is dirt upon Sheemish's head." And when it was dawn and voices were heard far off, Chu-bu became exultant with Earth's awakening things, and cried out till the sun was high, "Dirt, dirt, dirt, upon the head of Sheemish," and at noon he said, "So Sheemish would be a god." Thus was Sheemish confounded.

And with Tuesday one came and washed his head with rose-water, and he was worshipped again when they sang "There is also Sheemish." And yet was Chu-bu content, for he said, "The head of Sheemish has been defiled," and again, "His head was defiled, it is enough." And one evening lo! there was dirt on the head of Chu-bu also, and the thing was perceived of Sheemish.

It is not with the gods as it is with men. We are angry one with another and turn from our anger again, but the wrath of the gods is enduring. Chu-bu remembered and Sheemish did not forget. They spake as we do not speak, in silence yet heard of each other, nor were their thoughts as our thoughts. We should not judge them by merely human standards. All night long they spake and all night said these words only: "Dirty Chu-bu," "Dirty Sheemish." "Dirty Chu-bu," "Dirty Sheemish," all night long. Their wrath had not tired at dawn, and neither had wearied of his accusation. And gradually Chu-bu came to realize that he was nothing more than the equal of Sheemish. All gods are jealous, but this equality with the upstart Sheemish, a thing of painted wood a hundred years newer than Chu-bu, and this worship given to Sheemish in Chu-bu's own temple, were particularly bitter. Chu-bu was jealous even for a god; and when Tuesday came again, the third day of Sheemish's worship, Chu-bu could bear it no longer. He felt that his anger must be revealed at all costs, and he returned with all the vehemence of his will to achieving a little earthquake. The worshippers had just gone from his temple when Chu-bu settled his will to attain this miracle, now and then his meditations were disturbed by the now familiar dictum, "Dirty Chu-bu," but Chu-bu willed ferociously, not even stopping to say what he longed to say and had already said nine hundred times, and presently even these interruptions ceased.

They ceased because Sheemish had returned to a project that he had never definitely abandoned, the desire to assert himself and exalt himself over Chu-bu by performing a miracle, and the district being volcanic he had chosen a little earthquake as the miracle most easily accomplished by a small god.

Now an earthquake that is commanded by two gods has double the chance of fulfilment than when it is willed by one, and an incalculably greater chance than when two gods are pulling different ways; as, to take the case of older and greater gods, when the sun and the moon pull in the same direction we have the biggest tides.

Chu-bu knew nothing of the theory of tides, and was too much occupied with his miracle to notice what Sheemish was doing. And suddenly the miracle was an accomplished thing.

It was a very local earthquake, for there are other gods than Chu-bu or even Sheemish, and it was only a little one as the gods had willed, but it loosened some monoliths in a colonnade that supported one side of the temple and the whole of one wall fell in, and the low huts of the people of that city were shaken a little and some of their doors were jammed so that they would not open; it was enough, and for a moment it seemed that it was all; neither Chu-bu nor Sheemish commanded there should be more, but they had set in motion an old law older than Chu-bu, the law of gravity that that colonnade had held back for a hundred years, and the temple of Chu-bu quivered and then stood still, swayed once and was overthrown, on the heads of Chu-bu and Sheemish.

No one rebuilt it, for nobody dared go near such terrible gods. Some said that Chu-bu wrought the miracle, but some said Sheemish, and thereof schism was born; the weakly amiable, alarmed by the bitterness of rival sects, sought compromise and said that both had wrought it, but no one guessed the truth that the thing was done in rivalry.

And a saying arose, and both sects held this belief in common, that whoso toucheth Chu-bu shall die or whoso looketh upon Sheemish.

That is how Chu-bu came into my possession when I travelled once beyond the Hills of Ting. I found him in the fallen temple of Chu-bu with his hands and toes sticking up out of the rubbish, lying upon his back, and in that attitude just as I found him I keep him to this day on my mantelpiece, as he is less liable to be upset that way. Sheemish was broken, so I left him where he was.

And there is something so helpless about Chu-bu with his fat hands stuck up in the air that sometimes I am moved out of compassion to bow down to him and pray, saying, "O Chu-bu, thou that made everything, help thy servant."

Chu-bu cannot do much, though once I am sure that at a game of bridge he sent me the ace of trumps after I had not held a card worth having for the whole of the evening. And chance could have done as much as that for me, but I do not tell this to Chu-bu.

A Story of Land and Sea

IT is written in the first Book of Wonder how Captain Shard of the bad ship *Desperate Lark,* having looted the sea-coast city Bombasharna, retired from active life; and resigning piracy to younger men, with the goodwill of the North and South Atlantic, settled down with a captured queen on his floating island.

Sometimes he sank a ship for the sake of old times, but he no longer hovered along the trade-routes; and timid merchants watched for other men.

It was not age that caused him to leave his romantic profession; nor unworthiness of its traditions, nor gunshot wound, nor drink; but grim necessity and *force majeure.* Five navies were after him. How he gave them the slip one day in the Mediterranean, how he fought with the Arabs, how a ship's broadside was heard in Lat. 23 N. Long. 4 E. for the first time and the last, with other things unknown to Admiralties, I shall proceed to tell.

He had had his fling, had Shard, captain of pirates, and all his merry men wore pearls in their ear-rings; and now the English fleet was after him under full sail along the coast of Spain with a good north wind behind them. They were not gaining much on Shard's rakish craft, the bad ship *Desperate Lark,* yet they were closer than was to his liking, and they interfered with business.

For a day and a night they had chased him, when off Cape St. Vincent at about 6 a.m. Shard took that step that decided his retirement from active life, he turned for the Mediterranean. Had he held on southwards down the African coast it is doubtful whether in face of the interference of England, Russia, France,

Denmark and Spain, he could have made piracy pay; but in turning for the Mediterranean he took what we may call the penultimate step of his life which meant for him settling down. There were three great courses of action invented by Shard in his youth, upon which he pondered by day and brooded by night, consolations in all his dangers, secret even from his men, three means of escape as he hoped from any peril that might meet him on the sea. One of these was the floating island that the Book of Wonder tells of, another was so fantastic that we may doubt if even the brilliant audacity of Shard could ever have found it practicable, at least he never tried it so far as is known in that tavern by the sea in which I glean my news, and the third he determined on carrying out as he turned that morning for the Mediterranean. True, he might yet have practised piracy in spite of the step that he took, a little later when the seas grew quiet, but that penultimate step was like that small house in the country that the business man has his eye on; like some snug investment put away for old age, there are certain final courses in men's lives which after taking they never go back to business.

He turned then for the Mediterranean with the English fleet behind him, and his men wondered.

What madness was this—muttered Bill, the boatswain, in Old Frank's only ear—with the French fleet waiting in the Gulf of Lyons and the Spaniards all the way between Sardinia and Tunis: for they knew the Spaniards' ways. And they made a deputation and waited upon Captain Shard, all of them sober and wearing their costly clothes; and they said that the Mediterranean was a trap, and all he said was that the north wind should hold. And the crew said they were done.

So they entered the Mediterranean, and the English Fleet came up and closed the straits. And Shard went tacking along the Moroccan coast with a dozen frigates behind him. And the north wind grew in strength. And not till evening did he speak to his crew, and then he gathered them all together except the man at the helm, and politely asked them to come down to the hold. And there he showed them six immense steel axles and a dozen low iron wheels of enormous width which none had seen before; and he told his crew how all unknown to the world his keel had been specially fitted for these same axles and wheels, and how he meant soon to sail to the wide Atlantic again, though not by the way of the straits. And when they heard the name of the Atlantic all his merry men cheered, for they looked on the Atlantic as a wide safe sea.

And night came down and Captain Shard sent for his diver. With the sea getting up it was hard work for the diver, but by midnight things were done to Shard's satisfaction; and the diver said that of all the jobs he had done, . . . but finding no apt comparison, and being in need of a drink, silence fell on him and soon sleep, and his comrades carried him away to his hammock. All the next day the chase went on with the English well in sight, for Shard had lost time overnight with his wheels and axles, and the danger of meeting the Spaniards increased every hour; and evening came when every minute seemed dangerous, yet they still went tacking on towards the East where they knew the Spaniards must be.

And at last they sighted their topsails right ahead, and still Shard went on. It was a close thing, but night was coming on, and the Union Jack which he hoisted helped Shard with the Spaniards for the last few anxious minutes, though it seemed to anger the English, but as Shard said, "There's no pleasing everyone," and then the twilight shivered into darkness.

"Hard to starboard," said Captain Shard.

The north wind which had risen all day was now blowing a gale. I do not know what part of the coast Shard steered for, but Shard knew, for the coasts of the world were to him what Margate is to some of us.

At a place where the desert rolling up from mystery and from death, yea from the heart of Africa, emerges upon the sea, no less grand than she, no less terrible, even there they sighted the land quite close, almost in darkness. Shard ordered every man to the hinder part of the ship and all the ballast too; and soon the *Desperate Lark,* her prow a little high out of the water, doing her eighteen knots before the wind, struck a sandy beach and shuddered; she heeled over a little, then righted herself, and slowly headed into the interior of Africa.

The men would have given three cheers, but after the first Shard silenced them and, steering the ship himself, he made them a short speech while the broad wheels pounded slowly over the African sand, doing barely five knots in a gale. The perils of the sea, he said, had been greatly exaggerated. Ships had been sailing the sea for hundreds of years, and at sea you knew what to do, but on land this was different. They were on land now and they were not to forget it. At sea you might make as much noise as you pleased and no harm was done, but on land anything might happen. One of the perils of the land that he instanced was that of hanging. For every hundred men that they hung on land, he said, not more than twenty would be hung at sea. The men were to sleep at their guns. They would not go far that night; for the risk of being wrecked at night was another danger peculiar to the land, while at sea you might sail from set of sun till dawn: yet it was essential to get out of sight of the sea, for if anyone knew they were there they'd have cavalry after them. And he had sent back Smerdrak (a young lieutenant of pirates) to cover their tracks where they came up from the sea. And the merry men vigorously nodded their heads though they did not dare to cheer, and presently Smerdrak came running up and they threw him a rope by the stern. And when they had done fifteen knots they anchored, and Captain Shard gathered his men about him and, standing by the land-wheel in the bows, under the large and clear Algerian stars, he explained his system of steering. There was not much to be said for it; he had with considerable ingenuity detached and pivoted the portion of the keel that held the leading axle and could move it by chains which were controlled from the land-wheel, thus the front pair of wheels could be deflected at will, but only very slightly, and they afterwards found that in a hundred yards they could only turn their ship four yards from her course. But let not captains of comfortable battleships, or owners even of yachts, criticize too harshly a man who was not of their time and who knew not modern contrivances; it should be remembered also that Shard was no longer at sea. His steering may have been clumsy but he did what he could.

When the use and limitations of his land-wheel had been made clear to his men, Shard bade them all turn in except those on watch. Long before dawn he woke them and by the very first gleam of light they got their ship under way, so that when those two fleets that had made so sure of Shard closed in like a great crescent on the Algerian coast there was no sign to see of the *Desperate Lark* either on sea or land; and the flags of the Admiral's ship broke out into a hearty English oath.

The gale blew for three days and, Shard using more sail by daylight, they scudded over the sands at little less than ten knots, though on the report of rough water ahead (as the look-out man called rocks, low hills or uneven surface before he adapted himself to his new surroundings) the rate was much decreased. Those were long summer days and Shard, who was anxious while the wind held good to outpace the rumour of his own appearance, sailed for nineteen hours a day, lying to at ten in the evening and hoisting sail again at 3 a.m., when it first began to be light.

In those three days he did five hundred miles; then the wind dropped to a breeze, though it still blew from the north, and for a week they did no more than two knots an hour. The merry men began to murmur then. Luck had distinctly favoured Shard at first, for it sent him at ten knots through the only populous districts well ahead of crowds except those who chose to run, and the cavalry were away on a local raid. As for the runners they soon dropped off when Shard pointed his cannon though he did not dare to fire, up there near the coast; for much as he jeered at the intelligence of the English and Spanish Admirals in not suspecting his manoeuvre, the only one as he said that was possible in the circumstances, yet he knew that cannon had an obvious sound which would give his secret away to the weakest mind. Certainly luck had befriended him, and when it did so no longer he made out of the occasion all that could be made; for instance, while the wind held good he had never missed opportunities to revictual; if he passed by a village its pigs and poultry were his, and whenever he passed by water he filled his tanks to the brim, and now that he could only do two knots he sailed all night with a man and a lantern before him: thus in that week he did close on four hundred miles while another man would have anchored at night and have missed five or six hours out of the twenty-four. Yet his men murmured. Did he think the wind would last for ever, they said. And Shard only smoked. It was clear that he was thinking, and thinking hard. "But what is he thinking about?" said Bill to Bad Jack. And Bad Jack answered: "He may think as hard as he likes, but thinking won't get us out of the Sahara if this wind were to drop."

And towards the end of that week Shard went to his chart-room and laid a new course for his ship a little to the east and towards cultivation. And one day towards evening they sighted a village, and twilight came and the wind dropped altogether. Then the murmurs of the merry men grew to oaths and nearly to mutiny. "Where were they now?" they asked, and were they being treated like poor honest men?

Shard quieted them by asking what they wished to do them-selves, and when no one had any better plan than going to the villagers and saying that they had been blown out of their course by a storm, Shard unfolded his scheme to them.

Long ago he had heard how they drove carts with oxen in Africa; oxen were very numerous in these parts wherever there was any cultivation, and for this reason when the wind had begun to drop he had laid his course for the village: that night the moment it was dark they were to drive off fifty yoke of oxen; by midnight they must all be yoked to the bows and then away they would go at a good round gallop.

So fine a plan as this astonished the men and they all apolo-gized for their want of faith in Shard, shaking hands with him every one, and spitting on their hands before they did so in token of goodwill.

The raid that night succeeded admirably; but ingenious as Shard was on land, and a past-master at sea, yet it must be admitted that lack of experience in this class of seamanship led him to make a mistake, a slight one it is true, and one that a little practice would have prevented altogther: the oxen could not gallop. Shard swore at them, threatened them with his pistol, said they should have no food, and all to no avail: that night and as long as they pulled the bad ship *Desperate Lark* they did one knot an hour and no more. Shard's failures like everything that came his way were used as stones in the edifice of his future success, he went at once to his chart-room and worked out all his calculations anew.

The matter of the oxen's pace made pursuit impossible to avoid. Shard therefore countermanded his order to his lieutenant to cover the tracks in the sand, and the *Desperate Lark* plodded on into the Sahara on her new course trusting to her guns.

The village was not a large one, and the little crowd that was sighted astern next morning disappeared after the first shot from the cannon in the stern. At first Shard made the oxen wear rough iron bits, another of his mistakes, and strong bits too, "For if they run away," he had said, "we might as well be driving before a gale, and there's no saying where we'd find ourselves," but after a day or two he found that the bits were no good and, like the practical man he was, immediately corrected his mistake.

And now the crew sang merry songs all day, bringing out mandolins and clarionettes and cheering Captain Shard. All were jolly except the captain himself whose face was moody and perplexed; he alone expected to hear more of those villagers; and the oxen were drinking up the water every day; he alone feared that there was no more to be had, and a very unpleasant fear that is when your ship is becalmed in a desert. For over a week they went on like this, doing ten knots a day, and the music and singing got on the captain's nerves, but he dared not tell his men what the trouble was. And then one day the oxen drank up the last of the water. And Lieutenant Smerdrak came and reported the fact.

"Give them rum," said Shard, and he cursed the oxen. "What is good enough for me," he said, "should be good enough for them," and he swore that they should have rum.

"Aye, aye, sir," said the young lieutenant of pirates.

Shard should not be judged by the orders he gave that day; for nearly a fortnight he had watched the doom that was coming slowly towards him, discipline cut him off from anyone that might have shared his fear and discussed it, and all the while he had had to navigate his ship, which even at sea is an arduous responsibility. These things had fretted the calm of that clear judgment that had once baffled five navies. Therefore he cursed the oxen and ordered them rum, and Smerdrak had said "Aye, aye, sir," and gone below.

Towards sunset Shard was standing on the poop, thinking of death; it would not come to him by thirst; mutiny first, he thought. The oxen were refusing rum for the last time, and the men were beginning to eye Captain Shard in a very ominous way, not muttering, but each man looking at him with a side-long look of the eye as though there were only one thought among them all that had no need of words. A score of geese like a long letter "V" were crossing the evening sky, they slanted their necks and all went twisting downwards somewhere about the horizon. Captain Shard rushed to his chart-room, and pres-

ently the men came in at the door with Old Frank in front
looking awkward and twisting his cap in his hand.

"What is it?" said Shard as though nothing were wrong.

Then Old Frank said what he had come to say: "We want to
know what you be going to do."

And the men nodded grimly.

"Get water for the oxen," said Captain Shard, "as the swine
won't have rum, and they'll have to work for it, the lazy beasts.
Up anchor!"

And at the word water a look came into their faces like when
some wanderer suddenly thinks of home.

"Water!" they said.

"Why not?" said Captain Shard. And none of them ever knew
that but for those geese, that slanted their necks and suddenly
twisted downwards, they would have found no water that night
nor ever after, and the Sahara would have taken them as she
has taken so many and shall take so many more. All that night
they followed their new course: at dawn they found an oasis and
the oxen drank.

And here, on this green acre or so with its palm trees and its
well, beleaguered by thousands of miles of desert and holding out
through the ages, here they decided to stay: for those who have
been without water for a while in one of Africa's deserts come
to have for that simple fluid such a regard as you, O reader,
might not easily credit. And here each man chose a site where
he would build his hut, and settle down, and marry perhaps,
and even forget the sea; when Captain Shard having filled his
tanks and barrels peremptorily ordered them to weigh anchor.
There was much dissatisfaction, even some grumbling, but when
a man has twice saved his fellows from death by the sheer freshness of his mind they come to have a respect for his judgment
that is not shaken by trifles. It must be remembered that in
the affair of the dropping of the wind and again when they ran
out of water these men were at their wits' end: so was Shard on
the last occasion, but that they did not know. All this Shard
knew, and he chose this occasion to strengthen the reputation
that he had in the minds of the men of that bad ship by explaining to them his motives, which usually he kept secret. The
oasis, he said, must be a port of call for all the travellers within
hundreds of miles: how many men did you see gathered together

in any part of the world where there was a drop of whiskey to be had! And water here was rarer than whiskey in decent countries and, such was the peculiarity of the Arabs, even more precious. Another thing he pointed out to them, the Arabs were a singularly inquisitive people and if they came upon a ship in the desert they would probably talk about it; and the world having a wickedly malicious tongue would never construe in its proper light their difference with the English and Spanish fleets, but would merely side with the strong against the weak.

And the men sighed, and sang the capstan song, and hoisted the anchor and yoked the oxen up, and away they went doing their steady knot, which nothing could increase. It may be thought strange that with all sail furled in dead calm and while the oxen rested they should have cast anchor at all. But custom is not easily overcome and long survives its use. Rather enquire how many such useless customs we ourselves preserve: the flaps, for instance, to pull up the tops of hunting boots though the tops no longer pull up, the bows on our evening shoes that neither tie nor untie. They said they felt safer that way, and there was an end of it.

Shard lay a course of south by west and they did ten knots that day, the next day they did seven or eight and Shard hove to. Here he intended to stop; they had huge supplies of fodder on board for the oxen, for his men he had a pig or so, plenty of poultry, several sacks of biscuits and ninety-eight oxen (for two were already eaten), and they were only twenty miles from water. Here he said they would stay till folks forgot their past, someone would invent something or some new thing would turn up to take folks' minds off them and the ships he had sunk: he forgot that there are men who are well paid to remember.

Half-way between him and the oasis he established a little depot where he buried his water-barrels. As soon as a barrel was empty he sent half a dozen men to roll it by turns to the depot. This they would do at night, keeping hid by day, and next night they would push on to the oasis, fill the barrel and roll it back. Thus only ten miles away he soon had a store of water, unknown to the thirstiest native of Africa, from which he could safely replenish his tanks at will. He allowed his men to sing and even within reason to light fires. Those were jolly nights while the rum held out; sometimes they saw gazelles watching them curiously, sometimes a lion went by over the sand, the sound of his roar added to their sense of the security of their ship; all round them level, immense lay the Sahara. "This is better than an English prison," said Captain Shard.

And still the dead calm lasted, not even the sand whispered at night to little winds; and when the rum gave out and it looked like trouble, Shard reminded them what little use it had been to them when it was all they had and the oxen wouldn't look at it.

And the days wore on with singing, and even dancing at times, and at nights round a cautious fire in a hollow of sand, with only one man on watch, they told tales of the sea. It was all a relief after arduous watches and sleeping by the guns, a rest to strained nerves and eyes; and all agreed, for all that they missed their rum, that the best place for a ship like theirs was the land.

This was in latitude 23 north, longitude 4 east, where, as I have said, a ship's broadside was heard for the first time and the last. It happened this way.

They had been there several weeks and had eaten perhaps ten or a dozen oxen and all that while there had been no breath of wind and they had seen no one: when one morning about two bells when the crew were at breakfast the look-out man reported cavalry on the port side. Shard, who had already surrounded his ship with sharpened stakes, ordered all his men on board; the young trumpeter, who prided himself on having picked up the ways of the land, sounded "Prepare to receive cavalry"; Shard sent a few men below with pikes to the lower port-holes, two more aloft with muskets, the rest to the guns; he changed the "grape" or "canister" with which the guns were loaded in case of a surprise, for shot, cleared the decks, drew in ladders, and before the cavalry came within range everything was ready for them. The oxen were always yoked in order that Shard could manoeuvre his ship at a moment's notice.

When first sighted the cavalry were trotting, but they were coming on now at a slow canter. Arabs in white robes on good horses. Shard estimated that there were two or three hundred of them. At six hundred yards Shard opened with one gun; he had had the distance measured, but had never practised for fear of being heard at the oasis: the shot went high. The next one fell short and ricochetted over the Arabs' heads. Shard had the range then, and by the time the ten remaining guns of his broadside were given the same elevation as that of his second gun the Arabs had come to the spot where the last shot pitched. The broadside hit the horses, mostly low, and ricochetted on amongst them; one cannon-ball striking a rock at the horses' feet shattered it and sent fragments flying amongst the Arabs with the peculiar scream of things set free by projectiles from their motionless harmless state, and the cannon-ball went on with them with a great howl; this shot alone killed three men.

"Very satisfactory," said Shard, rubbing his chin. "Load with grape," he added sharply.

The broadside did not stop the Arabs nor even reduce their speed, but they crowded in closer together as though for company in their time of danger, which they should not have done. They were four hundred yards off now, three hundred and fifty; and then the muskets began, for the two men in the crow's-nest had thirty loaded muskets besides a few pistols; the muskets all stood round them leaning against the rail; they picked them up and fired them one by one. Every shot told, but still the Arabs came on. They were galloping now. It took some time to load the guns in those days. Three hundred yards, two hundred and fifty, men dropping all the way, two hundred yards; Old Frank for all his one ear had terrible eyes; it was pistols now, they had fired all their muskets; a hundred and fifty; Shard had marked the fifties with little white stones. Old Frank and Bad Jack up aloft felt pretty uneasy when they saw the Arabs had come to that little white stone, they both missed their shots.

"All ready?" said Captain Shard.

"Aye, aye, sir," said Smerdrak.

"Right," said Captain Shard, raising a finger.

A hundred and fifty yards is a bad range at which to be caught by grape (or "case" as we call it now), the gunners can hardly miss and the charge has time to spread. Shard estimated afterwards that he got thirty Arabs by that broadside alone and as many horses.

There were close on two hundred of them still on their horses, yet the broadside of grape had unsettled them, they surged round the ship but seemed doubtful what to do. They carried swords and scimitars in their hands, though most had strange long muskets slung behind them; a few unslung them and began firing wildly. They could not reach Shard's merry men with their swords. Had it not been for that broadside that took them when it did they might have climbed up from their horses and carried the bad ship by sheer force of numbers, but they would have had to have been very steady, and the broadside spoiled all that. Their best course was to have concentrated all their efforts in setting fire to the ship, but this they did not attempt. Part of them swarmed all round the ship brandishing their swords and looking vainly for an easy entrance; perhaps they expected a door, they were not seafaring people; but their leaders were evidently set on driving off the oxen, not dreaming that the *Desperate Lark* had other means of travelling. And this to some extent they succeeded in doing. Thirty they drove off, cutting the traces, twenty they killed on the spot with their scimitars though the bow gun caught them twice as they did their work, and ten more were unluckily killed by Shard's bow gun. Before they could fire a third time from the bows they all galloped away, firing back at the oxen with their muskets and killing three more, and what troubled Shard more than the loss of his oxen was the way that they manoeuvred, galloping off just when the bow gun was ready and riding off by the port bow where the broadside could not get them, which seemed to him to show more knowledge of guns than they could have learned on that bright morning. What, thought Shard to himself, if they should bring big guns against the *Desperate Lark!* And the mere thought of it made him rail at Fate. But the merry men all cheered when they rode away. Shard had only twenty-two oxen left, and then a score or so of the Arabs dismounted while the rest rode further on leading their horses. And the dismounted men lay down on the port bow behind some rocks two hundred yards away and began to shoot at the oxen. Shard had just enough of them left to manoeuvre his ship with an effort, and he turned his ship a few points to the starboard so as to get a broadside at the rocks. But grape was of no use here, as the only way he could get an Arab was by hitting one of the rocks with shot behind which an Arab was lying, and the rocks were not easy to hit except by chance, and as often as he manoeuvred his ship the Arabs changed their ground. This went on all day while the mounted Arabs hovered out of range watching what

Shard would do; and all the while the oxen were growing fewer, so good a mark were they, until only ten were left and the ship could manoeuvre no longer. But then they all rode off.

The merry men were delighted, they calculated that one way and another they had unhorsed a hundred Arabs, and on board there had been no more than one man wounded: Bad Jack had been hit in the wrist; probably by a bullet meant for the men at the guns, for the Arabs were firing high. They had captured a horse and had found quaint weapons on the bodies of the dead Arabs and an interesting kind of tobacco. It was evening now and they talked over the fight, made jokes about their luckier shots, smoked their new tobacco and sang: altogether it was the jolliest evening they'd had. But Shard alone on the quarter-deck paced to and fro pondering, brooding and wondering. He had chopped off Bad Jack's wounded hand and given him a hook out of store, for captain does doctor upon these occasions, and Shard, who was ready for most things, kept half a dozen or so of neat new limbs, and of course a chopper. Bad Jack had gone below swearing a little and said he'd lie down for a bit, the men were smoking and singing on the sand, and Shard was there alone. The thought that troubled Shard was: What would the Arabs do? They did not look like men to go away for nothing. And at back of all his thoughts was one that reiterated guns, guns, guns. He argued with himself that they could not drag them all that way on the sand, that the *Desperate Lark* was not worth it, that they had given it up. Yet he knew in his heart that that was what they would do. He knew there were fortified towns in Africa, and as for its being worth it, he knew that there was no pleasant thing left now to those defeated men except revenge, and if the *Desperate Lark* had come over the sand, why not guns? He knew that the ship could never hold out against guns and cavalry, a week perhaps, two weeks, even three: what difference did it make how long it was? And the men sang:

> Away we go,
> Oho, Oho, Oho,
> A drop of rum for you and me,
> And the world's as round as the letter O,
> And round it runs the sea.

A melancholy settled down on Shard.

About sunset Lieutenant Smerdrak came up for orders. Shard ordered a trench to be dug along the port side of the ship. The men wanted to sing and grumbled at having to dig, especially as Shard never mentioned his fear of guns, but he fingered his pistols and in the end Shard had his way. No one on board could shoot like Captain Shard. That is often the way with captains of pirate ships, it is a difficult position to hold. Discipline is essential to those that have the right to fly the skull-and-cross-bones, and Shard was the man to enforce it. It was starlight by the time the trench was dug to the captain's satisfaction, and the men that it was to protect when the worst came to the worst swore all the time as they dug. And when it was finished they clamoured to make a feast on some of the killed oxen, and this Shard let them do. And they lit a huge fire for the first time, burning abundant scrub, they thinking that the Arabs daren't return, Shard knowing that concealment was now useless. All that night they feasted and sang, and Shard sat up in his chart-room making his plans.

When morning came they rigged up the cutter, as they called the captured horse, and told off her crew. As there were only two men that could ride at all these became the crew of the cutter. Spanish Dick and Bill the Boatswain were the two.

Shard's orders were that turn and turn about they should take command of the cutter and cruise about five miles off to the north-east all the day, but at night they were to come in. And they fitted the horse up with a flagstaff in front of the saddle so that they could signal from her, and carried an anchor behind for fear she should run away.

And as soon as Spanish Dick had ridden off Shard sent some men to roll all the barrels back from the depot, where they were buried in the sand, with orders to watch the cutter all the time, and, if she signalled, to return as fast as they could.

They buried the Arabs that day, removing their water-bottles and any provisions they had, and that night they got all the water-barrels in, and for days nothing happened. One event of extraordinary importance did indeed occur: the wind got up one day, but it was due south, and as the oasis lay to the north of them, and beyond that they might pick up the camel track, Shard decided to stay where he was. If it had looked to him like lasting Shard might have hoisted sail, but it dropped at evening

as he knew it would, and in any case it was not the wind he
wanted. And more days went by, two weeks without a breeze.
The dead oxen would not keep and they had had to kill three
more; there were only seven left now.

Never before had the men been so long without rum. And
Captain Shard had doubled the watch, besides making two more
men sleep at the guns. They had tired of their simple games,
and most of their songs; and their tales that were never true
were no longer new. And then one day the monotony of the
desert came down upon them.

There is a fascination in the Sahara: a day there is delightful,
a week is pleasant, a fortnight is a matter of opinion, but it was
running into months. The men were perfectly polite, but the
boatswain wanted to know when Shard thought of moving on.
It was an unreasonable question to ask of the captain of any
ship in a dead calm in a desert, but Shard said he would set a
course and let him know in a day or two. And a day or two
went by over the monotony of the Sahara, who for monotony
is unequalled by all the parts of the earth. Great marshes cannot
equal it, nor plains of grass nor the sea; the Sahara alone lies
unaltered by the seasons, she has no altering surface, no flowers
to fade or grow, year in year out she is changeless for hundreds
and hundreds of miles. And the boatswain came again and took
off his cap and asked Captain Shard to be so kind as to tell them
about his new course. Shard said he meant to stay until they had
eaten three more of the oxen as they could only take three of them
in the hold, there were only six left now. But what if there was
no wind? the boatswain said. And at that moment the faintest
breeze from the north ruffled the boatswain's forelock as he
stood with his cap in his hand.

"Don't talk about the wind to *me*," said Captain Shard: and
Bill was a little frightened for Shard's mother had been a gipsy.

But it was only a breeze astray, a trick of the Sahara. And another week went by and they ate two more oxen.

They obeyed Captain Shard ostentatiously now, but they wore
ominous looks. Bill came again and Shard answered him in
Romany.

Things were like this one hot Sahara morning when the cutter
signalled. The look-out man told Shard and Shard read the
message. "Cavalry astern" it read, and then a little later she
signalled "With guns."

"Ah," said Captain Shard.

One ray of hope Shard had; the flags on the cutter fluttered. For the first time for five weeks a light breeze blew from the north, very light, you hardly felt it. Spanish Dick rode in and anchored his horse to starboard and the cavalry came on slowly from the port.

Not till the afternoon did they come in sight, and all the while that little breeze was blowing.

"One knot," said Shard at noon. "Two knots," he said at six bells, and still it grew and the Arabs trotted nearer. By five o'clock the merry men of the bad ship *Desperate Lark* could make out twelve long old-fashioned guns on low-wheeled carts dragged by horses, and what looked like lighter guns carried on camels. The wind was blowing a little stronger now.

"Shall we hoist sail, sir?" said Bill.

"Not yet," said Shard.

By six o'clock the Arabs were just outside the range of cannon and there they halted. Then followed an anxious hour or so, but the Arabs came no nearer. They evidently meant to wait till dark to bring their guns up. Probably they intended to dig a gun epaulement from which they could safely pound away at the ship.

"We could do three knots," said Shard half to himself, he was walking up and down his quarter-deck with very fast short paces. And then the sun set and they heard the Arabs praying, and Shard's merry men cursed at the top of their voices to show that they were as good men as they.

The Arabs had come no nearer, waiting for night. They did not know how Shard was longing for it too, he was gritting his teeth and sighing for it, he even would have prayed, but that he feared that it might remind Heaven of him and his merry men.

Night came and the stars. "Hoist sail," said Shard. The men sprang to their places, they had had enough of that silent lonely spot. They took the oxen on board and let the great sails down; and like a lover coming from over sea, long dreamed of, long expected, like a lost friend seen again after many years, the north wind came into the pirates' sails. And before Shard could stop it a ringing English cheer went away to the wondering Arabs.

They started off at three knots, and soon they might have done four, but Shard would not risk it at night. All night the wind held good, and doing three knots from ten to four they were far out of sight of the Arabs when daylight came. And then Shard hoisted more sail and they did four knots, and by eight bells they were doing four and a half. The spirits of those volatile men rose high, and discipline became perfect. So long as there was wind in the sails and water in the tanks Captain Shard felt safe at least from mutiny. Great men can only be overthrown while their fortunes are at their lowest. Having failed to depose Shard when his plans were open to criticism and he himself scarce knew what to do next, it was hardly likely they could do it now; and whatever we think of his past and his way of living we cannot deny that Shard was among the great men of the world.

Of defeat by the Arabs he did not feel so sure. It was useless to try to cover his tracks even if he had had time, the Arab cavalry could have picked them up anywhere. And he was afraid of their camels with those light guns on board, he had heard they could do seven knots and keep it up most of the day, and if as much as one shot struck the mainmast . . . and Shard taking his mind off useless fears worked out on his chart when the Arabs were likely to overtake them. He told his men that the wind would hold good for a week, and, gipsy or no, he certainly knew as much about the wind as is good for a sailor to know.

Alone in his chart-room he worked it out like this: mark two hours to the good for surprise and finding the tracks and delay in starting, say three hours if the guns were mounted in their epaulements, then the Arabs should start at seven. Supposing the camels go twelve hours a day at seven knots they would do eighty-four knots a day, while Shard doing three knots from ten to four, and four knots the rest of the time, was doing ninety and actually gaining. But when it came to it he wouldn't risk more than two knots at night while the enemy were out of sight, for he rightly regarded anything more than that as dangerous when sailing on land at night, so he too did eighty-four knots a day. It was a pretty race. I have not troubled to see if Shard added up his figures wrongly or if he underrated the pace of camels, but whatever it was the Arabs gained slightly, for on the fourth day Spanish Jack, five knots astern on what they called the cutter, sighted the camels a very long way off and signalled the fact to Shard. They had left their cavalry behind as Shard supposed they would. The wind held good, they had still two oxen left, and could always eat their "cutter," and they had a fair, though not ample, supply of water; but the appearance of the Arabs was a blow to Shard, for it showed him that there was no getting away from them, and of all things he dreaded guns. He made light of it to the men: said they would sink the lot before they had been in action half an hour: yet he feared that once the guns came up it was only a question of time before his rigging was cut or his steering gear disabled.

One point the *Desperate Lark* scored over the Arabs and a very good one too, darkness fell just before they could have sighted her, and now Shard used the lantern ahead as he dared not do on the first night when the Arabs were close, and with the help of it managed to do three knots. The Arabs encamped in the evening and the *Desperate Lark* gained twenty knots. But the next evening they appeared again, and this time they saw the sails of the *Desperate Lark*.

On the sixth day they were close. On the seventh they were closer. And then, a line of verdure across their bows, Shard saw the Niger River.

Whether he knew that for a thousand miles it rolled its course through forest, whether he even knew that it was there at all; what his plans were, or whether he lived from day to day like a man whose days are numbered, he never told his men. Nor can I get an indication on this point from the talk that I hear from sailors in their cups in a certain tavern I know of. His face was expressionless, his mouth shut, and he held his ship to her course. That evening they were up to the edge of the tree-trunks and the Arabs camped and waited ten knots astern, and the wind had sunk a little.

There Shard anchored a little before sunset and landed at once. At first he explored the forest a little on foot. Then he sent for Spanish Dick. They had slung the cutter on board some days ago when they found she could not keep up. Shard could not ride, but he sent for Spanish Dick and told him he must take him as a passenger. So Spanish Dick slung him in front of the saddle "before the mast," as Shard called it, for they still carried a mast on the front of the saddle, and away they galloped together. "Rough weather," said Shard, but he surveyed the forest

as he went, and the long and short of it was he found a place
where the forest was less than half a mile thick and the *Desperate
Lark* might get through: but twenty trees must be cut. Shard
marked the trees himself, sent Spanish Dick right back to watch
the Arabs and turned the whole of his crew on to those twenty
trees. It was a frightful risk, the *Desperate Lark* was empty, with
an enemy no more than ten knots astern, but it was a moment
for bold measures and Shard took the chance of being left without his ship in the heart of Africa in the hope of being repaid
by escaping altogether.

The men worked all night on those twenty trees, those that
had no axes bored with bradawls and blasted, and then relieved
those that had.

Shard was indefatigable, he went from tree to tree, showing
exactly what way every one was to fall, and what was to be done
with them when they were down. Some had to be cut down because their branches would get in the way of the masts, others
because their trunks would be in the way of the wheels; in the
case of the last the stumps had to be made smooth and low with
saws and perhaps a bit of the trunk sawn off and rolled away.
This was the hardest work they had. And they were all large
trees; on the other hand, had they been small, there would have
been many more of them and they could not have sailed in and
out, sometimes for hundreds of yards, without cutting any at all:
and all this Shard calculated on doing if only there was time.

The light before dawn came and it looked as if they would
never do it at all. And then dawn came and it was all done but
one tree, the hard part of the work had all been done in the night
and a sort of final rush cleared everything up except that one
huge tree. And then the cutter signalled the Arabs were moving.
At dawn they had prayed, and now they had struck their camp.
Shard at once ordered all his men to the ship except ten whom he
left at the tree; they had some way to go and the Arabs had been
moving some ten minutes before they got there. Shard took in
the cutter, which wasted five minutes, hoisted sail short-handed
and that took five minutes more, and slowly got under way.

The wind was dropping still, and by the time the *Desperate
Lark* had come to the edge of that part of the forest through
which Shard had laid his course the Arabs were no more than

five knots away. He had sailed east half a mile, which he ought to have done overnight so as to be ready, but he could not spare time or thought or men away from those twenty trees. Then Shard turned into the forest and the Arabs were dead astern. They hurried when they saw the *Desperate Lark* enter the forest.

"Doing ten knots," said Shard as he watched them from the deck. The *Desperate Lark* was doing no more than a knot and a half, for the wind was weak under the lee of the trees. Yet all went well for a while. The big tree had just come down some way ahead, and the ten men were sawing bits off the trunk.

And then Shard saw a branch that he had not marked on the chart, it would just catch the top of the mainmast. He anchored at once and sent a man aloft who sawed it half-way through and did the rest with a pistol, and now the Arabs were only three knots astern. For a quarter of a mile Shard steered them through the forest till they came to the ten men and that bad big tree; another foot had yet to come off one corner of the stump, for the wheels had to pass over it. Shard turned all hands on to the stump, and it was then that the Arabs came within shot. But they had to unpack their gun. And before they had it mounted Shard was away. If they had charged things might have been different. When they saw the *Desperate Lark* under way again the Arabs came on to within three hundred yards and there they mounted two guns. Shard watched them along his stern gun but would not fire. They were six hundred yards away before the Arabs could fire, and then they fired too soon and both guns missed. And Shard and his merry men saw clear water only ten fathoms ahead. Then Shard loaded his stern gun with canister instead of shot and at the same moment the Arabs charged on their camels; they came galloping down through the forest waving long lances. Shard left the steering to Smerdrak and stood by the stern gun; the Arabs were within fifty yards and still Shard did not fire; he had most of his men in the stern with muskets beside him. Those lances carried on camels were altogether different from swords in the hands of horsemen, they could reach the men on deck. The men could see the horrible barbs on the lance-heads, they were almost at their faces when Shard fired; and at the same moment the *Desperate Lark* with her dry and sun-cracked keel in air on the high bank of the Niger fell forward like a diver. The gun went off through the tree-tops, a wave came over the bows and swept the stern, the *Desperate Lark* wriggled and righted herself, she was back in her element.

The merry men looked at the wet decks and at their dripping clothes. "Water," they said almost wonderingly.

The Arabs followed a little way through the forest, but when they saw that they had to face a broadside instead of one stern gun and perceived that a ship afloat is less vulnerable to cavalry even than when on shore, they abandoned ideas of revenge, and comforted themselves with a text out of their sacred book which tells how in other days and other places our enemies shall suffer even as we desire.

For a thousand miles with the flow of the Niger and the help of occasional winds, the *Desperate Lark* moved seawards. At first he sweeps east a little and then southwards, till you come to Akassa and the open sea.

I will not tell you how they caught fish and ducks, raided a village here and there and at last came to Akassa, for I have said much already of Captain Shard. Imagine them drawing nearer and nearer the sea, bad men all, and yet with a feeling for something where we feel for our king, our country or our home, a feeling for something that burned in them not less ardently than our feelings in us, and that something the sea. Imagine them nearing it till sea birds appeared and they fancied they felt sea breezes and all sang songs again that they had not sung for weeks. Imagine them heaving at last on the salt Atlantic again.

I have said much already of Captain Shard and I fear lest I shall weary you, O my reader, if I tell you any more of so bad a man. I, too, at the top of a tower all alone am weary.

And yet it is right that such a tale should be told. A journey almost due south from near Algiers to Akassa in a ship that we should call no more than a yacht. Let it be a stimulus to younger men.

Guarantee to the Reader

Since writing down for your benefit, O my reader, all this long tale that I heard in the tavern by the sea, I have travelled in Algeria and Tunisia as well as in the Desert. Much that I saw in those countries seems to throw doubt on the tale that the sailor told me. To begin with, the Desert does not come within hundreds of miles of the coast, and there are more mountains to cross than you would suppose, the Atlas mountains in particular. It is just possible Shard might have got through by El Cantara, following the camel road which is many centuries old; or he may have gone by Algiers and Bou Saada and through the mountain pass El Finita Dem, though that is a bad enough way for camels to go (let alone bullocks with a ship), for which reason the Arabs call it Finita Dem—the Path of Blood.

I should not have ventured to give this story the publicity of print had the sailor been sober when he told it, for fear that he should have deceived you, O my reader; but this was never the case with him, as I took good care to ensure: *in vino veritas* is a sound old proverb, and I never had cause to doubt his word unless that proverb lies.

If it should prove that he has deceived me, let it pass; but if he has been the means of deceiving you, there are little things about him that I know, the common gossip of that ancient tavern whose leaded bottle-glass windows watch the sea, which I will tell at once to every judge of my acquaintance, and it will be a pretty race to see which of them will hang him.

Meanwhile, O my reader, believe the story, resting assured that if you are taken in the thing shall be a matter for the hangman.

The Distressing Tale of Thangobrind the Jeweller, and of the Doom that Befell Him

WHEN Thangobrind the jeweller heard the ominous cough, he turned at once upon that narrow way. A thief was he, of very high repute, being patronised by the lofty and elect, for he stole nothing smaller than the Moomoo's egg, and in all his life stole only four kinds of stone—the ruby, the diamond, the emerald, and the sapphire; and, as jewellers go, his honesty was great. Now there was a Merchant Prince who had come to Thangobrind and had offered his daughter's soul for the diamond that is larger than the human head and was to be found on the lap of the spider-idol, Hlo-hlo, in his temple of Moung-ga-ling; for he had heard that Thangobrind was a thief to be trusted.

Thangobrind oiled his body and slipped out of his shop, and went secretly through byways and got as far as Snarp, before anybody knew that he was out on business again or missed his sword from its place under the counter. Thence he moved only by night, hiding by day and rubbing the edges of his sword, which he called Mouse because it was swift and nimble. The jeweller had subtle methods of travelling; nobody saw him cross the plains of Zid; nobody saw him come to Mursk or Tlun. O, but he loved shadows! Once the moon peeping out unexpectedly from a tempest had betrayed an ordinary jeweller; not so did it undo Thangobrind: the watchmen only saw a crouching shape that snarled and laughed: " 'Tis but a hyena," they said. Once in the city of Ag one of the guardians seized him, but Thangobrind was oiled and slipped from his hand; you scarcely heard his bare feet patter away. He knew that the Merchant Prince awaited his return, his little eyes open all night and glittering

with greed; he knew how his daughter lay chained up and screaming night and day. Ah, Thangobrind knew. And had he not
been out on business he had almost allowed himself one or two
little laughs. But business was business, and the diamond that
he sought still lay on the lap of Hlo-hlo, where it had been for
the last two million years since Hlo-hlo created the world and
gave unto it all things except that precious stone called Dead
Man's Diamond. The jewel was often stolen, but it had a knack
of coming back again to the lap of Hlo-hlo. Thangobrind knew
this, but he was no common jeweller and hoped to outwit Hlo-
hlo, perceiving not the trend of ambition and lust and that they
are vanity.

How nimbly he threaded his way through the pits of Snood!—
now like a botanist, scrutinising the ground; now like a dancer,
leaping from crumbling edges. It was quite dark when he went
by the towers of Tor, where archers shoot ivory arrows at strangers
lest any foreigner should alter their laws, which are bad, but not
to be altered by mere aliens. At night they shoot by the sound of
the strangers' feet. O, Thangobrind, Thangobrind, was ever a
jeweller like you! He dragged two stones behind him by long
cords, and at these the archers shot. Tempting indeed was the
snare that they set in Woth, the emeralds loose-set in the city's
gate; but Thangobrind discerned the golden cord that climbed
the wall from each and the weights that would topple upon him
if he touched one, and so he left them, though he left them
weeping, and at last came to Theth. There all men worship
Hlo-hlo; though they are willing to believe in other gods, as
missionaries attest, but only as creatures of the chase for the
hunting of Hlo-hlo, who wears Their halos, so these people say,
on golden hooks along his hunting-belt. And from Theth he
came to the city of Moung and the temple of Moung-ga-ling, and
entered and saw the spider-idol, Hlo-hlo, sitting there with Dead
Man's Diamond glittering on his lap, and looking for all the
world like a full moon, but a full moon seen by a lunatic who had
slept too long in its rays, for there was in Dead Man's Diamond
a certain sinister look and a boding of things to happen that are
better not mentioned here. The face of the spider-idol was lit by
that fatal gem; there was no other light. In spite of his shocking
limbs and that demoniac body his face was serene and apparently
unconscious.

A little fear came into the mind of Thangobrind the jeweller, a passing tremor—no more; business was business and he hoped for the best. Thangobrind offered honey to Hlo-hlo and prostrated himself before him. Oh, he was cunning! When the priests stole out of the darkness to lap up the honey they were stretched senseless on the temple floor, for there was a drug in the honey that was offered to Hlo-hlo. And Thangobrind the jeweller picked Dead Man's Diamond up and put it on his shoulder and trudged away from the shrine; and Hlo-hlo the spider-idol said nothing at all, but he laughed softly as the jeweller shut the door. When the priests awoke out of the grip of the drug that was offered with the honey to Hlo-hlo, they rushed to a little secret room with an outlet on the stars and cast a horoscope of the thief. Something that they saw in the horoscope seemed to satisfy the priests.

It was not like Thangobrind to go back by the road by which he had come. No, he went by another road, even though it led to the narrow way, night-house and spider-forest.

The city of Moung went towering up behind him, balcony above balcony, eclipsing half the stars, as he trudged away with his diamond. He was not easy as he trudged away. Though when a soft pittering as of velvet feet arose behind him he refused to acknowledge that it might be what he feared, yet the instincts of his trade told him that it is not well when any noise whatever follows a diamond by night, and this was one of the largest that had ever come to him in the way of business. When he came to the narrow way that leads to spider-forest, Dead Man's Diamond feeling cold and heavy, and the velvety footfall seeming fearfully close, the jeweller stopped and amost hesitated. He looked behind him; there was nothing there. He listened attentively; there was no sound now. Then he thought of the screams of the Merchant Prince's daughter, whose soul was the diamond's price, and smiled and went stoutly on. There watched him, apathetically, over the narrow way, that grim and dubious woman whose house is the Night. Thangobrind, hearing no longer the sound of suspicious feet, felt easier now. He was all but come to the end of the narrow way, when the woman listlessly uttered that ominous cough.

The cough was too full of meaning to be disregarded. Thangobrind turned round and saw at once what he feared. The spider-idol had not stayed at home. The jeweller put his diamond gently upon the ground and drew his sword called Mouse. And then began that famous fight upon the narrow way, in which the grim old woman whose house was Night seemed to take so little interest. To the spider-idol you saw at once it was all a horrible joke. To the jeweller it was grim earnest. He fought and panted and was pushed back slowly along the narrow way, but he wounded Hlo-hlo all the while with terrible long gashes all over his deep, soft body till Mouse was slimy with blood. But at last the persistent laughter of Hlo-hlo was too much for the jeweller's nerves, and, once more wounding his demoniac foe, he sank aghast and exhausted by the door of the house called Night at the feet of the grim old woman, who having uttered once that ominous cough interfered no further with the course of events. And there carried Thangobrind the jeweller away those whose duty it was, to the house where the two men hang, and, taking down from his hook the left-hand one of the two, they put that venturous jeweller in his place; so that there fell on him the doom that he feared, as all men know though it is so long since, and there abated somewhat the ire of the envious gods.

And the only daughter of the Merchant Prince felt so little gratitude for this great deliverance that she took to respectability of a militant kind, and became aggressively dull, and called her home the English Riviera, and had platitudes worked in worsted upon her tea-cosy, and in the end never died, but passed away at her residence.

The Sword of Welleran

WHERE the great plain of Tarphet runs up, as the sea in estuaries, among the Cyresian mountains, there stood long since the city of Merimna well-nigh among the shadows of the crags. I have never seen a city in the world so beautiful as Merimna seemed to me when first I dreamed of it. It was a marvel of spires and figures of bronze, and marble fountains, and trophies of fabulous wars, and broad streets given over wholly to the Beautiful. Right through the centre of the city there went an avenue fifty strides in width, and along each side of it stood likenesses in bronze of the Kings of all the countries that the people of Merimna had ever known. At the end of that avenue was a colossal chariot with three bronze horses driven by the winged figure of Fame, and behind her in the chariot the huge form of Welleran, Merimna's ancient hero, standing with extended sword. So urgent was the mien and attitude of Fame, and so swift the pose of the horses, that you had sworn that the chariot was instantly upon you, and that its dust already veiled the faces of the Kings. And in the city was a mighty hall wherein were stored the trophies of Merimna's heroes. Sculptured it was and domed, the glory of the art of masons a long while dead, and on the summit of the dome the image of Rollory sat gazing across the Cyresian mountains toward the wide lands beyond, the lands that knew his sword. And beside Rollory, like an old nurse, the figure of Victory sat, hammering into a golden wreath of laurels for his head the crowns of fallen Kings.

Such was Merimna, a city of sculptured Victories and warriors of bronze. Yet in the time of which I write the art of war had been forgotten in Merimna, and the people almost slept. To and fro and up and down they would walk through the marble streets, gazing at memorials of the things achieved by their country's swords in the hands of those that long ago had loved Merimna well. Almost they slept, and dreamed of Welleran, Soorenard, Mommolek, Rollory, Akanax, and young Iraine. Of the lands beyond the mountains that lay all round about them they knew nothing, save that they were the theatre of the terrible deeds of Welleran, that he had done with his sword. Long since these lands had fallen back into the possession of the nations that had been scourged by Merimna's armies. Nothing now remained to Merimna's men save their inviolate city and the glory of the remembrance of their ancient fame. At night they would place sentinels far out in the desert, but these always slept at their posts dreaming of Rollory, and three times every night a guard would march around the city clad in purple, bearing lights and singing songs of Welleran. Always the guard went unarmed, but as the sound of their song went echoing across the plain towards the looming mountains, the desert robbers would hear the name of Welleran and steal away to their haunts. Often dawn would come across the plain, shimmering marvellously upon Merimna's spires, abashing all the stars, and find the guard still singing songs of Welleran, and would change the colour of their purple robes and pale the lights they bore. But the guard would go back leaving the ramparts safe, and one by one the sentinels in the plain would awake from dreaming of Rollory and shuffle back into the city quite cold. Then something of the menace would pass away from the faces of the Cyresian mountains, that from the north and the west and the south lowered upon Merimna, and clear in the morning the statues and the pillars would arise in the old inviolate city. You would wonder that an unarmed guard and sentinels that slept could defend a city that was stored with all the glories of art, that was rich in gold and bronze, a haughty city that had erst oppressed its neighbours, whose people had forgotten the art of war. Now this is the reason that, though all her other lands had long been taken from her, Merimna's city was safe. A strange thing was believed or feared by the fierce tribes beyond the mountains, and it was credited among them that at certain stations round Merimna's ramparts there still rode Welleran, Soorenard, Mommolek, Rollory, Akanax, and young Iraine. Yet it was close on a hundred years since Iraine, the youngest of Merimna's heroes, fought his last battle with the tribes.

Sometimes indeed there arose among the tribes young men who doubted and said: "How may a man for ever escape death?"

But graver men answered them: "Hear us, ye whose wisdom has discerned so much, and discern for us how a man may escape death when two score horsemen assail him with their swords, all of them sworn to kill him, and all of them sworn upon their country's gods; as often Welleran hath. Or discern for us how two men alone may enter a walled city by night, and bring away from it that city's king, as did Soorenard and Mommolek. Surely men that have escaped so many swords and so many sleety arrows shall escape the years and Time."

And the young men were humbled and became silent. Still, the suspicion grew. And often when the sun set on the Cyresian mountains, men in Merimna discerned the forms of savage tribesmen black against the light, peering towards the city.

All knew in Merimna that the figures round the ramparts were only statues of stone, yet even there a hope lingered among a few that some day their old heroes would come again, for certainly none had ever seen them die. Now it had been the wont of these six warriors of old, as each received his last wound and knew it to be mortal, to ride away to a certain deep ravine and cast his body in, as somewhere I have read great elephants do, hiding their bones away from lesser beasts. It was a ravine steep and narrow even at the ends, a great cleft into which no man could come by any path. There rode Welleran alone, panting hard; and there later rode Soorenard and Mommolek, Mommolek with a mortal wound upon him not to return, but Soorenard was unwounded and rode back alone from leaving his dear friend resting among the mighty bones of Welleran. And there rode Soorenard, when his day was come, with Rollory and Akanax, and Rollory rode in the middle and Soorenard and Akanax on either side. And the long ride was a hard and weary thing for Soorenard and Akanax, for they both had mortal wounds; but the long ride was easy for Rollory, for he was dead. So the bones of these five heroes whitened in an enemy's land, and very still they were, though they had troubled cities, and none knew where they lay saving only Iraine, the young captain, who was but twenty-five when Mommolek, Rollory, Akanax rode away. And among them were strewn their saddles and their bridles, and all the accoutrements of their horses, lest any man should ever find them afterwards and say in some foreign city: "Lo! the bridles or the saddles of Merimna's captains, taken in war," but their beloved trusty horses they turned free.

Forty years afterwards, in the hour of a great victory, his last wound came upon Iraine, and the wound was terrible and would not close. And Iraine was the last of the captains, and rode away alone. It was a long way to the dark ravine, and Iraine feared that he would never come to the resting-place of the old heroes, and he urged his horse on swiftly, and clung to the saddle with his hands. And often as he rode he fell asleep, and dreamed of earlier days, and of the times when he first rode forth to the great wars of Welleran, and of the time when Welleran first spake to him, and of the faces of Welleran's comrades when they led charges in the battle. And ever as he awoke a great longing arose in his soul as it hovered on his body's brink, a longing to lie among the bones of the old heroes. At last when he saw the dark ravine making a scar across the plain, the soul of Iraine slipped out through his great wound and spread its wings, and pain departed from the poor hacked body and, still urging his horse forward, Iraine died. But the old true horse cantered on till suddenly he saw before him the dark ravine and put his forefeet out on the very edge of it and stopped. Then the body of Iraine came toppling forward over the right shoulder of the horse, and his bones mingle and rest as the years go by with the bones of Merimna's heroes.

Now there was a little boy in Merimna named Rold. I saw him first, I, the dreamer, that sit before my fire asleep, I saw him first as his mother led him through the great hall where stand the trophies of Merimna's heroes. He was five years old, and they stood before the great glass casket wherein lay the sword of Welleran, and his mother said: "The sword of Welleran." And Rold said: "What should a man do with the sword of Welleran?" And his mother answered: "Men look at the sword and remember Welleran." And they went on and stood before the great red cloak of Welleran, and the child said: "Why did Welleran wear this great red cloak?" And his mother answered: "It was the way of Welleran."

When Rold was a little older he stole out of his mother's house quite in the middle of the night when all the world was still, and Merimna asleep dreaming of Welleran, Soorenard, Mommolek, Rollory, Akanax, and young Iraine. And he went down to the ramparts to hear the purple guard go by singing of Welleran. And the purple guard came by with lights, all singing in the stillness, and dark shapes out in the desert turned and fled. And Rold went back again to his mother's house with a great yearning towards the name of Welleran, such as men feel for very holy things.

And in time Rold grew to know the pathway all round the ramparts, and the six equestrian statues that were there guarding Merimna still. These statues were not like other statues, they were so cunningly wrought of many-coloured marbles that none might be quite sure until very close that they were not living men. There was a horse of dappled marble, the horse of Akanax. The horse of Rollory was of alabaster, pure white, his armour was wrought out of a stone that shone, and his horseman's cloak was made of a blue stone, very precious. He looked northward.

But the marble horse of Welleran was pure black, and there sat Welleran upon him looking solemnly westwards. His horse it was whose cold neck Rold most loved to stroke, and it was Welleran whom the watchers at sunset on the mountains the most clearly saw as they peered towards the city. And Rold loved the red nostrils of the great black horse and his rider's jasper cloak.

Now beyond the Cyresians the suspicion grew that Merimna's heroes were dead, and a plan was devised that a man should go by night and come close to the figures upon the ramparts and see whether they were Welleran, Soorenard, Mommolek, Rollory, Akanax, and young Iraine. And all were agreed upon the plan, and many names were mentioned of those who should go, and the plan matured for many years. It was during these years that watchers clustered often at sunset upon the mountains but came no nearer. Finally, a better plan was made, and it was decided that two men who had been by chance condemned to death should be given a pardon if they went down into the plain by night and discovered whether or not Merimna's heroes lived. At first the two prisoners dared not go, but after a while one of them, Seejar, said to his companion, Sajar-Ho: "See now, when the King's axeman smites a man upon the neck that man dies."

And the other said that this was so. Then said Seejar: "And even though Welleran smite a man with his sword no more befalleth him than death."

Then Sajar-Ho thought for a while. Presently he said: "Yet the eye of the King's axeman might err at the moment of his stroke or his arm fail him, and the eye of Welleran hath never erred nor his arm failed. It were better to bide here."

Then said Seejar: "Maybe that Welleran is dead and that some other holds his place upon the ramparts, or even a statue of stone."

But Sajar-Ho made answer: "How can Welleran be dead when he even escaped from two score horsemen with swords that were sworn to slay him, and all sworn upon our country's gods?"

And Seejar said: "This story his father told my grandfather concerning Welleran. On the day that the fight was lost on the plains of Kurlistan he saw a dying horse near to the river, and the horse looked piteously toward the water but could not reach it. And the father of my grandfather saw Welleran go down to the river's brink and bring water from it with his own hand and give it to the horse. Now we are in as sore a plight as was that horse, and as near to death; it may be that Welleran will pity us, while the King's axeman cannot because of the commands of the King."

Then said Sajar-Ho: "Thou wast ever a cunning arguer. Thou broughtest us into this trouble with thy cunning and thy devices, we will see if thou canst bring us out of it. We will go."

So news was brought to the King that the two prisoners would go down to Merimna.

That evening the watchers led them to the mountain's edge, and Seejar and Sajar-Ho went down towards the plain by the way of a deep ravine, and the watchers watched them go. Presently their figures were wholly hid in the dusk. Then night came up, huge and holy, out of waste marshes to the eastwards and low lands and the sea; and the angels that watched over all men through the day closed their great eyes and slept, and the angels that watched over all men through the night awoke and ruffled their deep blue feathers and stood up and watched. But the plain became a thing of mystery filled with fears. So the two spies went down the deep ravine, and coming to the plain sped stealthily across it. Soon they came to the line of sentinels asleep upon the sand, and one stirred in his sleep calling on Rollory, and a great dread seized upon the spies and they whispered "Rollory lives," but they remembered the King's axeman and went on. And next they came to the great bronze statue of Fear, carved by some sculptor of the old glorious years in the attitude of flight towards the mountains, calling to her children as she fled. And the children of Fear were carved in the likeness of the armies of all the trans-Cyresian tribes with their backs toward Merimna, flocking after Fear. And from where he sat on his horse behind the ramparts the sword of Welleran was stretched out over their heads as ever it was wont. And the two spies kneeled down in the sand and kissed the huge bronze foot of the statue of Fear, saying: "O Fear, Fear." And as they knelt they saw lights far off along the ramparts coming nearer and nearer, and heard men singing of Welleran. And the purple guard came nearer and went by with their lights, and passed on into the distance round the ramparts still singing of Welleran. And all the while the two spies clung to the foot of the statue, muttering: "O Fear, Fear." But when they could hear the name of Welleran no more they arose and came to the ramparts and climbed over them and came at once upon the figure of Welleran, and they bowed low to the ground, and Seejar said: "O Welleran, we came to see whether thou didst yet live." And for a long while they waited with their faces to the earth. At last Seejar looked up toward Welleran's terrible sword, and it was still stretched out pointing to the carved armies that followed after Fear. And Seejar bowed to the ground again and touched the horse's hoof, and it seemed cold to him. And he moved his hand higher and touched the leg of the horse, and it seemed quite cold. At last he touched Welleran's foot, and the armour on it seemed hard and stiff. Then as Welleran moved not and spake not, Seejar climbed up at last and touched his hand, the terrible hand of Welleran, and it was marble. Then Seejar laughed aloud, and he and Sajar-Ho sped down the empty pathway and found Rollory, and he was marble too. Then they climbed down over the ramparts and went back across the plain, walking contemptuously past the figure of Fear, and heard the guard returning round the ramparts for the third time, singing of Welleran; and Seejar said: "Ay, you may sing of Welleran, but Welleran is dead and a doom is on your city."

And they passed on and found the sentinel still restless in the night and calling on Rollory. And Sajar-Ho muttered: "Ay, you may call on Rollory, but Rollory is dead and naught can save your city."

And the two spies went back alive to their mountains again, and as they reached them the first ray of the sun came up red over the desert behind Merimna and lit Merimna's spires. It was the hour when the purple guard were wont to go back into the city with their tapers pale and their robes a brighter colour, when the cold sentinels came shuffling in from dreaming in the desert; it was the hour when the desert robbers hid themselves away going back to their mountain caves, it was the hour when gauze-winged insects are born that only live for a day, it was the hour when men die that are condemned to death, and in this hour a great peril, new and terrible, arose for Merimna and Merimna knew it not.

Then Seejar turning said: "See how red the dawn is and how red the spires of Merimna. They are angry with Merimna in Paradise and they bode its doom."

So the two spies went back and brought the news to their King, and for a few days the Kings of those countries were gathering their armies together; and one evening the armies of four Kings were massed together at the top of the deep ravine, all crouching below the summit waiting for the sun to set. All wore resolute and fearless faces, yet inwardly every man was praying to his gods, unto each one in turn.

Then the sun set, and it was the hour when the bats and the dark creatures are abroad and the lions come down from their lairs, and the desert robbers go into the plains again, and fevers rise up winged and hot out of chill marshes, and it was the hour when safety leaves the thrones of Kings, the hour when dynasties change. But in the desert the purple guard came swinging out of Merimna with their lights to sing of Welleran, and the sentinels lay down to sleep.

Now into Paradise no sorrow may ever come, but may only beat like rain against its crystal walls, yet the souls of Merimna's heroes were half aware of some sorrow far away as some sleeper feels that some one is chilled and cold yet knows not in his sleep that it is he. And they fretted a little in their starry home. Then unseen there drifted earthward across the setting sun the souls of Welleran, Soorenard, Mommolek, Rollory, Akanax, and young Iraine. Already when they reached Merimna's ramparts it was just dark, already the armies of the four Kings had begun to move, jingling, down the deep ravine. But when the six warriors saw their city again, so little changed after so many years, they looked towards her with a longing that was nearer to tears than any that their souls had known before, crying to her:

"O Merimna, our city: Merimna, our walled city.

"How beautiful thou art with all thy spires, Merimna. For thee we left the earth, its kingdoms and little flowers, for thee we have come away for awhile from Paradise.

"It is very difficult to draw away from the face of God—it is like a warm fire, it is like dear sleep, it is like a great anthem, yet there is a stillness all about it, a stillness full of lights.

"We have left Paradise for awhile for thee, Merimna.

"Many women have we loved, Merimna, but only one city.

"Behold now all the people dream, all our loved people. How beautiful are dreams! In dreams the dead may live, even the long dead and the very silent. Thy lights are all sunk low, they have all gone out, no sound is in thy streets. Hush! Thou art like a maiden that shutteth up her eyes and is asleep, that draweth her breath softly and is quite still, being at ease and untroubled.

"Behold now the battlements, the old battlements. Do men defend them still as we defended them? They are worn a little, the battlements," and drifting nearer they peered anxiously. "It is not by the hand of man that they are worn, our battlements. Only the years have done it and indomitable Time. Thy battlements are like the girdle of a maiden, a girdle that is round about her. See now the dew upon them, they are like a jewelled girdle.

"Thou art in great danger, Merimna, because thou art so beautiful. Must thou perish tonight because we no more defend thee, because we cry out and none hear us, as the bruised lilies cry out and none have known their voices?"

Thus spake those strong-voiced, battle-ordering captains, calling to their dear city, and their voices came no louder than the whispers of little bats that drift across the twilight in the evening. Then the purple guard came near, going round the ramparts for the first time in the night, and the old warriors called to them, "Merimna is in danger! Already her enemies gather in

"We Are But Dreams, Let Us Go Among Dreams"

"Welleran! And the Sword of Welleran!"

the darkness." But their voices were never heard because they were only wandering ghosts. And the guard went by and passed unheeding away, still singing of Welleran.

Then said Welleran to his comrades: "Our hands can hold swords no more, our voices cannot be heard, we are stalwart men no longer. We are but dreams, let us go among dreams. Go all of you, and thou too, young Iraine, and trouble the dreams of all the men that sleep, and urge them to take the old swords of their grandsires that hang upon the walls, and to gather at the mouth of the ravine; and I will find a leader and make him take my sword."

Then they passed up over the ramparts and into their dear city. And the wind blew about, this way and that, as he went, the soul of Welleran who had upon his day withstood the charges of tempestuous armies. And the souls of his comrades, and with them young Iraine, passed up into the city and troubled the dreams of every man who slept, and to every man the souls said in their dreams: "It is hot and still in the city. Go out now into the desert, into the cool under the mountains, but take with thee the old sword that hangs upon the wall for fear of the desert robbers."

And the god of that city sent up a fever over it, and the fever brooded over it and the streets were hot; and all that slept awoke from dreaming that it would be cool and pleasant where the breezes came down the ravine out of the mountains: and they took the old swords that their grandsires had, according to their dreams, for fear of the desert robbers. And in and out of dreams passed the souls of Welleran's comrades, and with them young Iraine, in great haste as the night wore on; and one by one they troubled the dreams of all Merimna's men and caused them to arise and go out armed, all save the purple guard who, heedless of danger, sang of Welleran still, for waking men cannot hear the souls of the dead.

But Welleran drifted over the roofs of the city till he came to the form of Rold lying fast asleep. Now Rold was grown strong and was eighteen years of age, and he was fair of hair and tall like Welleran, and the soul of Welleran hovered over him and went into his dreams as a butterfly flits through trellis-work into a garden of flowers, and the soul of Welleran said to Rold in his dreams: "Thou wouldst go and see again the sword of Welleran, the great curved sword of Welleran. Thou wouldst go and look at it in the night with the moonlight shining upon it."

And the longing of Rold in his dreams to see the sword caused him to walk still sleeping from his mother's house to the hall wherein were the trophies of the heroes. And the soul of Welleran urging the dreams of Rold caused him to pause before the great red cloak, and there the soul said among the dreams: "Thou art cold in the night; fling now a cloak around thee."

And Rold drew round about him the huge red cloak of Welleran. Then Rold's dreams took him to the sword, and the soul said to the dreams: "Thou hast a longing to hold the sword of Welleran: take up the sword in thy hand."

But Rold said: "What should a man do with the sword of Welleran?"

And the soul of the old captain said to the dreams: "It is a good sword to hold: take up the sword of Welleran."

And Rold, still sleeping and speaking aloud, said: "It is not lawful; none may touch the sword."

And Rold turned to go. Then a great and terrible cry arose in the soul of Welleran, all the more bitter for that he could not utter it, and it went round and round his soul finding no utterance, like a cry evoked long since by some murderous deed in some old haunted chamber that whispers through the ages heard by none.

And the soul of Welleran cried out to the dreams of Rold: "Thy knees are tied! Thou are fallen in a marsh! Thou canst not move."

And the dreams of Rold said to him: "Thy knees are tied, thou art fallen in a marsh," and Rold stood still before the sword. Then the soul of the warrior wailed among Rold's dreams, as Rold stood before the sword.

"Welleran is crying for his sword, his wonderful curved sword. Poor Welleran, that once fought for Merimna, is crying for his sword in the night. Thou wouldst not keep Welleran without his beautiful sword when he is dead and cannot come for it, poor Welleran who fought for Merimna."

And Rold broke the glass casket with his hand and took the sword, the great curved sword of Welleran; and the soul of the warrior said among Rold's dreams: "Welleran is waiting in the deep ravine that runs into the mountains, crying for his sword."

And Rold went down through the city and climbed over the ramparts, and walked with his eyes wide open but still sleeping over the desert to the mountains.

Already a great multitude of Merimna's citizens were gathered in the desert before the deep ravine with old swords in their hands, and Rold passed through them as he slept holding the sword of Welleran, and the people cried in amaze to one another as he passed: "Rold hath the sword of Welleran!"

And Rold came to the mouth of the ravine, and there the voices of the people woke him. And Rold knew nothing that he had done in his sleep, and looked in amazement at the sword in his hand and said: "What art thou, thou beautiful thing? Lights shimmer in thee, thou art restless. It is the sword of Welleran, the curved sword of Welleran!"

And Rold kissed the hilt of it, and it was salt upon his lips with the battle-sweat of Welleran. And Rold said: "What should a man do with the sword of Welleran?"

And all the people wondered at Rold as he sat there with the sword in his hand muttering, "What should a man do with the sword of Welleran?"

Presently there came to the ears of Rold the noise of a jingling up in the ravine, and all the people, the people that knew naught of war, heard the jingling coming nearer in the night; for the four armies were moving on Merimna and not yet expecting an enemy. And Rold gripped upon the hilt of the great curved sword, and the sword seemed to lift a little. And a new thought came into the hearts of Merimna's people as they gripped their grandsires' swords. Nearer and nearer came the heedless armies of the four Kings, and old ancestral memories began to arise in the minds of Merimna's people in the desert with their swords in their hands sitting behind Rold. And all the sentinels were awake holding their spears, for Rollory had put their dreams to flight, Rollory that once could put to flight armies and now was but a dream struggling with other dreams.

And now the armies had come very near. Suddenly Rold leaped up, crying: "Welleran! And the sword of Welleran!" And the savage, lusting sword that had thirsted for a hundred years went up with the hand of Rold and swept through a tribesman's ribs. And with the warm blood all about it there came a joy into the curved soul of that mighty sword, like to the joy of a swimmer coming up dripping out of warm seas after living for long in a dry land. When they saw the red cloak and that terrible sword a cry ran through the tribal armies, "Welleran lives!" And there arose the sounds of the exulting of victorious men, and the panting of those that fled, and the sword singing softly to itself as it whirled dripping through the air. And the last that I saw of the battle as it poured into the depth and darkness of the ravine was the sword of Welleran sweeping up and falling, gleaming blue in the moonlight whenever it arose and afterwards gleaming red, and so disappearing into the darkness.

But in the dawn Merimna's men came back, and the sun aris- ing to give new life to the world, shone instead upon the hideous things that the sword of Welleran had done. And Rold said: "O sword, sword! How horrible thou art! Thou art a terrible thing to have come among men. How many eyes shall look upon gardens no more because of thee? How many fields must go empty that might have been fair with cottages, white cottages with children all about them? How many valleys must go deso- late that might have nursed warm hamlets, because thou hast slain long since the men that might have built them? I hear the wind crying against thee, thou sword! It comes from the empty valleys. It comes over the bare fields. There are chil- dren's voices in it. They were never born. Death brings an end to crying for those that had life once, but these must cry for ever. O sword! sword! why did the gods send thee among men?" And the tears of Rold fell down upon the proud sword but could not wash it clean.

And now that the ardour of battle had passed away, the spirits of Merimna's people began to gloom a little, like their leader's, with their fatigue and with the cold of the morning; and they looked at the sword of Welleran in Rold's hand and said: "Not any more, not any more for ever will Welleran now return, for his sword is in the hand of another. Now we know indeed that he is dead. O Welleran, thou wast our sun and moon and all our stars. Now is the sun fallen down and the moon broken, and all the stars are scattered as the diamonds of a necklace that is snapped off one who is slain by violence."

Thus wept the people of Merimna in the hour of their great victory, for men have strange moods, while beside them their old inviolate city slumbered safe. But back from the ramparts and beyond the mountains and over the lands that they had conquered of old, beyond the world and back again to Paradise, went the souls of Welleran, Soorenard, Mommolek, Rollory, Akanax, and young Iraine.

The Fortress Unvanquishable, Save For Sacnoth

In a wood older than record, a foster brother of the hills, stood the village of Allathurion; and there was peace between the people of that village and all the folk who walked in the dark ways of the wood, whether they were human or of the tribes of the beasts or of the race of the fairies and the elves and the little sacred spirits of trees and streams. Moreover, the village people had peace among themselves and between them and their lord, Lorendiac. In front of the village was a wide and grassy space, and beyond this the great wood again, but at the back the trees came right up to the houses, which, with their great beams and wooden framework and thatched roofs, green with moss, seemed almost to be a part of the forest.

Now in the time I tell of, there was trouble in Allathurion, for of an evening fell dreams were wont to come slipping through the tree trunks and into the peaceful village; and they assumed dominion of men's minds and led them in watches of the night through the cindery plains of Hell. Then the magician of that village made spells against those fell dreams; yet still the dreams came flitting through the trees as soon as the dark had fallen, and led men's minds by night into terrible places and caused them to praise Satan openly with their lips.

And men grew afraid of sleep in Allathurion. And they grew worn and pale, some through the want of rest, and others from fear of the things they saw on the cindery plains of Hell.

Then the magician of the village went up into the tower of his house, and all night long those whom fear kept awake could see his window high up in the night glowing softly alone. The next day, when the twilight was far gone and night was gathering fast, the magician went away to the forest's edge, and uttered there the spell that he had made. And the spell was a compulsive, terrible thing, having a power over evil dreams and over spirits of ill; for it was a verse of forty lines in many languages, both living and dead, and had in it the word wherewith the people of the plains are wont to curse their camels, and the shout wherewith the whalers of the north lure the whales shoreward to be killed, and a word that causes elephants to trumpet; and every one of the forty lines closed with a rhyme for "wasp."

And still the dreams came flitting through the forest, and led men's souls into the plains of Hell. Then the magician knew that the dreams were from Gaznak. Therefore he gathered the people of the village, and told them that he had uttered his mightiest spell—a spell having power over all that were human or of the tribes of the beasts; and that since it had not availed the dreams must come from Gaznak, the greatest magician among the spaces of the stars. And he read to the people out of the Book of Magicians, which tells the comings of the comet and foretells his coming again. And he told them how Gaznak rides upon the comet, and how he visits Earth once in every two hundred and thirty years, and makes for himself a vast, invincible fortress and sends out dreams to feed on the minds of men, and may never be vanquished but by the sword Sacnoth.

And a cold fear fell on the hearts of the villagers when they found that their magician had failed them.

Then spake Leothric, son of the Lord Lorendiac, and twenty years old was he: "Good Master, what of the sword Sacnoth?"

And the village magician answered: "Fair Lord, no such sword as yet is wrought, for it lies as yet in the hide of Tharagavverug, protecting his spine."

Then said Leothric: "Who is Tharagavverug, and where may he be encountered?"

And the magician of Allathurion answered: "He is the dragon-crocodile who haunts the Northern marshes and ravages the homesteads by their marge. And the hide of his back is of steel, and his under parts are of iron; but along the midst of his back, over his spine, there lies a narrow strip of unearthly steel. This strip of steel is Sacnoth, and it may be neither cleft nor molten, and there is nothing in the world that may avail to break it, nor

even leave a scratch upon its surface. It is of the length of a good
sword, and of the breadth thereof. Shouldst thou prevail against
Tharagavverug, his hide may be melted away from Sacnoth in
a furnace; but there is only one thing that may sharpen Sacnoth's
edge, and this is one of Tharagavverug's own steel eyes; and the
other eye thou must fasten to Sacnoth's hilt, and it will watch for
thee. But it is a hard task to vanquish Tharagavverug, for no
sword can pierce his hide; his back cannot be broken, and he can
neither burn nor drown. In one way only can Tharagavverug
die, and that is by starving."

Then sorrow fell upon Leothric, but the magician spoke on:

"If a man drive Tharagavverug away from his food with a
stick for three days, he will starve on the third day at sunset. And
though he is not vulnerable, yet in one spot he may take hurt,
for his nose is only of lead. A sword would merely lay bare the
uncleavable bronze beneath, but if his nose be smitten constantly
with a stick he will always recoil from the pain, and thus may
Tharagavverug, to left and right, be driven away from his food."

Then Leothric said: "What is Tharagavverug's food?"

And the magician of Allathurion said: "His food is men."

But Leothric went straightway thence, and cut a great staff from
a hazel tree, and slept early that evening. But the next morning,
awaking from troubled dreams, he arose before the dawn, and,
taking with him provisions for five days, set out through the forest
northwards towards the marshes. For some hours he moved
through the gloom of the forest, and when he emerged from it
the sun was above the horizon shining on pools of water in the
waste land. Presently he saw the claw-marks of Tharagavverug
deep in the soil, and the track of his tail between them like a
furrow in a field. Then Leothric followed the tracks till he heard
the bronze heart of Tharagavverug before him, booming like a
bell.

And Tharagavverug, it being the hour when he took the first
meal of the day, was moving toward a village with his heart tolling. And all the people of the village were come out to meet him,
as it was their wont to do; for they abode not the suspense of
awaiting Tharagavverug and of hearing him sniffing brazenly
as he went from door to door, pondering slowly in his metal
mind what habitant he should choose. And none dared to flee,
for in the days when the villagers fled from Tharagavverug, he,

having chosen his victim, would track him tirelessly, like a doom. Nothing availed them against Tharagavverug. Once they climbed the trees when he came, but Tharagavverug went up to one, arching his back and leaning over slightly, and rasped against the trunk until it fell. And when Leothric came near, Tharagavverug saw him out of one of his small steel eyes and came towards him leisurely, and the echoes of his heart swirled up through his open mouth. And Leothric stepped sideways from his onset, and came between him and the village and smote him on the nose, and the blow of the stick made a dint in the soft lead. And Tharagavverug swung clumsily away, uttering one fearful cry like the sound of a great church bell that had become possessed of a soul that fluttered upward from the tombs at night—an evil soul, giving the bell a voice. Then he attacked Leothric, snarling, and again Leothric leapt aside, and smote him on the nose with his stick. Tharagavverug uttered like a bell howling. And whenever the dragon-crocodile attacked him, or turned towards the village, Leothric smote him again.

So all day long Leothric drove the monster with a stick, and he drove him farther and farther from his prey, with his heart tolling angrily and his voice crying out for pain.

Towards evening Tharagavverug ceased to snap at Leothric, but ran before him to avoid the stick, for his nose was sore and shining; and in the gloaming the villagers came out and danced to cymbal and psaltery. When Tharagavverug heard the cymbal and psaltery, hunger and anger came upon him, and he felt as some lord might feel who was held by force from the banquet in his own castle and heard the creaking spit go round and round and the good meat crackling on it. And all that night he attacked Leothric fiercely, and ofttimes nearly caught him in the darkness; for his gleaming eyes of steel could see as well by night as by day. And Leothric gave ground slowly till the dawn, and when the light came they were near the village again; yet not so near to it as they had been when they encountered, for Leothric drove Tharagavverug farther in the day than Tharagavverug had forced him back in the night. Then Leothric drove him again with his stick till the hour came when it was the custom of the dragon-crocodile to find his man. One third of his man he would eat at the time he found him, and the rest at noon and evening. But when the hour came for finding his man a great

fierceness came on Tharagavverug, and he grabbed rapidly at
Leothric, but could not seize him, and for a long while neither
of them would retire. But at last the pain of the stick on his
leaden nose overcame the hunger of the dragon-crocodile, and
he turned from it howling. From that moment Tharagavverug
weakened. All that day Leothric drove him with his stick, and
at night both held their ground; and when the dawn of the third
day was come the heart of Tharagavverug beat slower and fainter.
It was as though a tired man was ringing a bell. Once Tharagavverug nearly seized a frog, but Leothric snatched it away just in
time. Towards noon the dragon-crocodile lay still for a long
while, and Leothric stood near him and leaned on his trusty
stick. He was very tired and sleepless, but had more leisure now
for eating his provisions. With Tharagavverug the end was
coming fast, and in the afternoon his breath came hoarsely, rasping in his throat. It was as the sound of many huntsmen blowing
blasts on horns, and towards evening his breath came faster but
fainter, like the sound of a hunt going furious to the distance
and dying away, and he made desperate rushes towards the village; but Leothric still leapt about him, battering his leaden nose.
Scarce audible now at all was the sound of his heart: it was like
a church bell tolling beyond hills for the death of some one
unknown and far away. Then the sun set and flamed in the village windows, and a chill went over the world, and in some small
garden a woman sang; and Tharagavverug lifted up his head
and starved, and his life went from his invulnerable body, and
Leothric lay down beside him and slept. And later in the starlight the villagers came out and carried Leothric, sleeping, to the
village, all praising him in whispers as they went. They laid him
down upon a couch in a house, and danced outside in silence,
without psaltery or cymbal. And the next day, rejoicing, to
Allathurion they hauled the dragon-crocodile. And Leothric went
with them, holding his battered staff; and a tall, broad man, who
was smith of Allathurion, made a great furnace, and melted
Tharagavverug away until only Sacnoth was left, gleaming among
the ashes. Then he took one of the small eyes that had been
chiselled out, and filed an edge on Sacnoth, and gradually the
steel eye wore away facet by facet, but ere it was quite gone it
had sharpened redoubtably Sacnoth. But the other eye they set
in the butt of the hilt, and it gleamed there bluely.

And that night Leothric arose in the dark and took the sword, and went westwards to find Gaznak; and he went through the dark forest till the dawn, and all the morning and till the afternoon. But in the afternoon he came into the open and saw in the midst of The Land Where No Man Goeth the fortress of Gaznak, mountainous before him, little more than a mile away.

And Leothric saw that the land was marsh and desolate. And the fortress went up all white out of it, with many buttresses, and was broad below but narrowed higher up, and was full of gleaming windows with the light upon them. And near the top of it a few white clouds were floating, but above them some of its pinnacles reappeared. Then Leothric advanced into the marshes, and the eye of Tharagavverug looked out warily from the hilt of Sacnoth; for Tharagavverug had known the marshes well, and the sword nudged Leothric to the right or pulled him to the left away from the dangerous places, and so brought him safely to the fortress walls.

And in the wall stood doors like precipices of steel, all studded with boulders of iron, and above every window were terrible gargoyles of stone; and the name of the fortress shone on the wall, writ large in letters of brass: "The Fortress Unvanquishable, Save For Sacnoth."

Then Leothric drew and revealed Sacnoth, and all the gargoyles grinned, and the grin went flickering from face to face right up into the cloud-abiding gables.

And when Sacnoth was revealed and all the gargoyles grinned, it was like the moonlight emerging from a cloud to look for the first time upon a field of blood, and passing swiftly over the wet faces of the slain that lie together in the horrible night. Then Leothric advanced towards a door, and it was mightier than the marble quarry, Sacremona, from which of old men cut enormous slabs to build the Abbey of the Holy Tears. Day after day they wrenched out the very ribs of the hill until the Abbey was builded, and it was more beautiful than anything in stone. Then the priests blessed Sacremona, and it had rest, and no more stone was ever taken from it to build the houses of men. And the hill stood looking southwards lonely in the sunlight, defaced by that mighty scar. So vast was the door of steel. And the name of the door was The Porte Resonant, the Way of Egress for War.

Then Leothric smote upon the Porte Resonant with Sacnoth,

and the echo of Sacnoth went ringing through the halls, and all the dragons in the fortress barked. And when the baying of the remotest dragon had faintly joined in the tumult, a window opened far up among the clouds below the twilit gables, and a woman screamed, and far away in Hell her father heard her and knew that her doom was come.

And Leothric went on smiting terribly with Sacnoth, and the grey steel of the Porte Resonant, the Way of Egress for War, that was tempered to resist the swords of the world, came away in ringing slices.

Then Leothric, holding Sacnoth in his hand, went in through the hole that he had hewn in the door, and came into the unlit, cavernous hall.

An elephant fled trumpeting. And Leothric stood still, holding Sacnoth. When the sound of the feet of the elephant had died away in the remoter corridors, nothing more stirred, and the cavernous hall was still.

Presently the darkness of the distant halls became musical with the sound of bells, all coming nearer and nearer.

Still Leothric waited in the dark, and the bells rang louder and louder, echoing through the halls, and there appeared a procession of men on camels riding two by two from the interior of the fortress, and they were armed with scimitars of Assyrian make and were all clad with mail, and chain-mail hung from their helmets about their faces, and flapped as the camels moved. And they all halted before Leothric in the cavernous hall, and the camel bells clanged and stopped. And the leader said to Leothric:

"The Lord Gaznak has desired to see you die before him. Be pleased to come with us, and we can discourse by the way of the manner in which the Lord Gaznak has desired to see you die."

And as he said this he unwound a chain of iron that was coiled upon his saddle, and Leothric answered:

"I would fain go with you, for I am come to slay Gaznak."

Then all the camel-guard of Gaznak laughed hideously, disturbing the vampires that were asleep in the measureless vault of the roof. And the leader said:

"The Lord Gaznak is immortal, save for Sacnoth, and weareth armour that is proof even against Sacnoth himself, and hath a sword the second most terrible in the world."

Then Leothric said: "I am the Lord of the sword Sacnoth."

And he advanced towards the camel-guard of Gaznak, and Sacnoth lifted up and down in his hand as though stirred by an exultant pulse. Then the camel-guard of Gaznak fled, and the riders leaned forward and smote their camels with whips, and they went away with a great clamour of bells through colonnades and corridors and vaulted halls, and scattered into the inner darknesses of the fortress. When the last sound of them had died away, Leothric was in doubt which way to go, for the camel-guard was dispersed in many directions, so he went straight on till he came to a great stairway in the midst of the hall. Then Leothric set his foot in the middle of a wide step, and climbed steadily up the stairway for five minutes. Little light was there in the great hall through which Leothric ascended, for it only entered through arrow slits here and there, and in the world outside evening was waning fast. The stairway led up to two folding doors, and they stood a little ajar, and through the crack Leothric entered and tried to continue straight on, but could get no farther, for the whole room seemed to be full of festoons of ropes which swung from wall to wall and were looped and draped from the ceiling. The whole chamber was thick and black with them. They were soft and light to the touch, like fine silk, but Leothric was unable to break any one of them, and though they swung away from him as he pressed forward, yet by the time he had gone three yards they were all about him like a heavy cloak. Then Leothric stepped back and drew Sacnoth, and Sacnoth divided the ropes without a sound, and without a sound the severed pieces fell to the floor. Leothric went forward slowly, moving Sacnoth in front of him up and down as he went. When he was come into the middle of the chamber, suddenly, as he parted with Sacnoth a great hammock of strands, he saw a spider before him that was larger than a ram, and the spider looked at him with eyes that were little, but in which there was much sin, and said:

"Who are you that spoil the labour of years all done to the honour of Satan?"

And Leothric answered: "I am Leothric, son of Lorendiac."

And the spider said: "I will make a rope at once to hang you with."

Then Leothric parted another bunch of strands, and came nearer to the spider as he sat making his rope, and the spider, looking up from his work, said: "What is that sword which is able to sever my ropes?"

And Leothric said: "It is Sacnoth."

Thereat the black hair that hung over the face of the spider parted to left and right, and the spider frowned; then the hair fell back into its place, and hid everything except the sin of the little eyes which went on gleaming lustfully in the dark. But before Leothric could reach him, he climbed away with his hands, going up by one of his ropes to a lofty rafter, and there sat, growling. But clearing his way with Sacnoth, Leothric passed through the chamber, and came to the farther door; and the door being shut, and the handle far up out of his reach, he hewed his way through it with Sacnoth in the same way as he had through the Porte Resonant, the Way of Egress for War. And so Leothric came into a well-lit chamber, where Queens and Princes were banqueting together, all at a great table; and thousands of candles were glowing all about, and their light shone in the wine that the Princes drank and on the huge gold candelabra, and the royal faces were irradiant with the glow, and the white table-cloth and the silver plates and the jewels in the hair of the Queens, each jewel having a historian all to itself, who wrote no other chronicles all his days. Between the table and the door there stood two hundred footmen in two rows of one hundred facing one another. Nobody looked at Leothric as he entered through the hole in the door, but one of the Princes asked a question of a footman, and the question was passed from mouth to mouth by all the hundred footmen till it came to the last one nearest Leothric; and he said to Leothric, without looking at him:

"What do you seek here?"

And Leothric answered: "I seek to slay Gaznak."

And footman to footman repeated all the way to the table: "He seeks to slay Gaznak."

And another question came down the line of footmen: "What is your name?"

And the line that stood opposite took his answer back.

Then one of the Princes said: "Take him away where we shall not hear his screams."

And footman repeated it to footman till it came to the last two, and they advanced to seize Leothric.

Then Leothric showed to them his sword, saying, "This is

Sacnoth," and both of them said to the man nearest: "It is Sac-noth," then screamed and fled away.

And two by two, all up the double line, footman to footman repeated, "It is Sacnoth," then screamed and fled, till the last two gave the message to the table, and all the rest had gone. Hurriedly then arose the Queens and Princes, and fled out of the chamber. And the goodly table, when they were all gone, looked small and disorderly and awry. And to Leothric, pondering in the desolate chamber by what door he should pass onwards, there came from far away the sounds of music, and he knew that it was the magical musicians playing to Gaznak while he slept.

Then Leothric, walking towards the distant music, passed out by the door opposite to the one through which he had cloven his entrance, and so passed into a chamber vast as the other, in which were many women, weirdly beautiful. And they all asked him of his quest, and when they heard that it was to slay Gaznak, they all besought him to tarry among them, saying that Gaznak was immortal, save for Sacnoth, and also that they had need of a knight to protect them from the wolves that rushed round and round the wainscot all the night and sometimes broke in upon them through the mouldering oak. Perhaps Leothric had been tempted to tarry had they been human women, for theirs was a strange beauty, but he perceived that instead of eyes they had little flames that flickered in their sockets, and knew them to be the fevered dreams of Gaznak. Therefore he said:

"I have a business with Gaznak and with Sacnoth," and passed on through the chamber.

And at the name of Sacnoth those women screamed, and the flames of their eyes sank low and dwindled to sparks.

And Leothric left them, and, hewing with Sacnoth, passed through the farther door.

Outside he felt the night air on his face, and found that he stood upon a narrow way between two abysses. To left and right of him, as far as he could see, the walls of the fortress ended in a profound precipice, though the roof still stretched above him; and before him lay the two abysses full of stars, for they cut their way through the whole Earth and revealed the under sky; and threading its course between them went the way, and it sloped upward and its sides were sheer. And beyond the abysses, where the way led up to the farther chambers of the fortress, Leothric heard the musicians playing their magical tune. So he stepped on to the way, which was scarcely a stride in width, and moved along it holding Sacnoth naked. And to and fro beneath him in each abyss whirred the wings of vampires passing up and down, all giving praise to Satan as they flew. Presently he perceived the dragon Thok lying upon the way, pretending to sleep, and his tail hung down into one of the abysses.

And Leothric went towards him, and when he was quite close Thok rushed at Leothric.

And he smote deep with Sacnoth, and Thok tumbled into the abyss, screaming, and his limbs made a whirring in the darkness as he fell, and he fell till his scream sounded no louder than a whistle and then he could be heard no more. Once or twice Leothric saw a star blink for an instant and reappear again, and this momentary eclipse of a few stars was all that remained in the world of the body of Thok. And Lunk, the brother of Thok, who had lain a little behind him, saw that this must be Sacnoth and fled lumbering away. And all the while that he walked between the abysses, the mighty vault of the roof of the fortress still stretched over Leothric's head, all filled with gloom. Now, when the farther side of the abyss came into view, Leothric saw a chamber that opened with innumerable arches upon the twin abysses, and the pillars of the arches went away into the distance and vanished in the gloom to left and right.

Far down the dim precipice on which the pillars stood he could see windows small and closely barred, and between the bars there showed at moments, and disappeared again, things that I shall not speak of.

There was no light here except for the great Southern stars that shown below the abysses, and here and there in the chamber through the arches lights that moved furtively without the sound of footfall.

Then Leothric stepped from the way, and entered the great chamber.

Even to himself he seemed but a tiny dwarf as he walked under one of those colossal arches.

The last faint light of evening flickered through a window painted in sombre colours commemorating the achievements of Satan upon Earth. High up in the wall the window stood, and the streaming lights of candles lower down moved stealthily away.

Other light there was none, save for a faint blue glow from the steel eye of Tharagavverug that peered restlessly about it from the hilt of Sacnoth. Heavily in the chamber hung the clammy odour of a large and deadly beast.

Leothric moved forward slowly with the blade of Sacnoth in front of him feeling for a foe, and the eye in the hilt of it looking out behind.

Nothing stirred.

If anything lurked behind the pillars of the colonnade that held aloft the roof, it neither breathed nor moved.

The music of the magical musicians sounded from very near.

Suddenly the great doors on the far side of the chamber opened to left and right. For some moments Leothric saw nothing move, and waited clutching Sacnoth. Then Wong Bongerok came towards him, breathing.

This was the last and faithfullest guard of Gaznak, and came from slobbering just now his master's hand.

More as a child than a dragon was Gaznak wont to treat him, giving him often in his fingers tender pieces of man all smoking from his table.

Long and low was Wong Bongerok, and subtle about the eyes, and he came breathing malice against Leothric out of his faithful breast, and behind him roared the armoury of his tail, as when sailors drag the cable of the anchor all rattling down the deck.

And well Wong Bongerok knew that he now faced Sacnoth, for it had been his wont to prophesy quietly to himself for many years as he lay curled at the feet of Gaznak.

And Leothric stepped forward into the blast of his breath, and lifted Sacnoth to strike.

But when Sacnoth was lifted up, the eye of Tharagavverug in the butt of the hilt beheld the dragon and perceived his subtlety.

For he opened his mouth wide, and revealed to Leothric the ranks of his sabre teeth, and his leather gums flapped upwards. But while Leothric made to smite at his head, he shot forward scorpion-wise over his head the length of his armoured tail. All this the eye perceived in the hilt of Sacnoth, who smote suddenly sideways. Not with the edge smote Sacnoth, for, had he done so, the severed end of the tail had still come hurtling on, as some pine tree that the avalanche has hurled point foremost from the cliff right through the broad breast of some mountaineer. So had

Leothric been transfixed; but Sacnoth smote sideways with the flat of his blade, and sent the tail whizzing over Leothric's left shoulder; and it rasped upon his armour as it went, and left a groove upon it. Sideways then at Leothric smote the foiled tail of Wong Bongerok, and Sacnoth parried, and the tail went shrieking up the blade and over Leothric's head. Then Leothric and Wong Bongerok fought sword to tooth, and the sword smote as only Sacnoth can, and the evil faithful life of Wong Bongerok the dragon went out through the wide wound.

Then Leothric walked on past that dead monster, and the armoured body still quivered a little. And for a while it was like all the ploughshares in a county working together in one field behind tired and struggling horses; then the quivering ceased, and Wong Bongerok lay still to rust.

And Leothric went on to the open gates, and Sacnoth dripped quietly along the floor.

By the open gates through which Wong Bongerok had entered, Leothric came into a corridor echoing with music. This was the first place from which Leothric could see anything above his head, for hitherto the roof had ascended to mountainous heights and had stretched indistinct in the gloom. But along the narrow corridor hung huge bells low and near to his head, and the width of each brazen bell was from wall to wall, and they were one behind the other. And as he passed under each the bell uttered, and its voice was mournful and deep, like to the voice of a bell speaking to a man for the last time when he is newly dead. Each bell uttered once as Leothric came under it, and their voices sounded solemnly and wide apart at ceremonious intervals. For if he walked slow, these bells came closer together, and when he walked swiftly they moved farther apart. And the echoes of each bell tolling above his head went on before him whispering to the others. Once when he stopped they all jangled angrily till he went on again.

Between these slow and boding notes came the sound of the magical musicians. They were playing a dirge now very mournfully.

And at last Leothric came to the end of the Corridor of the Bells, and beheld there a small black door. And all the corridor behind him was full of the echoes of the tolling, and they all muttered to one another about the ceremony; and the dirge of the musicians came floating slowly through them like a procession of foreign elaborate guests, and all of them boded ill to Leothric.

The black door opened at once to the hand of Leothric, and he found himself in the open air in a wide court paved with marble. High over it shone the moon, summoned there by the hand of Gaznak.

There Gaznak slept, and around him sat his magical musicians, all playing upon strings. And, even sleeping, Gaznak was clad in armour, and only his wrists and face and neck were bare.

But the marvel of that place was the dreams of Gaznak; for beyond the wide court slept a dark abyss, and into the abyss there poured a white cascade of marble stairways, and widened out below into terraces and balconies with fair white statues on them, and descended again in a wide stairway, and came to lower terraces in the dark, where swart uncertain shapes went to and fro. All these were the dreams of Gaznak, and issued from his mind, and, becoming gleaming marble, passed over the edge of the abyss as the musicians played. And all the while out of the mind of Gaznak, lulled by that strange music, went spires and pinnacles beautiful and slender, ever ascending skywards. And the marble dreams moved slow in time to the music. When the bells tolled and the musicians played their dirge, ugly gargoyles came out suddenly all over the spires and pinnacles, and great shadows passed swiftly down the steps and terraces, and there was hurried whispering in the abyss.

When Leothric stepped from the black door, Gaznak opened his eyes. He looked neither to left nor right, but stood up at once facing Leothric.

Then the magicians played a deathspell on their strings, and there arose a humming along the blade of Sacnoth as he turned the spell aside. When Leothric dropped not down, and they heard the humming of Sacnoth, the magicians arose and fled, all wailing, as they went, upon their strings.

Then Gaznak drew out screaming from its sheath the sword that was the mightiest in the world except for Sacnoth, and slowly walked towards Leothric; and he smiled as he walked, although his own dreams had foretold his doom. And when Leothric and Gaznak came together, each looked at each, and neither spoke a word; but they smote both at once, and their swords met, and each sword knew the other and from whence he came. And whenever the sword of Gaznak smote on the blade of Sacnoth it rebounded gleaming, as hail from off slated roofs; but whenever it fell upon the armour of Leothric, it stripped it off in sheets. And upon Gaznak's armour Sacnoth fell oft and furiously, but ever he came back snarling, leaving no mark behind, and as Gaznak fought he held his left hand hovering close over his head. Presently Leothric smote fair and fiercely at his enemy's neck, but Gaznak, clutching his own head by the hair, lifted it high aloft, and Sacnoth went cleaving through an empty space. Then Gaznak replaced his head upon his neck, and all the while fought nimbly with his sword; and again and again Leothric swept with Sacnoth at Gaznak's bearded neck, and ever the left hand of Gaznak was quicker than the stroke, and the head went up and the sword rushed vainly under it.

And the ringing fight went on till Leothric's armour lay all round him on the floor and the marble was splashed with his blood, and the sword of Gaznak was notched like a saw from meeting the blade of Sacnoth. Still Gaznak stood unwounded and smiling still.

At last Leothric looked at the throat of Gaznak and aimed with Sacnoth, and again Gaznak lifted his head by the hair; but not at his throat flew Sacnoth, for Leothric struck instead at the lifted hand, and through the wrist of it went Sacnoth whirring, as a scythe goes through the stem of a single flower.

And bleeding, the severed hand fell to the floor; and at once blood spurted from the shoulders of Gaznak and dripped from the fallen head, and the tall pinnacles went down into the earth, and the wide fair terraces all rolled away, and the court was gone like the dew, and a wind came and the colonnades drifted thence, and all the colossal halls of Gaznak fell. And the abysses closed up suddenly as the mouth of a man who, having told a tale, will for ever speak no more.

Then Leothric looked around him in the marshes where the night mist was passing away, and there was no fortress nor sound of dragon or mortal, only beside him lay an old man, wizened and evil and dead, whose head and hand were severed from his body.

And gradually over the wide lands the dawn was coming up, and ever growing in beauty as it came, like to the peal of an organ played by a master's hand, growing louder and lovelier as the soul of the master warms, and at last giving praise with all its mighty voice.

Then the birds sang, and Leothric went homeward, and left the marshes and came to the dark wood, and the light of the dawn ascending lit him upon his way. And into Allathurion he came ere noon, and with him brought the evil wizened head, and the people rejoiced, and their nights of trouble ceased.

This is the tale of the vanquishing of The Fortress Unvanquishable, Save For Sacnoth, and of its passing away, as it is told and believed by those who love the mystic days of old.

Others have said, and vainly claim to prove, that a fever came to Allathurion, and went away; and that this same fever drove Leothric into the marshes by night, and made him dream there and act violently with a sword.

And others again say that there hath been no town of Allathurion, and that Leothric never lived.

Peace to them. The gardener hath gathered up this autumn's leaves. Who shall see them again, or who wot of them? And who shall say what hath befallen in the days of long ago?

The Injudicious Prayers of
Pombo the Idolater

POMBO the idolater had prayed to Ammuz a simple prayer, a
necessary prayer, such as even an idol of ivory could very easily
grant, and Ammuz had not immediately granted it. Pombo had
therefore prayed to Tharma for the overthrow of Ammuz, an
idol friendly to Tharma, and in doing this offended against the
etiquette of the gods. Tharma refused to grant the little prayer.
Pombo prayed frantically to all the gods of idolatry, for though
it was a simple matter, yet it was very necessary to a man. And
gods that were older than Ammuz rejected the prayers of Pombo,
and even gods that were younger and therefore of greater repute.
He prayed to them one by one, and they all refused to hear him;
nor at first did he think at all of that subtle, divine etiquette
against which he had offended. It occurred to him all at once as
he prayed to his fiftieth idol, a little green-jade god whom the
Chinese know, that all the idols were in league against him.
When Pombo discovered this he resented his birth bitterly, and
made lamentation and alleged that he was lost. He might have
been seen then in any part of London haunting curiosity-shops
and places where they sold idols of ivory or of stone, for he dwelt
in London with others of his race though he was born in Burmah
among those who hold Ganges holy. On drizzly evenings of
November's worst his haggard face could be seen in the glow of
some shop pressed close against the glass, where he would sup-
plicate some calm cross-legged idol till policemen moved him on.
And after closing hours back he would go to his dingy room, in
that part of our capital where English is seldom spoken, to sup-
plicate little idols of his own. And when Pombo's simple, neces-

sary prayer was equally refused by the idols of museums, auction-rooms, shops, then he took counsel with himself and purchased incense and burned it in a brazier before his own cheap little idols, and played the while upon an instrument such as that wherewith men charm snakes. And still the idols clung to their etiquette.

Whether Pombo knew about this etiquette and considered it frivolous in the face of his need, or whether his need, now grown desperate, unhinged his mind, I know not, but Pombo the idolater took a stick and suddenly turned iconoclast.

Pombo the iconoclast immediately left his house, leaving his idols to be swept away with the dust and so to mingle with Man, and went to an arch-idolater of repute who carved idols out of rare stones, and put his case before him. The arch-idolater who made idols of his own rebuked Pombo in the name of Man for having broken his idols—"for hath not Man made them?" the arch-idolater said; and concerning the idols themselves he spoke long and learnedly, explaining divine etiquette, and how Pombo had offended, and how no idol in the world would listen to Pombo's prayer. When Pombo heard this he wept and made bitter outcry, and cursed the gods of ivory and the gods of jade, and the hand of Man that made them, but most of all he cursed their etiquette that had undone, as he said, an innocent man; so that at last that arch-idolater, who made idols of his own, stopped in his work upon an idol of jasper for a king that was weary of Wosh, and took compassion on Pombo, and told him that though no idol in the world would listen to his prayer, yet only a little way over the edge of it a certain disreputable idol sat who knew nothing of etiquette, and granted prayers that no respectable god would ever consent to hear. When Pombo heard this he took two handfuls of the arch-idolater's beard and kissed them joyfully, and dried his tears and became his old impertinent self again. And he that carved from jasper the usurper of Wosh explained how in the village of World's End, at the furthest end of Last Street, there is a hole that you take to be a well, close by the garden wall, but that if you lower yourself by your hands over the edge of the hole, and feel about with your feet till they find a ledge, that is the top step of a flight of stairs that takes you down over the edge of the World. "For all that men know, those stairs may have a purpose and even a bottom step," said the arch-

idolater, "but discussion about the lower flights is idle." Then
the teeth of Pombo chattered, for he feared the darkness, but he
that made idols of his own explained that those stairs were always
lit by the faint blue gloaming in which the World spins. "Then,"
he said, "you will go by Lonely House and under the bridge that
leads from the House to Nowhere, and whose purpose is not
guessed; thence past Maharrion, the god of flowers, and his high-
priest, who is neither bird nor cat; and so you will come to the
little idol Duth, the disreputable god that will grant your prayer."
And he went on carving again at his idol of jasper for the king
who was weary of Wosh; and Pombo thanked him and went
singing away, for in his vernacular mind he thought that "he
had the gods."

It is a long journey from London to World's End, and Pombo
had no money left, yet within five weeks he was strolling along
Last Street; but how he contrived to get there I will not say, for
it was not entirely honest. And Pombo found the well at the end
of the garden beyond the end house of Last Street, and many
thoughts ran through his mind as he hung by his hands from the
edge, but chiefest of all those thoughts was one that said the gods
were laughing at him through the mouth of the arch-idolater,
their prophet, and the thought beat in his head till it ached like
his wrists . . . and then he found the step.

And Pombo walked downstairs. There, sure enough, was the
gloaming in which the world spins, and stars shone far off in it
faintly; there was nothing before him as he went downstairs but
that strange blue waste of gloaming, with its multitudes of stars,
and comets plunging through it on outward journeys, and comets
returning home. And then he saw the lights of the bridge to
Nowhere, and all of a sudden he was in the glare of the shimmering parlour-window of Lonely House; and he heard voices there
pronouncing words, and the voices were nowise human, and but
for his bitter need he had screamed and fled. Halfway between
the voices and Maharrion, whom he now saw standing out from
the world, covered in rainbow halos, he perceived the weird grey
beast that is neither cat nor bird. As Pombo hesitated, chilly with
fear, he heard those voices grow louder in Lonely House, and at
that he stealthily moved a few steps lower, and then rushed past
the beast. The beast intently watched Maharrion hurling up
bubbles that are every one a season of spring in unknown constel-

lations, calling the swallows home to unimagined fields, watched him without even turning to look at Pombo, and saw him drop into the Linlunlarna, the river that rises at the edge of the World, the golden pollen that sweetens the tide of the river and is carried away from the World to be a joy to the Stars. And there before Pombo was the little disreputable god who cares nothing for etiquette and will answer prayers that are refused by all the respectable idols. And whether the view of him, at last, excited Pombo's eagerness, or whether his need was greater than he could bear that it drove him so swiftly downstairs, or whether, as is most likely, he ran too fast past the beast, I do not know, and it does not matter to Pombo; but at any rate he could not stop, as he had designed, in attitude of prayer at the feet of Duth, but ran on past him down the narrowing steps, clutching at smooth bare rocks till he fell from the World as, when our hearts miss a beat, we fall in dreams and wake up with a dreadful jolt; but there was no waking up for Pombo, who still fell on towards the incurious stars, and his fate is even one with the fate of Slith.

How Plash-Goo Came to the
Land of None's Desire

In a thatched cottage of enormous size, so vast that we might consider it a palace, but only a cottage in the style of its building, its timbers and the nature of its interior, there lived Plash-Goo.

Plash-Goo was of the children of the giants, whose sire was Uph. And the lineage of Uph had dwindled in bulk for the last five hundred years, till the giants were now no more than fifteen feet high; but Uph ate elephants which he caught with his hands.

Now on the tops of the mountains above the house of Plash-Goo, for Plash-Goo lived in the plains, there dwelt the dwarf whose name was Lrippity-Kang.

And the dwarf used to walk at evening on the edge of the tops of the mountains, and would walk up and down along it, and was squat and ugly and hairy, and was plainly seen of Plash-Goo.

And for many weeks the giant had suffered the sight of him, but at length grew irked at the sight (as men are by little things) and could not sleep of a night and lost his taste for pigs. And at last there came the day, as anyone might have known, when Plash-Goo shouldered his club and went up to look for the dwarf.

And the dwarf though briefly squat was broader than may be dreamed, beyond all breadth of man, and stronger than men may know; strength in its very essence dwelt in that little frame, as a spark in the heart of a flint: but to Plash-Goo he was no more than misshapen, bearded and squat, a thing that dared to defy all natural laws by being more broad than long.

When Plash-Goo came to the mountain he cast his chimahalk down (for so he named the club of his heart's desire) lest the dwarf should defy him with nimbleness; and stepped towards

Lrippity-Kang with gripping hands, who stopped in his mountainous walk without a word, and swung round his hideous
breadth to confront Plash-Goo.

Already then Plash-Goo in the deeps of his mind had seen
himself seize the dwarf in one large hand and hurl him with his
beard and his hated breadth sheer down the precipice that
dropped away from that very place to the Land of None's Desire.
Yet it was otherwise that Fate would have it. For the dwarf
parried with his little arms the grip of those monstrous hands,
and gradually working along the enormous limbs came at length
to the giant's body where by dwarfish cunning he obtained a
grip; and turning Plash-Goo about, as a spider does some great
fly, till his little grip was suitable to his purpose, he suddenly
lifted the giant over his head. Slowly at first, by the edge of that
precipice whose base sheer distance hid, he swung his giant victim round his head, but soon faster and faster; and at last when
Plash-Goo was streaming round the hated breadth of the dwarf
and the no less hated beard was flapping in the wind, Lrippity-
Kang let go. Plash-Goo shot over the edge and for some way
further, out towards Space, like a stone; then he began to fall.
It was long before he believed and truly knew that this was really
he that fell from this mountain, for we do not associate such
dooms with ourselves; but when he had fallen for some while
through the evening and saw below him, where there had been
nothing to see, or *began* to see, the glimmer of tiny fields, then
his optimism departed; till later on when the fields were greener
and larger he saw that this was indeed (and growing how terribly
nearer) that very land to which he had destined the dwarf.

At last he saw it unmistakable, close, with its grim houses and
its dreadful ways, and its green fields shining in the light of the
evening. His cloak was streaming from him in whistling shreds.

So Plash-Goo came to the Land of None's Desire.

Bethmoora

THERE is a faint freshness in the London night as though some strayed reveller of a breeze had left his comrades in the Kentish uplands and had entered the town by stealth. The pavements are a little damp and shiny. Upon one's ears that at this late hour have become very acute there hits the tap of a remote footfall. Louder and louder grow the taps, filling the whole night. And a black cloaked figure passes by, and goes tapping into the dark. One who has danced goes homewards. Somewhere a ball has closed its doors and ended. Its yellow lights are out, its musicians are silent, its dancers have all gone into the night air, and Time has said of it, "Let it be past and over, and among the things that I have put away."

Shadows begin to detach themselves from their great gathering places. No less silently than those shadows that are thin and dead, move homewards the stealthy cats. Thus have we even in London our faint forebodings of the dawn's approach, which the birds and the beasts and the stars are crying aloud to the untrammelled fields.

At what moment I know not I perceive that the night itself is irrecoverably overthrown. It is suddenly revealed to me by the weary pallor of the street lamps that the streets are silent and nocturnal still, not because there is any strength in night, but because men have not yet arisen from sleep to defy him. So have I seen dejected and untidy guards still bearing antique muskets in palatial gateways, although the realms of the monarch that they guard have shrunk to a single province which no enemy yet has troubled to overrun.

And it is now manifest from the aspect of the street lamps, those abashed dependants of night, that already English mountain peaks have seen the dawn, that the cliffs of Dover are standing white to the morning, that the sea-mist has lifted and is pouring inland.

And now men with a hose have come and are sluicing out the streets.

Behold now night is dead.

What memories, what fancies throng one's mind! A night but just now gathered out of London by the hostile hand of Time. A million common artificial things all cloaked for a while in mystery, like beggars robed in purple, and seated on dread thrones. Four million people asleep, dreaming perhaps. What worlds have they gone into? Whom have they met? But my thoughts are far off with Bethmoora in her loneliness, whose gates swing to and fro. To and fro they swing, and creak and creak in the wind, but no one hears them. They are of green copper, very lovely, but no one sees them now. The desert wind pours sand into their hinges, no watchman comes to ease them. No guard goes round Bethmoora's battlements, no enemy assails them. There are no lights in her houses, no footfall in her streets; she stands there dead and lonely beyond the Hills of Hap, and I would see Bethmoora once again, but dare not.

It is many a year, as they tell me, since Bethmoora became desolate.

Her desolation is spoken of in taverns where sailors meet, and certain travellers have told me of it.

I had hoped to see Bethmoora once again. It is many a year ago, they say, when the vintage was last gathered in from the vineyards that I knew, where it is all desert now. It was a radiant day, and the people of the city were dancing by the vineyards, while here and there one played upon the kalipac. The purple flowering shrubs were all in bloom, and the snow shone upon the Hills of Hap.

Outside the copper gates they crushed the grapes in vats to make the syrabub. It had been a goodly vintage.

In little gardens at the desert's edge men beat the tambang and the tittibuk, and blew melodiously the zootibar.

All there was mirth and song and dance, because the vintage had been gathered in, there would be ample syrabub for the winter months, and much left over to exchange for turquoises and emeralds with the merchants who come down from Oxuhahn. Thus they rejoiced all day over their vintage on the narrow strip of cultivated ground that lay between Bethmoora and the desert which meets the sky to the South. And when the heat of the day began to abate, and the sun drew near to the snows on the Hills of Hap, the note of the zootibar still rose clear from the gardens, and the brilliant dresses of the dancers still wound among the flowers. All that day three men on mules had been noticed crossing the face of the Hills of Hap. Backwards and forwards they moved as the track wound lower and lower, three little specks of black against the snow. They were seen first in the very early morning up near the shoulder of Peol Jagganoth, and seemed to be coming out of Utnar Véhi. All day they came. And in the evening, just before lights come out and colours change, they appeared before Bethmoora's copper gates. They carried staves, such as messengers bear in those lands, and seemed sombrely clad when the dancers all came round them with their green and lilac dresses. Those Europeans who were present and heard the message given were ignorant of the language, and only caught the name of Utnar Véhi. But it was brief, and passed rapidly from mouth to mouth, and almost at once the people burnt their vineyards and began to flee away from Bethmoora, going for the most part northwards, though some went to the East. They ran down out of their fair white houses, and streamed through the copper gate; the throbbing of the tambang and the tittibuk suddenly ceased with the note of the zootibar, and the clinking kalipac stopped a moment after. The three strange travellers went back the way they came the instant their message was given. It was the hour when a light would have appeared in some high tower, and window after window would have poured into the dusk its lion-frightening light, and the copper gates would have been fastened up. But no lights came out in windows there that night and have not ever since, and those copper gates were left wide and have never shut, and the sound arose of the red fire crackling in the vineyards, and the pattering of feet fleeing softly. There were no cries, no other sounds at all, only the rapid and determined flight. They fled as swiftly and quietly as a herd of wild cattle flee when they suddenly see a man. It was as though something had befallen which had been feared for generations, which could only be escaped by instant flight, which left no time for indecision.

Then fear took the Europeans also, and they too fled. And what the message was I have never heard.

Many believe that it was a message from Thuba Mleen, the mysterious emperor of those lands, who is never seen by man, advising that Bethmoora should be left desolate. Others say that the message was one of warning from the gods, whether from friendly gods or from adverse ones they know not.

And others hold that the Plague was ravaging a line of cities over in Utnar Véhi, following the South-west wind which for many weeks had been blowing across them towards Bethmoora.

Some say that the terrible gnousar sickness was upon the three travellers, and that their very mules were dripping with it, and suppose that they were driven to the city by hunger, but suggest no better reason for so terrible a crime.

But most believe that it was a message from the desert himself, who owns all the Earth to the southwards, spoken with his peculiar cry to those three who knew his voice—men who had been out on the sand-wastes without tents by night, who had been by day without water, men who had been out there where the desert mutters, and had grown to know his needs and his malevolence. They say that the desert had a need for Bethmoora, that he wished to come into her lovely streets, and to send into her temples and her houses his storm-winds draped with sand. For he hates the sound and the sight of men in his old evil heart, and he would have Bethmoora silent and undisturbed, save for the weird love he whispers at her gates.

If I knew what that message was that the three men brought on mules, and told in the copper gate, I think that I should go and see Bethmoora once again. For a great longing comes on me here in London to see once more that white and beautiful city; and yet I dare not, for I know not the danger I should have to face, whether I should risk the fury of unknown dreadful gods, or some disease unspeakable and slow, or the desert's curse, or torture in some little private room of the Emperor Thuba Mleen, or something that the travellers have not told—perhaps more fearful still.

Idle Days on the Yann

So I came down through the wood to the bank of Yann and found, as had been prophesied, the ship *Bird of the River* about to loose her cable.

The captain sate cross-legged upon the white deck with his scimitar lying beside him in its jewelled scabbard, and the sailors toiled to spread the nimble sails to bring the ship into the central stream of Yann, and all the while sang ancient soothing songs. And the wind of the evening descending cool from the snow-fields of some mountainous abode of distant gods came suddenly, like glad tidings to an anxious city, into the wing-like sails.

And so we came into the central stream, whereat the sailors lowered the greater sails. But I had gone to bow before the captain, and to inquire concerning the miracles, and appearances among men, of the most holy gods of whatever land he had come from. And the captain answered that he came from Fair Belzoond, and worshipped gods that were the least and humblest, who seldom sent the famine or the thunder, and were easily appeased with little battles. And I told how I came from Ireland, which is of Europe, whereat the captain and all the sailors laughed, for they said, "There are no such places in all the land of dreams." When they had ceased to mock me, I explained that my fancy mostly dwelt in the desert of Cuppar-Nombo, about a beautiful blue city called Golthoth the Damned, which was sentinelled all round by wolves and their shadows, and had been utterly desolate for years and years, because of a curse which the gods once spoke in anger and could never since recall. And sometimes my dreams took me as far as Pungar Vees, the red walled city where the fountains are, which trades with the Isles and

Thul. When I said this they complimented me upon the abode of my fancy, saying that, though they had never seen these cities, such places might well be imagined. For the rest of that evening I bargained with the captain over the sum that I should pay him for my fare if God and the tide of Yann should bring us safely as far as the cliffs by the sea, which are named Bar-Wul-Yann, the Gate of Yann.

And now the sun had set, and all the colours of the world and heaven had held a festival with him, and slipped one by one away before the imminent approach of night. The parrots had all flown home to the jungle on either bank, the monkeys in rows in safety on high branches of the trees were silent and asleep, the fireflies in the deeps of the forest were going up and down, and the great stars came gleaming out to look on the face of Yann. Then the sailors lighted lanterns and hung them round the ship, and the light flashed out on a sudden and dazzled Yann, and the ducks that fed along his marshy banks all suddenly arose, and made wide circles in the upper air, and saw the distant reaches of the Yann and the white mist that softly cloaked the jungle, before they returned again into their marshes.

And then the sailors knelt on the decks and prayed, not all together, but five or six at a time. Side by side there kneeled down together five or six, for there only prayed at the same time men of different faiths, so that no god should hear two men praying to him at once. As soon as any one had finished his prayer, another of the same faith would take his place. Thus knelt the row of five or six with bended heads under the fluttering sail, while the central stream of the River Yann took them on towards the sea and their prayers rose up from among the lanterns and went towards the stars. And behind them in the after end of the ship the helmsman prayed aloud the helmsman's prayer, which is prayed by all who follow his trade upon the River Yann, of whatever faith they be. And the captain prayed to his little lesser gods, to the gods that bless Belzoond.

And I, too, felt that I would pray. Yet I liked not to pray to a jealous God there where the frail affectionate gods whom the heathen love were being humbly invoked; so I bethought me, instead, of Sheol Nugganoth, whom the men of the jungle have long since deserted, who is now unworshipped and alone; and to him I prayed.

And upon us praying the night came suddenly down, as it comes upon all men who pray at evening and upon all men who do not; yet our prayers comforted our own souls when we thought of the Great Night to come.

And so Yann bore us magnificently onwards, for he was elate with molten snow that the Poltiades had brought him from the Hills of Hap; and the Marn and Migris were swollen full with floods; and he bore us in his might past Kyph and Pir, and we saw the lights of Goolunza.

Soon we all slept except the helmsman, who kept the ship in the mid-stream of Yann.

When the sun rose the helmsman ceased to sing, for by song he cheered himself in the lonely night. When the song ceased we suddenly all awoke, and another took the helm, and the helmsman slept.

We know that soon we should come to Mandaroon. We made a meal, and Mandaroon appeared. Then the captain commanded, and the sailors loosed again the greater sails, and the ship turned and left the stream of Yann and came into a harbour beneath the ruddy walls of Mandaroon. Then while the sailors went and gathered fruits I came alone to the gate of Mandaroon. A few huts were outside it, in which lived the guard. A sentinel with a long white beard was standing in the gate, armed with a rusty pike. He wore large spectacles, which were covered with dust. Through the gate I saw the city. A deathly stillness was over all of it. The ways seemed untrodden, and moss was thick on door-steps; in the market-place huddled figures lay asleep. A scent of incense came wafted through the gateway, of incense and burned poppies, and there was a hum of the echoes of distant bells. I said to the sentinel in the tongue of the region of Yann, "Why are they all asleep in this still city?"

He answered: "None may ask questions in this gate for fear they wake the people of the city. For when the people of this city wake the gods will die. And when the gods die men may dream no more." And I began to ask him what gods that city worshipped, but he lifted his pike because none might ask questions there. So I left him and went back to the *Bird of the River.*

Certainly Mandaroon was beautiful with her white pinnacles peering over her ruddy walls and the green of her copper roofs.

When I came back again to the *Bird of the River,* I found the sailors were returned to the ship. Soon we weighed anchor, and sailed out again, and so came once more to the middle of the river. And now the sun was moving toward his heights, and there had reached us on the River Yann the song of those countless myriads of choirs that attend him in his progress round the world. For the little creatures that have many legs had spread their gauze wings easily on the air, as a man rests his elbows on a balcony and gave jubilant, ceremonial praises to the sun, or else they moved together on the air in wavering dances intricate and swift, or turned aside to avoid the onrush of some drop of water that a breeze had shaken from a jungle orchid, chilling the air and driving it before it, as it fell whirring in its rush to the earth; but all the while they sang triumphantly. "For the day is for us," they said, "whether our great and sacred father the Sun shall bring up more like us from the marshes, or whether all the world shall end to-night." And there sang all those whose notes are known to human ears, as well as those whose far more numerous notes have been never heard by man.

To these a rainy day had been as an era of war that should desolate continents during all the lifetime of a man.

And there came out also from the dark and steaming jungle to behold and rejoice in the Sun the huge and lazy butterflies. And they danced, but danced idly, on the ways of the air, as some haughty queen of distant conquered lands might in her poverty and exile dance, in some encampment of the gipsies, for the mere bread to live by, but beyond that would never abate her pride to dance for a fragment more.

And the butterflies sung of strange and painted things, of purple orchids and of lost pink cities and the monstrous colours of the jungle's decay. And they, too, were among those whose voices are not discernible by human ears. And as they floated above the river, going from forest to forest, their splendour was matched by the inimical beauty of the birds who darted out to pursue them. Or sometimes they settled on the white and wax-like blooms of the plant that creeps and clambers about the trees of the forest; and their purple wings flashed out on the great blossoms as, when the caravans go from Nurl to Thace, the gleaming silks flash out upon the snow, where the crafty merchants spread them one by one to astonish the mountaineers of the Hills of Noor.

But upon men and beasts the sun sent a drowsiness. The river monsters along the river's marge lay dormant in the slime. The sailors pitched a pavillion, with golden tassels, for the captain upon the deck, and then went, all but the helmsman, under a sail that they had hung as an awning between two masts. Then they told tales to one another, each of his own city or of the miracles of his god, until all were fallen asleep. The captain offered me the shade of his pavillion with the gold tassels, and there we talked for awhile, he telling me that he was taking merchandise to Perdóndaris, and that he would take back to fair Belzoond things appertaining to the affairs of the sea. Then, as I watched through the pavillion's opening the brilliant birds and butterflies that crossed and re-crossed over the river, I fell asleep, and dreamed that I was a monarch entering his capital underneath arches of flags, and all the musicians of the world were there, playing melodiously their instruments; but no one cheered.

In the afternoon, as the day grew cooler again, I awoke and found the captain buckling on his scimitar, which he had taken off him while he rested.

And now we were approaching the wide court of Astahahn, which opens upon the river. Strange boats of antique design were chained there to the steps. As we neared it we saw the open marble court, on three sides of which stood the city fronting on colonnades. And in the court and along the colonnades the people of that city walked with solemnity and care according to the rites of ancient ceremony. All in that city was of ancient device; the carving on the houses, which, when age had broken it, remained unrepaired, was of the remotest times, and everywhere were represented in stone beasts that have long since passed away from Earth—the dragon, the griffin, and the hippogriffin, and the different species of gargoyle. Nothing was to be found, whether material or custom, that was new in Astahahn. Now they took no notice at all of us as we went by, but continued their processions and ceremonies in the ancient city, and the sailors, knowing their custom, took no notice of them. But I called, as we came near, to one who stood beside the water's edge, asking him what men did in Astahahn and what their merchandise was, and with whom they traded. He said, "Here we have fettered and manacled Time, who would otherwise slay the gods."

I asked him what gods they worshipped in that city, and he said, "All those gods whom Time has not yet slain." Then he

Bird of the River

The Gate of Yann

turned from me and would say no more, but busied himself in behaving in accordance with ancient custom. And so, according to the will of Yann, we drifted onwards and left Astahahn. The river widened below Astahahn, and we found in greater quantities such birds as prey on fishes. And they were very wonderful in their plumage, and they came not out of the jungle, but flew, with their long necks stretched out before them, and their legs lying on the wind behind, straight up the river over the midstream.

And now the evening began to gather in. A thick white mist had appeared over the river, and was softly rising higher. It clutched at the trees with long impalpable arms, it rose higher and higher, chilling the air; and white shapes moved away into the jungle as though the ghosts of shipwrecked mariners were searching stealthily in the darkness for the spirits of evil that long ago had wrecked them on the Yann.

As the sun sank behind the field of orchids that grew on the matted summit of the jungle, the river monsters came wallowing out of the slime in which they had reclined during the heat of the day, and the great beasts of the jungle came down to drink. The butterflies a while since were gone to rest. In little narrow tributaries that we passed night seemed already to have fallen, though the sun which had disappeared from us had not yet set.

And now the birds of the jungle came flying home far over us, with the sunlight glistening pink upon their breasts, and lowered their pinions as soon as they saw the Yann, and dropped into the trees. And the widgeon began to go up the river in great companies, all whistling, and then would suddenly wheel and all go down again. And there shot by us the small and arrow-like teal; and we heard the manifold cries of flocks of geese, which the sailors told me had recently come in from crossing over the Lispasian ranges; every year they come by the same way, close by the peak of Mluna, leaving it to the left, and the mountain eagles know the way they come and—men say—the very hour, and every year they expect them by the same way as soon as the snows have fallen upon the Northern Plains. But soon it grew so dark that we saw these birds no more, and only heard the whirring of their wings, and of countless others besides, until they all settled down along the banks of the river, and it was the hour when the birds of the night went forth. Then the sailors lit the lanterns for the night, and huge moths appeared, flapping about the ship, and at moments their gorgeous colours would be revealed by the lanterns, then they would pass into the night again, where all was black. And again the sailors prayed, and thereafter we supped and slept, and the helmsman took our lives into his care.

When I awoke I found that we had indeed come to Perdóndaris, that famous city. For there it stood upon the left of us, a city fair and notable, and all the more pleasant for our eyes to see after the jungle that was so long with us. And we were anchored by the market-place, and the captain's merchandise was all displayed, and a merchant of Perdóndaris stood looking at it. And the captain had his scimitar in his hand, and was beating with it in anger upon the deck, and the splinters were flying up from the white planks; for the merchant had offered him a price for his merchandise that the captain declared to be an insult to himself and his country's gods, whom he now said to be great and terrible gods, whose curses were to be dreaded. But the merchant waved his hands, which were of great fatness, showing the pink palms, and swore that of himself he thought not at all, but only of the poor folk in the huts beyond the city to whom he wished to sell the merchandise for as low a price as possible, leaving no remuneration for himself. For the merchandise was mostly the thick toomarund carpets that in the winter keep the wind from the floor, and tollub which the people smoke in pipes. Therefore the merchant said if he offered a piffek more the poor folk must go without their toomarunds when the winter came, and without their tollub in the evenings, or else he and his aged father must starve together. Thereat the captain lifted his scimitar to his own throat, saying that he was now a ruined man, and that nothing remained to him but death. And while he was carefully lifting his beard with his left hand, the merchant eyed the merchandise again; and said that rather than see so worthy a captain die, a man for whom he had conceived an especial love when first he saw the manner in which he handled his ship, he and his aged father should starve together and therefore he offered fifteen piffeks more.

When he said this the captain prostrated himself and prayed to his gods that they might yet sweeten this merchant's bitter heart—to his little lesser gods, to the gods that bless Belzoond.

At last the merchant offered yet five piffeks more. Then the captain wept, for he said that he was deserted of his gods; and the merchant also wept, for he said that he was thinking of his aged father, and of how he soon would starve, and he hid his weeping face with both his hands, and eyed the tollub again between his fingers. And so the bargain was concluded, and the merchant took the toomarund and tollub, paying for them out of a great clinking purse. And these were packed up into bales again, and three of the merchant's slaves carried them upon their heads into the city. And all the while the sailors had sat silent, cross-legged in a crescent upon the deck, eagerly watching the bargain, and now a murmur of satisfaction arose among them, and they began to compare it among themselves with other bargains that they had known. And I found out from them that there are seven merchants in Perdóndaris, and that they had all come to the captain one by one before the bargaining began, and each had warned him privately against the others. And to all the merchants the captain had offered the wine of his own country, that they make in fair Belzoond, but could in no wise persuade them to it. But now that the bargain was over, and the sailors were seated at the first meal of the day, the captain appeared among them with a cask of that wine, and we broached it with care and all made merry together. And the captain was glad in his heart because he knew that he had much honour in the eyes of his men because of the bargain that he had made. So the sailors drank the wine of their native land, and soon their thoughts were back in fair Belzoond and the little neighbouring cities of Durl and Duz.

But for me the captain poured into a little glass some heavy yellow wine from a small jar which he kept apart among his sacred things. Thick and sweet it was, even like honey, yet there was in its heart a mighty, ardent fire which had authority over souls of men. It was made, the captain told me, with great subtlety by the secret craft of a family of six who lived in a hut on the mountains of Hian Min. Once in these mountains, he said, he followed the spoor of a bear, and he came suddenly on a man of that family who had hunted the same bear, and he was at the end of a narrow way with precipice all about him, and his spear was sticking in the bear, and the wound not fatal, and he had no other weapon. And the bear was walking towards the man, very slowly because his wound irked him—yet he was now very close. And what the captain did he would not say, but every year as soon as the snows are hard, and travelling is easy on the Hian Min, that man comes down to the market in the plains, and always leaves for the captain in the gate of fair Belzoond a vessel of that priceless secret wine.

And as I sipped the wine and the captain talked, I remembered me of stalwart noble things that I had long since resolutely planned, and my soul seemed to grow mightier within me and to dominate the whole tide of the Yann. It may be that I then slept. Or, if I did not, I do not now minutely recollect every detail of that morning's occupations. Towards evening, I awoke and wishing to see Perdóndaris before we left in the morning, and being unable to wake the captain, I went ashore alone. Certainly Perdóndaris was a powerful city; it was encompassed by a wall of great strength and altitude, having in it hollow ways for troops to walk in, and battlements along it all the way, and fifteen strong towers on it in every mile, and copper plaques low down where men could read them, telling in all the languages of those parts of the Earth—one language on each plaque—the tale of how an army once attacked Perdóndaris and what befell that army. Then I entered Perdóndaris and found all the people dancing, clad in brilliant silks, and playing on the tambang as they danced. For a fearful thunderstorm had terrified them while I slept, and the fires of death, they said, had danced over Perdóndaris, and now the thunder had gone leaping away large and black and hideous, they said, over the distant hills, and had turned round snarling at them, showing his gleaming teeth, and had stamped, as he went, upon the hilltops until they rang as though they had been bronze. And often and again they stopped in their merry dances and prayed to the God they knew not, saying, "O, God that we know not, we thank Thee for sending the thunder back to his hills." And I went on and came to the market-place, and lying there upon the marble pavement I saw the merchant fast asleep and breathing heavily, with his face and the palms of his hands towards the sky, and slaves were fanning him to keep away the flies. And from the market-place I came to a silver temple and then to a palace of onyx, and there were many wonders in Perdóndaris, and I would have stayed and seen them all, but as I came to the outer wall of the city I suddenly saw in it a huge ivory gate. For a while I paused and admired it, then I came nearer and perceived the dreadful truth. The gate was carved out of one solid piece!

I fled at once through the gateway and down to the ship, and even as I ran I thought that I heard far off on the hills behind me the tramp of the fearful beast by whom that mass of ivory was shed, who was perhaps even then looking for his other tusk. When I was on the ship again I felt safer, and I said nothing to the sailors of what I had seen.

And now the captain was gradually awakening. Now night was rolling up from the East and North, and only the pinnacles of the towers of Perdóndaris still took the fallen sunlight. Then I went to the captain and told him quietly of the thing I had seen. And he questioned me at once about the gate, in a low voice, that the sailors might not know; and I told him how the weight of the thing was such that it could not have been brought from afar, and the captain knew that it had not been there a ·year ago. We agreed that such a beast could never have been killed by any assault of man, and then the gate must have been a fallen tusk, and one fallen near and recently. Therefore he decided that it were better to flee at once; so he commanded, and the sailors went to the sails, and others raised the anchor to the deck, and just as the highest pinnacle of marble lost the last rays of the sun we left Perdóndaris, that famous city. And night came down and cloaked Perdóndaris and hid it from our eyes, which as things have happened will never see it again; for I have heard since that something swift and wonderful has suddenly wrecked Perdóndaris in a day—towers and walls, and people.

And the night deepened over the River Yann, a night all white with stars. And with the night there rose the helmsman's song. As soon as he had prayed he began to sing to cheer himself all through the lonely night. But first he prayed, praying the helmsman's prayer. And this is what I remember of it, rendered into English with a very feeble equivalent of the rhythm that seemed so resonant in those tropic nights.

To whatever god may hear.

Wherever there be sailors whether of river or sea: whether their way be dark or whether through storm: whether their peril be of beast or of rock; or from enemy lurking on land or pursuing on sea: wherever the tiller is cold or the helmsman stiff: wherever sailors sleep or helmsmen watch: guard, guide, and return us to the old land, that has known us: to the far homes that we know.

> To all the gods that are.
> To whatever god may hear.

So he prayed, and there was silence. And the sailors laid them down to rest for the night. The silence deepened, and was only broken by the ripples of Yann that lightly touched our prow. Sometimes some monster of the river coughed.

Silence and ripples, ripples and silence again.

And then his loneliness came upon the helmsman, and he began to sing. And he sang the market songs of Durl and Duz, and the old dragon-legends of Belzoond.

Many a song he sang, telling to spacious and exotic Yann the little tales and trifles of his city of Durl. And the songs welled up over the black jungle and came into the clear cold air above, and the great bands of stars that look on Yann began to know the affairs of Durl and Duz, and of the shepherds that dwelt in the fields between, and the flocks that they had, and the loves that they had loved, and all the little things that they hoped to do. And as I lay wrapped up in skins and blankets, listening to those songs, and watching the fantastic shapes of the great trees like to black giants stalking through the night, I suddenly fell asleep.

When I awoke great mists were trailing away from the Yann. And the flow of the river was tumbling now tumultuously, and little waves appeared; for Yann had scented from afar the ancient crags of Glorm, and knew that their ravines lay cool before him wherein he should meet the merry wild Irillion rejoicing from fields of snow. So he shook off from him the torpid sleep that had come upon him in the hot and scented jungle, and forgot its orchids and its butterflies, and swept on turbulent, expectant, strong; and soon the snowy peaks of the Hills of Glorm came glittering into view. And now the sailors were waking up from sleep. Soon we all eat, and then the helmsman laid him down to sleep while a comrade took his place, and they all spread over him their choicest furs.

And in a while we heard the sound that the Irillion made as she came down dancing from the fields of snow.

And then we saw the ravine in the Hills of Glorm lying precipitous and smooth before us, into which we were carried by the leaps of Yann. And now we left the steamy jungle and breathed the mountain air; the sailors stood up and took deep breaths of it, and thought of their own far-off Acroctian hills on which were Durl and Duz—below them in the plains stands fair Belzoond.

A great shadow brooded between the cliffs of Glorm, but the crags were shining above us like gnarled moons, and almost lit the gloom. Louder and louder came the Irillion's song, and the sound of her dancing down from the fields of snow. And soon we saw her white and full of mists, and wreathed with rainbows delicate and small that she had plucked up near the mountain's summit from some celestial garden of the Sun. Then she went away seawards with the huge grey Yann and the ravine widened, and opened upon the world, and our rocking ship came through to the light of the day.

And all that morning and all the afternoon we passed through the marshes of Pondoovery; and Yann widened there, and flowed solemnly and slowly, and the captain bade the sailors beat on bells to overcome the dreariness of the marshes.

At last the Irusian mountains came in sight, nursing the villages of Pen-Kai and Blut, and the wandering streets of Mlo, where priests propitiate the avalanche with wine and maize. Then night came down over the plains of Tlun, and we saw the lights of Cappadarnia. We heard the Pathnites beating upon drums as we passed the Imaut and Golzunda, then all but the helmsman slept. And villages scattered along the banks of the Yann heard all that night in the helmsman's unknown tongue the little songs of cities that they knew not.

I awoke before dawn with a feeling that I was unhappy before I remembered why. Then I recalled that by the evening of the approaching day, according to all foreseen probabilities, we should come to Bar-Wul-Yann, and I should part from the captain and his sailors. And I had liked the man because he had given me of his yellow wine that was set apart among his sacred things, and many a story he had told me about his fair Belzoond between the Acroctian hills and the Hian Min. And I had liked the ways that his sailors had, and the prayers that they prayed at evening side by side, grudging not one another their alien gods. And I had a liking too for the tender way in which they often spoke of Durl and Duz, for it is good that men should love their native cities and the little hills that hold those cities up.

And I had come to know who would meet them when they returned to their homes, and where they thought the meetings would take place, some in a valley of the Acroctian hills where the road comes up from Yann, others in the gateway of one or another of the three cities, and others by the fireside in the home. And I thought of the danger that had menaced us all alike outside Perdóndaris, a danger that, as things have happened, was very real.

And I thought too of the helmsman's cheery song in the cold and lonely night, and how he had held our lives in his careful hands. And as I thought of this the helmsman ceased to sing, and I looked up and saw a pale light had appeared in the sky, and the lonely night had passed; and the dawn widened, and the sailors awoke.

And soon we saw the tide of the Sea himself advancing resolute between Yann's borders, and Yann sprang lithely at him and they struggled awhile; then Yann and all that was his were pushed back northward, so that the sailors had to hoist the sails and, the wind being favorable, we still held onwards.

And we passed Góndara and Narl and Haz. And we saw memorable, holy Golnuz, and heard the pilgrims praying.

When we awoke after the midday rest we were coming near to Nen, the last of the cities on the River Yann. And the jungle was all about us once again, and about Nen; but the great Mloon ranges stood up over all things, and watched the city from beyond the jungle.

Here we anchored, and the captain and I went up into the city and found that the Wanderers had come into Nen.

And the Wanderers were a weird, dark tribe, that once in every seven years came down from the peaks of Mloon, having crossed by a pass that is known to them from some fantastic land that lies beyond. And the people of Nen were all outside their houses, and all stood wondering at their own streets. For the men and women of the Wanderers had crowded all the ways, and every one was doing some strange thing. Some danced astounding dances that they had learned from the desert wind, rapidly curving and swirling till the eye could follow no longer. Others

played upon instruments beautiful wailing tunes that were full
of horror, which souls had taught them lost by night in the desert,
that strange far desert from which the Wanderers came.

None of their instruments were such as were known in Nen
nor in any part of the region of the Yann; even the horns out of
which some were made were of beasts that none had seen along
the river, for they were barbed at the tips. And they sang, in the
language of none, songs that seemed to be akin to the mysteries
of night and to the unreasoned fear that haunts dark places.

Bitterly all the dogs of Nen distrusted them. And the Wanderers
told one another fearful tales, for though no one in Nen knew
ought of their language yet they could see the fear on the listeners'
faces, and as the tale wound on the whites of their eyes showed
vividly in terror as the eyes of some little beast whom the hawk
has seized. Then the teller of the tale would smile and stop, and
another would tell his story, and the teller of the first tale's lips
would chatter with fear. And if some deadly snake chanced to
appear the Wanderers would greet him as a brother, and the
snake would seem to give his greetings to them before he passed
on again. Once that most fierce and lethal of tropic snakes, the
giant lythra, came out of the jungle and all down the street, the
central street of Nen, and none of the Wanderers moved away
from him, but they all played sonorously on drums, as though he
had been a person of much honour; and the snake moved through
the midst of them and smote none.

Even the Wanderers' children could do strange things, for if
any one of them met with a child of Nen the two would stare at
each other in silence with large grave eyes; then the Wanderers'
child would slowly draw from his turban a live fish or snake. And
the children of Nen could do nothing of that kind at all.

Much I should have wished to stay and hear the hymn with
which they greet the night, that is answered by the wolves on
the heights of Mloon, but it was now time to raise the anchor
again that the captain might return from Bar-Wul-Yann upon the
landward tide. So we went on board and continued down the
Yann. And the captain and I spoke little, for we were thinking
of our parting, which should be for long, and we watched instead the splendour of the westerning sun. For the sun was a ruddy
gold, but a faint mist cloaked the jungle, lying low, and into it
poured the smoke of the little jungle cities, and the smoke of

them met together in the mist and joined into one haze, which became purple, and was lit by the sun, as the thoughts of men become hallowed by some great and sacred thing. Some times one column from a lonely house would rise up higher than the cities' smoke, and gleam by itself in the sun.

And now as the sun's last rays were nearly level, we saw the sight that I had come to see, for from two mountains that stood on either shore two cliffs of pink marble came out into the river, all glowing in the light of the low sun, and they were quite smooth and of mountainous altitude, and they nearly met, and Yann went tumbling between them and found the sea.

And this was Bar-Wul-Yann, the Gate of Yann, and in the distance through that barrier's gap I saw the azure indescribable sea, where little fishing-boats went gleaming by.

And the sun set, and the brief twilight came, and the exultation of the glory of Bar-Wul-Yann was gone, yet still the pink cliffs glowed, the fairest marvel that the eye beheld—and this in a land of wonders. And soon the twilight gave place to the coming out of stars, and the colours of Bar-Wul-Yann went dwindling away. And the sight of those cliffs was to me as some chord of music that a master's hand had launched from the violin, and which carries to Heaven or Faëry the tremulous spirits of men.

And now by the shore they anchored and went no further, for they were sailors of the river and not of the sea, and knew the Yann but not the tides beyond.

And the time was come when the captain and I must part, he to go back again to his fair Belzoond in sight of the distant peaks of the Hian Min, and I to find my way by strange means back to those hazy fields that all poets know, wherein stand small mysterious cottages through whose windows, looking westwards, you may see the fields of men, and looking eastwards see glittering elfin mountains, tipped with snow, going range on range into the region of Myth, and beyond it into the kingdom of Fantasy, which pertain to the Lands of Dream. Long we regarded one another, knowing that we should meet no more, for my fancy is weakening as the years slip by, and I go ever more seldom into the Lands of Dream. Then we clasped hands, uncouthly on his part, for it is not the method of greeting in his country, and he commended my soul to the care of his own gods, to his little lesser gods, the humble ones, to the gods that bless Belzoond.

The Hashish Man

I WAS at dinner in London the other day. The ladies had gone upstairs, and no one sat on my right; on my left there was a man I did not know, but he knew my name somehow, apparently, for he turned to me after a while, and said, "I read a story of yours about Bethmoora in a review."

Of course I remembered the tale. It was about a beautiful Oriental city that was suddenly deserted in a day—nobody quite knew why. I said, "Oh, yes," and slowly searched in my mind for some more fitting acknowledgement of the compliment that his memory had paid me.

I was greatly astonished when he said, "You were wrong about the gnousar sickness; it was not that at all."

I said, "Why! Have you been there?"

And he said, "Yes; I do it with hashish. I know Bethmoora well." And he took out of his pocket a small box full of some black stuff that looked like tar, but had a stranger smell. He warned me not to touch it with my finger, as the stain remained for days. "I got it from a gipsy," he said. "He had a lot of it, as it had killed his father." But I interrupted him, for I wanted to know for certain what it was that had made desolate that beautiful city, Bethmoora, and why they fled from it swiftly in a day. "Was it because of the Desert's curse?" I asked. And he said, "Partly it was the fury of the Desert and partly the advice of the Emperor Thuba Mleen, for that fearful beast is in some way connected with the Desert on his mother's side." And he told me this strange story: "You remember the sailor with the black scar, who was there on the day that you described when the messengers came on mules to the gate of Bethmoora, and all the people fled. I met this man in a tavern, drinking rum, and he told me all about the flight from Bethmoora, but knew no more than you did what the message was, or who had sent it. However, he said he would see Bethmoora once more whenever he touched again at an eastern port, even if he had to face the Devil. He often said that he would face the Devil to find out the mystery of that message that emptied Bethmoora in a day. And in the end he had to face Thuba Mleen, whose weak ferocity he had not imagined. For one day the sailor told me he had found a ship, and I met him no more after that in the tavern drinking rum. It was about that time that I got the hashish from the gipsy, who had a quantity that he did not want. It takes one literally out of oneself. It is like wings. You swoop over distant countries and into other worlds. Once I found out the secret of the universe. I have forgotten what it was, but I know that the Creator does not take Creation seriously, for I remember that He sat in Space with all His work in front of Him and laughed. I have seen incredible things in fearful worlds. As it is your imagination that takes you there, so it is only by your imagination that you can get back. Once out in æther I met a battered, prowling spirit, that had belonged to a man whom drugs had killed a hundred years ago; and he led me to regions that I had never imagined; and we parted in anger beyond the Pleiades, and I could not imagine my way back. And I met a huge grey shape that was the Spirit of some great people, perhaps of a whole star, and I besought It to show me my way home, and It halted beside me like a sudden wind and pointed, and, speaking quite softly, asked me if I discerned a certain tiny light, and I saw a far star faintly, and then It said to me, 'That is the Solar System,' and strode tremendously on. And somehow I imagined my way back, and only just in time, for my body was already stiffening in a chair in my room; and the fire had gone out and everything was cold, and I had to move each finger one by one, and there were pins and needles in them, and dreadful pains in the nails, which began to thaw; and at last I could move one arm, and reached a bell, and for a long time no one came, because every one was in bed. But at last a man appeared, and they got a doctor; and *he* said that it was hashish poisoning, but it would have been all right if I hadn't met that battered, prowling spirit.

"I could tell you astounding things that I have seen, but you want to know who sent that message to Bethmoora. Well, it was Thuba Mleen. And this is how I know. I often went to the city after that day that you wrote of (I used to take hashish of an evening in my flat), and I always found it uninhabited. Sand had poured into it from the desert, and the streets were yellow and smooth, and through open, swinging doors the sand had drifted.

"One evening I had put the guard in front of the fire, and settled into a chair and eaten my hashish, and the first thing that I saw when I came to Bethmoora was the sailor with the black scar, strolling down the street, and making footprints in the yellow sand. And now I knew that I should see what secret power it was that kept Bethmoora uninhabited.

"I saw that there was anger in the Desert, for there were storm clouds heaving along the skyline, and I heard a muttering amongst the sand.

"The sailor strolled on down the street, looking into the empty houses as he went; sometimes he shouted and sometimes he sang, and sometimes he wrote his name on a marble wall. Then he sat down on a step and ate his dinner. After a while he grew tired of the city, and came back up the street. As he reached the gate of green copper three men on camels appeared.

"I could do nothing. I was only a consciousness, invisible, wandering: my body was in Europe. The sailor fought well with his fists, but he was over-powered and bound with ropes, and led away through the Desert.

"I followed for as long as I could stay, and found that they were going by the way of the Desert round the Hills of Hap towards Utnar Véhi, and then I knew that the camel men belonged to Thuba Mleen.

"I work in an insurance office all day, and I hope you won't forget me if ever you want to insure—life, fire, or motor—but that's no part of my story. I was desperately anxious to get back to my flat, though it is not good to take hashish two days running; but I wanted to see what they would do to the poor fellow, for I had heard bad rumours about Thuba Mleen. When at last I got away I had a letter to write; then I rang for my servant, and told him that I must not be disturbed, though I left my door unlocked in case of accidents. After that I made up a good fire, and sat down and partook of the pot of dreams. I was going to the palace of Thuba Mleen.

"I was kept back longer than usual by noises in the street, but suddenly I was up above the town; the European countries rushed by beneath me, and there appeared the thin white palace spires of horrible Thuba Mleen. I found him presently at the end of a little narrow room. A curtain of red leather hung behind him, on which all the names of God, written in Yannish, were worked with a golden thread. Three windows were small and high. The Emperor seemed no more than about twenty, and looked small and weak. No smiles came on his nasty yellow face, though he tittered continually. As I looked from his low forehead to his quivering under lip, I became aware that there was some horror about him, though I was not able to perceive what it was. And then I saw it—the man never blinked; and though later on I watched those eyes for a blink, it never happened once.

"And then I followed the Emperor's rapt glance, and I saw the sailor lying on the floor, alive but hideously rent, and the royal torturers were at work all round him. They had torn long strips from him, but had not detached them, and they were torturing the ends of them far away from the sailor." The man that I met at dinner told me many things which I must omit. "The sailor was groaning softly, and every time he groaned Thuba Mleen tittered. I had no sense of smell, but I could hear and see, and I do not know which was the most revolting—the terrible condition of the sailor or the happy unblinking face of horrible Thuba Mleen.

"I wanted to go away, but the time was not yet come, and I had to stay where I was.

"Suddenly the Emperor's face began to twitch violently and his under lip quivered faster, and he whimpered with anger, and cried with a shrill voice, in Yannish, to the captain of his torturers that there was a spirit in the room. I feared not, for living men cannot lay hands on a spirit, but all the torturers were appalled at his anger, and stopped their work, for their hands trembled with fear. Then two men of the spear-guard slipped from the room, and each of them brought back presently a golden bowl, with knobs on it, full of hashish; and the bowls were large enough for heads to have floated in had they been filled with blood. And the two men fell to rapidly, each eating with two great spoons—there was enough in each spoonful to have given dreams to a hundred men. And there came upon them soon the hashish state, and their spirits hovered, preparing to go free, while I feared horribly, but ever and anon they fell back again to the bodies, recalled by some noise in the room. Still the men ate, but lazily now, and without ferocity. At last the great spoons dropped out of their hands, and their spirits rose and left them. I could not flee. And the spirits were more horrible than the men, because they were young men, and not yet wholly moulded to fit their fearful souls. Still the sailor groaned softly, evoking little titters from the Emperor Thuba Mleen. Then the two spirits rushed at me, and swept me thence as gusts of wind sweep butterflies, and away we went from that small, pale, heinous man. There was no escaping from these spirits' fierce insistence. The energy in my minute lump of the drug was overwhelmed by the huge spoonsful that these men had eaten with both hands. I was whirled over Arvle Woondery, and brought to the lands of Snith, and swept on still until I came to Kragua, and beyond this to those bleak lands that are nearly unknown to fancy. And we came at last to those ivory hills that are named the Mountains of Madness, and I tried to struggle against the spirits of that frightful Emperor's men, for I heard on the other side of the ivory hills the pittering of those beasts that prey on the mad, as they prowled up and down. It was no fault of mine that my little lump of hashish could not fight with their horrible spoonsful. . . ."

Some one was tugging at the hall-door bell. Presently a servant came and told our host that a policeman in the hall wished to speak to him at once. He apologised to us, and went outside, and we heard a man in heavy boots, who spoke in a low voice to him. My friend got up and walked over to the window, and opened it, and looked outside. "I should think it will be a fine night," he said. Then he jumped out. When we put our astonished heads out of the window to look for him, he was already out of sight.

A Narrow Escape

It was underground.

In that dank cavern down below Belgrave Square the walls were dripping. But what was that to the magician? It was secrecy that he needed, not dryness. There he pondered upon the trend of events, shaped destinies and concocted magical brews.

For the last few years the serenity of his ponderings had been disturbed by the noise of the motor-bus; while to his keen ears there came the earthquake-rumble, far off, of the train in the tube, going down Sloane Street; and what he heard of the world above his head was not to its credit.

He decided one evening over his evil pipe, down there in his dank dark chamber, that London had lived long enough, had abused its opportunities, had gone too far, in fine, with its civilization. And so he decided to wreck it.

Therefore he beckoned up his acolyte from the weedy end of the cavern, and, "Bring me," he said, "the heart of the toad that dwelleth in Arabia and by the mountains of Bethany." The acolyte slipped away by the hidden door, leaving that grim old man with his frightful pipe, and whither he went who knows but the gipsy people, or by what path he returned; but within a year he stood in the cavern again, slipping secretly in by the trap while the old man smoked, and he brought with him a little fleshy thing that rotted in a casket of pure gold.

"What is it?" the old man croaked.

"It is," said the acolyte, "the heart of the toad that dwelt once in Arabia and by the mountains of Bethany."

The old man's crooked fingers closed on it, and he blessed the acolyte with his rasping voice and claw-like hand uplifted; the motor-bus rumbled above on its endless journey; far off the train shook Sloane Street.

"Come," said the old magician, "it is time." And there and then they left the weedy cavern, the acolyte carrying cauldron, gold poker and all things needful, and went abroad in the light. And very wonderful the old man looked in his silks.

Their goal was the outskirts of London; the old man strode in front and the acolyte ran behind him, and there was something magical in the old man's stride alone, without his wonderful dress, the cauldron and wand, the hurrying acolyte and the small gold poker.

Little boys jeered till they caught the old man's eye. So there went on through London this strange procession of two, too swift for any to follow. Things seemed worse up there than they did in the cavern, and the further they got on their way towards London's outskirts the worse London got. "It is time," said the old man, "surely."

And so they came at last to London's edge and a small hill watching it with a mournful look. It was so mean that the acolyte longed for the cavern, dank though it was and full of terrible sayings that the old man said when he slept.

They climbed the hill and put the cauldron down, and put therein the necessary things, and lit a fire of herbs that no chemist will sell nor decent gardener grow, and stirred the cauldron with the golden poker. The magician retired a little apart and muttered, then he strode back to the cauldron and, all being ready, suddenly opened the casket and let the fleshy thing fall in to boil.

Then he made spells, *then* he flung up his arms; the fumes from the cauldron entering in at his mind he said raging things that he had not known before and runes that were dreadful (the acolyte screamed); there he cursed London from fog to loam-pit, from zenith to the abyss; motor-bus, factory, shop, parliament, people. "Let them all perish," he said, "and London pass away, tram lines and bricks and pavement, the usurpers too long of the fields, let them all pass away and the wild hares come back, blackberry and briar-rose.

"Let it pass," he said, "pass now, pass utterly."

In the momentary silence the old man coughed, then waited with eager eyes; and the long long hum of London hummed as it always has since first the reed-huts were set up by the river, changing its note at times but always humming, louder now than it was in years gone by, but humming night and day though its voice be cracked with age; so it hummed on.

And the old man turned him round to his trembling acolyte and terribly said as he sank into the earth: "YOU HAVE NOT BROUGHT ME THE HEART OF THE TOAD THAT DWELLETH IN ARABIA AND BY THE MOUNTAINS OF BETHANY!"

JORKENS

The Sign

ONE day as I entered the Billiards Club about lunch-time, I noticed at once that the conversation was a good bit deeper than usual. In fact they were all discussing transmigration. They were men of many topics, varying from the price of more than one commodity on the Stock Exchange to the best place to buy oysters, yet the intricacies of the afterlife of a Brahmin were a little outside their range. A glance at Jorkens showed me what it was all about; if they had gone out of their own depth, it was as much as anything to get out of Jorkens', just as anyone taking the air on an esplanade might walk out to sea to avoid an acquaintance with too long a story to tell. The reason for wishing to get out of Jorkens' depth was naturally that one or two of the others had tales of their own to tell.

"Transmigration," said Jorkens. "It's a thing one hears lots of talk of and seldom sees."

Terbut opened his mouth and said nothing.

"It happened to come my way once," went on Jorkens.

"To come your way?" said Terbut.

"I'll tell you," said Jorkens. "When I was quite young I knew a man called Horcher, who impressed me a great deal. One of the things for instance that used to impress me about him was the way in which, if one were talking of politics and wondering what was going to happen, he would quietly say what the Government were going to do, when there hadn't been a word about it in any paper: that was always impressive; and still more so if one was guessing what was going to happen in Europe; he would come in then with his information in just the same quiet way."

"And was he right?" asked Terbut.

"Well," replied Jorkens, "I won't say that. But it isn't every-one who would venture to prophesy at all. And any way he impressed me a great deal by it at the time, and older men than me. And another thing he was very good at; he would give me advice on any conceivable subject. I'm not saying the advice was good, but it showed the vast range of his interests and his glad-ness to share them with others, that to hear of anything that you wished to do was enough to call forth his immediate advice about it. I lost a good deal of money, one way and another, on bits of advice of his; and yet there was a spontaneity about it, and a certain apparent depth, that could not fail to impress you. Well, one of those days, being very young and all the world equally new to me, and the faith of the Brahmins no stranger to me than the theory of man's descent, I started talking to Horcher on the subject of transmigration. He smiled at my ignorance, as he always did, in a friendly sort of way, and then told me all about it. The Brahmins, he said were wrong in a great many particu-lars, not having studied the question scientifically or being in-tellectually qualified to understand its more difficult aspects. I will not tell you the theory of transmigration as he explained it to me, because you can read it yourselves in textbooks; it's not what he told me that was new, so much as the quiet certainty with which he told it, and the rather exciting impression he left on my mind that he had discovered it all for himself. But two things I will tell you about it; and one was that, on account of the interest he had always taken in conditions that affected the welfare of the lower classes he would, 'if (as he put it) there was any justice hereafter,' be rewarded by a considerable promotion in his next existence. 'For if,' he said, 'there were to be no reward in a subsequent state for an interest in such things during this one, there would be no sense in it.' I remember we walked in a garden as he told me all this, and the path was full of snails, which were probably all moving towards some poplars a little way off, for every tree had several of them climbing up the trunks, as though they all made this journey at that time of the year, which was early October. I remember him stepping on the snails as he walked, not from any cruelty, for he was not cruel, but because it could not matter to forms of life that were so absurdly low. And the other thing that he told me was that he had invented a signal, or rather that he had invented a way of branding it into his memory. The signal was no more than the Greek letter ϕ, but he was a man of enormous industry and he had trained or hypnotized himself into remembering this one sign with such vehemence that he was convinced he would make it automatically, even in another existence. In this life he frequently made it quite unconsciously, tracing it on a wall with his finger, or even in the air: he had trained himself to do that. And he told me that if ever he saw me in his next life, and remembered me (and he smiled pleasantly as though he thought that such a remembrance was possible) he would make that sign to me, whatever our respective stations might be."

"And what did he think he was going to be?" I asked Jorkens.

"He never would tell me that," Jorkens replied. "But I knew he was sure that it was to be something of the most tremendous importance, I knew that from the condescension that showed through the kindness of his manner when he said he would make the sign to me; and then there was a certain slow grace with which he lifted his hand, when he made the sign in the air, which more than suggested someone seated upon a throne. I don't think he would have wanted to be bothered with me at all in that triumphant second life of his, but for his pride in having stamped that sign by sheer industry into his very soul, so that he could not help making it now, and felt confident that habit would endure wherever his soul went, and he naturally wanted posterity to know what he had achieved. Every half hour or so he would, quite unconsciously, make the sign as we walked; he had certainly trained himself to do that."

"And had he any justification for thinking he would sit on a throne," I asked, "if he had a second life?"

"Well," said Jorkens, "he was a very busy man, and it isn't for me to say to what extent his interest in other men's lives was philanthropy or interference: I took him at his own valuation then, so I don't like to value him otherwise now he's dead. His own view was that pretty well all men were fools, so that somebody must look after them, and that at much personal inconvenience he was prepared to do so himself, and that any system that did not reward a man who was so philanthropic as that must be a silly system. Mind you I don't think he did think that Creation was silly, because he believed that he *was* going to be rewarded: the most I've heard him say against it was that he could have arranged many things much better than they are arranged if he had had the ordering of the world, and he gave me a few instances.

"Well, he impressed on me this sign, which he said would prove transmigration to be of the utmost value to science; though I think that what may have interested him more was that I should see to what heights he had deservedly risen. And, mind you, he had got me to believe him. I thought over it a lot, and often I pictured myself in my later years attending a levée or other great function at the Court of some foreign country, and suddenly receiving from the sovereign, I alone of all that assembly, that signal of recognition that would mean nothing to all the rest.

"He died at a good age, and I was still under thirty; and I decided to do what he had advised me, and to watch in my own old age the careers of men holding high places in Europe (for he didn't think much of Asia), born after his death and showing certain abilities which might be expected from himself in another life, with all the advantages of his experience in this one. For I said to myself 'if he's right about transmigration, he'll be right about what it can do for him.' And, do you know, he *was* right about transmigration. I was walking in that very garden the year after he died, thinking of the Greek letter ϕ; as he had told me always to think of it, the distinct circle and the upright bar through the midst of it. Often I would make the sign with my fingers, as he used to do, to keep it in my mind; I made it that day on the old red garden-wall. I watched a snail on the wall making its slow journey, and remembered his contempt for them, and was somehow glad to think that he had not despised the poor things more than he seemed to despise men. The glittering track it was making up the wall, and which gathered the sunlight to it, was to him not worth noticing, but then much of the work of men was to him equally foolish. I looked still at the bright track of the snail's progress, until I realized that he would have said that only a fool or a poet would waste his time with such trifles, and then I turned away. As I turned away I saw by one of those glances that stray from the corners of our eyes that the snail was making a very distinct curve. I looked again, and set little store by what I had seen, for chance could have done that much, but the snail had made a very distinct quarter of a circle on his way up the wall. It was so neat a bit of a circle that I went on watching, till it was as good a semicircle as it had been a quarter of a circle. It was not till it began to turn downwards that I grew excited. And then I did grow very excited indeed; for the snail had been obviously climbing the wall. What did it want to turn downwards for? The diameter of the circle was about four inches. On and on went the snail. With my mind so full of the sign I could not possibly ignore that, if the snail went on and completed the circle, it would be half the sign. And it was just the size, too, of the sign that Horcher used to make in that regal way with his forefinger. And the snail went on. When only half an inch remained to complete the circle, it may sound silly, but I made the sign myself, in the air with my finger. I knew the snail couldn't see it: if it really was Horcher, I knew it could only be the habit, self-hypnotized into the very ego, that was making that sign, and nothing to do with any intellect. Then I put the absurd idea clean out of my mind. Yet the snail went on. And then it completed the circle. 'Well,' I said, 'the snail has moved in a circle: lots of animals do: dogs do often: I expect birds do too: why shouldn't they? And I must keep steady.'

"Do you know that snail, as soon as it finished its round, went straight on up the wall, dividing that circle into two halves as neatly as you ever saw anything divided. I stood and stared with my mouth and my eyes wide open. Below ran the perfectly vertical track by which the snail climbed the wall, then the circle, and now the continuation of the vertical line dividing the circle in two. It came to the top of the circle. What now? The snail went straight on upwards. It came to a point a couple of inches above the top of the circle and there it stopped, having made a perfect ϕ, having proved the dream of the Brahmin to be a reality. 'Poor old Horcher,' I said."

"Did you do anything for the snail?" asked Terbut.

"I thought for a moment of killing it," said Jorkens, "to give Horcher a better chance with his third life. And then I realized that there was something about his outlook that it might take hundreds of lives to purify. You can't go on and on killing snails, you know."

The Neapolitan Ice

I HAVE had on other occasions to mention topics carefully chosen by members of the Billiards Club with the sole intent of steering conversation where Jorkens might be unable to follow. I do not refer again to this unsporting device with any intention of deprecating it, but only because it was the beginning of a story by Jorkens of an experience that may be of interest to such as care to study his somewhat unusual character. The topic at lunch-time on the day in question was Polar exploration. I will not record the conversation in any detail, because it was scarcely original; after all, there is no need to be original when you are discussing something at a club; for instance one of our members said: "It must be pretty hard to keep warm."

"Yes, it's damned hard," said Jorkens.

It was clearly on the tip of Terbut's tongue to say, "How do you know?" One could see that. But rather than risk letting Jorkens in with a story, he closed his lips again with the remark unsaid.

"You'd keep warm with whiskey, wouldn't you?" said one of us.

"Oh, I don't know," said Jorkens. "Whiskey's a rather overrated drink."

One of the things I like about Jorkens is the immensely surprising remarks that he sometimes makes.

"Whiskey overrated!" we said.

"Well, yes, compared to some drinks," said Jorkens.

"What, for instance?" said Terbut, who really wanted to know.

"For keeping you warm in ice and snow," said Jorkens, "and

probably keeping off frostbite, I know nothing like a liqueur a man gave me once at a dinner in a little restaurant that there used to be in Punt Street: it's closed down long ago: there's a hair-cutter's shop there now. It was a wonderful drink, a drink like honey and roses and a very gentle fire, a cosy, quiet fire mildly flickering. I never knew anything like it. Unfortunately I don't know its name. He was a bit of a traveller, this man. I don't know where the bottle came from; the waiter brought it in, but I was never able to get another like it in that restaurant, or elsewhere; my host was very secretive about it. He did not have it brought in till the end of dinner. It came in with the Neapolitan ice. I should like to have had a glass of it beside me all through dinner; so would any of you if once you had tasted it, as none of you have; but it only came in with the ices." And Jorkens uttered a small sigh.

"Did you never find out the name of it?" asked Terbut a little greedily.

"Well, no," said Jorkens. "It was all a matter of business. There was a business deal that this man was rather keen on; and he wanted to get my attitude just right, so he brought out this liqueur. There are a good many secrets in business, and this liqueur was one of them. As a matter of fact the fellow overdid it, and the deal never came off, but I had one wonderful drink. I should have liked a lot more of it; but they only brought it with the ices. It was a good dinner he gave me. Well, naturally; because he was pretty keen on this deal. We had turtle soup; fresh turtle, you know; red mullet; good enough in its way, only too many bones; and then we had hare; just the common hare, but they could cook it at that restaurant that there used to be in Punt Street. And really I think that was about all; and then the Neapolitan ice. Quite a small dinner; but good, you know." And he saw Terbut about to interrupt, and turned to him and forestalled him with the remark: "Perhaps you don't know a Neapolitan ice, Terbut."

And Terbut took this to be an aspersion on his ignorance of the world that Jorkens had travelled so much, and blurted out, "Of course I do. It's green and white and pink. The white is supposed to be vanilla, and of course the pink is strawberry; as for the green, I don't quite know what that is, but . . ."

"We are not meant to," said Jorkens.

"We are a long way from the Arctic," Terbut retorted.

"I was about to tell you," said Jorkens. "The liqueur came in with the ices. And the moment I put it down, it woke the imagination as I've known nothing else able to. It liberated the very spirit. I may have had two glasses; that I don't remember. But that restaurant, Punt Street, all London, fell behind me almost immediately, and my imagination or spirit or whatever carries one's ego, swept northward through England."

"How did you know you were going northward?" asked Terbut.

"How did I know?" asked Jorkens. "I could see. I was liberated; my spirit was free. I was far far up above England. I could see the shape of it, a long green belt going northwards, and Scotland too; green all the way until we came to the snow. I must have passed over that strip of six hundred miles of green in a few seconds: that is how spirits travel. Of course the fellow had let me have too much: there was no more business in me now, I was above all that sort of thing, and far above earth. And I was sweeping northwards. The seas froze almost at once; and instead of white foam there was ice, and snow on the ice for miles, and hundreds of miles; and still I went northwards. And there was the Arctic with the sun on the snow, a beautiful thing to see, the most wonderful journey that I have ever made. But liberations like this are never for long. Scarcely had I seen the beauty of that enormous vista of Arctic, when I felt that my spirit was falling. And fall it did, rapidly. And soon I was lying in the snow. I had not been conscious of my body when I was up at that glorious height travelling faster than birds migrating; but I was conscious of it now in the snow. The glittering whiteness of it began to weary my eyes; and my lips were freezing, for I was lying face downwards. I, who some seconds before had been superior to gravity, was now unable even to lift my face, and I knew that my lips were freezing. After the pain came numbness, the first symptom of frostbite."

"How could your lips be frostbitten," said Terbut, "if they were still indoors in London?"

"Well, they may not have been quite," said Jorkens; "but I went to a doctor next day, and he said that another three minutes would have been sure to have done it."

"I can't see how," said Terbut.

"I'm only telling you what happened," said Jorkens quite

calmly. "The ice was shining on the surface of the snow, and that beautiful scene, as it had been a while before, was now an intense weariness. The glare of the ice in my eyes was wearying my brain, and I could not lift up my face from it. That's the trouble with any drink; the more it lifts you up, the more it lets you down. But I had never been let down quite like that before: I could barely lift my eyes. But I lifted them, and I saw the Abendgluth, quite close and the snow all flushed with it. The white snow ended just by a ridge where my weary face was lying, and I saw the tremendous sight that they call the Abendgluth, on miles and miles of snow. It was worth while lying there with frozen lips only to see that everlasting wonder; miles and miles of rose-pink snow shining like dawn on earth; cold snow like a world-wide jewel, and a scent of strawberries."

"Strawberries!" said Terbut. "You must have a powerful imagination if you can imagine strawberries in the Arctic."

"Not at all," said Jorkens. "It was just sheer fact. It wasn't imagination at all. I was lying over the table with my face in the Neapolitan ice; I had slid over the green part, and my lips were on the vanilla, and just in front of my eyes was the strawberry end of it. The amount of strawberry of course in a strawberry ice varies according to the conscience of the man who makes it, and there was a distinct trace of strawberry in this one; but no vanilla."

Jorkens Consults a Prophet

It was the usual thing at the Billiards Club, a thing that happens too often: Jorkens was known to be coming up the stairs, and one or two members, simply with the deliberate intention of getting the conversation where he was unlikely to join in, that is to say away from Africa or any of the wilder lands, had chosen philosophy for their discussion. Free will or destiny was the general trend of their argument. I found it merely dull. But the moment Jorkens heard them, his eye brightened up.

"There is a lot to be said for destiny," said Jorkens, "but you can't ignore free will."

"What do you mean?" said one of the philosophers.

And then Terbut joined in.

"Do you know anything about either of them?" he said.

"Yes," said Jorkens. "As it happens I do. I thought I knew about one of them, and it turned out I didn't, but I had quite a considerable experience of the other. I'll tell you about it. It was like this. I was a good deal interested in destiny, not so much from the point of view from which you are looking at it, but as a practical proposition. I said to myself, things are bound to happen, and there's no stopping them; and if one could find out someone who knew what those things were, there'd be a great deal of money in it. And, mind you, it was not I that was having wild fancies about it: plenty of people claimed to know the future, and do so still. Well, I investigated the claims of one of them. I went to him and I said, 'You foretell the future?'

" 'I do,' he said.

" 'Can you tell what is going to win the Derby?' I asked.

" 'I can,' he said.

"Well, it wasn't the Derby that I wanted to know about, it was a race-meeting a long way from here, but it served my purpose just as well, and I asked him if he could tell me what was going to win that. So he brought out a lot of silks and began unwrapping them, all of them different colours; and when he had taken off about nine of them, there was a crystal, not quite smooth, but lightly carved on the surface with things like leaves; rather like an artichoke. Then he lit a powder in a little agate saucer, which made a smoke with a queer smell and made everything dim all round, but not the crystal. The crystal remained as bright as ever. When he moved it slightly in his hand things moved in the crystal: you could see them quite clearly. And then he told me the name of the horse that would win that race, and the name of the second and the third. He did more than that, he showed me the actual race in the crystal with the three horses leading it past the post and their colours clear and distinct. Now, that was a queer thing to do. The horses were unmistakable: I recognized all three of them afterwards; but, to make sure, I jotted down the colours that the jockeys were wearing. He let me see that race again and again. It was clear and bright, in spite of the smoke all round me; in fact the grass was greener than it ever is naturally, and the colours the jockeys wore were more like enamel than silk. But you simply couldn't mistake them. Of course I paid him; I paid him a good deal; in fact the blackguard demanded £5, and wouldn't take less. But, after all, the information was worth it. Then I got out of the room as fast as I could, away from the scented smoke, to breathe the fresh air, and because I didn't like the fellow at all. I had the name of the winning horse from the conjurer's lips, and I had seen the race with my own eyes. Did I tell you that he let me see the race over and over again, so that I got the colours quite clear? I bought some coloured chalks and jotted down sketches of them. I very soon found what the horses were, and who their owners were and what their colours; and the colours I had seen in the crystal were perfectly right. Well, do you know, I didn't have a penny on that race. I just went and watched it. And there were the horses, every single one of them, just as I had seen them in the crystal. And the man was perfectly right about the name of the winner, and of the second and third. It was an odd and surprising experience to see that race in the crystal repeated before my eyes, all the horses I had seen, all the colours and even the exact distances between each, which I had noticed in the crystal and made rough notes of. I was a good deal surprised, but I didn't waste any time wondering: I saw that I was on a good thing, and I went straight back to that rather sinister fellow that burned the scented smoke. I said, 'I want to see another race, and I will give you £10 this time.' I did that so as not to have any argument as to whether or not he would show me another, for I knew now that it was an excessively good thing. Well, he burned the smoke again in the agate saucer while he held the crystal in his hand; and the room grew dim once more and the crystal shone brighter and I saw another race. Again he told me the names of the three winners, and again I jotted them down and made little sketches of all the colours with the coloured pencils, which I had in my pocket this time. It was a big race, a very big one, and it was coming on in about three weeks' time. Well, I concentrated on the winner. Of course I could have got fabulous odds, if I had backed all those three horses to come in in the right order, but I didn't want to give too much away: I didn't want people to suspect that I had had dealings with a clairvoyant, and so to find out that my bet was a bet on a certainty. I had a good deal of money in those days, and I concentrated on the winner. I put all the money I had on him, spreading it over various bookies, and I borrowed a good deal more; and the odds were six to one. What with the cash I had borrowed and what with the stuff I owned, I stood to be ten times richer on the afternoon of that race than I had been on the same morning. I am not going to tell you what race it was; because, if what I tell you gets out, I don't want some fellow to get up and say that that's not the way races are run there. They are run in that way of course, only I don't want to say so.

"The day before I made my final arrangements with the bookies I went back to the damned fellow with the crystal and scented smoke, to ask him if he was sure of what he had been talking about, that is to say that Pullover would win that race, with a jockey wearing blue and yellow hoops. He said he knew well what he was talking about, and that that horse would win. And he asked me if the other race had not gone exactly as he had predicted, which of course made me look rather silly and

quite unreasonably anxious. But it was then that he touched
on a topic that I think you were just talking about. He said that
free will was some sort of force that was almost equal, I think he
said, to destiny; and that if I were to take a gun and shoot the
horse as he came by, or injure it severely before the race, then
of course it would not win, but that according to the will and the
actions of everybody else in the world, and every horse, that
horse would win the race. Only two men, he and I, knew anything of the future, as far as that horse was concerned: he certainly would do nothing whatever, and took an oath accordingly,
and, provided that I exerted no free will against what was
planned for the horse, it was destined that it must win. He also
repeated the names of the second and third, with which I had
nothing to do, for the reason that I have told you. The whole
thing seemed very reasonable and, indeed, obvious. Of course
if I took violent measures against whatever was ordained, the
thing could not happen; just as, if you divert a river, it won't
go its old way to the sea; but leave it alone, and it will.

"The day of the race I went and saw the horses in the ring.
And I had seen every one of them in the crystal. The colours of
three of the jockeys I had of course sketched in coloured pencil,
and I had the sketch in my pocket. And there the three jockeys
were, all walking about. The winner was absolutely unmistakable, even without the blue and yellow hoops: he was a bright
chestnut with a clear white star on his forehead.

"I watched the race. And the second horse that I had seen
in the crystal, white with red spots, and the third horse, green
jacket and cap with white sleeves, were coming along nicely; but
the odd thing was that my winner suddenly went a bit short far
out in the country, and I saw him through my glasses dropping
back. When the man had said 'if you shoot the horse, he won't
win,' I had said to the damned fellow, 'Do you think I should
be such a fool?' But I had done a more foolish thing really. I
had backed the horse too heavily for the bookies. They couldn't
afford to let him win. If I said that that jockey with his blue
and yellow hoops had received any money from them, he would
turn out to be still alive and would sue me for libel. But he
had a young family; and a thousand-pound note comes in wonderfully handy in bringing up two or three children. Yes, the
second horse was first, and the third horse was second, and then

came the field: the race was wonderfully like what I had seen in the crystal, only that my chestnut horse with the white star, ridden by blue and yellow hoops, was right back with a little bunch that came cantering past at the end. Of course it was all my own fault: I'd played free will against destiny. And, as I was never able to make out in what proportions they work, I never had anything to do with that kind of thing any more."

The Walk to Lingham

"There's a kind of idea that I can't tell a story," said Jorkens, "without some kind of a drink. How such ideas get about I haven't the faintest notion. A story crossed my mind only this afternoon, if you call an actual experience a story. It's a little bit out of the way, and if you'd care to hear it I'll tell it you. But I can assure you that a drink is absolutely unnecessary."

"Oh, I know," I said.

"All I ask," said Jorkens, "is that if you pass it on, you'll tell it in such a way that people will believe you. There have been people, I don't say many, but there have been people that treated those tales I told you as pure fabrication. One man even compared me to Munchausen, compared me favourably I admit, but still he made the comparison. Painful to me, and painful, I should think, to your publisher. It's the way you told those tales; they were true enough every one of them; but it was the way you told them, that somehow started those doubts. You'll be more careful in future, won't you?"

"Yes," I said, "I'll make a note of it."

And with that he started the story.

"Yes, it's distinctly out of the way. Distinctly. But I imagine you will not disbelieve it on that account. Otherwise everyone that ever told a story of any experience he'd had would have to select the dullest and most ordinary, so as to be believed; an account of a railway journey, we'll say, from Penge to Victoria station. We've not come to that, I trust."

"No, no," I said.

"Very well," said Jorkens.

A couple of other members sat down near us then, and Jorkens said: "I can remember as if it was yesterday a long road in the East of England, with a border of poplars. It must have been three miles long, and poplars standing along it all the way on both sides of the road; right across flat fen-country. They had drained the fens, but patches of marsh remained, and here and all along ditches the pennons of the rushes were waving, like an army that had warred with ill success against man, scattered but not annihilated. And they hadn't contented themselves with draining the fens, for they had begun to cut down the poplars. That was what they were at when I first saw the road, with its two straight rows of poplars over the plain like green and silvery plumes, and I must say they were felling them very neatly. They were bringing them down across the road, as it was easier that way to get them on to the carts, and the amount of traffic they interfered with wasn't worth bothering over: in any case they could see it coming for three miles each way, if any ever came, and I never saw any, except the thing that I'll tell you about. Well, they were cutting one down that had to fall between two others across the road without making a mess of their branches, and there was only just room to do it with not two feet to spare. And they did it so neatly that it never touched a leaf: it came down with a huge sigh between the two other trees, and all the little leaves that were turned towards it waved and fluttered anxiously as it went past them with that great last breath. It was done so neatly that I took off my hat and cheered. Anyone might have done so. One doesn't set out to rejoice over those that are down, at least not openly. But one does not always stop to think, and it was perhaps five minutes before I began to be ashamed of that cry of triumph of mine echoing down the doomed avenue.

"It was the last tree they felled that day, and soon I was walking back alone to the village of Lingham where stood the nearest human habitations, three miles away over the fenland. And the glimmers of evening began to mellow the poplars. The woodmen with their carts and their fallen trees went the other way; their loud clear voices in talk, and their calls to their horses, soon fading out of all hearing. And then I was in a silence all unbroken but for my own footfall, and but for the faintest sound that seemed sometimes to murmur behind me, that I took for the sound of the wind in the tops of the poplars, though there was no wind blowing.

"I hadn't gone a mile when I had a sense, based on no clue, yet a deeply intense feeling, growing stronger and stronger for the last ten minutes, growing up from a mere suspicion to sheer intuitive certainty, that I was being furtively followed. I looked round and saw nothing. Or rather, partly obscured by a slight curve of the road I must have seen what I afterwards saw too clearly, and yet never credited what was happening. After that the more my sense of being followed increased, the less I dared look round. And none of the kinds of men that I tried to imagine as being what was after me seemed quite to fit my fears. I hadn't gone another quarter mile; I'd barely done another four hundred yards, when: but look here, I'm damned dry. I never had another experience like it, and looking back on it even today has parched my throat till I can hardly speak. I doubt if any of you have ever known anything of the kind."

"I'm sure we haven't," I said, and signed to the waiter, for there was no doubt that there was something in Jorkens' memory that could shake him even now. When he was quite himself again the first thing he did was to thank me, like the good old fellow he is, and then he went on with his tale.

"I hadn't gone another four hundred yards, when it was clear to me with some awful certainty that whatever was after me was nothing human. The shock of that was perhaps worse than the first knowledge that I was followed. There was no longer the very faintest doubt of pursuit; I could hear the measured steps. But they were not human. And, you know, looking over the fields all empty of men, level and low and marshy, I got the feeling, one got it very easily all alone as I was, that if there was anything there that had something against man, I was the one on whom its anger must fall. And the more that the fading illumination of evening made all things dim and mysterious the more that feeling got hold of me. I think I may say that I bore up fairly well, going resolutely on with those steps getting louder behind me. Only I daren't look round. I was afraid when I knew I was followed; I freely admit it; I was more afraid when I knew it was nothing human, yet I held on with a certain determination not to give way to my fears, except that one about not looking round. It wasn't the memory of anything I've told you yet that made my throat go dry just now." Jorkens stopped and took another long drink: in fact he emptied his tumbler.

"A frightful terror was still in store for me, a blasting fear that so shook me then that I nearly dropped on the road, and that sometimes even now comes shivering back on me, and often haunts my nights. We, you know, we are all so proud of the animal kingdom, and so absolutely preoccupied with it, that any attack from outside leaves us staggered and gasping. It was so with me now, when I learned that whatever was after me was certainly nothing animal. I heard the clod clod of the steps, and a certain prolonged swish, but never a sound of breathing. It was fully time to look round, and yet I daren't. The hard heavy steps had nothing of the softness of flesh. Paws they were not, nor even hooves. And they were so near now that there must have been sounds of large breathing, had it been anything animal. And at such moments there are spiritual wisdoms that guide us, intuitions, inner feelings; call them what you will. They told me clearly, that this was none of us. Nothing soft and mortal. Nor was it. Nor was it.

"Those moments of making up my mind to look round, while I walked on at the same steady pace, were the most frightful in my life. I could not turn my head. And then I stopped and turned completely round. I don't know why I did it that way. There was perhaps a certain boldness in the movement that gave me some mastery over myself which just saved me from panic, and that would have of course been the end of me. Had I run I must have been done for. I spun right round and back again, and saw what was after me.

"I told you how I had cheered when the poplar fell. I was standing right under its neighbour. And men had been cutting down poplars for weeks. I remembered the look of that tree by which I had stood and cheered; chanced to note the hang of its branches. And I recognized it now. It was right in the middle of the road. One root was lifted up, with clods of earth clinging to it, and it was stumping after me down the road to Lingham. Don't think from any calmness I have as I tell you this that I was calm then. To say that I wasn't utterly racked with terror, would be merely to tell you a lie. One thing alone my reeling mind remained master of, and that was that one must not run. Old tales came back to me of men that were followed by lions, and my mind was able to hold them, and to act as they had taught. Never run. It was the last piece of wisdom left to my poor wits.

"Of course I tried to quicken my pace unnoticed. Whether I succeeded or not I do not know: the tree was terribly close. I turned round no more, but I knew what it looked like from the sound of its awful steps, coming up crab-like and elephantine and stumping grimly down, and I knew from the sigh in the leaves that the twigs were all bending back as it hurried after me. And I never ran.

"And the others seemed to be watching me. There was not that air of aloofness that inanimate things, if they really be inanimate, should have towards us; far less was there the respect that is due to man. I was terribly alone amongst the anger of all those poplars; and, mind you, I'd never cut one of them.

"My knees weren't too weak to have run: I could have done it: it was only my good sense that held me back, the last steady sense that was left to me. I knew that if I ran I should be helpless before the huge pursuit of the tree. It stands to reason, looking at it reasonably, as one can sitting here, that anything that is after you, whatever it is, is not going to let you get right away from it, and the more you try to escape the more you must excite it. And then there were the others: I didn't know what they would do. They were merely watchful as yet, but I was so frightfully alone there, with nothing human in sight, that it was best to go calmly on as though nothing was wrong, and making the most of that arrogance, as I suppose one must call it, that marks our attitude towards all inanimate things. As evening darkened the snipe began to drum, over the empty waste that lay flat and lonely all round me. And I might have felt some companionship, in my awful predicament, from these little voices of the animal kingdom, only that somehow or other I could not feel so certain as to what side they'd be on. And it is a very uneasy sound, the drumming of snipe, when you cannot be sure that it is friendly: the whole air moans with it. Certainly nothing in the sound decreased the pursuit of the tree, as one might have hoped it would, had any allies of the animal kingdom been gathering to befriend me. Rooks moved over, utterly unconcerned, and still the pursuit continued. I began to forget, in my terror, that I was a man. I remembered only that I was animal. I had some foolish hope that, as the rooks went over and the snipe's feathers cut through the air, these awful watchful poplars and the terror that came behind me might drop back to their proper station. Yet the sound of the snipe seemed only to add to the loneliness, and the rooks seemed only to aid the gathering darkness, and nothing turned the poplar as yet from its terrible usurpation. I was left to my miserable subterfuges; walking with a limp as though tired, and yet making a longer or quicker step with one leg than the other. Sometimes longer, sometimes quicker; varying it; and seeing which deceived the best. But these poor antics are not much good; for whatever is quietly following you is likely to judge your pace by the space between it and its prey, as much as by watching your gait, and to match its own accordingly. So, though I did increase my lead now and then, there soon grew louder again the swish of the air in the branches, and that clod clod that I hear at nights even now, whenever my dreams are troubled, a sound to be instantly recognized from any other whatever.

"Three miles doesn't sound far: it's no more than from here to Kensington: but I knew a man who was followed for far less by only a lion, and he swore it was longer than any walk he had ever walked before, or any ten. And only a lion, with breath and blood like himself; death perhaps, yet a death such as comes to thousands; but here was I with a terror from outside human experience, a thing against which no man had ever had to steel himself, a thing that I never knew I should one day have to face. And still I did not run.

"A change at last seemed coming over the loneliness. It wasn't merely the lights that began to shine from Lingham, nor the smoke from chimneys, the banner of man in the air; nor any warmth from the houses that could beat out as far as this: it was a certain feeling wider than warmth could go, a certain glow that one felt from the presence of man. And it was not only I that felt it: the poplars along the road were no longer watching me with quite that excited interest with which a while ago they had seemed to expect my slaughter."

"How did they show it?" said Terbut who can never leave Jorkens alone.

"If you had studied poplars for years and years," said Jorkens, "or if you had watched them as I watched them on that walk, when vast stretches of time seem condensed in one dreadful experience, you too would have been able to tell when poplars were watching you. I have seldom seen it since, and never again so as to be quite certain, but it was unmistakable then, a certain strained tensity in every leaf, twigs like the fingers of a spectre saying Hush to a village; you could not mistake it. But now the leaves were moving again in the soft evening air, the twigs seemed to be menacing nothing, and nothing about the trees was pointing or hinting or waiting; if you can use so mild a word as 'waiting' for their dreadfully strained expectancy. And better than all that, I had a hope—I could not yet call it any more— that my frightful pursuer was slowly dropping behind. And as I neared the windows the hope grew. Their mellow light, some reflecting the evening, some shining from lamps already, seemed throwing far over the marshes the influence of man. I heard a dog bark then, and, immediately after, the healthy clip clap clop of a good cart-horse, going home to his byre. The influence of these sounds on all nature can scarcely be estimated. I knew at once that there had been no revolution. I knew the animal kingdom was still supreme. I heard now unmistakably a certain hesitance come in the frightful footsteps behind me. And still I plodded on with my regular steps, whatever my pulse was doing. And now I began to hear the sound of geese and ducks, more cart-horses and now and then a boy shouting at them, and dogs joining in, and I knew I was back again within the lines of the animal kingdom; and had it not been for that terrible clod clod clod that I still heard behind me though fainter, I could have almost brought myself to disbelieve in the tree. Yes, as easily as you can, Terbut," for Jorkens saw he was about to say something, "sitting safely here." And in the end Terbut said nothing.

"When at last I reached the village the steps were far fainter, and yet I was still pursued, and only my fears could guess how far the revengeful tree would dare to penetrate into Lingham to face the arrogant mastery, and even the incredulity, of our kind. I hurried on, still without running, till I came to an inn with a good stout door. For a moment I stood and looked at it, door, roof and front wall, to satisfy myself that it could not easily be battered in, and when I saw it was really the shelter I sought, I slipped in like a rabbit.

"The brave appearance I kept up in front of the poplar dropped from me like a falling cloak, as I sat or lay on a wooden chair by a table, part of me on the table and part on the chair; till people came up and began to speak to me. But I couldn't speak. Three or four working men, in there for their glass of beer, and the landlord of the Mug of Ale, all came round me. I couldn't speak at all.

"They were very good to me. And when I found that the words would come again I said I had had an attack. I didn't say of what, as I might have blundered on to something that whiskey was bad for, and my life depended on a drink. And they gave me one. I will indeed say that for them. They gave me a tumbler of neat whiskey. I just drank it. And they gave me another. Do you know, the two glasses had no effect on me whatever. Not the very slightest. I wanted another, but before I took that there was one thing I had to be sure of. Was there anything waiting for me outside? I daren't ask straight out.

"'A nice village,' I said, lifting up my head from the table. 'Nice tree outside.'

"'No tree out there,' said one of the men.

"'No tree?' I said. 'I'll bet you five shillings there is.'

"'No,' he said, and stuck to it. He didn't even want to bet.

"'I thought I noticed something like a:' I daren't even say the word poplar, so I said 'a tree' instead. 'Just outside the door,' I added.

"'No, no tree,' he repeated.

"'I'll bet you ten shillings,' I said.

"He took that.

"'Well, go and have a look, governor,' he said.

"You don't think I was going outside that door again. So I said, 'No, you shall decide. I mayn't trust your memory against mine, but if you go outside and look, and say whether it's there or not, that's quite good enough for me.'

"He smiled and thought me a bit dotty. Oh Lord, what would he have thought me if I'd told him the bare truth.

"Well, he came back with the news that thrilled all through me, the golden glorious news that I'd lost my ten shillings. And at that I paid my bet and had my third tumbler of whiskey, which I did not dare to risk while I didn't know how things were. And that third whiskey won. It beat my misery, it beat my fatigue and my terror, and the awful suspicion which partly haunted my reason, that this unquestioned dominion that animal life believes itself to have established was possibly overthrown. It beat everything, and I dropped into a deep sleep there at the table.

"I woke next day at noon immensely refreshed, where the good fellows had laid me upstairs on a bed. I looked out over ruddy tiles; there was a yard below, with poultry, among walls of red brick, and a goat was tied up there, and a woman went out to feed him; and from beyond came all the ancient sounds of the farm, against which time can do nothing. I revelled in all these sounds of animal mastery, and felt a safety there in the light of that bright morning that somehow told me my dreadful experience was over.

"Of course you may say it was all a dream; but one doesn't remember a dream all those years like that. No, that frightful poplar had something against man, and with cause enough I'll admit.

"What it would have done if I'd run doesn't bear thinking of."

And Jorkens didn't think of it; with a cheery wave of his hand he made the sign to the waiter, that drowns memory.

How Ryan Got out of Russia

"ONCE again," said Jorkens suddenly, either in answer to some remark that I had not heard or to some fierce memory that awoke in his mind, "once again I must protest that anyone who finds anything unusual in any story that I may ever have happened to tell knows little of the stories that men do tell, daily, hourly, in fact all the time. All the twenty-four hours of every day there is someone telling some tale here in London, not to mention everywhere else, that is far less credible than anything I ever told. Then why do they single me out for what I can only call incredulity? Can you answer me that? No. And can you tell me any tale I have ever told you that has been definitely disproved in a properly scientific manner? No," he added before giving anyone very much time, not that anyone seemed ready with any case in point. "And I'll tell you what," Jorkens went on; "I'm ready to prove what I say. I'm ready to take anyone now and show him someone within a mile from here who is telling stranger tales than I've ever told, at this very minute. And if he isn't, he'll begin as soon as we ask him. As many of you as you like. Now, who'll come?"

"Very well, very well," Jorkens went on. "You'll none of you come. Then please never say, or allow anyone else to say, that I tell any more unusual tales than other people. Because I've given you an opportunity of putting it to the proof; and you won't take it. Very well. Waiter."

In another moment Jorkens would have settled down to a large whiskey; he would have soothed himself with it; he would then have slept a little: when he awoke he would have forgotten his anger, for he is never angry for long, and with his anger he would have forgotten the whole episode, including the man to whom he offered to take us. I don't say that Jorkens' tales are unusual, or that they are usual; I leave the reader to judge that; but I do say that anyone whose tales were more unusual would certainly have something to tell that was distinctly out of the way. So before Jorkens had caught the waiter's eye, before any whiskey had had time to be brought to him, I said: "That is unsporting of them, Jorkens. You have offered to prove that your stories are not unusual, as stories go. They should give you a chance to prove it. I'll come."

Jorkens looked for a moment a little regretfully in the direction of the screen at the far end of the room, behind which were the waiters, and then said: "Very well." So away we went from the Billiards Club, and soon we were in a taxi, going towards Soho, with Tutton, another member, who at the last moment came too.

I thought that even in the taxi Jorkens was regretting his whiskey, for he sat silent; but when we got to the dingy café to which he had directed the driver, a dark little place called The Universe, and we went in and he saw at once the man he was looking for, he brightened up a good deal. The man was seated alone at one of the tables eating some odd foreign dish. "Look at his forehead," said Jorkens.

"Yes," I said. "He hasn't got one."

"Well, a pair of bulging eyebrows," said Jorkens. "But no forehead. As you say. Not a man to imagine anything."

"Not in the least," I said.

"No, no," said Tutton.

"Very well," said Jorkens.

He took hold of a couple of chairs then, and dragged them up to the man's table, while I brought one for myself.

"A couple of friends," said Jorkens, "who would like to hear your tale." And all at the same moment he made a sign with one finger to a waiter whose home I would have placed as the East of Europe, though I could get no nearer than that; and the sign meant evidently absinthe, for one came. The man had not spoken yet; then he tasted the absinthe; tasted it again, to be sure it was all right; then started at once. "I was in a Russian prison," he said. "The walls were ten feet thick. And I was sentenced to death."

"Begin at the beginning," said Jorkens.

"Sentenced to die next morning, as a matter of fact," the man went on; "so there wasn't much time. And I was working on the mortar round one of the big stones with the edge of a button off my trousers."

"At the beginning," said Jorkens.

"Oh," said the man; and he looked up from his absinthe, his clipped black moustache wet with it, his eyes groping with memory. Then he started again.

"I never knew who I was spying for," he said.

"Tell them how you came to be spying," said Jorkens.

"I got into a chess-club in Paris," said the man. And he took another drink from his glass of absinthe, and it all seemed to come back to him. "It was a dark low sty of a place. I only went there twice. It was only the second time I ever went there that I looked up from the game I was playing, at one of the other tables. I was having a good enough game and getting a bit the best of it, and I turned to look at one of the other tables 'while my man was making his move, a table level with mine on the other side of the gangway, and got the shock of my life. I saw all of a sudden that one of the two players didn't know the move of the knight. He was moving it anyhow, and his opponent was taking no notice. Well, it wasn't a chess-club.

"I'd been introduced to the place by a man of whom I knew nothing. No help there. The man I was playing with was a chess-player all right, but one summer doesn't make a swallow. I glanced at a few other boards, and saw pretty much the same thing going on as I had seen at the table beside me. Chess was a blind. What did go on there? I was a long way from the door, and I felt most damnably alone."

"You've never told me, you know," said Jorkens, "what you were doing in Paris."

"Just looking round to see what would turn up," said the man.

"Oh well, go on," replied Jorkens.

He took another sip at the absinthe, and went on.

"I began looking round at the door then, and seeing how many men there were sitting between me and it. I couldn't have done anything worse. I couldn't have made myself more conspicuous if I'd made a dash for it. They followed the turn of my eyes, and all seemed to read my thoughts. And a man got

up from another table presently, and loafed my way as though
he were not coming up to me. But I knew he was. He passed
my table, but turned round at once, and spoke to me. 'Are
you one of us?' he said.

"It was no use saying Yes. You can't invent passwords. They'd
have plenty of them all right. I knew the kind of people they
were the moment I discovered what they were not.

"So I said, 'No, but I wish to be.'

"It was the only thing to do. But it let me in for a lot of oaths,
of which I can tell you nothing; with penalties attached, you
know. And I became a member, of the lowest degree, of an
association of which I still know practically nothing at all. All
I really knew of its aims was that they seemed to be to give orders
to members of the degree to which I belonged. And you had to
obey those orders. Otherwise, several unpleasant things, behind
the screen at the end of that dingy room, the far end from the
door of course, and the Seine afterwards.

"Well, I got away from that room, and I went back to Mimi.
I haven't told you about Mimi. And I said to her: 'Mimi, that
chess-club isn't a chess-club; it's something else, and I've got to
leave Paris.'

"And she said at once: 'Don't you go. People like that would
be sure to watch you. Don't let them see you trying to get away.
It's not safe.'

"And, do you know, she was right. But all I said to her was:
'People like that, Mimi? But I've not told you what they
are like.'

"And all she would say was: 'I know that type,' and went on
urging me not to try to go.

"She was right, sure enough. They were watching me. I saw
Mimi gazing out of the window next morning, and saying
nothing; just gazing, till I went up and gazed too. And there
was a man outside looking too unconcerned, looking a shade too
thoughtfully up at the sky; and I knew Mimi was right.

"So I merely stayed with Mimi. And one day the order came.
I was to go round to the chess-club that evening to receive instructions from the Grand Master. Well, I went. I had a pretty
shrewd idea as to what those instructions would be. But I went.

"Well, there he was all dressed up, at the dark end of the room;
dingy and curtained off, and a couple of candles.

" 'You will go to Russia,' he said; and before he had time to
get in another word I slipped in with what I had to say. 'Not
to assassinate anybody,' I said. I slipped in with it then because,
once he had given me my orders, there was an end of it. If I
disobeyed after that, it was the Seine, with certain accessories:
if I let him see now that I wouldn't do it for certain, there seemed
the ghost of a chance. Why put themselves to the trouble of
carrying a sack all the way to the Seine at night, I thought, if
they knew they had nothing to gain by it? It was a slender
chance. He seemed surprised, and was silent a moment. 'And
if he has already signed the death-warrants of two hundred
thousand innocent men and women?' he said.

" 'That's his affair,' I said. 'I attend to mine.'

" 'You wouldn't kill even such a man?' he said.

" 'No,' I answered.

"He was silent again; so were the others; the sort of silence
that seemed like earthquake, or any awful natural disaster; and
the sort of robes they were wearing rustled against the silence.
It was only two seconds, probably, before he spoke again.

" 'I have not commanded you to assassinate anyone,' he said.

"So it worked, my slender chance.

" 'You are to destroy something deadlier than a man,' he said.
'But perhaps your scruples won't let you hurt a machine?'

"The words sound simple, but he said them nastily enough.

" 'I obey,' I said.

" 'You will go to Russia,' he repeated. 'There is a machine in
Novarsinsk that makes certain munitions. There are only three
of them in Russia. They are the three deadliest machines in the
world. You will wreck one of them.'

"He ceased speaking. Others gave me my passport, money,
railway tickets, and a varnished walking-stick, half of which was
a steel bar. I was to break off the bar later on and secrete it in
my clothing, and drop it one day into the machine. And they
gave me a testimonial that seemed to make me out one of the
world's best experts in the handling of that particular machine,
signed by some fellow that seemed to cut a good deal of ice in
Russia; forged of course. I knew something of engineering, but
not that much.

" 'What will I do with the machine?' I asked.

"But they were busy closing down their meeting. 'You won't

be there long,' said one of them, 'before you drop the bar in.
Then you get back here as quickly as possible.' And he rather
hustled me out. He was the man that saw me off next day, by the
train across Europe. I tried to tell Mimi something about it
without giving anything away. There's a lot I haven't told you:
I told Mimi still less. And yet she seemed to guess a good deal
of it. And the odd thing was she said I'd come back all right.
Lord knows how she knew. And I remembered what she said,
through the oddest experiences, and when a thousand to one
against her being right looked like a safe bet to lay.

"Well I went all through Europe, past the German rye-fields,
silvery green; and a great many other things; but I wasn't
thinking so much of scenery, as of my chances of ever seeing it
again, coming the other way. You see, I fancied I should come
out of Russia by train, if I ever came out at all. You can waste
your time guessing how I did come out, if you like. Certainly
I never guessed it.

"Well, I arrived and showed my testimonial. It looked a good
one to me when first I saw it, but nothing to what it looked to
them: I was evidently just the one man in the world they were
waiting for; they seemed a bit short of engineers. They brought
me along to their machine; and, except that it was a machine and
needed oiling, I knew very very little about it. It was a huge
affair, as big as the engines of a small ship; and there it was
roaring away underneath me, and they looking at it as though
—well, there simply weren't any standards of comparison; they
hadn't any religion, and no king, and didn't care overmuch about
human life, so it's no use saying it was like one of their children
to them, or a god or anything else; but I saw, from the way they
looked at it, roughly what they would do to anybody that hurt it.
Well, I went round oiling it, but as that was about all I was able
to do for it, for a wage of £2000 a year, I thought the sooner
I wrecked it and cleared out the better. And so I did. Not the
clearing out; they saw to that; but the wrecking of it. I pushed
the steel bar, a foot and a half of it, in through a grating with my
forefinger at the end of it, with which I gave it a good send off;
and it went down like an arrow in amongst the great cogs of the
wheels, till a heaving piston hid it out of my sight, and it didn't
heave any more, and the roar of the engine that had been like a
huge purr changed its note suddenly. I didn't like that change

of note coming as quick as it did. I don't know what else I
expected. I see now that I might as well have tried to kill a tiger
in the Zoo with a spike, and expect that none of the keepers
would notice, as expect to smash a machine like that quietly.
Of course I was alone when I did it, but the thing began roaring
like a wounded gorilla that has been trapped in a china shop;
and the Bolshies rushed in on me. Of course I said I knew
nothing about it; and they didn't try to mob me. They said
there would have to be a trial, and they took me to prison; but
they were rather polite than otherwise. I got the idea that they
would never be able to prove anything, and that my chances were
quite good. What I was worrying mostly about was that they
might keep me a long time in prison before they had any trial,
several months perhaps; but they were in more of a hurry to
deal with me than I knew. As for my chances, the first shadow
came over them when one of the Russians came to the prison to
question me. 'You can prove nothing whatever,' I had remarked
to him.

" 'Prove things!' he answered. 'We don't waste time proving
things when we know perfectly well what has happened.'

" 'You have to in a court of law,' I said.

" 'Have to? Why?' he asked.

" 'Because you might punish an innocent man otherwise,' I
told him.

"He laughed rather a nasty laugh at that. 'And if we stopped
the course of the law for that,' he said, 'we'd stop ploughing the
steppes with our motor-tractors for fear of killing a worm.'

"I was on the point of telling him things were different in
England, and stopped myself in time and did a good deal of
thinking.

"And then the trial came on, very soon, as I said. I'd worked
out a good enough defence. Who had ever seen me with a steel
bar? How could I have concealed it? Why should I wreck a
machine that was to pay me £2000 a year? And a lot more points
besides. But somehow when I looked at them in their law-court
I got the idea that they were up to all that. And at the very last
moment I felt I must do something better.

"The charge was read out and the judge looked straight at me.
'Did you do it?' he said.

" 'Yes,' I replied, on the spur of the moment.

" 'Why?' he asked.

" 'I was compelled to, by capitalists,' I answered.

"They were interested at once. 'Of what country?' he asked me.

" 'England,' I said; and watched how the answer went down.

" 'Who gave you your orders?' asked the judge.

" 'The Archbishop of Canterbury,' I said, and saw that I had said the right thing. I didn't expect to get off scot-free, but if I could get the blame on to English capitalists I felt sure they would spare my life.

" 'Where did he give you your orders?' said the judge.

" 'At the back of his cathedral,' I answered.

"It was just right. They'd never have heard of Lambeth, and they'd have known that a secular conversation of that sort would not have gone on within the cathedral; but the shadow of its huge walls, at the back, out of the way, would have been the perfect scene for it. And they believed me too. I could see that.

" 'What were his exact words?' said the judge.

"And that was where I crashed. I had nothing prepared, and with the judge's eyes on my face I had no time to prepare it now.

" 'Those accursed Russians have a machine,' I began; but I saw from a change in their faces that it was no good. And one watches men's faces pretty closely when one's life hangs on what they are thinking about. You see, I hadn't like to blackguard them too much to their faces; but my silly politeness ruined me. I should have given them the talk that they would have expected from a prominent personage of a capitalist country, instead of mincing my words as I did. Look what they had done to religion. They would have expected the archbishop to talk pretty stiffly about them, and I was altogether too mild. So all I got for trying to spare their feelings was a death sentence. I saw they had stopped believing me; and somehow, after that, my answers were merely silly. And in a minute or two the judge took a pull at his cigarette and leaned back and looked at me, then shot the smoke out of his lungs and said two words in Russian.

" 'Tell him it's death,' I heard one of them say. And the sentry standing beside me, with a very nasty-looking bayonet fixed, took out his cigarette and said: 'It's death,' and went on with his smoking.

"They hadn't got my real name yet, and now they asked for it, just when it seemed not to matter any longer. I gave them the name of Bourk."

"And what name do you give us?" asked Jorkens.

The man thought for a moment, and then said: "Ryan."

"This is where the tale gets a little unusual," said Jorkens to us. And the man went on.

"When they took me back to the prison, I knew I hadn't got very long. The English idea on these occasions is to give a man a little time to look after his soul; but in Russia, where you don't have one, they weren't likely to keep me waiting.

"I'd looked at the stones in my prison wall pretty thoughtfully; square grey blocks that had once had plaster over them; and now I decided to work the mortar away and get one out, after which some of the others should come more easily, and see where the hole led to. I had ten buttons on my trousers; metal ones; and by bending one of them double I got some sort of a point, and I started to scrape away the mortar at once, so as not to waste time, which was precious. The mortar came easily, being old and full of damp, and presently I began to hope. I had a chair in the cell, and I kept it handy: whenever I heard the lock in my door beginning to move I slewed the chair round and sat on it, with my back to the stone I was working on. The lock didn't move often; a man came twice a day with my food, and sometimes loafed in at an odd hour, making three times in all; but on this day he came in once oftener, attracted, I suppose, by the interesting news that they had condemned me to death. I always had my chair in place by the time the key had turned, and was sitting on it before the door began to open. By nightfall I had the stone loose, and had only used two buttons, and even they were by no means finished. That night I got it out, and worked till dawn on one of the stones behind it; then I tidied up the dust, eating some of it, and put the stone back, and had some sleep for an hour or two. But I didn't want to waste much time on sleep, as I didn't know how long I'd got; and early that morning I was at work again, this time on the next stone. And I was getting along splendidly.

"They are devils. They know how to make you despair. I had never despaired in all my life before. I had held back from despair as you keep from the brink of a precipice. But those

Russians brought me to it. They must have been watching me through some spy-hole they had; for the lock turned and one of them came in, and there was I sitting comfortably in my chair with my back to the loose stones, and the bent bit of button in my pocket. And he never said a word. Just threw a hammer and a good sharp chisel down on the floor in front of me, and walked out of the cell. Then I knew that those walls must be about ten feet thick, and that nothing was any good, and I left the hammer and chisel where they had fallen and gave myself up to despair. If he had put me into a lower dungeon, or manacled me, or flogged me, I could have held out against it, but that hammer and chisel somehow or other seemed the very last notes of doom.

"The man that came in with my food just looked at the chisel, as you might take a look at a snake, just to see that I wasn't near enough to use it on him; then he left it and the hammer lying there.

"Next day I was sitting there hopeless, when in walked another fellow, a good deal neater than the rest. I looked up.

" 'Do you want a reprieve?' he said.

"But I had seen the look on his face. I don't know what I thought he was going to ask for; to betray all those people in Paris, I suppose. But the look on his face was enough, and I said: 'No thank you.'

" 'Not want a reprieve?' he asked.

" 'No, not today, thank you,' I answered.

" 'If it's not today, you'll not want it at all,' he said. 'You're for the cellar tomorrow morning.'

"And he hung about near the door, to see if I'd change my mind. But I wouldn't. I felt sure that there must be some crab in it, from the look I had seen on his face.

"Well, a little while later another man came in, as though the first hadn't come in at all.

" 'I've got a reprieve for you,' he said.

" 'What have I got to do for it?' I asked him.

" 'We want to explore a distant place; perhaps to colonize it,' he said. 'We want you to go there first, and light a fire as a sign when you get there.'

" 'What else?' I asked.

" 'Nothing else,' he said.

" 'How do I get there?' said I.

" 'We send you,' he said.

" 'Where is it?' I asked.

" 'The moon,' he replied.

" 'Nonsense,' I said.

" 'Yes, to capitalists,' he answered. 'They're all two hundred years behind Russia; and imperialism is as far as they can think. But the moon is well within the scope of our scientists.'

" 'How would you get me there?' I asked.

" 'Shoot you out of a gun,' he said.

" 'Well, there's two reasons why you couldn't do that,' I told him.

" 'Well?' he said with a superior smile.

" 'Firstly,' I said, 'the thing would smash to fragments on landing; or more likely melt.'

" 'There's a parachute that you can release from a spring inside,' he said, 'as soon as you see you're close. The head of the shell is crystal.'

" 'Well, there's another reason,' I said. 'Starting off at a thousand feet per second would merely finish one. Why, even a railway train . . .'

" 'You don't,' he said. 'You're moving at three to four hundred miles an hour when you enter the gun.'

" 'How do you manage that?' I asked.

"Always the slow superior smile, as though their scientists were all grown up and the people in other countries only children.

" 'We've rails,' he said, 'and the shell is on very low wheels. It runs on those rails over what is almost a precipice, four or five hundred feet of it, and that's how it gets its pace. The moment it enters the tunnel a steel door falls behind it. The tunnel's the gun. As in any gun, the near end, the chamber, is larger, and the powder is stacked there all round you; but when you get to the barrel it exactly fits the shell, even to a groove for the wheels. The powder is ignited behind you the moment you pass, slow-burning big blocks of black powder, slow-burning I mean when compared with modern explosives, and by the time you leave the muzzle you have your maximum speed. Is that simple enough for you?'

" 'Is the gun rifled?' I asked.

"Again the smile, as though he spoke to a child. 'Of course,' he said. 'The grooves for the wheels are twisted round the barrel.'

" 'Then the spin will addle my brains,' I said, 'and I shan't unloose any parachute.'

" 'There's a gyroscope in your cabin,' he answered.

" 'What? The outside spins, while the gyroscope holds the cabin?'

" 'Of course,' he said.

" 'And what will I breathe?' I asked.

" 'Oxygen,' he replied.

" 'And eat and drink?'

" 'We give you supplies,' said he.

" 'And how long will they last on the moon?' I asked.

" 'We'll send over more shells,' he said.

" 'Supposing one of them hits me,' I said.

" 'Very unlikely,' he answered. 'Whereas our man in the cellar was working hard all through the busy time, perhaps fifty thousand cases, and he's never missed yet.'

"I could see they were pretty keen for me to go, from that tactful reference to the swine in the cellar. Well, I wasn't keen on the cellar, and I accepted. A bit longer to live, and that was to the good, and any way I would get out of Russia.

"They released me from the prison and housed me decently; as a matter of fact there was tapestry all over the walls; but it wasn't any easier to escape; they saw to that all right. There was a court-yard all round the palace in which they kept me, and a thirty-foot wall beyond, and plenty of soldiers walking about between.

"What they were keenest on was my lighting a fire when I got there: they gave me a packet of powder to spread over a hundred yards square, and they were going to watch with their telescopes. They were keen on Russia being the first to do it, and keen on proving they had. Any Russians that they could spare they had probably killed already, so they had to send people like me. If I lit the fire they would send other men after me; if I didn't, they would send over no more provisions. They fed me well, very well indeed; in fact they seemed as fond of me as a farmer is of a good fat turkey when it is getting near Christmas. They took me out and showed me their apparatus; a huge high iron scaffold on a hill, with a lift running up it, and the rails running airily down over a flimsy viaduct, and their long steel tunnel lying along the fields, slanting very slightly upwards, just enough for the shell to clear the low hills in the West on its way to the new moon. New, you see, so that it would most of it be in darkness and they would be able to see my fire. And there was the shell all ready, waiting at the end of its rail. And they opened it and showed me my bunk inside, like the smallest berth on a boat you ever saw; barely room to turn round; a nasty place to spend ten days or a fortnight. And the gadgets they showed me too, the oxygen gas-mask for use on the moon, and the switch for releasing the parachute that was to steady the shell before landing. When it came to the switch for the parachute I pointed out that there wasn't much air on the moon. 'Not much,' said one of them, the same man that first offered me the reprieve; 'but we have evidence that there is some. Four or five hundred feet would be all you'd want for the parachute,' brushing aside lightly enough what was probably the principal drawback. I bet he'd have worried more about that air if he'd been the one that was going.

"Then we went down and had a look at the tunnel, with its steel door up in the air like a guillotine, the door that was to fall behind me the moment the shell ran in, and would close the breech of the gun. We walked in and saw the big blocks of black powder lying beside the rails and stacked round the walls, and then the sudden narrowing of the tunnel.

" 'The bigger the blocks of powder the slower they burn,' said my friend, if one can use such a word of the man who had sneeringly offered reprieve. 'The explosion gradually increases in force all the time you are in the gun.'

"I may say that that moon-shooting tunnel was over two hundred yards long.

"There seemed sense in what they told me about the gun, but I couldn't get over my fear that the lunar atmosphere would be too thin for the parachute, and that I should crash through it and melt on landing. I watched them talking among themselves in the tunnel and knew what they were saying, though I didn't know Russian: they were boasting that the U.S.S.R would do it.

" 'It's a thousand to one against getting there,' I blurted out to the man who talked English.

" 'Russia will do it,' he answered. 'Our scientists don't leave things to prayer or chance, like the people in capitalist countries. If it's a thousand to one we'll send a thousand men, and get one

there, and then a thousand more, and as many thousands as we
need to get enough there to colonize it.'

"So that was the sort of men they were.

"Well, there seemed nothing for it but to try to live as long
as I could. 'Will you give me a fortnight's holiday before I
start?' I said.

"And to my surprise they said Yes. Well, next day Eisen called
for me rather early; that's what the sneering man called himself,
the man whose reprieve I'd refused; and he said that he wanted
to show me all over the shell again, so that I should know all
about it, and that after that we'd go to a theatre, and to a
dance with some girls he knew. He talked of the girls all the way
to the high gaunt tower, and they really seemed very nice. One
in particular, he said, would be very glad to meet me: he knew
her tastes. He said this just as I got inside the shell; he had been
describing her all the way up in the lift. The moon, a little past
full, was high in the sky behind us as I got in, the long gun
pointing away from it. Eisen put his hand in and began showing
me things; then he questioned me about everything in the shell,
because he said that I had to know all about it before I went on
my holiday, and he kept on explaining about spreading the
powder on a hundred yards square on the moon. 'She's a very
pretty one, that girl,' he said all of a sudden. Then he showed
me how the door shut.

"There was a grinding of wheels at once. Lord! we were off! I
thought at first that it was an accident, but I've found that,
however easily people fool you, you find it out when you think
it over, sometimes long afterwards. Having the moon behind me
was one thing that helped to fool me. It never occurred to me
that the gun might be aiming at just where the moon would be
ten days to a fortnight later, when the shell would be due to
arrive. Well, it was a sickening feeling, dropping down the rails
from that tower. I lay there on the sort of bed, wondering when
we'd come to the tunnel. As a matter of fact I remember nothing
of that. It was all very well for them to talk of the increase of
speed being gradual, but somewhere or other in that tunnel I
must have had a jolt that was a bit too much for my brains; for
I opened my eyes feeling very sleepy indeed, and when I
remembered what had been happening and looked out through
the crystal window, there was nothing but sky in sight.

"That damned Russian had turned on the oxygen, or I

wouldn't have been alive. How many hours or days had passed
since leaving earth I had no idea, nor any idea how far we were
away from it. Nor could I see the moon. All I knew was that
I was rushing through space at the pace of a bullet, and all I felt
was the most absolute stillness, the most absolute stillness that
I have ever known; and no sound but the purr of my gyroscope
that was keeping my cabin steady while the shell rotated. No
sound of any wind or the passage of air; so I knew I was outside
Earth's atmosphere. An intolerable glitter oppressed me, a glare
still and unflickering, sunlight rushing through space unhindered
by clouds or air. I shut my eyes to escape it, but could not sleep;
and so hours went by. And then a shadow came over us that I
felt through my closed eyes, and I looked through the crystal
again, and at once the stars came out. This blessed shadow
wrapped us for half an hour, and passed away again and the
glare returned."

"What made the shadow?" I asked.

And Ryan looked up wearily from his absinthe, weary still, it
seemed, from the memory of that long journey, unsheltered in
sunlight: "Sunset," he said, "and then in half an hour it came
up on the other side. We were as far as that from Earth."

"How awful," I couldn't help saying.

"But I was out of Russia," he said. "Still I couldn't see the
moon. I didn't know where I was, or how long we'd been going.
I ate some food: I didn't know how many hours or days I had
been without it; and I drank some water, and it tasted good.
And then a curious thing happened. I'd been lying back in my
bunk, facing the way we were going, with my feet a lot higher
than my head."

"You should never sleep like that," said Jorkens.

"No," replied Ryan, "and it probably helped to keep me
unconscious much longer than I should have been otherwise.
But I don't know. But now I was sliding down more and more
to the other end, and pressing against my feet. The head of the
shell had been higher than its base, and was now evidently lower.
I drank a lot more water during the next few hours, which I
seemed to want more than food; and nothing else changed. And
then my bed seemed to be a little steeper, and I was pressing a
little harder against my feet. And suddenly through the crystal
head of the shell the weary steely glitter disappeared, and a soft

grey took its place. The relief to the eye, and the brain itself, was immense. But I had no idea where I was, or what was happening. And then sound came again, the sound of what could only be air. And the soft grey darkened. It came to me with extraordinary suddenness, and nearly too late, that it was time to use the parachute. It worked, and there was a bump that broke the end of my bed. We had landed. The first thing I did was to slip on the oxygen gas-mask, that they had given me to wear when walking about on the moon. I could see nothing at all, for most of the crystal nose of the shell was buried, and the rest of it was all blurred, with some atmospheric disturbance that looked like rain. Then I opened the door that Eisen had shut in Russia, and walked out wearing my gas-mask; and sure enough it was rain, and it splashed on my eye-pieces and dimmed them at once, and it seemed to be evening. From a soft patch of soil in which we had luckily landed I stepped at once on an expanse that I could feel rather than see to be utterly devoid of all vegetation. In fact it was exactly the sandy or gravelly waste that I had expected to find by the shore of some dried-up lunar sea. But our anticipations do not always guide us aright; for suddenly just behind me I heard the words: 'Are you aware you are trespassing?'

"Yes, it was England. England all over. And a man who couldn't have been either a Russian or an inhabitant of the moon came towards me, looking at me out of his eye-glass, along his gravel drive. My shell had landed in one of his flower-beds, and the parachute draped all over it looked like a fallen tent. Well, I'm not a lunatic. So I didn't say to him: 'I have come out of a gun in Russia, but I was looking for the moon.' No, I said: 'I'm very sorry, sir, but I'm down from London, camping; and I didn't know it was private. I'll go away at once.' He gave one disgusted look at his flower-bed, and went away with his nose in the air. You see I'd told him exactly what he'd expected, as when I told the Russians about the Archbishop of Canterbury, and there was no more for him to say. Well, I didn't like to leave that shell for the Press of the world to write about. I was none too sure I mightn't get extradited over that business of the steel bar. So I got hold of the powder that was to light up the moon, and mixed it with everything inflammable in the shell and put the oxygen canisters on top of it; and, protecting it all from the rain with the parachute, I set the whole thing alight. It made a fine glow in the sky; but they wouldn't have seen that in Russia: they were looking for it in the wrong place. And I doubt if what was left of the shell, after that, got into even the local papers. And by the evening of the next day I saw **Mimi again,** as she had told me I would."

"Now, you know, that's unusual," said Jorkens to Tutton and me. "I should say distinctly unusual."

A Mystery of the East

November had come round again, and the woods away beyond London were a glory, and London had drawn round her ancient shoulders the grey cloak she wears at this season. It was dim in the room at the club where we sat after lunch, the curtains round the one window seemed tall masses of shadow, and we were talking about the mystery of the East. It was really more than mystery we were discussing; for one who had met it in Port Said, another in Aden, a third who believed he had seen it in Kilindini, and a collector of butterflies who had met it all over India, were telling tales of pure magic. It is my object in recording tales I hear at my club to relate only those that are true so far as we know, and that seem to me to be interesting, but none of these stories of magic fulfilled either of these conditions, and I do not therefore retell them; yet I mention them because they gradually woke Jorkens, who happened to be asleep, and drew from him what is to me a very interesting statement.

"They understand magic perfectly," he asserted.

"What? Who do?" we said, startled by the vehement statement from the man that we thought was still sleeping.

"The East," said Jorkens. "I mean to say those in the East whose business it is. Just as one says that the West understands machinery. Of course you'd find millions in Europe who could not run a machine, but engineers can."

"And in the East?" I said, to keep him to the point.

"In the East," said Jorkens, "the magicians understand magic."

"Can you give us a case in point?" asked Terbut. And I'm glad he did, for one often hears of the mystery of the East, but seldom, as now, a definite story of magic, with every detail that anybody could ask for.

"Certainly I can," replied Jorkens, now wide awake.

I have little doubt that Terbut hoped, in a tale of magic, to catch Jorkens out with something he could not prove, more thoroughly than he could ever hope to catch him over some more solid tale of travel or sport. How completely he failed I leave the reader to judge.

And then Jorkens began his story.

"On a bank of the Ganges, not so long ago, I was standing looking at that pearl of a river; there flowed the water of it a yard or two from my feet, and there flowed the beauty of it right through me. It was evening, and river and sky were not only unearthly, as you might suppose, but they somehow seemed realler than earth, with a reality that all the while was growing and growing and growing. So that if ever I had left the world we know for the world of fancies and song that seems sometimes to drift so near to it, then is the time I'd have gone. But I was brought back suddenly to reality by stepping on to a man who was sitting beside the river, while my gaze was far off in the twilight. In fact I fell over him, and all light of the Ganges was gone clean out of my mind; but he still sat motionless there with his eyes as full of the beauty of river and sky as they had probably been for hours. That is, I suppose, one of the principal differences between us and people like that; we can probably appreciate the glory of such a river under that sort of sky, with the fires of the burning-ghats beginning to glow, and a young moon floating slender over their temples, we can probably appreciate it almost as well as they can; but we don't seem able to cling to it. Well, as I was saying, I was brought back to earth in every sense of the word, and there was this man, naked above the waist, sitting as though; well, there's only one way to describe it; sitting as though I had not been there at all. One of those what-d'you-call-'ems, I said to myself. And all of a sudden the idea came to test him."

"How did you do that?" asked Terbut.

"Nothing simpler," said Jorkens. "Well, in one way it wasn't so simple, because I had to explain to him what a sweepstake was, and what numbers were, in fact practically everything; and I don't suppose he really understood; but one thing I did make him understand, and that was that the number on a ticket that I showed him was the same as the number on a ticket in another part of the world, and that it was his job to make that other ticket come first out of a drum, first among millions. I got him to understand that, because he asked me why, and I told him that there was money on it. When a man starts asking questions you can nearly always make him understand, because you can see just where he has stuck, and can help him on every time. So he said that he had not the power to make the money of use to me, and I said: 'Never you mind about that.' And the rest he promised to do. The ticket with that very number should come first of all out of the drum, or there was no power in Ganges. And then he took my ticket out of my hand and held it up high in that glow of sunset and small moon and fires, and gave it back and went on with his meditation. I wanted to thank him, but it was no use whatever; his spirit was somewhere far off: I might as well have tried to talk to one of his Indian gods.

"Well, I may as well tell you that that sweepstake was to be worth £30,000; and I walked away pretty pleased, for I could see that if there is anything whatever in magic, or whatever it is that these people practise, then I was sure of the prize; he had given his word for that. Of course I still thought that there might possibly be nothing in it; but, if there was, there could be no possible doubt that he was one of them, or that he had exerted his power just as he said.

"Well, I left the Ganges next day; I left India within the week; and you may imagine I was pretty full of my chances of getting £30,000. Was there anything in the mystery of the East or was there not? That was the point. Now there was a man in the ship who knew, if anyone knew, a man called Lupton. He knew the East as well as anyone born on this side of the world is likely to know it; and, in particular, he knew about this very thing; I mean magic. Unfortunately I'd never met him, and I hardly liked to go up and beard him, he was too distinguished for that; and there was I watching him walking by me every day, and knowing that he carried the secret of my £30,000, the simple knowledge of whether or not the East could do what it claimed. Well, sooner or later on board a ship you get to know everybody, though we were into the Mediterranean before I was introduced to him; and almost the first thing I said to him was,

'Is there anything in this magic that they say they can do in the East?'

"It very nearly shut him up altogether, for he thought that I was speaking of magic lightly. But he luckily saw I was serious. I suppose he saw some light from that thirty thousand that there must have been in my eyes. For after a moment's silence, as though he were not going to answer, he turned and, speaking in a quite friendly way, said: 'You might, just as well, doubt wireless.'

"So then I asked him what I wanted to know: was it possible for a man to exert any influence in the East that could cause a ticket to come first out of a drum in Dublin? And I remember still the very words of his answer: 'It is a very rare power,' he said; 'yet not only can it be done, but I know a man now living who is able to do it.'

"Well, I asked him then about my friend by the Ganges, but he knew nothing about him. His man lived in North Africa. My man might be able to do it too, he said, but there were very few of them. There was one obvious crab in the situation, and a difficult one to deal with: why didn't he go to his African friend himself, and lift that thirty thousand? He was a distinguished man and I'd only just been introduced to him, and it wasn't too easy a question to ask. But I managed it. Of course my question was all wrapped up, but I got it out. And he answered me quite sincerely. 'I'm settling down now near London,' he said, 'on my pension and what I've put by, and I don't say that if anyone offered me thirty thousand I shouldn't be grateful to him; only, living as much in the East as I have done, one has taken a good deal of quinine in one's time, and in the end it's bad for the nerves; and if I got thirty thousand like that, out of the East by magic, I'd always be worrying as to whether the East might get level. I know it's silly of me, but there it is. You probably don't feel like that.'

" 'No, I don't think I do,' I said. I couldn't say any more, for fear of hurting his feelings. But thirty thousand, you know; and afraid that the East might try to get it back! Well, let the East try: that was all *I* felt about it. But first of all let's get it. So I said, 'What part of North Africa were you saying that this man lived in?'

"He smiled at my persistence, and told me. 'Not very far in,' he said. 'A night and half a day by train from the coast. You had better get out at El Kántara; and a few days ride on a mule from there will bring you to the Ouled Naïl Mountains, where he lives.'

" 'What part of the mountains?' I asked. For he had stopped speaking, and a mountain range seemed rather an incomplete address.

" 'Oh, there's no difficulty in finding him,' he said. 'He's a holy man, and well enough known. You merely ask one of the nomads for Hamid ben Ibrahim, when you get to the feet of the mountains. Besides, you can see his house for twenty miles. It's only ten foot high, and about eight yards broad and long; but it's white-washed, under brown mountains, and the desert is flat in front of it all the way to the Niger. You'll find Hamid all right.'

" 'They don't all do it for nothing, I suppose,' said I; 'like my friend on the Ganges.'

"You see, I hadn't very much cash in hand after my trip to India, not counting my hope of the thirty thousand pounds.

" 'No,' he said. 'But he'll do it for this.'

"And he gave me a little packet out of his pocket; a powder, as I could feel through the paper.

" 'What is it?' I said.

" 'Bismuth,' he answered. 'His digestion's bad. But he's too holy to take an aperient; never has had one in his life, or smoked; and of course brandy is out of the question. So he is rather hard to cure. As you probably know, all Europeans are held to be doctors over there; so the first thing he'll do is to tell you his symptoms and ask you to cure him; and I think bismuth may do it. If it does, he'll work that ticket for you. In fact he knows a good deal more about magic than any of us know of medicine. And you might ask the ship's doctor for anything else that might be good for him. He's pretty fat, and takes no exercise. Do what you can for the old fellow.'

" 'I certainly will,' I said. It seemed only fair.

" 'And I should buy a tent in Algiers,' he said, 'rather than hire one from an Arab. You'll find it will cost you about a quarter as much. Or an eighth. It depends how good you are at bargaining.'

"Daylight had gone while we talked, without my noticing it; and I looked up and saw bands of stars where there had been scarlet and gold. And a chill came with the stars, and Lupton's face went grey; for the chill after sunset seemed the one thing he was unable to stand, though you'd have thought the opposite, living as he had lived, more in tents than in houses. So he went below, and his last words to me were: 'He can do it all right. You need have no doubt of that.'

"Well, I troubled Lupton no more; oddly enough I rather avoided him, for any conversation we might have had would have sounded so trivial after this mystery of the East that he had revealed to me, while all those millions of stars slipped softly out to shine in the Mediterranean. And before the end of the week we came to Marseilles. Well, I got out there. If I'd gone on to England I'd only have had to come back again, in order to get to Africa; and the finances wouldn't have run to it. My only difficulty was how to get another ticket in that sweepstake, as I didn't want the two spells working on the same ticket; but, do you know, I was able to buy one from a man in Marseilles, who seemed to have lost faith in his luck. So with that I slipped across to Algiers by a line that goes backwards and forwards from Marseilles to the African coast, and cheers itself against any monotony it may find in that by calling itself the Compagnie Générale Transatlantique. I hadn't entirely lost faith in my friend by the Ganges; I had kept his ticket and wanted to see what he could do; but naturally, after having that talk with one of the foremost orientalists, I relied a great deal more on the man he had recommended me. When first I had seen the man by the Ganges it had hardly seemed possible to me that he could fail, so overpowering seemed his eyes, and so much his spirit seemed dwelling only temporarily in that body that sat by the river, and able to exert its power on one place as well as another. But now I was all under the influence of Lupton, and only wanted to find the man in the Ouled Naïl Mountains.

"Well, I bought a cheap tent in Algiers and took the train one evening, and the next afternoon I came in sight of the mountains, going up like spires from El Kántara. There I told the Arabs that I was a doctor, travelling to the desert in search of health. It was easy enough for them to believe me, for I had given proof of medical knowledge by that very remark; for, do you know, there is more health in the Sahara than in the whole length of Harley Street. But in any case it was perfectly true what Lupton had told me, that every European is credited, in those parts, with being a doctor. But I was a very special kind of doctor, and I had brought a few aperients and some extra quinine in order to prove it further. One day, with the wind in the date palms under those barren precipices, I started off on mules with three Arabs, riding south-westwards. Somehow El Kántara always reminds me of gold in iron vaults, the green mass of a thousand date-palms, these people's only wealth, and all round them rocks that have never known as much green as you sometimes see on a salt-cellar."

"You were telling us," I said, "of the man you were looking for in the Ouled Naïl Mountains."

"I beg your pardon," said Jorkens. "Yes, we were riding south-westwards. As soon as we got through the pass we were in the desert, and we rode keeping the mountains on our right. We were never far from water: old torrents that had come with storms in the mountains had scooped out hundreds of basins in all the dry ravines; and over every one you came to someone had placed a flat stone, to protect the water that lay there from being drunk up by the sun. We had an easy journey, camping whenever the mules were tired; and as we ambled past the flocks of the nomads the rumour of my skill as a doctor went on swiftly before me. Ah, those evenings in the desert, with the afterglow on the mountains; and here it's all dark and noisy and full of houses."

"You found the Ouled Naïl Mountains?" I said.

"Ah, yes," said Jorkens. "Yes, yes, of course. We kept out in the desert, and one day there was the whole range of them lying on our right. We kept out in the desert till I saw the white house. I saw it suddenly one evening. There had been no sign of anything on the mountains; and then the sun set, and far away to the north-east of us, I saw the house stand out exactly as Lupton described it, with its door and its two small windows, miles and miles away.

"I moved into the mountains to get water next day; and then I said that I had found the health that I sought and would go back to El Kántara, and we went along under the mountains, on a course that brought me close to the little house. Of course we and our mules were visible from the house on the rocks all the morning, and my reputation as a physician had arrived there long before, so that as soon as I drew near, the holy man came running out of his house, so far as a man of that shape may be said to be able to run. Well, I talked a good deal of Arabic, of a sort, and he talked a good deal of bad French, and we understood one another perfectly. Diagnosis is always a good thing in medicine, as any doctor will tell you, but it is particularly effective when you are able to do it before the patient has spoken at all. You see, I knew all about this man from Lupton. So I told him all his symptoms. And then I gave him some medicine right away, and he made some coffee for me and we sat and talked for five hours. Whether it was the medicine or the diagnosis, he was feeling better already, and when it came to offering me some fee I told him that my skill to heal was rather the result of magic than the study of medicine, and that therefore I took no fee; but that if, as some rumour among the nomads rather seemed to have indicated, he was himself a brother magician, I should be well content to be shown a little of his own magic; and I brought out the ticket I had bought in Marseilles from the man who had given up faith in it.

"He looked at the number of the ticket, and understood the whole thing at once, very unlike the man on the Ganges. Yes; he could do it. And I wouldn't have taken an offer then of twenty thousand pounds for that ticket.

"And he was right; he *could* do it. Lupton was right. There's magic in the East of which we know nothing.

"I went back to El Kántara then, back to London, third class of course all the way, and put those two tickets in a bank, and waited for the draw in the lottery."

"But wait a moment," said Terbut. "You say he *could* do it."

"Certainly," said Jorkens. "And the man by the Ganges too."

"Then you got sixty thousand pounds," said Terbut; "not only thirty."

"Well, read for yourself," said Jorkens. "I kept the cutting to this day." And he took a cutting from an Irish paper out of an old leather wallet he had. He gave it to Terbut, and Terbut read it aloud. "At the fateful moment," he read, "a hundred nurses paraded before the drum, dressed as early-Victorian bicyclists, and marched past Mr. O'Riotty, who took the salute, attended by two machine-guns. A door in the drum was then opened, and the first nurse put in her hand to bring out the fortunate number. She accidentally brought out two tickets, and Mr. O'Riotty ordered them both to be put back."

"You needn't read any further," said Jorkens.

"What?" said Terbut.

"No," replied Jorkens. "The mistake I made. The mistake I made," he repeated. "Oh, but of course it's easy to see it now."

"I see," began Terbut thoughtfully. "You think that both of them . . ."

But Jorkens only let out an impatient gasp.

"Never mind," I said. "Have a whiskey."

"A whiskey!" said Jorkens. "What is the use of that?"

The remark staggered me. It seemed to me to mark one of those changes that come suddenly in a man's life, like a milestone flashing upon a rapid traveller, and that bring to a close some period of his story. With what more momentous event could I close this book?

GODS

Pegana

The Gods of Pegana

PREFACE

THERE be islands in the Central Seas, whose waters are bounded by no shore and where no ships come—this is the faith of their people.

IN the mists before the Beginning, Fate and Chance cast lots to decide whose the Game should be; and he that won strode through the mists to MANA-YOOD-SUSHAI and said: "Now make gods for Me, for I have won the cast and the Game is to be Mine." Who it was that won the cast, and whether it was Fate or whether Chance that went through the mists before the Beginning to MANA-YOOD-SUSHAI—none knoweth.

BEFORE there stood gods upon Olympus, or ever Allah was Allah, had wrought and rested MANA-YOOD-SUSHAI.

There are in Pegana—Mung and Sish and Kib, and the maker of all small gods, who is MANA-YOOD-SUSHAI. Moreover, we have a faith in Roon and Slid.

And it has been said of old that all things that have been were wrought by the small gods, excepting only MANA-YOOD-SUSHAI, who made the gods and hath thereafter rested.

And none may pray to MANA-YOOD-SUSHAI but only to the gods whom he hath made.

But at the Last will MANA-YOOD-SUSHAI forget to rest, and will make again new gods and other worlds, and will destroy the gods whom he hath made.

And the gods and the worlds shall depart, and there shall be only MANA-YOOD-SUSHAI.

OF SKARL THE DRUMMER

WHEN MANA-YOOD-SUSHAI had made the gods and Skarl, Skarl made a drum, and began to beat upon it that he might drum for ever. Then because he was weary after the making of the gods, and because of the drumming of Skarl, did MANA-YOOD-SUSHAI grow drowsy and fall asleep.

And there fell a hush upon the gods when they saw that MANA rested, and there was silence on Pegāna save for the drumming of Skarl. Skarl sitteth upon the mist before the feet of MANA-YOOD-SUSHAI, above the gods of Pegāna, and there he beateth his drum. Some say that the Worlds and the Suns are but the echoes of the drumming of Skarl, and others say that they be dreams that arise in the mind of MANA because of the drumming of Skarl, as one may dream whose rest is troubled by sound of song, but none knoweth, for who hath heard the voice of MANA-YOOD-SUSHAI, or who hath seen his drummer?

Whether the season be winter or whether it be summer, whether it be morning among the worlds or whether it be night, Skarl still beateth his drum, for the purposes of the gods are not yet fulfilled. Sometimes the arm of Skarl grows weary; but still he beateth his drum, that the gods may do the work of the gods, and the worlds go on, for if he cease for an instant then MANA-YOOD-SUSHAI will start awake, and there will be worlds nor gods no more.

But, when at the last the arm of Skarl shall cease to beat his drum, silence shall startle Pegāna like thunder in a cave, and MANA-YOOD-SUSHAI shall cease to rest.

Then shall Skarl put his drum upon his back and walk forth into the void beyond the worlds, because it is THE END, and the work of Skarl is over.

There there may arise some other god whom Skarl may serve, or it may be that he shall perish; but to Skarl it shall matter not, for he shall have done the work of Skarl.

OF THE MAKING OF THE WORLDS

WHEN MANA-YOOD-SUSHAI had made the gods there were only the gods, and They sat in the middle of Time, for there was as much Time before them as behind them, which having no end had neither a beginning.

And Pegāna was without heat or light or sound, save for the

The Dreams of MANA-YOOD-SUSHAI

Mung and the Beast of Mung

(from "The Revolt of the Home Gods")

drumming of Skarl; moreover Pegana was The Middle of All, for there was below Pegana what there was above it, and there lay before it that which lay beyond.

Then said the gods, making the signs of the gods and speaking with Their hands lest the silence of Pegana should blush; then said the gods to one another, speaking with Their hands: "Let Us make worlds to amuse Ourselves while MANA rests. Let Us make worlds and Life and Death, and colours in the sky; only let Us not break the silence upon Pegana."

Then raising Their hands, each god according to his sign, They made the worlds and the suns, and put a light in the houses of the sky.

Then said the gods: "Let Us make one to seek, to seek and never to find out concerning the wherefore of the making of the gods."

And They made by the lifting of Their hands, each god according to his sign, the Bright One with the flaring tail to seek from the end of the Worlds to the end of them again, to return again after a hundred years.

Man, when thou seest the comet, know that another seeketh besides thee nor ever findeth out.

Then said the gods, still speaking with Their hands: "Let there be now a Watcher to regard."

And They made the Moon, with his face wrinkled with many mountains and worn with a thousand valleys, to regard with pale eyes the games of the small gods, and to watch throughout the resting time of MANA-YOOD-SUSHAI; to watch, to regard all things, and be silent.

Then said the gods: "Let Us make one to rest. One not to move among the moving. One not to seek like the comet, nor to go round like the worlds; to rest while MANA rests."

And They made the Star of the Abiding and set it in the North.

Man, when thou seest the Star of the Abiding to the North, know that one resteth as doth MANA-YOOD-SUSHAI, and know that somewhere among the Worlds is rest.

Lastly the gods said: "We have made worlds and suns, and one to seek and another to regard, let Us now make one to wonder."

And They made Earth to wonder, each god by the uplifting of his hand according to his sign.

And Earth Was.

OF THE GAME OF THE GODS

A MILLION years passed over the first game of the gods. And MANA-YOOD-SUSHAI still rested, still in the middle of Time, and the gods still played with Worlds. The Moon regarded, and the Bright One sought, and returned again to his seeking.

Then Kib grew weary of the first game of the gods, and raised his hand in Pegana, making the sign of Kib, and Earth became covered with beasts for Kib to play with.

And Kib played with beasts.

But the other gods said one to another, speaking with their hands: "What is it that Kib has done?"

And They said to Kib: "What are these things that move upon The Earth yet move not in circles like the Worlds, that regard like the Moon and yet they do not shine?"

And Kib said: "This is Life."

But the gods said one to another: "If Kib has thus made beasts he will in time make Men, and will endanger the Secret of the gods."

And Mung was jealous of the work of Kib, and sent down Death among the beasts, but could not stamp them out.

A million years passed over the second game of the gods, and still it was the Middle of Time.

And Kib grew weary of the second game, and raised his hand in The Middle of All, making the sign of Kib, and made Men: out of beasts he made them, and Earth was covered with Men.

Then the gods feared greatly for the Secret of the gods, and set a veil between Man and his ignorance that he might not understand. And Mung was busy among Men.

But when the other gods saw Kib playing his new game They came and played it too. And this They will play until MANA arise to rebuke Them, saying: *"What do ye playing with Worlds and Suns and Men and Life and Death?"* And They shall be ashamed of Their playing in the hour of the laughter of MANA-YOOD-SUSHAI.

It was Kib who first broke the Silence of Pegana, by speaking with his mouth like a man.

And all the other gods were angry with Kib that he had spoken with his mouth.

And there was no longer silence in Pegana or the Worlds.

CONCERNING SISH
(The Destroyer of Hours)

TIME is the hound of Sish.

At Sish's bidding do the hours run before him as he goeth upon his way.

Never hath Sish stepped backward nor ever hath he tarried; never hath he relented to the things that once he knew nor turned to them again.

Before Sish is Kib, and behind him goeth Mung.

Very pleasant are all things before the face of Sish, but behind him they are withered and old.

And Sish goeth ceaselessly upon his way.

Once the gods walked upon the Earth as men walk and spake with their mouths like Men. That was in Wornath-Mavai. They walk not now.

And Wornath-Mavai was a garden fairer than all the gardens upon Earth.

Kib was propitious, and Mung raised not his hand against it, neither did Sish assail it with his hours.

Wornath-Mavai lieth in a valley and looketh towards the south, and on the slopes of it Sish rested among the flowers when Sish was young.

Thence Sish went forth into the world to destroy its cities, and to provoke his hours to assail all things, and to batter against them with the rust and with the dust.

And Time, which is the hound of Sish, devoured all things; and Sish sent up the ivy and fostered weeds, and dust fell from the hand of Sish and covered stately things. Only the valley where Sish rested when he and Time were young did Sish not provoke his hours to assail.

There he restrained his old hound Time, and at its borders Mung withheld his footsteps.

Wornath-Mavai still lieth looking towards the south, a garden among gardens, and still the flowers grow about its slopes as they grew when the gods were young; and even the butterflies live in Wornath-Mavai still. For the minds of the gods relent towards their earliest memories, who relent not otherwise at all.

Wornath-Mavai still lieth looking towards the south; but if

thou shouldst ever find it thou art then more fortunate than the
gods, because they walk not in Wornath-Mavai now.

Once did the prophet think that he discerned it in the distance
beyond mountains, a garden exceeding fair with flowers; but
Sish arose, and pointed with his hand, and set his hound to
pursue him, who hath followed ever since.

Time is the hound of the gods; but it hath been said of old
that he will one day turn upon his masters, and seek to slay the
gods, excepting only MANA-YOOD-SUSHAI, whose dreams are the
gods themselves—dreamed long ago.

THE DEEDS OF MUNG
(Lord of all Deaths between Pegana and the Rim)

ONCE, as Mung went his way athwart the Earth and up and
down its cities and across its plains, Mung came upon a man who
was afraid when Mung said: "I am Mung!"

And Mung said: "Were the forty million years before thy
coming intolerable to thee?"

And Mung said: "Not less tolerable to thee shall be the forty
million years to come!"

Then Mung made against him the sign of Mung and the Life
of the Man was fettered no longer with hands and feet.

At the end of the flight of the arrow there is Mung, and in
the houses and the cities of Men. Mung walketh in all places
at all times. But mostly he loves to walk in the dark and still,
along the river mists when the wind hath sank, a little before
night meeteth with the morning upon the highway between
Pegana and the Worlds.

Sometimes Mung entereth the poor man's cottage; Mung
also boweth very low before The King. Then do the Lives of
the poor man and of The King go forth among the Worlds.

And Mung said: "Many turnings hath the road that Kib hath
given every man to tread upon the earth. Behind one of these
turnings sitteth Mung."

One day as a man trod upon the road that Kib had given him
to tread he came suddenly upon Mung. And when Mung said:
"I am Mung!" the man cried out: "Alas, that I took this road,
for had I gone by any other way then had I not met with Mung."

And Mung said: "Had it been possible for thee to go by any
other way then had the Scheme of Things been otherwise and

the gods had been other gods. When MANA-YOOD-SUSHAI forgets
to rest and makes again new gods it may be that They will send
thee again into the Worlds; and then thou mayest choose some
other way, and so not meet with Mung."

Then Mung made the sign of Mung. And the Life of that man
went forth with yesterday's regrets and all old sorrows and
forgotten things—whither Mung knoweth.

And Mung went onward with his work to sunder Life from
flesh, and Mung came upon a man who became stricken with
sorrow when he saw the shadow of Mung. But Mung said:
"When at the sign of Mung thy Life shall float away there will
also disappear thy sorrow at forsaking it." But the man cried
out: "O Mung! tarry for a little, and make not the sign of Mung
against me *now*, for I have a family upon the Earth with whom
sorrow will remain, though mine should disappear because of
the sign of Mung."

And Mung said: "With the gods it is always Now. And before
Sish hath banished many of the years the sorrows of thy family
for thee shall go the way of thine." And the man beheld Mung
making the sign of Mung before his eyes, which beheld things
no more.

THE REVOLT OF THE HOME GODS

THERE be three broad rivers of the plain, born before memory
or fable, whose mothers are three grey peaks and whose father
was the storm. Their names be Eimes, Zanes, and Segástrion.

And Eimes is the joy of lowing herds; and Zanes hath bowed
his neck to the yoke of man, and carries the timber from the
forest far up below the mountain; and Segástrion sings old songs
to shepherd boys, singing of his childhood in a low ravine and
of how he once sprang down the mountain sides and far away
into the plain to see the world, and of how one day at last he will
find the sea. These be the rivers of the plain, wherein the plain
rejoices. But old men tell, whose fathers heard it from the
ancients, how once the lords of the three rivers of the plain
rebelled against the law of the Worlds, and passed beyond their
boundaries, and joined together and whelmed cities and slew
men, saying: "We now play the game of the gods and slay men
for our pleasure, and we be greater than the gods of Pegana."

And all the plain was flooded to the hills.

And Eimes, Zanes, and Segástrion sat upon the mountains, and spread their hands over their rivers that rebelled by their command.

But the prayer of men going upward found Pegana, and cried in the ear of the gods: "There be three home gods who slay us for Their pleasure, and say that they be mightier than Pegana's gods, and play Their game with men."

Then were all the gods of Pegana very wroth; but They could not whelm the lords of the three rivers, because being home gods, though small, they were immortal.

And still the home gods spread their hands across their rivers, with their fingers wide apart, and the waters rose and rose, and the voice of their torrent grew louder, crying: "Are we not Eimes, Zanes and Segástrion?"

Then Mung went down into a waste of Afrik, and came upon the drought Umbool as he sat in the desert upon iron rocks, clawing with miserly grasp at the bones of men and breathing hot.

And Mung stood before him as his dry sides heaved, and ever as they sank his hot breath blasted dead sticks and bones.

Then Mung said: "Friend of Mung! go thou and grin before the faces of Eimes, Zanes, and Segástrion till they see whether it be wise to rebel against the gods of Pegana."

And Umbool answered: "I am the beast of Mung."

And Umbool came and crouched upon a hill upon the other side of the waters and grinned across them at the rebellious home gods.

And whenever Eimes, Zanes, and Segástrion stretched out their hands over their rivers they saw before their faces the grinning of Umbool; and because the grinning was like death in a hot and hideous land therefore they turned away and spread their hands no more over their rivers, and the waters sank and sank.

But when Umbool had grinned for thirty days the waters fell back into the river beds and the lords of the rivers slunk away back again to their homes: still Umbool sat and grinned.

Then Eimes sought to hide himself in a great pool beneath a rock, and Zanes crept into the middle of a wood, and Segástrion lay and panted on the sand—still Umbool sat and grinned.

And Eimes grew lean, and was forgotten, so that the men of the plain would say: "Here once was Eimes"; and Zanes scarce had strength to lead his river to the sea; and as Segástrion lay and panted, a man stepped over his stream, and Segástrion said:

"It is the foot of a man that has passed across my neck, and I have sought to be greater than the gods of Pegana."

Then said the gods of Pegana: "It is enough. We are the gods of Pegana, and none are equal."

Then Mung sent Umbool back to his waste in Afrik to breathe again upon the rocks, and parch the desert, and to sear the memory of Afrik into the brains of all who ever bring their bones away.

And Eimes, Zanes, and Segástrion sang again, and walked once more in their accustomed haunts, and played the game of Life and Death with fishes and frogs, but never essayed to play it any more with men, as do the gods of Pegana.

OF THE THING THAT IS NEITHER GOD NOR BEAST

SEEING that wisdom is not in cities nor happiness in wisdom, and because Yadin the prophet was doomed by the gods, ere he was born, to go in search of wisdom, he followed the caravans to Bodraháhn. There in the evening, when the camels rest, when the wind of the day ebbs out into the desert sighing amid the palms its last farewells and leaving the caravans still, he sent his prayer with the wind to drift into the desert calling to Hoodrazai.

And down the wind his prayer went calling: "Why do the gods endure, and play their game with men? Why doth not Skarl forsake his drumming, and MANA cease to rest?" and the echo of seven deserts answered: "Who knows? Who knows?"

But out of the waste beyond the seven deserts where Ranorada looms enormous in the dusk, at evening his prayer was heard; and from the rim of the waste whither had gone his prayer, came three flamingoes flying, and their voices said: "Going South, Going South" at every stroke of their wings.

But as they passed by the prophet they seemed so cool and free and the desert so blinding and hot that he stretched up his arms towards them. Then it seemed happy to fly and pleasant to follow behind great white wings, and he was with the three flamingoes up in the cool above the desert, and their voices cried before him: "Going South, Going South," and the desert below him mumbled: "Who knows? Who knows?"

Sometimes the earth stretched up towards them with peaks of mountains, sometimes it fell away in steep ravines, blue rivers sang to them as they passed above them, or very faintly came the song of breezes in lone orchards, and far away the sea sang mighty dirges of old forsaken isles. But it seemed that in all the world there was nothing only to be going South.

It seemed that somewhere the South was calling to her own, and that they were going South.

But when the prophet saw that they had passed above the edge of Earth, and that far away to the North of them lay the Moon, he perceived that he was following no mortal birds but some strange messengers of Hoodrazai whose nest had lain in one of Pegana's vales below the mountains whereon sit the gods.

Still they went South, passing by all the Worlds and leaving them to the North, till only Araxes, Zadres, and Hyráglion lay still to the South of them, where great Ingazi seemed only a point of light, and Yo and Mindo could be seen no more.

Still they went South till they passed below the South and came to the Rim of the Worlds.

There there is neither South nor East nor West, but only North and Beyond: there is only North of it where lie the Worlds, and Beyond it where lies the Silence; and the Rim is a mass of rocks that were never used by the gods when They made the Worlds, and on it sat Trogool. Trogool is the Thing that is neither god nor beast, who neither howls nor breathes, only IT turns over the leaves of a great book, black and white, black and white for ever until THE END.

And all that is to be is written in the book, as also all that was.

When IT turneth a black page it is night, and when IT turneth a white page it is day.

Because it is written that there are gods—there are the gods.

Also there is writing about thee and me until the page where our names no more are written.

Then as the prophet watched IT, Trogool turned a page— a black one, and night was over, and day shone on the Worlds.

Trogool is the Thing that men in many countries have called by many names, IT is the Thing that sits behind the gods, whose book is the Scheme of Things.

But when Yadin saw that old remembered days were hidden away with the part that IT had turned, and knew that upon one whose name is writ no more the last page had turned for ever a thousand pages back, then did he utter his prayer in the face of Trogool who only turns the pages and never answers prayer.

"It"

The Ship of Yoharneth-Lanai
(*from "The River"*)

He prayed in the face of Trogool: "Only turn back thy pages to the name of one which is writ no more, and far away upon a place named Earth shall rise the prayers of a little people that acclaim the name of Trogool, for there is indeed far off a place called Earth where men shall pray to Trogool."

Then spake Trogool who turns the pages and never answers prayer, and his voice was like the murmurs of the waste at night when echoes have been lost: "Though the whirlwind of the South should tug with his claws at a page that hath been turned yet shall he not be able ever to turn it back."

Then because of words in the book that said that it should be so, Yadin found himself lying in the desert where one gave him water, and afterwards carried him on a camel into Bodraháhn.

There some said that he had but dreamed when thirst had seized him while he wandered among the rocks in the desert. But certain aged men of Bodraháhn say that indeed there sitteth somewhere a Thing that is called Trogool, that is neither god nor beast, that turneth the leaves of a book, black and white, black and white, until he come to the words: MAI DOON IZAHN, which means The End For Ever, and book and gods and worlds shall be no more.

KABOK THE PROPHET

WHEN Alhireth-Hotep was among the Things that Were, and still men sought to know, they said unto Kabok: "Be thou as wise as was Alhireth-Hotep."

And Kabok grew wise in his own sight and in the sight of men.

And Kabok said: "Mung maketh his sign against men or withholdeth it by the advice of Kabok."

And he said unto one: "Thou hast sinned against Kabok, therefore will Mung make the sign of Mung against thee." And to another: "Thou hast brought Kabok gifts, therefore shall Mung forbear to make against thee the sign of Mung."

One night as Kabok fattened upon the gifts that men had brought him he heard the tread of Mung treading in the garden of Kabok about his house at night.

And because the night was very still it seemed most evil to Kabok that Mung should be treading in his garden, without the advice of Kabok, about his house at night.

And Kabok, who knew All Things, grew afraid, for the treading was very loud and the night still, and he knew not what lay behind the back of Mung, which none had ever seen.

But when the morning grew to brightness, and there was light upon the Worlds, and Mung trod no longer in the garden, Kabok forgot his fears, and said: "Perhaps it was but a herd of cattle that stampeded in the garden of Kabok."

And Kabok went about his business, which was that of knowing All Things, and telling All Things unto men, and making light of Mung.

But that night Mung trod again in the garden of Kabok, about his house at night, and stood before the window of the house like a shadow standing erect, so that Kabok knew indeed that it was Mung.

And a great fear fell upon the throat of Kabok, so that his speech was hoarse; and he cried out: "Thou art Mung!"

And Mung slightly inclined his head, and went on to tread in the garden of Kabok, about his house at night.

And Kabok lay and listened with horror at his heart.

But when the second morning grew to brightness, and there was light upon the Worlds, Mung went from treading in the garden of Kabok; and for a little while Kabok hoped, but looked with great dread for the coming of the third night.

And when the third night was come, and the bat had gone to his home, and the wind had sunk, the night was very still.

And Kabok lay and listened, to whom the wings of the night flew very slow.

But, ere night met the morning upon the highway between Pegana and the Worlds, there came the tread of Mung in the garden of Kabok towards Kabok's door.

And Kabok fled out of his house as flees a hunted beast and flung himself before Mung.

And Mung made the sign of Mung, pointing towards The End.

And the fears of Kabok had rest from troubling Kabok any more, for they and he were among accomplished things.

OF HOW IMBAUN BECAME HIGH PROPHET IN ARADEC OF ALL THE GODS SAVE ONE

IMBAUN was to be made High Prophet in Aradec, of All the gods save One.

From Ardra, Rhoodra, and the lands beyond came all High

Prophets of the Earth to the Temple in Aradec of All the gods save One.

And there they told Imbaun how The Secret of Things was upon the summit of the dome of the Hall of Night, but faintly writ, and in an unknown tongue.

Midway in the night, between the setting and the rising sun, they led Imbaun into the Hall of Night, and said to him, chaunting all together: "Imbaun, Imbaun, Imbaun, look up to the roof, where is writ The Secret of Things, but faintly, and in an unknown tongue."

And Imbaun looked up, but darkness was so deep within the Hall of Night that Imbaun saw not even the High Prophets who came from Ardra, Rhoodra, and the lands beyond, nor saw he aught in the Hall of Night at all.

Then called the High Prophets: "What seest thou, Imbaun?"

And Imbaun said: "I see naught."

Then called the High Prophets: "What knowest thou, Imbaun?"

And Imbaun said: "I know naught."

Then spake the High Prophet of Eld of All the gods save One, who is first on Earth of prophets: "O Imbaun! we have all looked upwards in the Hall of Night towards the Secret of Things, and ever it was dark, and the secret faint and in an unknown tongue. And know thou knowest what all High Priests know."

And Imbaun answered: "I know."

So Imbaun became High Prophet in Aradec of All the gods save One, and prayed for all the people, who knew not that there was darkness in the Hall of Night or that the secret was writ faint and in an unknown tongue.

These are the words of Imbaun that he wrote in a book that all the people might know:

"In the twentieth night of the nine hundredth moon, as night came up the valley, I performed the mystic rites of each of the gods in the temple as is my wont, lest any of the gods should grow angry in the night and whelm us while we slept.

"And as I uttered the last of certain secret words I fell asleep in the temple, for I was weary, with my head against the altar or Dorozhand. Then in the stillness, as I slept, there entered Dorozhand by the temple door in the guise of a man, and touched me on the shoulder, and I awoke.

"But when I saw that his eyes shone blue and lit the whole

of the temple I knew that he was a god though he came in mortal guise. And Dorozhand said: 'Prophet of Dorozhand, behold! that the people may know.' And he showed me the paths of Sish stretching far down into the future time.

"Then he bade me arise and follow whither he pointed, speaking no words but commanding with his eyes.

"Therefore upon the twentieth night of the nine hundredth moon I walked with Dorozhand adown the paths of Sish into the future time.

"And ever beside the way did men slay men. And the sum of their slaying was greater than the slaying of the pestilence or any of the evils of the gods.

"And cities arose and shed their houses in dust, and ever the desert returned again to its own, and covered over and hid the last of all that had troubled its repose.

"And still men slew men.

"And I came at last to a time when men set their yoke no longer upon beasts but made them beasts of iron.

"And after that did men slay men with mists.

"Then, because the slaying exceeded their desire, there came peace upon the world that was brought by the hand of the slayer, and men slew men no more.

"And cities multiplied, and overthrew the desert and conquered its repose.

"And suddenly I beheld that THE END was near, for there was a stirring above Pegana as of One who grows weary of resting, and I saw the hound Time crouch to spring, with his eyes upon the throats of the gods, shifting from throat to throat, and the drumming of Skarl grew faint.

"And if a god may fear, it seemed that there was fear upon the face of Dorozhand, and he seized me by the hand and led me back along the paths of Time that I might not see THE END.

"Then I saw cities rise out of the dust again and fall back into the desert whence they had arisen; and again I slept in the Temple of All the gods save One, with my head against the altar of Dorozhand.

"Then again the Temple was alight, but not with light from the eyes of Dorozhand; only dawn came all blue out of the East and shone through the arches of the Temple. Then I awoke and performed the morning rites and mysteries of All the gods save One, lest any of the gods be angry in the day and take away the Sun.

"And I knew that because I who had been so near to it had not beheld THE END a man should never behold it or know the doom of the gods. This They have hidden."

OF HOW IMBAUN SPAKE OF DEATH TO THE KING

THERE trod such pestilence in Aradec that the King as he looked abroad out of his palace saw men die. And when the King saw death he feared that one day even the King should die. Therefore he commanded guards to bring before him the wisest prophet that should be found in Aradec.

Then heralds came to the temple of All the gods save One, and cried aloud, having first commanded silence, crying: "Rhazahan, King over Aradec, Prince by right of Ildun and Ildaun, and Prince by conquest of Pathia, Ezek, and Azhan, Lord of the Hills, to the High Prophet of All the gods save One sends salutations."

Then they bore him before the King.

The King said unto the prophet: "O Prophet of All the gods save One, shall I indeed die?"

And the prophet answered: "O King! thy people may not rejoice for ever, and some day the King will die."

And the King answered: "This may be so, but certainly *thou* shalt die. It may be that one day I shall die, but till then the lives of the people are in my hands."

Then guards led the prophet away.

And there arose prophets in Aradec who spake not of death to Kings.

OF OOD

MEN say that if thou comest to Sundári, beyond all the plains, and shalt climb to his summit before thou art seized by the avalanche which sitteth always on his slopes, then there lie before thee many peaks. And if thou shalt climb these and cross their valleys (of which there be seven and also seven peaks) thou shalt come at last to the land of forgotten hills, where amid many valleys and white snow there standeth the "Great Temple of One God Only."

Therein is a dreaming prophet who doeth naught, and a drowsy priesthood about him.

These be the priests of MANA-YOOD-SUSHAI. Within the temple it is forbidden to work, also it is forbidden to pray. Night differeth not from day within its doors. They rest as MANA rests. And the name of their prophet is Ood.

Ood is a greater prophet than any of all the prophets of Earth, and it hath been said by some that were Ood and his priests to pray, chaunting all together and calling upon MANA-YOOD-SUSHAI, MANA-YOOD-SUSHAI would then awake, for surely he would hear the prayers of his own prophet—then would there be Worlds no more.

There is also another way to the land of forgotten hills, which is a smooth road and a straight, that lies through the heart of the mountains. But for certain hidden reasons it were better for thee to go by the peaks and snow, even though thou shouldst perish by the way, than that thou shouldst seek to come to the home of Ood by the smooth, straight road.

THE RIVER

THERE arises a river in Pegana that is neither a river of water nor yet a river of fire, and it flows through the skies and the Worlds to the Rim of the Worlds,—a river of silence. Through all the Worlds are sounds, the noises of moving, and the echoes of voices and song; but upon the River is no sound ever heard, for there all echoes die.

The River arises out of the drumming of Skarl, and flows for ever between banks of thunder, until it comes to the waste beyond the Worlds, behind the farthest star, down to the Sea of Silence.

I lay in the desert beyond all cities and sounds, and above me flowed the River of Silence through the sky; and on the desert's edge night fought against the Sun, and suddenly conquered.

Then on the River I saw the dream-built ship of the God Yoharneth-Lahai, whose great prow lifted grey into the air above the River of Silence.

Her timbers were olden dreams dreamed long ago, and poets' fancies made her tall, straight masts, and her rigging was wrought out of the people's hopes.

Upon her deck were rowers with dream-made oars, and the

rowers were the people of men's fancies, and princes of old story and people who had died, and people who had never been.

These swung forward and swung back to row Yoharneth-Lahai through the Worlds with never a sound of rowing. For ever on every wind float up to Pegana the hopes and the fancies of the people which have no home in the Worlds, and there Yoharneth-Lahai weaves them into dreams, to take them to the people again.

And every night in his dream-built ship Yoharneth-Lahai setteth forth, with all his dreams on board, to take again their old hopes back to the people and all forgotten fancies.

But ere the day comes back to her own again, and all the conquering armies of the dawn hurl their red lances in the face of night, Yoharneth-Lahai leaves the sleeping Worlds, and rows back up the River of Silence, that flows from Pegana into the Sea of Silence that lies beyond the Worlds.

And the name of the River is Imrana, the River of Silence. All they that be weary of the sound of cities and very tired of clamour creep down in the night-time to Yoharneth-Lahai's ship, and going aboard it, lie down upon the deck, and pass from sleeping to the River, while Mung, behind them, makes the sign of Mung because they would have it so. And, lying there upon the deck among their own remembered fancies, and songs that were never sung, they drift up Imrana ere the dawn, where the sound of the cities comes not, nor the voice of the thunder is heard, nor the midnight howl of Pain as he gnaws at the bodies of men, and far away and forgotten bleat the small sorrows that trouble all the Worlds.

But where the River flows through Pegana's gates, between the great twin constellations Yum and Gothum, where Yum stands sentinel upon the left and Gothum upon the right, there sits Sirami, the lord of All Forgetting. And, when the ship draws near, Sirami looketh with his sapphire eyes into the faces and beyond them of those that were weary of cities, and as he gazes, as one that looketh before him remembering naught, he gently waves his hands. And amid the waving of Sirami's hands there fall from all that behold him all their memories, save certain things that may not be forgot even beyond the Worlds.

It hath been said that when Skarl ceases to drum, and MANA-YOOD-SUSHAI awakes, and the gods of Pegana know that it is THE END, then the gods will enter galleons of gold, and with dream-born rowers glide down Imrana (who knows whither or why?) till they come where the River enters the Silent Sea, and shall there be gods of nothing, where nothing is, and never a sound shall come. And far away upon the River's banks shall bay their old hound Time, that shall seek to rend his masters; while MANA-YOOD-SUSHAI shall think some other plan concerning gods and worlds.

THE BIRD OF DOOM AND THE END

FOR at the last shall the thunder, fleeing to escape from the doom of the gods, roar horribly among the Worlds; and Time, the hounds of the gods, shall bay hungrily at his masters because he is lean with age.

And from the innermost of Pegana's vales shall the bird of doom, Mosahn, whose voice is like the trumpet, soar upward with boisterous beatings of his wings above Pegana's mountains and the gods, and there with his trumpet voice acclaim THE END.

Then in the tumult and amid the fury of Their hound the gods shall make for the last time in Pegana the sign of all the gods, and go with dignity and quiet down to Their galleons of gold, and sail away down the River of Silence, not ever to return.

Then shall the River overflow its banks, and a tide come setting in from the Silent Sea, till all the Worlds and the Skies are drowned in Silence; while MANA-YOOD-SUSHAI in the Middle of All sits deep in thought. And the hound Time, when all the Worlds and cities are swept away whereon he used to raven, having no more to devour shall suddenly die.

But there are some that hold—and this is the heresy of the Saigoths—that when the gods go down at the last into their galleons of gold Mung shall turn alone, and, setting his back against Trehágobol and wielding the Sword of Severing which is called Death, shall fight out his last fight with the hound Time, his empty scabbard Sleep clattering loose beside him.

There under Trehágobol they shall fight alone when all the gods are gone.

And the Saigoths say that for two days and nights the hound shall leer and snarl before the face of Mung—days and nights that shall be lit by neither sun nor moons, for these shall go dipping down the sky with all the Worlds as the galleons glide away, because the gods that made them are gods no more.

And then shall the hound, springing, tear out the throat of Mung, who, making for the last time the sign of Mung, shall bring down Death crashing through the shoulders of the hound, and in the blood of Time that Sword shall rust away.

Then shall MANA-YOOD-SUSHAI be all alone, with neither Death nor Time, and never the hours singing in his ears, nor the swish of the passing lives.

But far away from Pegana shall go the galleons of gold that bear the gods away, upon whose faces shall be utter calm, because They are the gods knowing that it is THE END.

Time and the Gods

ONCE when the gods were young and only Their swarthy servant Time was without age, the gods lay sleeping by a broad river upon earth. There in a valley that from all the earth the gods had set apart for Their repose the gods dreamed marble dreams. And with domes and pinnacles the dreams arose and stood up proudly between the river and the sky, all shimmering white to the morning. In the city's midst the gleaming marble of a thousand steps climbed to the citadel where arose four pinnacles beckoning to heaven, and midmost between the pinnacles there stood the dome, vast, as the gods had dreamed it. All around, terrace by terrace, there went marble lawns well guarded by onyx lions and carved with effigies of all the gods striding amid the symbols of the worlds. With a sound like tinkling bells, far off in a land of shepherds hidden by some hill, the waters of many fountains turned again home. Then the gods awoke and there stood Sardathrion. Not to common men have the gods given to walk Sardathrion's streets, and not to common eyes to see her fountains. Only to those to whom in lonely passes in the night the gods have spoken, leaning through the stars, to those that have heard the voices of the gods above the morning or seen Their faces bending above the sea, only to those hath it been given to see Sardathrion, to stand where her pinnacles gathered together in the night fresh from the dreams of gods. For round the valley a great desert lies through which no common traveller may come, but those whom the gods have chosen feel suddenly a great longing at heart, and crossing the mountains that divide the desert from the world, set out across it driven by the gods, till hidden in the desert's midst they find the valley at last and look with eyes upon Sardathrion.

In the desert beyond the valley grow a myriad thorns, and all pointing towards Sardathrion. So may many that the gods have loved come to the marble city, but none can return, for other cities are no fitting home for men whose feet have touched Sardathrion's marble streets, where even the gods have not been ashamed to come in the guise of men with Their cloaks wrapped about Their faces. Therefore no city shall ever hear the songs that are sung in the marble citadel by those in whose ears have rung the voices of the gods. No report shall ever come to other lands of the music of the fall of Sardathrion's fountains, when the waters which went heavenward return again into the lake where the gods cool Their brows sometimes in the guise of men. None may ever hear the speech of the poets of that city, to whom the gods have spoken.

It stands a city aloof. There hath been no rumour of it—I alone have dreamed of it, and I may not be sure that my dreams are true.

Above the Twilight the gods were seated in the after years, ruling the worlds. No longer now They walked at evening in the Marble City hearing the fountains splash, or listening to the singing of the men they loved, because it was in the after years and the work of the gods was to be done.

But often as they rested a moment from doing the work of the gods, from hearing the prayers of men or sending here the Pestilence or there Mercy, They would speak awhile with one another of the olden years saying, "Rememberest thou not Sardathrion?" and another would answer "Ah! Sardathrion, and all Sardathrion's mist-draped marble lawns whereon we walk not now."

Then the gods turned to do the work of the gods, answering the prayers of men or smiting them, and ever They sent Their swarthy servant Time to heal or overwhelm. And Time went forth into the worlds to obey the commands of the gods, yet he cast furtive glances at his masters, and the gods distrusted Time because he had known the worlds or ever the gods became.

One day when furtive Time had gone into the worlds to nimbly smite some city whereof the gods were weary, the gods above the Twilight speaking to one another said:

"Surely we are the lords of Time and gods of the worlds besides. See how our city Sardathrion lifts over other cities. Others arise and perish but Sardathrion standeth yet, the first and the last of cities. Rivers are lost in the sea and streams forsake the hills, but ever Sardathrion's fountains arise in our dream city. As was Sardathrion when the gods were young, so are her streets to-day as a sign that we are the gods."

Suddenly the swart figure of Time stood up before the gods, with both hands dripping with blood and a red sword dangling idly from his fingers, and said:

"Sardathrion is gone! I have overthrown it!"

And the gods said:

"Sardathrion? Sardathrion, the marble city? Thou, thou hast overthrown it? Thou, the slave of the gods?"

And the oldest of the gods said:

"Sardathrion, Sardathrion, and is Sardathrion gone?"

And furtively Time looked him in the face and edged towards him fingering with his dripping fingers the hilt of his nimble sword.

Then the gods feared with a new fear that he that had overthrown Their city would one day slay the gods. And a new cry went wailing through the Twilight, the lament of the gods for Their dream city, crying:

"Tears may not bring again Sardathrion.

"But this the gods may do who have seen, and seen with unrelenting eyes, the sorrows of ten thousand worlds—thy gods may weep for thee.

"Tears may not bring again Sardathrion.

"Believe it not, Sardathrion, that ever thy gods sent this doom to thee; he that hath overthrown thee shall overthrow thy gods.

"How oft when Night came suddenly on Morning playing in the fields of Twilight did we watch thy pinnacles emerging from the darkness, Sardathrion, Sardathrion, dream city of the gods, and thine onyx lions looming limb by limb from the dusk.

"How often have we sent our child the Dawn to play with thy fountain tops; how often hath Evening, loveliest of our goddesses, strayed long upon thy balconies.

"Let one fragment of thy marbles stand up above the dust for thine old gods to caress, as a man when all else is lost treasures one lock of the hair of his beloved.

"Sardathrion, the gods must kiss once more the place where thy streets were once.

"There were wonderful marbles in thy streets, Sardathrion.

"Sardathrion, Sardathrion, the gods weep for thee."

The Coming of the Sea

ONCE there was no sea, and the gods went walking over the green plains of earth.

Upon an evening of the forgotten years the gods were seated on the hills, and all the little rivers of the world lay coiled at Their feet asleep, when Slid, the new god, striding through the stars, came suddenly upon earth lying in a corner of space. And behind Slid there marched a million waves, all following Slid and tramping up the twilight; and Slid touched earth in one of her great green valleys that divide the south, and here he encamped for the night with all his waves about him. But to the gods as They sat upon Their hilltops a new cry came crying over the green spaces that lay below the hills, and the gods said:

"This is neither the cry of life nor yet the whisper of death. What is this new cry that the gods have never commanded, yet which comes to the ears of the gods?"

And the gods together shouting made the cry of the south calling the south wind to them. And again the gods shouted all together making the cry of the north, calling the north wind to Them; and thus They gathered to Them all Their winds and sent these four down into the low plains to find what thing it was that called with the new cry, and to drive it away from the gods.

Then all the winds harnessed up their clouds and drave forth till they came to the great green valley that divides the south in twain, and there found Slid with all his waves about him. Then for a great space Slid and the four winds struggled with one another till the strength of the winds was gone, and they limped back to the gods, their masters, and said:

Slid

The Tomb of Morning Zai
(*from "The Secret of the Gods"*)

"We have met this new thing that has come upon the earth and have striven against its armies, but could not drive them forth; and the new thing is beautiful but very angry, and is creeping towards the gods."

But Slid advanced and led his armies up the valley, and inch by inch and mile by mile he conquered the lands of the gods. Then from Their hills the gods sent down a great array of cliffs of hard, red rocks, and bade them march against Slid. And the cliffs marched down till they came and stood before Slid and leaned their heads forward and frowned and stood staunch to guard the lands of the gods against the might of the sea, shutting Slid off from the world. Then Slid sent some of his smaller waves to search out what stood against him, and the cliffs shattered them. But Slid went back and gathered together a hoard of his greatest waves and hurled them against the cliffs, and the cliffs shattered them. And again Slid called up out of his deep a mighty array of waves and sent them roaring against the guardians of the gods, and the red rocks frowned and smote them. And once again Slid gathered his greater waves and hurled them against the cliffs; and when the waves were scattered like those before them the feet of the cliffs were no longer standing firm, and their faces were scarred and battered. Then into every cleft that stood in the rocks Slid sent his hugest wave and others followed behind it, and Slid himself seized hold of huge rocks with his claws and tore them down and stamped them under his feet. And when the tumult was over the sea had won, and over the broken remnants of those red cliffs the armies of Slid marched on and up the long green valley.

Then the gods heard Slid exulting far away and singing songs of triumph over Their battered cliffs, and ever the tramp of his armies sounded nearer and nearer in the listening ears of the gods.

Then the gods called to Their downlands to save Their world from Slid, and the downlands gathered themselves together and marched away, a great white line of gleaming cliffs, and halted before Slid. Then Slid advanced no more and lulled his legions, and while his waves were low he softly crooned a song such as once long ago had troubled the stars and brought down tears out of the twilight.

Sternly the white cliffs stood on guard to save the world of the gods, but the song that once had troubled the stars went moaning on awaking pent desires, till full at the feet of the gods the melody fell. Then the blue rivers that lay curled asleep opened their gleaming eyes, uncurled themselves and shook their rushes, and, making a stir among the hills, crept down to find the sea. And passing across the world they came at last to where the white cliffs stood, and, coming behind them, split them here and there and went through their broken ranks to Slid at last. And the gods were angry with Their traitorous streams.

Then Slid ceased from singing the song that lures the world, and gathered up his legions, and the rivers lifted up their heads with the waves, and all went marching on to assail the cliffs of the gods. And wherever the rivers had broken the ranks of the cliffs, Slid's armies went surging in and broke them up into islands and shattered the islands away. And the gods on Their hill-tops heard once more the voice of Slid exulting over Their cliffs.

Already more than half the world lay subject to Slid, and still his armies advanced; and the people of Slid, the fishes and the long eels, went in and out of arbours that once were dear to the gods. Then the gods feared for Their dominion, and to the innermost sacred recesses of the mountains, to the very heart of the hills, the gods trooped off together and there found Tintaggon, a mountain of black marble, staring far over the earth, and spake thus to him with the voices of the gods:

"O eldest born of our mountains, when first we devised the earth we made thee, and thereafter fashioned fields and hollows, valleys and other hills, to lie about thy feet. And now, Tintaggon, thine ancient lords, the gods, are facing a new thing which overthrows the old. Go therefore, thou, Tintaggon, and stand up against Slid, that the gods be still the gods and the earth still green."

And hearing the voices of his sires, the elder gods, Tintaggon strode down through the evening, leaving a wake of twilight broad behind him as he strode: and going across the green earth came down to Ambrady at the valley's edge, and there met the foremost of Slid's fierce armies conquering the world.

And against him Slid hurled the force of a whole bay, which lashed itself high over Tintaggon's knees and streamed around his flanks and then fell and was lost. Tintaggon still stood firm for the honour and dominion of his lords, the elder gods. Then

Slid went to Tintaggon and said: "Let us now make a truce. Stand thou back from Ambrady and let me pass through thy ranks that mine armies may now pass up the valley which opens on the world, that the green earth that dreams around the feet of older gods shall know the new god Slid. Then shall mine armies strive with thee no more, and thou and I shall be the equal lords of the whole earth when all the world is singing the chaunt of Slid, and thy head alone shall be lifted above mine armies when rival hills are dead. And I will deck thee with all the robes of the sea, and all the plunder that I have taken in rare cities shall be piled before thy feet. Tintaggon, I have conquered all the stars, my song swells through all the space besides, I come victorious from Mahn and Khanagat on the furthest edge of the worlds, and thou and I are to be equal lords when the old gods are gone and the green earth knoweth Slid. Behold me gleaming azure and fair with a thousand smiles, and swayed by a thousand moods." And Tintaggon answered: "I am staunch and black and have one mood, and this—to defend my masters and their green earth."

Then Slid went backward growling and summoned together the waves of a whole sea and sent them singing full in Tintaggon's face. Then from Tintaggon's marble front the sea fell backwards crying on to a broken shore, and ripple by ripple straggled back to Slid saying: "Tintaggon stands."

Far out beyond the battered shore that lay at Tintaggon's feet Slid rested long and sent the nautilus to drift up and down before Tintaggon's eyes, and he and his armies sat singing idle songs of dreamy islands far away to the south, and of the still stars whence they had stolen forth, of twilight evenings and of long ago. Still Tintaggon stood with his feet planted fair upon the valley's edge defending the gods and Their green earth against the sea.

And all the while that Slid sang his songs and played with the nautilus that sailed up and down he gathered his oceans together. One morning as Slid sang of old outrageous wars and of most enchanting peace and of dreamy islands and the south wind and the sun, he suddenly launched five oceans out of the deep all to attack Tintaggon. And the five oceans sprang upon Tintaggon and passed above his head. One by one the grip of the oceans loosened, one by one they fell back into the deep and still

Tintaggon stood, and on that morning the might of all five
oceans lay dead at Tintaggon's feet.

That which Slid had conquered he still held, and there is now
no longer a great green valley in the south, but all that Tintaggon
had guarded against Slid he gave back to the gods. Very calm
the sea lies now about Tintaggon's feet, where he stands all
black amid crumbled cliffs of white, with red rocks piled about
his feet. And often the sea retreats far out along the shore, and
often wave by wave comes marching in with the sound of the
tramping of armies, that all may still remember the great fight
that surged about Tintaggon once, when he guarded the gods and
the green earth against Slid.

Sometimes in their dreams the war-scarred warriors of Slid still
lift their heads and cry their battle cry; then do dark clouds
gather about Tintaggon's swarthy brow and he stands out
menacing, seen afar by the ships, where once he conquered Slid.
And the gods know well that while Tintaggon stands They and
Their world are safe; and whether Slid shall one day smite
Tintaggon is hidden among the secrets of the sea.

The Secret of the Gods

ZYNI MOË, the small snake, saw the cool river gleaming before
him afar off and set out over the burning sand to reach it.

Uldoon, the prophet, came out of the desert and followed up
the bank of the river towards his old home. Thirty years since
Uldoon had left the city, where he was born, to live his life in a
silent place where he might search for the Secret of the gods. The
name of his home was the City by the River, and in that city
many prophets taught concerning many gods, and men made
many secrets for themselves, but all the while none knew the
Secret of the gods. Nor might any seek to find it, for if any
sought men said of him:

"This man sins, for he giveth no worship to the gods that
speak to our prophets by starlight when none heareth."

And Uldoon perceived that the mind of a man is as a garden,
and that his thoughts are as the flowers, and the prophets of a
man's city are as many gardeners who weed and trim, and who
have made in the garden paths both smooth and straight, and
only along these paths is a man's soul permitted to go lest the
gardeners say, "This soul transgresseth." And from the paths
the gardeners weed out every flower that grows, and in the
garden they cut off all flowers that grow tall, saying:

"It is customary," and "it is written," and "this hath ever
been," or "that hath not been before."

Therefore Uldoon saw that not in that city might he discover
the Secret of the gods. And Uldoon said to the people:

"When the worlds began, the Secret of the gods lay written
clear over the whole earth, but the feet of many prophets have

trampled it out. Your prophets are all true men, but I go into the desert to find a truth which is truer than your prophets." Therefore Uldoon went into the desert and in storm and still he sought for many years. When the thunder roared over the mountains that limited the desert he sought the Secret in the thunder, but the gods spake not by the thunder. When the voices of the beasts disturbed the stillness under the stars he sought the Secret there, but the gods spake not by the beasts. Uldoon grew old and all the voices of the desert had spoken to Uldoon, but not the gods, when one night he heard Them whispering beyond the hills. And the gods whispered one to another, and turning Their faces earthward They all wept. And Uldoon though he saw not the gods yet saw Their shadows turn as They went back to a great hollow in the hills; and there, all standing in the valley's mouth, They said:

"Oh, Morning Zai, oh, oldest of the gods, the faith of thee is gone, and yesterday for the last time thy name was spoken upon earth." And turning earthward they all wept again. And the gods tore white clouds out of the sky and draped them about the body of Morning Zai and bore him forth from his valley behind the hills, and muffled the mountain peaks with snow, and beat upon their summits with drum sticks carved of ebony, playing the dirge of the gods. And the echoes rolled about the passes and the winds howled, because the faith of the olden days was gone, and with it had sped the soul of Morning Zai. So through the mountain passes the gods came at night bearing Their dead father. And Uldoon followed. And the gods came to a great sepulchre of onyx that stood upon four fluted pillars of white marble, each carved out of four mountains, and therein the gods laid Morning Zai because the old faith was fallen. And there at the tomb of Their father the gods spake and Uldoon heard the Secret of the gods, and it became to him a simple thing such as a man might well guess—yet hath not. Then the soul of the desert arose and cast over the tomb its wreath of forgetfulness devised of drifting sand, and the gods strode home across the mountains to Their hollow land. But Uldoon left the desert and travelled many days, and so came to the river where it passes beyond the city to seek the sea, and following its bank came near to his old home. And the people of the City by the River, seeing him far off, cried out:

"Hast thou found the Secret of the gods?"

And he answered:

"I have found it, and the Secret of the gods is this"—:

Zyni Moë, the small snake, seeing the figure and the shadow of a man between him and the cool river, raised his head and struck once. And the gods are pleased with Zyni Moë, and have called him the protector of the Secret of the gods.

In the Land of Time

THUS Karnith, King of Alatta, spake to his eldest son: "I bequeath to thee my City of Zoon, with its golden eaves, whereunder hum the bees. And I bequeath to thee also the land of Alatta, and all such other lands as thou art worthy to possess, for my three strong armies which I leave thee may well take Zindara and over-run Istahn, and drive back Onin from his frontier, and leaguer the walls of Yan, and beyond that spread conquest over the lesser lands of Hebith, Ebnon, and Karida. Only lead not thine armies against Zeenar, nor ever cross the Eidis."

Thereat in the city of Zoon in the land of Alatta, under his golden eaves, died King Karnith, and his soul went whither had gone the souls of his sires the elder Kings, and the souls of their slaves.

Then Karnith Zo, the new King, took the iron crown of Alatta and afterwards went down to the plains that encircle Zoon and found his three strong armies clamouring to be led against Zeenar, over the river Eidis.

But the new King came back from his armies, and all one night in the great palace alone with his iron crown, pondered long upon war; and a little before dawn he saw dimly through his palace window, facing east over the city of Zoon and across the fields of Alatta, to far off where a valley opened on Istahn. There, as he pondered, he saw the smoke arising tall and straight over small houses in the plain and the fields where the sheep fed. Later the sun rose shining over Alatta as it shone over Istahn, and there arose a stir about the houses both in Alatta and Istahn, and cocks crowed in the city and men went out into the fields among the bleating sheep; and the King wondered if men did otherwise in Istahn. And men and women met as they went out to work and the sound of laughter arose from streets and fields; the King's eyes gazed into the distance toward Istahn and still the smoke went upwards tall and straight from the small houses. And the sun rose higher that shone upon Alatta and Istahn, causing the flowers to open wide in each, and the birds to sing and the voices of men and women to arise. And in the market place of Zoon caravans were astir that set out to carry merchandise to Istahn, and afterwards passed camels coming to Alatta with many tinkling bells. All this the King saw as he pondered much, who had not pondered before. Westward the Agnid mountains frowned in the distance guarding the river Eidis; behind them the fierce people of Zeenar lived in a bleak land.

Later the King, going abroad through his new kingdom, came on the Temple of the gods of Old. There he found the roof shattered and the marble columns broken and tall weeds met together in the inner shrine, and the gods of Old, bereft of worship or sacrifice, neglected and forgotten. And the King asked of his councillors who it was that had overturned this temple of the gods or caused the gods Themselves to be thus forsaken. And they answered him:

"Time has done this."

Next the King came upon a man bent and crippled, whose face was furrowed and worn, and the King having seen no such sight within the court of his father said to the man:

"Who hath done this thing to you?"

And the old man answered:

"Time has ruthlessly done it."

But the King and his councillors went on, and next they came upon a body of men carrying among them a hearse. And the King asked his councillors closely concerning death, for these things had not before been expounded to the King. And the oldest of the councillors answered:

"Death, O King, is a gift sent by the gods by the hand of their servant Time, and some receive it gladly, and some are forced reluctantly to take it, and before others it is suddenly flung in the middle of the day. And with this gift that Time hath brought him from the gods a man must go forth into the dark to possess no other thing for so long as the gods are willing."

But the King went back to his palace and gathered the greatest of his prophets and his councillors and asked them more particularly concerning Time. And they told the King how that Time was a great figure standing like a tall shadow in the dusk or striding, unseen, across the world, and how that he was the slave of the gods and did Their bidding, but ever chose new masters, and how all the former masters of Time were dead and Their shrines forgotten. And one said:

"I have seen him once when I went down to play again in the garden of my childhood because of certain memories. And it was towards evening and the light was pale, and I saw Time standing over the little gate, pale like the light, and he stood between me and that garden and had stolen my memories of it because he was mightier than I."

And another said:

"I, too, have seen the Enemy of my House. For I saw him when he strode over the fields that I knew well and led a stranger by the hand to place him in my home to sit where my forefathers sat. And I saw him afterwards walk thrice round the house and stoop and gather up the glamour from the lawns and brush aside the tall poppies in the garden and spread weeds in his pathway where he strode through the remembered nooks."

And another said:

"He went one day into the desert and brought up life out of the waste places, and made it cry bitterly and covered it with the desert again."

And another said:

"I too saw him once seated in the garden of a child tearing the flowers, and afterwards he went away through many woodlands and stooped down as he went, and picked the leaves one by one from the trees."

And another said:

"I saw him once by moonlight standing tall and black amidst the ruins of a shrine in the old kingdom of Amarna, doing a deed by night. And he wore a look on his face such as murderers wear as he busied himself to cover over something with weeds and dust. Thereafter in Amarna the people of that old Kingdom missed their god, in whose shrine I saw Time crouching in the night, and they have not since beheld him."

And all the while from the distance at the city's edge rose a hum from the three armies of the King clamouring to be led against Zeenar. Thereat the King went down to his three armies and speaking to their chiefs said:

"I will not go down clad with murder to be King over other lands. I have seen the same morning arising on Istahn that also gladdened Alatta, and have heard Peace lowing among the flowers. I will not desolate homes to rule over an orphaned land and a land widowed. But I will lead you against the pledged enemy of Alatta who shall crumble the towers of Zoon and hath gone far to overthrow our gods. He is the foe of Zindara and Istahn and many-citadeled Yan, Hebith and Ebnon may not overcome him nor Karida be safe against him among her bleakest mountains. He is a foe mightier than Zeenar with frontiers stronger than the Eidis; he leers at all the peoples of the earth and mocks their gods and covets their builded cities. Therefore we will go forth and conquer Time and save the gods of Alatta from his clutch, and coming back victorious shall find that Death is gone and age and illness departed, and here we shall live for ever by the golden eaves of Zoon, while the bees hum among unrusted gables and never crumbling towers. There shall be neither fading nor forgetting, nor ever dying nor sorrow, when we shall have freed the people and pleasant fields of the earth from inexorable Time."

And the armies swore that they would follow the King to save the world and the gods.

So the next day the King set forth with his three armies and crossed many rivers and marched through many lands, and wherever they went they asked for news of Time.

And the first day they met a woman with her face furrowed and lined, who told them that she had been beautiful and that Time had smitten her in the face with his five claws.

Many an old man they met as they marched in search of Time. All had seen him but none could tell them more, except that some said he went that way and pointed to a ruined tower or to an old and broken tree.

And day after day and month by month the King pushed on with his armies, hoping to come at last on Time. Sometimes they encamped at night near palaces of beautiful design or beside gardens of flowers, hoping to find their enemy when he came to desecrate in the dark. Sometimes they came on cobwebs, sometimes on rusted chains and houses with broken roofs or crumbling walls. Then the armies would push on apace thinking that they were closer upon the track of Time.

As the weeks passed by and weeks grew to months, and always they heard reports and rumours of Time, but never found him, the armies grew weary of the great march, but the King pushed on and would let none turn back, saying always that the enemy was near at hand.

Month in, month out, the King led on his now unwilling armies, till at last they had marched for close upon a year and came to the village of Astarma very far to the north. There many of the King's weary soldiers deserted from his armies and settled down in Astarma and married Astarmian girls. By these soldiers we have the march of the armies clearly chronicled to the time when they came to Astarma, having been nigh a year upon the march. And the army left that village and the children cheered them as they went up the street, and five miles distant they passed over a ridge of hills and out of sight. Beyond this less is known, but the rest of this chronicle is gathered from the tales that the veterans of the King's armies used to tell in the evenings about the fires in Zoon and remembered afterwards by the men of Zeenar.

It is mostly credited in these days that such of the King's armies as went on past Astarma came at last (it is not known after how long a time) over a crest of a slope where the whole earth slanted green to the north. Below it lay green fields and beyond them moaned the sea with never shore nor island so far as the eye could reach. Among the green fields lay a village, and on this village the eyes of the King and his armies were turned as they came down the slope. It lay beneath them, grave with seared antiquity, with old-world gables stained and bent by the lapse of frequent years, with all its chimneys awry. Its roofs were tiled with antique stones covered over deep with moss, each little window looked with a myriad strange cut panes on the gardens shaped with quaint devices and overrun with weeds. On rusted hinges the doors swung to and fro and were fashioned of planks of immemorial oak with black knots gaping from their sockets. Against it all there beat the thistle-down, about it clambered the ivy or swayed the weeds; tall and straight out of the twisted chimneys arose blue columns of smoke, and blades of grass peeped upward between the huge cobbles of the unmolested street. Between the gardens and the cobbled street stood hedges higher than a horseman might look, of stalwart thorn, and upward through it clambered the convolvulus to peer into the garden from the top. Before each house there was cut a gap in the hedge, and in it swung a wicket gate of timber soft with the rain and years, and green like the moss. Over all of it there brooded age and the full hush of things bygone and forgotten. Upon this derelict that the years had cast up out of antiquity the King and his armies gazed long. Then on the hill slope the King made his armies halt, and went down alone with one of his chiefs into the village.

Presently there was a stir in one of the houses, and a bat flew out of the door into the daylight, and three mice came running out of the doorway down the step, an old stone cracked in two and held together by moss; and there followed an old man bending on a stick with a white beard coming to the ground, wearing clothes that were glossed with use, and presently there came others out of the other houses, all of them as old, and all hobbling on sticks. These were the oldest people that the King had ever beheld, and he asked them the name of the village and who they were; and one of them answered: "This is the City of the Aged in the Territory of Time."

And the King said, "Is Time then here?"

And one of the old men pointed to a great castle standing on a steep hill and said: "Therein dwells Time, and we are his people;" and they all looked curiously at King Karnith Zo, and the eldest of the villagers spoke again and said: "Whence do you come, you that are so young?" and Karnith Zo told him how he had come to conquer Time to save the world and the gods, and asked them whence they came.

And the villagers said:

"We are older than always, and know not whence we came, but we are the people of Time, and here from the Edge of Everything he sends out his hours to assail the world, and you may never conquer Time." But the King went back to his armies, and pointed toward the castle on the hill and told them that at last they had found the Enemy of the Earth; and they that were older than always went back slowly into their houses with the creaking of olden doors. And they went across the fields and passed the village. From one of his towers Time eyed them all the while, and in battle order they closed in on the steep hill as Time sat still in his great tower and watched.

But as the feet of the foremost touched the edge of the hill Time hurled five years against them, and the years passed over their heads and the army still came on, an army of older men. But the slope seemed steeper to the King and to every man in his army, and they breathed more heavily. And Time summoned up more years, and one by one he hurled them at Karnith Zo and at all his men. And the knees of the army stiffened, and their beards grew and turned grey, and the hours and days and the months went singing over their heads, and their hair turned whiter and whiter, and the conquering hours bore down, and the years rushed on and swept the youth of that army clear away till they came face to face under the walls of the castle of Time with a mass of howling years, and found the top of the slope too steep for aged men. Slowly and painfully, harassed with agues and chills, the King rallied his aged army that tottered down the slope.

Slowly the King led back his warriors over whose heads had shrieked the triumphant years. Year in, year out, they straggled southwards, always toward Zoon; they came, with rust upon their spears and long beards flowing, again into Astarma, and none knew them there. They passed again by towns and villages where once they had inquired curiously concerning Time, and none knew them there either. They came again to the palaces and gardens where they had waited for Time in the night, and found that Time had been there. And all the while they set a hope before them that they should come on Zoon again and see its golden eaves. And no one knew that unperceived behind them there lurked and followed the gaunt figure of Time cutting off stragglers one by one and overwhelming them with his hours, only men were missed from the army every day, and fewer and fewer grew the veterans of Karnith Zo.

But at last after many a month, one night as they marched in the dusk before the morning, dawn suddenly ascending shone on the eaves of Zoon, and a great cry ran through the army:

"Alatta, Alatta!"

But drawing nearer they found that the gates were rusted and weeds grew tall along the outer walls, many a roof had fallen, gables were blackened and bent, and the golden eaves shone not as heretofore. And the soldiers entering the city expecting to find their sisters and sweethearts of a few years ago saw only old women wrinkled with great age and knew not who they were.

Suddenly someone said:

"He has been here too."

And then they knew that while they searched for Time, Time had gone forth against their city and leaguered it with the years, and had taken it while they were far away and enslaved their women and children with the yoke of age. So all that remained of the three armies of Karnith Zo settled in the conquered city. And presently the men of Zeenar crossed over the river Eidis and easily conquering an army of aged men took all Alatta for themselves, and their kings reigned thereafter in the city of Zoon. And sometimes the men of Zeenar listened to the strange tales that the old Alattans told of the years when they made battle against Time. Such of these tales as the men of Zeenar remembered they afterwards set forth, and this is all that may be told of those adventurous armies that went to war with Time to save the world and the gods, and were overwhelmed by the hours and the years.

Sources

"The Gods of Pegana." From *The Gods of Pegana,* John W. Luce, Boston, [n.d.; 1st ed. was 1905]. This is a selection of material. Individual sections, however, have not been abridged.

"Time and the Gods," "The Coming of the Sea," "The Secret of the Gods" and "In the Land of Time." From *Time and the Gods,* John W. Luce and Co., Boston, 1913 [1st ed. was 1906].

"The Ghosts," "The Sword of Welleran" and "The Fortress Unvanquishable, Save For Sacnoth." From *The Sword of Welleran and Other Stories,* George Allen & Sons, London, 1908.

"Poor Old Bill," "Bethmoora," "Idle Days on the Yann" and "The Hashish Man." From *A Dreamer's Tales,* John W. Luce and Co., Boston, [1910].

"The Wonderful Window," "The Probable Adventure of the Three Literary Men," "The Coronation of Mr. Thomas Shap," "The Hoard of the Gibbelins," "How Nuth Would Have Practised His Art upon the Gnoles," "Chu-bu and Sheemish," "The Distressing Tale of Thangobrind the Jeweller, and of the Doom That Befell Him" and "The Injudicious Prayers of Pombo the Idolater." From *The Book of Wonder, A Chronicle of Little Adventures at the Edge of the World,* John W. Luce and Co., Boston, 1913 [1st ed. was 1912].

"The Three Sailors' Gambit," "The Three Infernal Jokes," "The Exiles' Club," "Thirteen at Table," "The Bureau d'Echange de Maux," "A Story of Land and Sea," "How Plash-

Goo Came to the Land of None's Desire" and "A Narrow Escape." From *Tales of Wonder*, Elkin Mathews, London, 1920 [1st ed. was 1916].

"The Walk to Lingham," "How Ryan Got out of Russia" and "A Mystery of the East." From *Jorkens Remembers Africa*, Longmans, Green & Co., New York, 1934.

"The Sign," "The Neapolitan Ice" and "Jorkens Consults a Prophet." From *Jorkens Has a Large Whiskey*, Putnams, New York and London. [1940].

A CATALOGUE OF SELECTED DOVER BOOKS
IN ALL FIELDS OF INTEREST

A CATALOGUE OF SELECTED DOVER BOOKS
IN ALL FIELDS OF INTEREST

AMERICA'S OLD MASTERS, James T. Flexner. Four men emerged unexpectedly from provincial 18th century America to leadership in European art: Benjamin West, J. S. Copley, C. R. Peale, Gilbert Stuart. Brilliant coverage of lives and contributions. Revised, 1967 edition. 69 plates. 365pp. of text.
21806-6 Paperbound $3.00

FIRST FLOWERS OF OUR WILDERNESS: AMERICAN PAINTING, THE COLONIAL PERIOD, James T. Flexner. Painters, and regional painting traditions from earliest Colonial times up to the emergence of Copley, West and Peale Sr., Foster, Gustavus Hesselius, Feke, John Smibert and many anonymous painters in the primitive manner. Engaging presentation, with 162 illustrations. xxii + 368pp.
22180-6 Paperbound $3.50

THE LIGHT OF DISTANT SKIES: AMERICAN PAINTING, 1760-1835, James T. Flexner. The great generation of early American painters goes to Europe to learn and to teach: West, Copley, Gilbert Stuart and others. Allston, Trumbull, Morse; also contemporary American painters—primitives, derivatives, academics—who remained in America. 102 illustrations. xiii + 306pp.
22179-2 Paperbound $3.00

A HISTORY OF THE RISE AND PROGRESS OF THE ARTS OF DESIGN IN THE UNITED STATES, William Dunlap. Much the richest mine of information on early American painters, sculptors, architects, engravers, miniaturists, etc. The only source of information for scores of artists, the major primary source for many others. Unabridged reprint of rare original 1834 edition, with new introduction by James T. Flexner, and 394 new illustrations. Edited by Rita Weiss. 6⅝ x 9⅝.
21695-0, 21696-9, 21697-7 Three volumes, Paperbound $13.50

EPOCHS OF CHINESE AND JAPANESE ART, Ernest F. Fenollosa. From primitive Chinese art to the 20th century, thorough history, explanation of every important art period and form, including Japanese woodcuts; main stress on China and Japan, but Tibet, Korea also included. Still unexcelled for its detailed, rich coverage of cultural background, aesthetic elements, diffusion studies, particularly of the historical period. 2nd, 1913 edition. 242 illustrations. lii + 439pp. of text.
20364-6, 20365-4 Two volumes, Paperbound $6.00

THE GENTLE ART OF MAKING ENEMIES, James A. M. Whistler. Greatest wit of his day deflates Oscar Wilde, Ruskin, Swinburne; strikes back at inane critics, exhibitions, art journalism; aesthetics of impressionist revolution in most striking form. Highly readable classic by great painter. Reproduction of edition designed by Whistler. Introduction by Alfred Werner. xxxvi + 334pp.
21875-9 Paperbound $2.50

VISUAL ILLUSIONS: THEIR CAUSES, CHARACTERISTICS, AND APPLICATIONS, Matthew Luckiesh. Thorough description and discussion of optical illusion, geometric and perspective, particularly; size and shape distortions, illusions of color, of motion; natural illusions; use of illusion in art and magic, industry, etc. Most useful today with op art, also for classical art. Scores of effects illustrated. Introduction by William H. Ittleson. 100 illustrations. xxi + 252pp.

21530-X Paperbound $2.00

A HANDBOOK OF ANATOMY FOR ART STUDENTS, Arthur Thomson. Thorough, virtually exhaustive coverage of skeletal structure, musculature, etc. Full text, supplemented by anatomical diagrams and drawings and by photographs of undraped figures. Unique in its comparison of male and female forms, pointing out differences of contour, texture, form. 211 figures, 40 drawings, 86 photographs. xx + 459pp. 5⅜ x 8⅜.

21163-0 Paperbound $3.50

150 MASTERPIECES OF DRAWING, Selected by Anthony Toney. Full page reproductions of drawings from the early 16th to the end of the 18th century, all beautifully reproduced: Rembrandt, Michelangelo, Dürer, Fragonard, Urs, Graf, Wouwerman, many others. First-rate browsing book, model book for artists. xviii + 150pp. 8⅜ x 11¼.

21032-4 Paperbound $2.50

THE LATER WORK OF AUBREY BEARDSLEY, Aubrey Beardsley. Exotic, erotic, ironic masterpieces in full maturity: Comedy Ballet, Venus and Tannhauser, Pierrot, Lysistrata, Rape of the Lock, Savoy material, Ali Baba, Volpone, etc. This material revolutionized the art world, and is still powerful, fresh, brilliant. With *The Early Work,* all Beardsley's finest work. 174 plates, 2 in color. xiv + 176pp. 8⅛ x 11.

21817-1 Paperbound $3.00

DRAWINGS OF REMBRANDT, Rembrandt van Rijn. Complete reproduction of fabulously rare edition by Lippmann and Hofstede de Groot, completely reedited, updated, improved by Prof. Seymour Slive, Fogg Museum. Portraits, Biblical sketches, landscapes, Oriental types, nudes, episodes from classical mythology—All Rembrandt's fertile genius. Also selection of drawings by his pupils and followers. "Stunning volumes," *Saturday Review.* 550 illustrations. lxxviii + 552pp. 9⅛ x 12¼.

21485-0, 21486-9 Two volumes, Paperbound $7.00

THE DISASTERS OF WAR, Francisco Goya. One of the masterpieces of Western civilization—83 etchings that record Goya's shattering, bitter reaction to the Napoleonic war that swept through Spain after the insurrection of 1808 and to war in general. Reprint of the first edition, with three additional plates from Boston's Museum of Fine Arts. All plates facsimile size. Introduction by Philip Hofer, Fogg Museum. v + 97pp. 9⅜ x 8¼.

21872-4 Paperbound $2.00

GRAPHIC WORKS OF ODILON REDON. Largest collection of Redon's graphic works ever assembled: 172 lithographs, 28 etchings and engravings, 9 drawings. These include some of his most famous works. All the plates from *Odilon Redon: oeuvre graphique complet,* plus additional plates. New introduction and caption translations by Alfred Werner. 209 illustrations. xxvii + 209pp. 9⅛ x 12¼.

21966-8 Paperbound $4.00

DESIGN BY ACCIDENT; A BOOK OF "ACCIDENTAL EFFECTS" FOR ARTISTS AND DESIGNERS, James F. O'Brien. Create your own unique, striking, imaginative effects by "controlled accident" interaction of materials: paints and lacquers, oil and water based paints, splatter, crackling materials, shatter, similar items. Everything you do will be different; first book on this limitless art, so useful to both fine artist and commercial artist. Full instructions. 192 plates showing "accidents," 8 in color. viii + 215pp. 8⅜ x 11¼.   21942-9 Paperbound $3.50

THE BOOK OF SIGNS, Rudolf Koch. Famed German type designer draws 493 beautiful symbols: religious, mystical, alchemical, imperial, property marks, runes, etc. Remarkable fusion of traditional and modern. Good for suggestions of timelessness, smartness, modernity. Text. vi + 104pp. 6⅛ x 9¼.
                    20162-7 Paperbound $1.25

HISTORY OF INDIAN AND INDONESIAN ART, Ananda K. Coomaraswamy. An unabridged republication of one of the finest books by a great scholar in Eastern art. Rich in descriptive material, history, social backgrounds; Sunga reliefs, Rajput paintings, Gupta temples, Burmese frescoes, textiles, jewelry, sculpture, etc. 400 photos. viii + 423pp. 6⅜ x 9¾.   21436-2 Paperbound $4.00

PRIMITIVE ART, Franz Boas. America's foremost anthropologist surveys textiles, ceramics, woodcarving, basketry, metalwork, etc.; patterns, technology, creation of symbols, style origins. All areas of world, but very full on Northwest Coast Indians. More than 350 illustrations of baskets, boxes, totem poles, weapons, etc. 378 pp.
                    20025-6 Paperbound $3.00

THE GENTLEMAN AND CABINET MAKER'S DIRECTOR, Thomas Chippendale. Full reprint (third edition, 1762) of most influential furniture book of all time, by master cabinetmaker. 200 plates, illustrating chairs, sofas, mirrors, tables, cabinets, plus 24 photographs of surviving pieces. Biographical introduction by N. Bienenstock. vi + 249pp. 9⅞ x 12¾.   21601-2 Paperbound $4.00

AMERICAN ANTIQUE FURNITURE, Edgar G. Miller, Jr. The basic coverage of all American furniture before 1840. Individual chapters cover type of furniture—clocks, tables, sideboards, etc.—chronologically, with inexhaustible wealth of data. More than 2100 photographs, all identified, commented on. Essential to all early American collectors. Introduction by H. E. Keyes. vi + 1106pp. 7⅞ x 10¾.
                21599-7, 21600-4 Two volumes, Paperbound $11.00

PENNSYLVANIA DUTCH AMERICAN FOLK ART, Henry J. Kauffman. 279 photos, 28 drawings of tulipware, Fraktur script, painted tinware, toys, flowered furniture, quilts, samplers, hex signs, house interiors, etc. Full descriptive text. Excellent for tourist, rewarding for designer, collector. Map. 146pp. 7⅞ x 10¾.
                    21205-X Paperbound $2.50

EARLY NEW ENGLAND GRAVESTONE RUBBINGS, Edmund V. Gillon, Jr. 43 photographs, 226 carefully reproduced rubbings show heavily symbolic, sometimes macabre early gravestones, up to early 19th century. Remarkable early American primitive art, occasionally strikingly beautiful; always powerful. Text. xxvi + 207pp. 8⅜ x 11¼.   21380-3 Paperbound $3.50

ALPHABETS AND ORNAMENTS, Ernst Lehner. Well-known pictorial source for decorative alphabets, script examples, cartouches, frames, decorative title pages, calligraphic initials, borders, similar material. 14th to 19th century, mostly European. Useful in almost any graphic arts designing, varied styles. 750 illustrations. 256pp. 7 x 10.   21905-4 Paperbound $4.00

PAINTING: A CREATIVE APPROACH, Norman Colquhoun. For the beginner simple guide provides an instructive approach to painting: major stumbling blocks for beginner; overcoming them, technical points; paints and pigments; oil painting; watercolor and other media and color. New section on "plastic" paints. Glossary. Formerly *Paint Your Own Pictures*. 221pp.   22000-1 Paperbound $1.75

THE ENJOYMENT AND USE OF COLOR, Walter Sargent. Explanation of the relations between colors themselves and between colors in nature and art, including hundreds of little-known facts about color values, intensities, effects of high and low illumination, complementary colors. Many practical hints for painters, references to great masters. 7 color plates, 29 illustrations. x + 274pp.
20944-X Paperbound $2.75

THE NOTEBOOKS OF LEONARDO DA VINCI, compiled and edited by Jean Paul Richter. 1566 extracts from original manuscripts reveal the full range of Leonardo's versatile genius: all his writings on painting, sculpture, architecture, anatomy, astronomy, geography, topography, physiology, mining, music, etc., in both Italian and English, with 186 plates of manuscript pages and more than 500 additional drawings. Includes studies for the Last Supper, the lost Sforza monument, and other works. Total of xlvii + 866pp. 7⅞ x 10¾.
22572-0, 22573-9 Two volumes, Paperbound $10.00

MONTGOMERY WARD CATALOGUE OF 1895. Tea gowns, yards of flannel and pillow-case lace, stereoscopes, books of gospel hymns, the New Improved Singer Sewing Machine, side saddles, milk skimmers, straight-edged razors, high-button shoes, spittoons, and on and on . . . listing some 25,000 items, practically all illustrated. Essential to the shoppers of the 1890's, it is our truest record of the spirit of the period. Unaltered reprint of Issue No. 57, Spring and Summer 1895. Introduction by Boris Emmet. Innumerable illustrations. xiii + 624pp. 8½ x 11⅝.
22377-9 Paperbound $6.95

THE CRYSTAL PALACE EXHIBITION ILLUSTRATED CATALOGUE (LONDON, 1851). One of the wonders of the modern world—the Crystal Palace Exhibition in which all the nations of the civilized world exhibited their achievements in the arts and sciences—presented in an equally important illustrated catalogue. More than 1700 items pictured with accompanying text—ceramics, textiles, cast-iron work, carpets, pianos, sleds, razors, wall-papers, billiard tables, beehives, silverware and hundreds of other artifacts—represent the focal point of Victorian culture in the Western World. Probably the largest collection of Victorian decorative art ever assembled— indispensable for antiquarians and designers. Unabridged republication of the Art-Journal Catalogue of the Great Exhibition of 1851, with all terminal essays. New introduction by John Gloag, F.S.A. xxxiv + 426pp. 9 x 12.
22503-8 Paperbound $4.50

A HISTORY OF COSTUME, Carl Köhler. Definitive history, based on surviving pieces of clothing primarily, and paintings, statues, etc. secondarily. Highly readable text, supplemented by 594 illustrations of costumes of the ancient Mediterranean peoples, Greece and Rome, the Teutonic prehistoric period; costumes of the Middle Ages, Renaissance, Baroque, 18th and 19th centuries. Clear, measured patterns are provided for many clothing articles. Approach is practical throughout. Enlarged by Emma von Sichart. 464pp. 21030-8 Paperbound $3.50

ORIENTAL RUGS, ANTIQUE AND MODERN, Walter A. Hawley. A complete and authoritative treatise on the Oriental rug—where they are made, by whom and how, designs and symbols, characteristics in detail of the six major groups, how to distinguish them and how to buy them. Detailed technical data is provided on periods, weaves, warps, wefts, textures, sides, ends and knots, although no technical background is required for an understanding. 11 color plates, 80 halftones, 4 maps. vi + 320pp. 6⅛ x 9⅛. 22366-3 Paperbound $5.00

TEN BOOKS ON ARCHITECTURE, Vitruvius. By any standards the most important book on architecture ever written. Early Roman discussion of aesthetics of building, construction methods, orders, sites, and every other aspect of architecture has inspired, instructed architecture for about 2,000 years. Stands behind Palladio, Michelangelo, Bramante, Wren, countless others. Definitive Morris H. Morgan translation. 68 illustrations. xii + 331pp. 20645-9 Paperbound $2.50

THE FOUR BOOKS OF ARCHITECTURE, Andrea Palladio. Translated into every major Western European language in the two centuries following its publication in 1570, this has been one of the most influential books in the history of architecture. Complete reprint of the 1738 Isaac Ware edition. New introduction by Adolf Placzek, Columbia Univ. 216 plates. xxii + 110pp. of text. 9½ x 12¾. 21308-0 Clothbound $10.00

STICKS AND STONES: A STUDY OF AMERICAN ARCHITECTURE AND CIVILIZATION, Lewis Mumford. One of the great classics of American cultural history. American architecture from the medieval-inspired earliest forms to the early 20th century; evolution of structure and style, and reciprocal influences on environment. 21 photographic illustrations. 238pp. 20202-X Paperbound $2.00

THE AMERICAN BUILDER'S COMPANION, Asher Benjamin. The most widely used early 19th century architectural style and source book, for colonial up into Greek Revival periods. Extensive development of geometry of carpentering, construction of sashes, frames, doors, stairs; plans and elevations of domestic and other buildings. Hundreds of thousands of houses were built according to this book, now invaluable to historians, architects, restorers, etc. 1827 edition. 59 plates. 114pp. 7⅞ x 10¾. 22236-5 Paperbound $3.00

DUTCH HOUSES IN THE HUDSON VALLEY BEFORE 1776, Helen Wilkinson Reynolds. The standard survey of the Dutch colonial house and outbuildings, with constructional features, decoration, and local history associated with individual homesteads. Introduction by Franklin D. Roosevelt. Map. 150 illustrations. 469pp. 6⅝ x 9¼. 21469-9 Paperbound $4.00

THE ARCHITECTURE OF COUNTRY HOUSES, Andrew J. Downing. Together with Vaux's *Villas and Cottages* this is the basic book for Hudson River Gothic architecture of the middle Victorian period. Full, sound discussions of general aspects of housing, architecture, style, decoration, furnishing, together with scores of detailed house plans, illustrations of specific buildings, accompanied by full text. Perhaps the most influential single American architectural book. 1850 edition. Introduction by J. Stewart Johnson. 321 figures, 34 architectural designs. xvi + 560pp.
22003-6 Paperbound $4.00

LOST EXAMPLES OF COLONIAL ARCHITECTURE, John Mead Howells. Full-page photographs of buildings that have disappeared or been so altered as to be denatured, including many designed by major early American architects. 245 plates. xvii + 248pp. 7⅞ x 10¾.
21143-6 Paperbound $3.50

DOMESTIC ARCHITECTURE OF THE AMERICAN COLONIES AND OF THE EARLY REPUBLIC, Fiske Kimball. Foremost architect and restorer of Williamsburg and Monticello covers nearly 200 homes between 1620-1825. Architectural details, construction, style features, special fixtures, floor plans, etc. Generally considered finest work in its area. 219 illustrations of houses, doorways, windows, capital mantels. xx + 314pp. 7⅞ x 10¾.
21743-4 Paperbound $4.00

EARLY AMERICAN ROOMS: 1650-1858, edited by Russell Hawes Kettell. Tour of 12 rooms, each representative of a different era in American history and each furnished, decorated, designed and occupied in the style of the era. 72 plans and elevations, 8-page color section, etc., show fabrics, wall papers, arrangements, etc. Full descriptive text. xvii + 200pp. of text. 8⅜ x 11¼.
21633-0 Paperbound $5.00

THE FITZWILLIAM VIRGINAL BOOK, edited by J. Fuller Maitland and W. B. Squire. Full modern printing of famous early 17th-century ms. volume of 300 works by Morley, Byrd, Bull, Gibbons, etc. For piano or other modern keyboard instrument; easy to read format. xxxvi + 938pp. 8⅜ x 11.
21068-5, 21069-3 Two volumes, Paperbound $10.00

KEYBOARD MUSIC, Johann Sebastian Bach. Bach Gesellschaft edition. A rich selection of Bach's masterpieces for the harpsichord: the six English Suites, six French Suites, the six Partitas (Clavierübung part I), the Goldberg Variations (Clavierübung part IV), the fifteen Two-Part Inventions and the fifteen Three-Part Sinfonias. Clearly reproduced on large sheets with ample margins; eminently playable. vi + 312pp. 8⅛ x 11.
22360-4 Paperbound $5.00

THE MUSIC OF BACH: AN INTRODUCTION, Charles Sanford Terry. A fine, nontechnical introduction to Bach's music, both instrumental and vocal. Covers organ music, chamber music, passion music, other types. Analyzes themes, developments, innovations. x + 114pp.
21075-8 Paperbound $1.25

BEETHOVEN AND HIS NINE SYMPHONIES, Sir George Grove. Noted British musicologist provides best history, analysis, commentary on symphonies. Very thorough, rigorously accurate; necessary to both advanced student and amateur music lover. 436 musical passages. vii + 407 pp.
20334-4 Paperbound $2.75

JOHANN SEBASTIAN BACH, Philipp Spitta. One of the great classics of musicology, this definitive analysis of Bach's music (and life) has never been surpassed. Lucid, nontechnical analyses of hundreds of pieces (30 pages devoted to St. Matthew Passion, 26 to B Minor Mass). Also includes major analysis of 18th-century music. 450 musical examples. 40-page musical supplement. Total of xx + 1799pp.
(EUK) 22278-0, 22279-9 Two volumes, Clothbound $17.50

MOZART AND HIS PIANO CONCERTOS, Cuthbert Girdlestone. The only full-length study of an important area of Mozart's creativity. Provides detailed analyses of all 23 concertos, traces inspirational sources. 417 musical examples. Second edition. 509pp. (USO) 21271-8 Paperbound $3.50

THE PERFECT WAGNERITE: A COMMENTARY ON THE NIBLUNG'S RING, George Bernard Shaw. Brilliant and still relevant criticism in remarkable essays on Wagner's Ring cycle, Shaw's ideas on political and social ideology behind the plots, role of Leitmotifs, vocal requisites, etc. Prefaces. xxi + 136pp.
21707-8 Paperbound $1.50

DON GIOVANNI, W. A. Mozart. Complete libretto, modern English translation; biographies of composer and librettist; accounts of early performances and critical reaction. Lavishly illustrated. All the material you need to understand and appreciate this great work. Dover Opera Guide and Libretto Series; translated and introduced by Ellen Bleiler. 92 illustrations. 209pp.
21134-7 Paperbound $1.50

HIGH FIDELITY SYSTEMS: A LAYMAN'S GUIDE, Roy F. Allison. All the basic information you need for setting up your own audio system: high fidelity and stereo record players, tape records, F.M. Connections, adjusting tone arm, cartridge, checking needle alignment, positioning speakers, phasing speakers, adjusting hums, trouble-shooting, maintenance, and similar topics. Enlarged 1965 edition. More than 50 charts, diagrams, photos. iv + 91pp. 21514-8 Paperbound $1.25

REPRODUCTION OF SOUND, Edgar Villchur. Thorough coverage for laymen of high fidelity systems, reproducing systems in general, needles, amplifiers, preamps, loudspeakers, feedback, explaining physical background. "A rare talent for making technicalities vividly comprehensible," R. Darrell, *High Fidelity*. 69 figures. iv + 92pp. 21515-6 Paperbound $1.25

HEAR ME TALKIN' TO YA: THE STORY OF JAZZ AS TOLD BY THE MEN WHO MADE IT, Nat Shapiro and Nat Hentoff. Louis Armstrong, Fats Waller, Jo Jones, Clarence Williams, Billy Holiday, Duke Ellington, Jelly Roll Morton and dozens of other jazz greats tell how it was in Chicago's South Side, New Orleans, depression Harlem and the modern West Coast as jazz was born and grew. xvi + 429pp.
21726-4 Paperbound $2.50

FABLES OF AESOP, translated by Sir Roger L'Estrange. A reproduction of the very rare 1931 Paris edition; a selection of the most interesting fables, together with 50 imaginative drawings by Alexander Calder. v + 128pp. 6½x9¼.
21780-9 Paperbound $1.50

AGAINST THE GRAIN (A REBOURS), Joris K. Huysmans. Filled with weird images, evidences of a bizarre imagination, exotic experiments with hallucinatory drugs, rich tastes and smells and the diversions of its sybarite hero Duc Jean des Esseintes, this classic novel pushed 19th-century literary decadence to its limits. Full unabridged edition. Do not confuse this with abridged editions generally sold. Introduction by Havelock Ellis. xlix + 206pp. 22190-3 Paperbound $2.00

VARIORUM SHAKESPEARE: HAMLET. Edited by Horace H. Furness; a landmark of American scholarship. Exhaustive footnotes and appendices treat all doubtful words and phrases, as well as suggested critical emendations throughout the play's history. First volume contains editor's own text, collated with all Quartos and Folios. Second volume contains full first Quarto, translations of Shakespeare's sources (Belleforest, and Saxo Grammaticus), Der Bestrafte Brudermord, and many essays on critical and historical points of interest by major authorities of past and present. Includes details of staging and costuming over the years. By far the best edition available for serious students of Shakespeare. Total of xx + 905pp.
21004-9, 21005-7, 2 volumes, Paperbound $7.00

A LIFE OF WILLIAM SHAKESPEARE, Sir Sidney Lee. This is the standard life of Shakespeare, summarizing everything known about Shakespeare and his plays. Incredibly rich in material, broad in coverage, clear and judicious, it has served thousands as the best introduction to Shakespeare. 1931 edition. 9 plates. xxix + 792pp. (USO) 21967-4 Paperbound $3.75

MASTERS OF THE DRAMA, John Gassner. Most comprehensive history of the drama in print, covering every tradition from Greeks to modern Europe and America, including India, Far East, etc. Covers more than 800 dramatists, 2000 plays, with biographical material, plot summaries, theatre history, criticism, etc. "Best of its kind in English," New Republic. 77 illustrations. xxii + 890pp.
20100-7 Clothbound $8.50

THE EVOLUTION OF THE ENGLISH LANGUAGE, George McKnight. The growth of English, from the 14th century to the present. Unusual, non-technical account presents basic information in very interesting form: sound shifts, change in grammar and syntax, vocabulary growth, similar topics. Abundantly illustrated with quotations. Formerly Modern English in the Making. xii + 590pp.
21932-1 Paperbound $3.50

AN ETYMOLOGICAL DICTIONARY OF MODERN ENGLISH, Ernest Weekley. Fullest, richest work of its sort, by foremost British lexicographer. Detailed word histories, including many colloquial and archaic words; extensive quotations. Do not confuse this with the Concise Etymological Dictionary, which is much abridged. Total of xxvii + 830pp. 6½ x 9¼.
21873-2, 21874-0 Two volumes, Paperbound $6.00

FLATLAND: A ROMANCE OF MANY DIMENSIONS, E. A. Abbott. Classic of science-fiction explores ramifications of life in a two-dimensional world, and what happens when a three-dimensional being intrudes. Amusing reading, but also useful as introduction to thought about hyperspace. Introduction by Banesh Hoffmann. 16 illustrations. xx + 103pp. 20001-9 Paperbound $1.00

POEMS OF ANNE BRADSTREET, edited with an introduction by Robert Hutchinson. A new selection of poems by America's first poet and perhaps the first significant woman poet in the English language. 48 poems display her development in works of considerable variety—love poems, domestic poems, religious meditations, formal elegies, "quaternions," etc. Notes, bibliography. viii + 222pp.

22160-1 Paperbound $2.00

THREE GOTHIC NOVELS: THE CASTLE OF OTRANTO BY HORACE WALPOLE; VATHEK BY WILLIAM BECKFORD; THE VAMPYRE BY JOHN POLIDORI, WITH FRAGMENT OF A NOVEL BY LORD BYRON, edited by E. F. Bleiler. The first Gothic novel, by Walpole; the finest Oriental tale in English, by Beckford; powerful Romantic supernatural story in versions by Polidori and Byron. All extremely important in history of literature; all still exciting, packed with supernatural thrills, ghosts, haunted castles, magic, etc. xl + 291pp.

21232-7 Paperbound $2.00

THE BEST TALES OF HOFFMANN, E. T. A. Hoffmann. 10 of Hoffmann's most important stories, in modern re-editings of standard translations: Nutcracker and the King of Mice, Signor Formica, Automata, The Sandman, Rath Krespel, The Golden Flowerpot, Master Martin the Cooper, The Mines of Falun, The King's Betrothed, A New Year's Eve Adventure. 7 illustrations by Hoffmann. Edited by E. F. Bleiler. xxxix + 419pp.

21793-0 Paperbound $2.50

GHOST AND HORROR STORIES OF AMBROSE BIERCE, Ambrose Bierce. 23 strikingly modern stories of the horrors latent in the human mind: The Eyes of the Panther, The Damned Thing, An Occurrence at Owl Creek Bridge, An Inhabitant of Carcosa, etc., plus the dream-essay, Visions of the Night. Edited by E. F. Bleiler. xxii + 199pp.

20767-6 Paperbound $1.50

BEST GHOST STORIES OF J. S. LEFANU, J. Sheridan LeFanu. Finest stories by Victorian master often considered greatest supernatural writer of all. Carmilla, Green Tea, The Haunted Baronet, The Familiar, and 12 others. Most never before available in the U. S. A. Edited by E. F. Bleiler. 8 illustrations from Victorian publications. xvii + 467pp.

20415-4 Paperbound $3.00

THE TIME STREAM, THE GREATEST ADVENTURE, AND THE PURPLE SAPPHIRE—THREE SCIENCE FICTION NOVELS, John Taine (Eric Temple Bell). Great American mathematician was also foremost science fiction novelist of the 1920's. The Time Stream, one of all-time classics, uses concepts of circular time; The Greatest Adventure, incredibly ancient biological experiments from Antarctica threaten to escape; The Purple Sapphire, superscience, lost races in Central Tibet, survivors of the Great Race. 4 illustrations by Frank R. Paul. v + 532pp.

21180-0 Paperbound $3.00

SEVEN SCIENCE FICTION NOVELS, H. G. Wells. The standard collection of the great novels. Complete, unabridged. First Men in the Moon, Island of Dr. Moreau, War of the Worlds, Food of the Gods, Invisible Man, Time Machine, In the Days of the Comet. Not only science fiction fans, but every educated person owes it to himself to read these novels. 1015pp.

20264-X Clothbound $5.00

LAST AND FIRST MEN AND STAR MAKER, TWO SCIENCE FICTION NOVELS, Olaf Stapledon. Greatest future histories in science fiction. In the first, human intelligence is the "hero," through strange paths of evolution, interplanetary invasions, incredible technologies, near extinctions and reemergences. Star Maker describes the quest of a band of star rovers for intelligence itself, through time and space: weird inhuman civilizations, crustacean minds, symbiotic worlds, etc. Complete, unabridged. v + 438pp. 21962-3 Paperbound $2.50

THREE PROPHETIC NOVELS, H. G. WELLS. Stages of a consistently planned future for mankind. *When the Sleeper Wakes,* and *A Story of the Days to Come,* anticipate *Brave New World* and *1984,* in the 21st Century; *The Time Machine,* only complete version in print, shows farther future and the end of mankind. All show Wells's greatest gifts as storyteller and novelist. Edited by E. F. Bleiler. x + 335pp. (USO) 20605-X Paperbound $2.25

THE DEVIL'S DICTIONARY, Ambrose Bierce. America's own Oscar Wilde— Ambrose Bierce—offers his barbed iconoclastic wisdom in over 1,000 definitions hailed by H. L. Mencken as "some of the most gorgeous witticisms in the English language." 145pp. 20487-1 Paperbound $1.25

MAX AND MORITZ, Wilhelm Busch. Great children's classic, father of comic strip, of two bad boys, Max and Moritz. Also Ker and Plunk (Plisch und Plumm), Cat and Mouse, Deceitful Henry, Ice-Peter, The Boy and the Pipe, and five other pieces. Original German, with English translation. Edited by H. Arthur Klein; translations by various hands and H. Arthur Klein. vi + 216pp. 20181-3 Paperbound $2.00

PIGS IS PIGS AND OTHER FAVORITES, Ellis Parker Butler. The title story is one of the best humor short stories, as Mike Flannery obfuscates biology and English. Also included, That Pup of Murchison's, The Great American Pie Company, and Perkins of Portland. 14 illustrations. v + 109pp. 21532-6 Paperbound $1.00

THE PETERKIN PAPERS, Lucretia P. Hale. It takes genius to be as stupidly mad as the Peterkins, as they decide to become wise, celebrate the "Fourth," keep a cow, and otherwise strain the resources of the Lady from Philadelphia. Basic book of American humor. 153 illustrations. 219pp. 20794-3 Paperbound $1.50

PERRAULT'S FAIRY TALES, translated by A. E. Johnson and S. R. Littlewood, with 34 full-page illustrations by Gustave Doré. All the original Perrault stories— Cinderella, Sleeping Beauty, Bluebeard, Little Red Riding Hood, Puss in Boots, Tom Thumb, etc.—with their witty verse morals and the magnificent illustrations of Doré. One of the five or six great books of European fairy tales. viii + 117pp. 8⅛ x 11. 22311-6 Paperbound $2.00

OLD HUNGARIAN FAIRY TALES, Baroness Orczy. Favorites translated and adapted by author of the *Scarlet Pimpernel.* Eight fairy tales include "The Suitors of Princess Fire-Fly," "The Twin Hunchbacks," "Mr. Cuttlefish's Love Story," and "The Enchanted Cat." This little volume of magic and adventure will captivate children as it has for generations. 90 drawings by Montagu Barstow. 96pp. (USO) 22293-4 Paperbound $1.95

THE RED FAIRY BOOK, Andrew Lang. Lang's color fairy books have long been children's favorites. This volume includes Rapunzel, Jack and the Bean-stalk and 35 other stories, familiar and unfamiliar. 4 plates, 93 illustrations x + 367pp.
21673-X Paperbound $2.50

THE BLUE FAIRY BOOK, Andrew Lang. Lang's tales come from all countries and all times. Here are 37 tales from Grimm, the Arabian Nights, Greek Mythology, and other fascinating sources. 8 plates, 130 illustrations. xi + 390pp.
21437-0 Paperbound $2.50

HOUSEHOLD STORIES BY THE BROTHERS GRIMM. Classic English-language edition of the well-known tales — Rumpelstiltskin, Snow White, Hansel and Gretel, The Twelve Brothers, Faithful John, Rapunzel, Tom Thumb (52 stories in all). Translated into simple, straightforward English by Lucy Crane. Ornamented with head-pieces, vignettes, elaborate decorative initials and a dozen full-page illustrations by Walter Crane. x + 269pp.
21080-4 Paperbound $2.50

THE MERRY ADVENTURES OF ROBIN HOOD, Howard Pyle. The finest modern versions of the traditional ballads and tales about the great English outlaw. Howard Pyle's complete prose version, with every word, every illustration of the first edition. Do not confuse this facsimile of the original (1883) with modern editions that change text or illustrations. 23 plates plus many page decorations. xxii + 296pp.
22043-5 Paperbound $2.50

THE STORY OF KING ARTHUR AND HIS KNIGHTS, Howard Pyle. The finest children's version of the life of King Arthur; brilliantly retold by Pyle, with 48 of his most imaginative illustrations. xviii + 313pp. 6⅛ x 9¼.
21445-1 Paperbound $2.50

THE WONDERFUL WIZARD OF OZ, L. Frank Baum. America's finest children's book in facsimile of first edition with all Denslow illustrations in full color. The edition a child should have. Introduction by Martin Gardner. 23 color plates, scores of drawings. iv + 267pp.
20691-2 Paperbound $2.25

THE MARVELOUS LAND OF OZ, L. Frank Baum. The second Oz book, every bit as imaginative as the Wizard. The hero is a boy named Tip, but the Scarecrow and the Tin Woodman are back, as is the Oz magic. 16 color plates, 120 drawings by John R. Neill. 287pp.
20692-0 Paperbound $2.50

THE MAGICAL MONARCH OF MO, L. Frank Baum. Remarkable adventures in a land even stranger than Oz. The best of Baum's books not in the Oz series. 15 color plates and dozens of drawings by Frank Verbeck. xviii + 237pp.
21892-9 Paperbound $2.00

THE BAD CHILD'S BOOK OF BEASTS, MORE BEASTS FOR WORSE CHILDREN, A MORAL ALPHABET, Hilaire Belloc. Three complete humor classics in one volume. Be kind to the frog, and do not call him names . . . and 28 other whimsical animals. Familiar favorites and some not so well known. Illustrated by Basil Blackwell. 156pp.
(USO) 20749-8 Paperbound $1.25

EAST O' THE SUN AND WEST O' THE MOON, George W. Dasent. Considered the best of all translations of these Norwegian folk tales, this collection has been enjoyed by generations of children (and folklorists too). Includes True and Untrue, Why the Sea is Salt, East O' the Sun and West O' the Moon, Why the Bear is Stumpy-Tailed, Boots and the Troll, The Cock and the Hen, Rich Peter the Pedlar, and 52 more. The only edition with all 59 tales. 77 illustrations by Erik Werenskiold and Theodor Kittelsen. xv + 418pp. 22521-6 Paperbound $3.00

GOOPS AND HOW TO BE THEM, Gelett Burgess. Classic of tongue-in-cheek humor, masquerading as etiquette book. 87 verses, twice as many cartoons, show mischievous Goops as they demonstrate to children virtues of table manners, neatness, courtesy, etc. Favorite for generations. viii + 88pp. 6½ x 9¼.
22233-0 Paperbound $1.25

ALICE'S ADVENTURES UNDER GROUND, Lewis Carroll. The first version, quite different from the final *Alice in Wonderland*, printed out by Carroll himself with his own illustrations. Complete facsimile of the "million dollar" manuscript Carroll gave to Alice Liddell in 1864. Introduction by Martin Gardner. viii + 96pp. Title and dedication pages in color. 21482-6 Paperbound $1.25

THE BROWNIES, THEIR BOOK, Palmer Cox. Small as mice, cunning as foxes, exuberant and full of mischief, the Brownies go to the zoo, toy shop, seashore, circus, etc., in 24 verse adventures and 266 illustrations. Long a favorite, since their first appearance in St. Nicholas Magazine. xi + 144pp. 6⅝ x 9¼.
21265-3 Paperbound $1.75

SONGS OF CHILDHOOD, Walter De La Mare. Published (under the pseudonym Walter Ramal) when De La Mare was only 29, this charming collection has long been a favorite children's book. A facsimile of the first edition in paper, the 47 poems capture the simplicity of the nursery rhyme and the ballad, including such lyrics as I Met Eve, Tartary, The Silver Penny. vii + 106pp. 21972-0 Paperbound $1.25

THE COMPLETE NONSENSE OF EDWARD LEAR, Edward Lear. The finest 19th-century humorist-cartoonist in full: all nonsense limericks, zany alphabets, Owl and Pussycat, songs, nonsense botany, and more than 500 illustrations by Lear himself. Edited by Holbrook Jackson. xxix + 287pp. (USO) 20167-8 Paperbound $2.00

BILLY WHISKERS: THE AUTOBIOGRAPHY OF A GOAT, Frances Trego Montgomery. A favorite of children since the early 20th century, here are the escapades of that rambunctious, irresistible and mischievous goat—Billy Whiskers. Much in the spirit of *Peck's Bad Boy*, this is a book that children never tire of reading or hearing. All the original familiar illustrations by W. H. Fry are included: 6 color plates, 18 black and white drawings. 159pp. 22345-0 Paperbound $2.00

MOTHER GOOSE MELODIES. Faithful republication of the fabulously rare Munroe and Francis "copyright 1833" Boston edition—the most important Mother Goose collection, usually referred to as the "original." Familiar rhymes plus many rare ones, with wonderful old woodcut illustrations. Edited by E. F. Bleiler. 128pp. 4½ x 6⅜. 22577-1 Paperbound $1.25

TWO LITTLE SAVAGES; BEING THE ADVENTURES OF TWO BOYS WHO LIVED AS INDIANS AND WHAT THEY LEARNED, Ernest Thompson Seton. Great classic of nature and boyhood provides a vast range of woodlore in most palatable form, a genuinely entertaining story. Two farm boys build a teepee in woods and live in it for a month, working out Indian solutions to living problems, star lore, birds and animals, plants, etc. 293 illustrations. vii + 286pp.

20985-7 Paperbound $2.50

PETER PIPER'S PRACTICAL PRINCIPLES OF PLAIN & PERFECT PRONUNCIATION. Alliterative jingles and tongue-twisters of surprising charm, that made their first appearance in America about 1830. Republished in full with the spirited woodcut illustrations from this earliest American edition. 32pp. 4½ x 6⅜.

22560-7 Paperbound $1.00

SCIENCE EXPERIMENTS AND AMUSEMENTS FOR CHILDREN, Charles Vivian. 73 easy experiments, requiring only materials found at home or easily available, such as candles, coins, steel wool, etc.; illustrate basic phenomena like vacuum, simple chemical reaction, etc. All safe. Modern, well-planned. Formerly *Science Games for Children*. 102 photos, numerous drawings. 96pp. 6⅛ x 9¼.

21856-2 Paperbound $1.25

AN INTRODUCTION TO CHESS MOVES AND TACTICS SIMPLY EXPLAINED, Leonard Barden. Informal intermediate introduction, quite strong in explaining reasons for moves. Covers basic material, tactics, important openings, traps, positional play in middle game, end game. Attempts to isolate patterns and recurrent configurations. Formerly *Chess*. 58 figures. 102pp. (USO) 21210-6 Paperbound $1.25

LASKER'S MANUAL OF CHESS, Dr. Emanuel Lasker. Lasker was not only one of the five great World Champions, he was also one of the ablest expositors, theorists, and analysts. In many ways, his Manual, permeated with his philosophy of battle, filled with keen insights, is one of the greatest works ever written on chess. Filled with analyzed games by the great players. A single-volume library that will profit almost any chess player, beginner or master. 308 diagrams. xli x 349pp.

20640-8 Paperbound $2.75

THE MASTER BOOK OF MATHEMATICAL RECREATIONS, Fred Schuh. In opinion of many the finest work ever prepared on mathematical puzzles, stunts, recreations; exhaustively thorough explanations of mathematics involved, analysis of effects, citation of puzzles and games. Mathematics involved is elementary. Translated by F. Göbel. 194 figures. xxiv + 430pp. 22134-2 Paperbound $3.00

MATHEMATICS, MAGIC AND MYSTERY, Martin Gardner. Puzzle editor for Scientific American explains mathematics behind various mystifying tricks: card tricks, stage "mind reading," coin and match tricks, counting out games, geometric dissections, etc. Probability sets, theory of numbers clearly explained. Also provides more than 400 tricks, guaranteed to work, that you can do. 135 illustrations. xii + 176pp.

20338-2 Paperbound $1.50

MATHEMATICAL PUZZLES FOR BEGINNERS AND ENTHUSIASTS, Geoffrey Mott-Smith. 189 puzzles from easy to difficult—involving arithmetic, logic, algebra, properties of digits, probability, etc.—for enjoyment and mental stimulus. Explanation of mathematical principles behind the puzzles. 135 illustrations. viii + 248pp.
20198-8 Paperbound $1.75

PAPER FOLDING FOR BEGINNERS, William D. Murray and Francis J. Rigney. Easiest book on the market, clearest instructions on making interesting, beautiful origami. Sail boats, cups, roosters, frogs that move legs, bonbon boxes, standing birds, etc. 40 projects; more than 275 diagrams and photographs. 94pp.
20713-7 Paperbound $1.00

TRICKS AND GAMES ON THE POOL TABLE, Fred Herrmann. 79 tricks and games— some solitaires, some for two or more players, some competitive games—to entertain you between formal games. Mystifying shots and throws, unusual caroms, tricks involving such props as cork, coins, a hat, etc. Formerly *Fun on the Pool Table.* 77 figures. 95pp.
21814-7 Paperbound $1.00

HAND SHADOWS TO BE THROWN UPON THE WALL: A SERIES OF NOVEL AND AMUSING FIGURES FORMED BY THE HAND, Henry Bursill. Delightful picturebook from great-grandfather's day shows how to make 18 different hand shadows: a bird that flies, duck that quacks, dog that wags his tail, camel, goose, deer, boy, turtle, etc. Only book of its sort. vi + 33pp. 6½ x 9¼.
21779-5 Paperbound $1.00

WHITTLING AND WOODCARVING, E. J. Tangerman. 18th printing of best book on market. "If you can cut a potato you can carve" toys and puzzles, chains, chessmen, caricatures, masks, frames, woodcut blocks, surface patterns, much more. Information on tools, woods, techniques. Also goes into serious wood sculpture from Middle Ages to present, East and West. 464 photos, figures. x + 293pp.
20965-2 Paperbound $2.00

HISTORY OF PHILOSOPHY, Julián Marías. Possibly the clearest, most easily followed, best planned, most useful one-volume history of philosophy on the market; neither skimpy nor overfull. Full details on system of every major philosopher and dozens of less important thinkers from pre-Socratics up to Existentialism and later. Strong on many European figures usually omitted. Has gone through dozens of editions in Europe. 1966 edition, translated by Stanley Appelbaum and Clarence Strowbridge. xviii + 505pp.
21739-6 Paperbound $3.00

YOGA: A SCIENTIFIC EVALUATION, Kovoor T. Behanan. Scientific but non-technical study of physiological results of yoga exercises; done under auspices of Yale U. Relations to Indian thought, to psychoanalysis, etc. 16 photos. xxiii + 270pp.
20505-3 Paperbound $2.50

Prices subject to change without notice.
Available at your book dealer or write for free catalogue to Dept. GI, Dover Publications, Inc., 180 Varick St., N. Y., N. Y. 10014. Dover publishes more than 150 books each year on science, elementary and advanced mathematics, biology, music, art, literary history, social sciences and other areas.